2.00

Quiller Bamboo

Quiller Novels by Adam Hall

The Quiller Memorandum
The 9th Directive
The Striker Portfolio
The Warsaw Document
The Tango Briefing
The Mandarin Cypher
The Kobra Manifesto
The Sinkiang Executive
The Scorpion Signal
The Peking Target
Quiller
Quiller's Run
Quiller KGB
Quiller Barracuda
Quiller Bamboo

Novels by Elleston Trevor

Chorus of Echoes
Redfern's Miracle
Tiger Street
A Blaze of Roses
The Passion and the Pity
The Big Pick-up
Squadron Airborne
The Killing-Ground
Gale Force
The Pillars of Midnight
The V.I.P.
The Billboard Madonna
The Burning Shore
The Flight of the Phoenix
The Shoot
The Freebooters
A Place for the Wicked
Bury Him Among Kings
Night Stop
Blue Jay Summer
The Theta Syndrome
The Sibling
The Damocles Sword
The Penthouse
Deathwatch

Quiller Bamboo

Adam Hall

William Morrow and Company, Inc.
New York

Copyright © 1991 by Trevor Productions, Inc.

All right reserved. No part of this book may be reproduced or utilized in any form or by any means, electronic or mechanical, including photocopying, record- ing, or by any information storage or retrieval system, without permission in writing from the Publisher. Inquiries should be addressed to Permissions Depart- ment, William Morrow and Company, Inc., 1350 Avenue of the Americas, New York, N.Y. 10019.

It is the policy of William Morrow and Company, Inc., and its imprints and affili- ates, recognizing the importance of preserving what has been written, to print the books we publish on acid-free paper, and we exert our best efforts to that end.

Library of Congress Cataloging-in-Publication Data

Hall, Adam.
    Quiller bamboo / Adam Hall.
        p.   cm.
    ISBN 0-688-09696-4
    I. Title.
PR6039.R518Q46 1991
823'.914--dc20   90-49142
                                                                      CIP

Printed in the United States of America

First Edition

1 2 3 4 5 6 7 8 9 10

BOOK DESIGN BY MARK STEIN STUDIOS

To
Anne and Alan
Threlfall

Contents

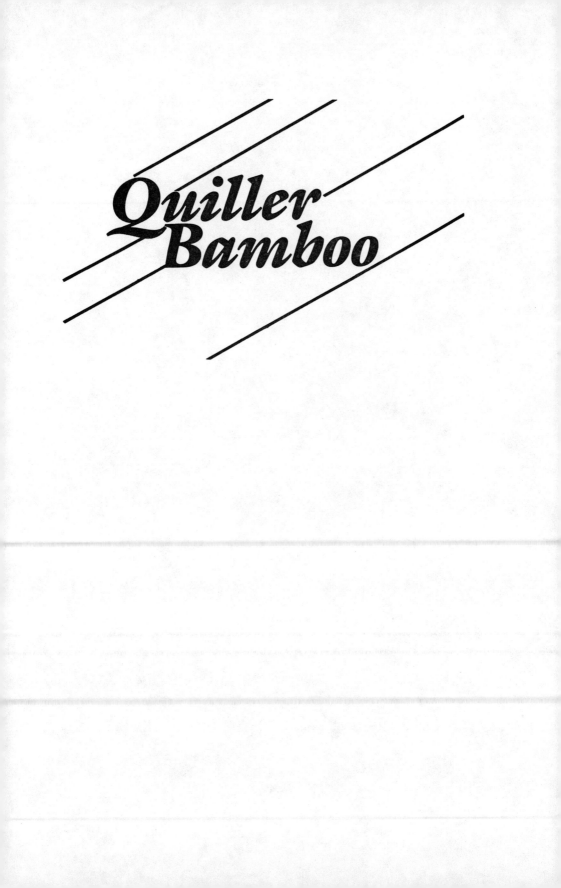

Quiller
Bamboo

Chapter 1

Hyde

It was 1:59 A.M. when the telephone woke me and I rolled over and answered it and Tilson said they wanted me there right away and I told him no, it was too soon.

The line went silent and then Tilson came back on again—I suppose he'd turned away to talk to someone.

"Fully urgent," he said.

The raw chill of a November fog came drifting through the open window, and I could hear a taxi throttling up along Knightsbridge in the distance.

"I've only been back ten days," I said.

Tilson's not often starchy but he said, "I think you know what fully urgent means," and rang off, so I got up and spent five minutes in the bathroom and went down to the car with my teeth clean but the stubble still there and brought the Aston up to a steady fifty along Piccadilly and went through the red when there was nothing coming and picked up a panda near the Ritz: he closed in and got his lights flashing but I didn't take any notice and he dropped back as he got the call from the dispatcher—Tilson had covered me as I knew he would, because "fully urgent" means that everyone's got to move.

The panda took up escort station behind me as far as Whitehall and then peeled off when I got to the building and saw Holmes manning the door.

"Mr. Hyde's office," he said and got me into the lift.

"What's it about?"

"Not absolutely sure. He wants you at the Foreign Office."

"So what am I doing here?"

"Briefing, clearance."

"I've only just got back. I told Tilson."

"Now you can tell Mr. Hyde."

We got out of the lift and went along the corridor with Holmes looking quiet and nervy, so I didn't ask him anything else. There were a lot of phones ringing behind the closed doors and Diane came out of Signals and darted into Codes and Cyphers with some papers in her hand, dropping a sheet and picking it up and not even seeing us as she went in there.

Someone else came out of the signals room and I heard a lot of beeping going on, more than usual at this time of night.

Holmes turned his head. "How much sleep have you had?"

"Few hours."

"Look in on me later if you want to. I've got to put a fire out in here."

He went into Signals and I kept on going. Not strictly a fire: someone had come unstuck in the field, Beirut, Sri Lanka, Bogotá, you name it, and he was lighting up his mission board for help.

Tilson was alone in Hyde's office, talking on one of the phones; by the look of him they'd dragged him out of bed too. I felt the adrenaline flushing the skin because I hadn't seen this kind of panic at the Bureau for months, but I was *not* going out again after only ten days, and they couldn't insist. Tilson nodded for me to have a chair but I stayed on my feet and went across to the window and looked at the street three stories below, deserted in the lamplight.

"I don't know," Tilson said on the phone, "it's only just come up. Quiller's here now, you should know; better tell Mr. Shepley."

I looked up at the reflection of Tilson's bland lopsided

face in the window. In this place Shepley was another name for God.

"Do you want him briefed and cleared first, or is he to go along to the FO right away?"

I didn't really mind what the answer was, since I was going back to bed in any case. I was technically at rest, which meant I'd got another twenty-one days before they could sign me up again and send me out, and I was going to spend at least a week at Norfolk wallowing in the luxury of sauna baths and Swedish massage and meditation to bring the nerves down to their normal pitch, plus a bit of refresher training with Kimura-sensei in the dojo and some close-combat work to get the reflexes back in tune.

"They're holding a board open," Tilson said on the phone, "and they've brought Dawson in from Paris—he knows the kind of signals we're liable to get from Hong Kong."

No way. Not Hong Kong. Norfolk. There was a drunk down there in the street, tottering with tremendous care along the pavement, holding on to the railings for a bit and then shoving off again.

Tilson cupped the phone and said, "Are you still under any kind of treatment?"

"Yes."

"What for?"

"Shark bite."

"What's your condition?"

"Look," I said, "we've got to talk."

Tilson took his hand away from the mouthpiece. "Yes, but I'll tell him the situation, or leave it to Mr. Hyde."

The drunk was on a course forty-five degrees in error, and when his foot slipped off the curb he went down like a felled tree and lay with his head in the gutter.

"No," Tilson said, "it began as a simple request for asylum."

I went across to the desk and picked up one of the other phones and pressed 9 and got the dial tone and pressed 999 and told them. Someone looked in at the door and Tilson shook his head and they went out again.

"I don't frankly know. We got it from MI6. They said they don't want to touch it."

"It's too far away," I said into the phone, "to see if he's bleeding, but he's going to get his head run over if he stays where he is."

Another phone started ringing and Tilson picked it up. "He's not here."

"Fifty yards north of the Cenotaph," I said.

"Well, let me deal with what's going on at this end and then I'll get back to you, or someone will." Tilson put the phone down.

"A minute ago," I said. "My pleasure."

"Who's that?" Tilson asked me.

"Drunk down there, just reporting it."

His eyes took on a stare. "Down where?"

"The thing is," I told him, "I got back precisely ten days ago and my nerves feel like barbed wire and the dressings are still being changed every day. Shall I spell that?"

Tilson leaned back in the chair and leveled his eyes.

"I quite understand. But you don't even want to know the score?" And he waited.

In a minute I said, "You really are a bastard."

We could hear a siren cut in and die away again as a police car came around Parliament Square into Whitehall, heading for the Cenotaph.

"I can't tell you much," Tilson said, "because they slapped a your-ears-only on this thing the minute it started coming in, but you're not the only one they got out of bed and Mr. Shepley himself has been alerted, so it's just conceivable that if they're going to pick you as the shadow executive you won't let the odd shark bite get in the way."

"It's the nerves," I said, "more than that." In an ideal world you could come off a mission and get a few nights' sleep and drink lots of Sanatogen and see Deirdre or someone and report back for work, but the Caribbean thing had been very busy and the whole organism still felt tender. "It's Hong Kong, is it?"

"That area."

"Who's available for the DIF?" If they could give me a really first-class director in the field it could make a difference.

"I'd have to check on that. But if you—" He broke off as the door opened again and Hyde came in.

"Did they alert Mr. Shepley?"

"Yes, sir."

"Is he on his way?"

"He just said he'd monitor his phone."

"All right." Hyde gave me a nod and stood for a minute looking around him at nothing at all, his large head tilted back and his tongue poking at his cheek, his big hands hanging by his sides and his feet splayed a little to support his weight. He didn't react when a phone rang and Tilson took it and told them he wanted priority calls only from now on and put the receiver back.

Hyde was in a dinner jacket; I suppose they'd beeped him at a nightclub or somewhere. He went on looking around him while he thought things over, then he brought his head down and told Tilson, "*This* is where the focus is, until we can open up the board in there. Can you handle it?"

Tilson said yes and Hyde turned to look at me. "You're resting, they said."

"Technically."

"Technically. What kind of shape are you in?"

"Not bad."

"Not good?"

"It depends on what I'd have to do."

He left a dead stare on me, miles away, and then his eyes focused again. "All I know," he said slowly, "or all I can *tell* you at this stage, because there's a blackout on, is that it's Far East and I'm running it and I want *you* in the field." There were beads of sweat on his forehead where the hair had thinned back; they always turned up the heating in this

15

bloody place in the wintertime, but it wasn't that. This thing had obviously been dropped into Hyde's lap without any warning and he was trying to size it up. "As far as I know," he said, "you wouldn't be going into anything terribly active in the opening phase, but"—his huge shoulders in a shrug— "nothing's ever predictable. I want you for this one very *much*, but I do *not* want you to go into the field if you don't feel ready for it."

I thought about it, because if I made a mistake at this stage it could be disastrous. "I'll have to know a bit more; then I can make a decision. Isn't there anyone else available?"

"It's not quite that, you see. There's no one else, in my opinion, who could do this one better than you. And you know the territory, I believe."

"Some of it. I've been to—"

"Tilson," Hyde said, "for God's sake tell them to turn the thermostats down to something reasonable. Say seventy." He swung his head back to me. "Sorry. You've been to—?"

"Bangkok, Singapore, Hong Kong, Thailand, but that's all."

"Not Beijing?"

"No."

"Seventy," Tilson was saying on the phone.

"Do you have any Chinese?"

"No."

His head tilted back again like a well-balanced boulder and he stared at the ceiling for a bit.

"Mr. Hyde's personal request."

He'd never run me, Hyde, but I knew that people liked him as a control. He'd run Fielding in Malaya and Parkes in Hungary and they both said he was good, knew his signals and support sources better than anyone and knew how to keep things going when there didn't seem to be a hope in hell of completing the mission. And he'd brought that bloody idiot Bates back alive across the border near Chernovtsy into Romania after he'd botched his signals and blown his escape route. We tend to appreciate a control like that.

"You are *still* the one I want," he said as his head came down again to look at me, "whether you have Chinese or not. It won't, I think, be crucial." To Tilson "Are they going to do it?"

"Yes, sir."

"Like a Turkish bath in here. Get Holmes on the line for me, will you?"

"He's in Signals," I said.

"Get him in Signals for me, then, and ask him where the *hell* they are and why they haven't kept me informed."

"Those people?"

"Those people."

Your-ears-only.

"There are only two others available for this one," Hyde told me, "and I don't much care for either of them. I want someone I can rely on when it comes to the crunch. Not," he said with his stare fixing me, "that you yourself are all that angelic to deal with, by repute."

"I don't suffer fools gladly."

"You have a tendency to bitch about accepting a new mission, so they say, but you seem to be in a fairly reasonable state of mind at the moment, considering you're meant to be at rest."

I suppose that was true, and it surprised me a bit because they'd dragged me out of bed and they didn't think a shark bite was any more interesting than a chilblain and here was a top control trying to con me into the field, *there's no one else, in my opinion, who could do this one better than you,* so forth, and the whole thing was a wonderful excuse for me to kick the door down and bite the rug and threaten all manner of mayhem, but I wasn't doing that. I suppose it was the moth-and-the-flame thing.

"I'm meant to be at rest, yes, but on the other hand Tilson said it was fully urgent and the signals room sounded like an electric organ when I passed it just now, and it's got me interested."

I was the moth.

In a moment he said slowly, "This mission has, shall we say, potentially major dimensions."

And that was the flame.

"Sticks out a mile," I said.

I was aware of the pulse in the carotid sinus, and that was normal at a time like this; but the psyche is more subtle than the cardiovascular system and I didn't know whether the elevated pulse was because of excitement or fear.

"Holmes," Tilson said, "has asked the switchboard to put their call through to his own office, to yours, and to Mr. Croder in Signals."

Hyde prodded his tongue into his cheek and in a moment said, "And Mr. Shepley is monitoring?"

"Yes, sir."

"Very well. I think," he said, turning to me again, "I'm going to do something rather nasty. I can't, you see, tell you anything useful about this one until and unless you have agreed to do it." Watching me carefully.

"Oh for Christ's sake—you want me to go in *blind*?"

Dipping his head, "Not quite. To go in under whatever conditions you care to name, provided of course I can meet them."

The pulse went up again by a few more beats, and the bloodstream became palpable, like a quiet fire coursing through the veins, not unpleasant. Not much more than an hour ago I'd been asleep in bed, the sores and the specters of the last mission still lingering but not offering any threat: I'd been safe; and now I was standing in this room with the choice of going on being safe for a little time longer, at least a few weeks, or letting these people pitch me headlong into the field again, of signing that form, the next-of-kin thing, without even knowing what I was taking on. I could tell the difference, now, between excitement and fear.

I was afraid. But there burned the flame, bright and beckoning. There are various forms, as I'm sure you know, of madness.

But there was still a chance. Conditions, Hyde had said.

"You would be my control, at the board?"

"Yes." His bright stare rested on me.

"No support in the field unless I ask for it."

"We can do that."

"In terms of my being expendable—" I said, and stopped right there. I'd tried this once with Shepley and he'd refused. It's something you don't have to sign your name to, but it's implicit in your general terms of service: if you're out there and in a red sector and you're blown and there's nothing you can do, London will try to get you out, but if it hasn't got the manpower or the firepower or it can't raise support or send specialists in or if there's a risk to the Bureau, to the mission, then they'll leave you there, crouched against a wall or sprawled on a rooftop right in the line of fire or trapped in a building with every door covered, wherever you are they will leave you there, and all you owe them, if there's time to pay, is to pop the capsule and protect the Sacred Bull, the Bureau, and go in silence and in peace. In terms of our being expendable, there is nothing we can ask. So I told Hyde, "Ignore that."

"Ignored."

Conditions.

"I pick my own DIF."

"There aren't very many," he said, "available."

"Ferris?"

"We sent him out to Tehran," Hyde said, "straight from your debriefing on *Barracuda*."

"Something major?"

"We wouldn't send Ferris out to wash the dishes." Perhaps he thought it sounded discourteous, so he said, "We reserve people like Ferris for people like you."

"Fane?"

A flash of surprise came into the stare. Fane had betrayed me once, but I'd had the edge and I'd survived, and he was no longer a danger: you're perfectly safe with someone you know you can't trust.

19

"Fane is down with the flu," Hyde said.

"Pepperidge?"

"Is available."

I looked at Tilson. "Is he in London?"

"Yes."

"Then I'll take him, if he's willing. He's fluent in Chinese and the dialects."

"Very well."

"Do we need to get him here tonight?"

"No. We needed *you* here because you are the key. If you so choose."

"If we can't get Pepperidge, who else is available?"

"No one," Tilson said from across the desk, "at your level."

Hyde: "If necessary, Mr. Croder would direct you in the field."

Croder. He was Chief of Signals. I was beginning to feel the size of this thing.

One of the phones rang and Tilson took it and said all right and rang off and looked up at Hyde. "They're on their way over there now."

Hyde angled his watch to the light. "Very well." He turned to me again. "Have you any further conditions?"

Silence in the room.

We can always refuse a mission. It can be in a locale too far away for our liking, or too hot, too cold, too hostile, too dangerous. Or we can simply be too tired, too exhausted after the last time out; or we can feel the tug of intuition not to take it, this one, not to risk it. We grow old, in this trade, before our time; we grow canny, cunning, cynical, steeped in subterfuge, versed in stealth. We grow obstinate, difficult; we grow intractable. And we grow afraid.

Their eyes on me, Tilson's, Hyde's, in the lamplight, in the silence of the room.

"No," I said, "there are no further conditions."

Hyde broke his stare. "You accept the mission?"

"Yes."

"Then we must be going," he said. "We're to meet these people at the Foreign Office as soon as we can get there. Did you come in your car?"

"Yes."

"Will you take me there?"

"Of course."

"Taxis are so laggardly. Tilson, will you set everything up? I'll brief Quiller as soon as we're back, then you can put him through Clearance."

On our way down Whitehall in the car, Hyde sat with his bulk hunched against the passenger door, watching the road and sometimes watching me as he talked.

"Go right here." I turned into Victoria Street. "Keep going," he said.

"Not the Foreign Office?"

"We just *said* the Foreign Office, but actually no. Too many moles. This matter, you see, is rather important, and we don't want people listening. Since you are now committed, I can give you the whole thing in a nutshell. If all goes to plan, we should be able to overthrow the Communist regime in Beijing and establish a democratic government within a matter of days."

Chapter 2

Underground

*T*here was the smell of burned metal from the high-voltage contacts, and the black mouth of the tunnel was lit intermittently by the flash of a welder's torch; I suppose there was a night crew along there, working on the rails. Here on the platform the scene was more formal: most of the people were in dark overcoats and two of them had rolled umbrellas. I was in a polo sweater and padded bomber jacket, since they'd got me out of my flat in such a hurry.

There were some men hanging around the mouth of the tunnel and the archway to the escalators; on our way down here, Hyde had told me the scene was protected by plain-clothes police. "We mustn't be disturbed, you see. I suppose it's odd," he'd said, "that in order to avoid any moles we're going underground."

It looked as if we were the last to arrive, and someone came forward to meet us.

"This is Mr. Jones," Hyde told him, and the other man shook hands with me and said:

"I'm Barstow, Private Secretary. Come and meet people."

Another flash lit the tunnel, and there was the crackle of the welding flame.

Barstow took us over to the group and made the introductions. "His Excellency Qiao Dejian, Ambassador from the People's Republic of China. The Right Honourable James Jarrow, Secretary of State for the United Kingdom. Mr. William Glover, MI6. Mr. Hou Jing, Chinese embassy counselor.

This is Mr. Hyde, and Mr. Jones. Shall we go and sit down?"

There was a holdup because the Secretary of State wanted the Chinese ambassador to go into the coach first, and little Qiao couldn't possibly allow it, so Barstow managed to shepherd them discreetly side by side through the sliding doors and the rest of us shuffled after them, with Hyde and me in the rear. Hyde's official capacity hadn't been mentioned and "Mr. Jones" is generally understood among the diplomatic crowd to be a cover name for some kind of agent.

There was another holdup inside the coach because Ambassador Qiao wouldn't sit down until the Secretary had, but Jarrow finally took his seat halfway along the coach and everyone else followed suit and someone pulled the sliding doors together manually and took up guard duty on the platform outside. I noticed that Qiao was looking deathly tired and the Secretary of State wasn't looking particularly tired but certainly tense. The Chinese counselor sat with a heavy black briefcase on his knees, clutching it with gloved hands.

Barstow, our Private Secretary, looked at his boss, and Jarrow nodded, but then there was another holdup while Ambassador Qiao got a handkerchief out and blew his nose and asked us to excuse him because he'd caught a cold. His English was perfect, I would have said Cambridge.

The scene was a degree surrealistic, and I think it put the Chinese off, being in a train underground instead of a nice formal office. The hand straps hung down above our heads like tiny gibbets in a row, and we could see our faces on this side reflected behind the people opposite, under the dim ceiling lights. The doors had been shut on us with a definitive thump, and we looked as if we'd been thrown together in purgatory, without knowing where the train was going to take us, heaven or hell.

Jarrow pulled out a gold cigarette case and asked if anybody minded and no one spoke so he lit up and Barstow started talking.

"So that we all know what's going on, I'll recap the main

points for you." He sat forward on the seat, hands on his knees and feet together, looking from one face to the next and giving each of us a precisely allotted share of his cool blue eyes. "Ambassador Qiao came to us two days ago and told us that after the democratic uprising in Beijing of last week, he feels he no longer wishes to represent the Communist regime at present in power there. His intention was to defect, and he asked us for asylum. His counselor, Mr. Hou Jing, has identical feelings. We conferred with MI6, who agreed it would be far more useful for all concerned if the ambassador remained at his post and made himself available to us as a source of information."

Qiao sat slumped on the seat, but I didn't think he was going to doze off. A lot of his fatigue must have been due to stress: a couple of days ago he'd been a bona fide ambassador and now he was in effect an intelligence agent working for the West. He didn't look the type who'd commit an act of betrayal too easily.

"He and his counselor declared themselves willing to do this," Barstow said, his eyes resting on mine and passing on to Hyde's. "The ambassador would probably like me to point out that in the present circumstances he regards his action as simply a shift of loyalties, from the Chinese government to the Chinese people."

No one spoke, though I thought we should have clapped or something. Jarrow flicked ash from his cigarette, looking at nobody.

"Ambassador Qiao," the Private Secretary went on, "has conferred with the Prime Minister, who is therefore acquainted with the situation, and who has pledged her assistance in any way possible with the ambassador's proposals. Mr. Hyde and Mr. Jones were called upon, and have declared themselves ready to implement those proposals by whatever means are open to them. I need hardly say, gentlemen, that the most extreme discretion must be used by all those present, when we are no longer protected by the security measures we enjoy at the present time."

If those measures, of course, were adequate. Maybe I was paranoid, but the fact remained that if this meeting had taken place a few years ago, the Foreign Office could have been represented here by Kim Philby.

"Before Ambassador Qiao presents his ideas, are there any questions?"

"What's going to be our timing?" Hyde asked him. "How quickly have we got to move?"

"Almost immediately, as far as I can gather, but we'll have a more precise idea from Ambassador Qiao."

It was getting stuffy in here, and I took off my bomber jacket. There was also a certain amount of heat generating from the nerves: Barstow had said we'd have to move almost immediately and by tonight the Bureau could have catapulted me straight into Beijing, and I didn't feel ready for that.

"If there are no other questions, I'll ask Ambassador Qiao to take over."

The Chinese got out his handkerchief again and when he'd finished he said with a note of apology, "I hope that the proposals I'm about to give you will offer a chance for my country to free itself of its present onerous regime, and at the same time break down the barriers between China and the rest of the world. But there are risks. There are very grave risks." He shifted to the edge of the seat and leaned his elbows on his knees, his small pale hands hanging loose; the light glinted across his glasses as he turned his head sometimes to look at us, though mostly he looked down. He didn't have the air of a renegade storming the barricades, but that was obviously what he was going to do, and as I watched his face, hollowed by fatigue, I felt something that doesn't often get through the scaly carapace of suspicion and distrust that forms around us in this dirty trade. It was compassion.

"In one sense," Qiao said, "the recent uprising is already causing more anguish than the one in June 1989, when the reaction by the government was confused and at first indecisive, and when the ensuing bloodshed evoked, at least, the attention and the sympathy of the rest of the world."

His head was lowered now and there was an edge to his tone that cut through the silence when he spoke again. "This time there was immediate reaction by the government; there was almost no media coverage of the event; there was almost no bloodshed, since the security forces were quick to move in; and very little news has leaked out from Beijing. Let me tell you, gentlemen, that this new uprising has in effect proved an infinitely greater tragedy than the last one, since most of the participants were intellectuals of high standing, with more chance and more hope than before of combating and ousting the government, only to see that hope shattered within days. And instead of visible bloodshed in the streets, we have a secret and most sinister operation under way that is bringing the intellectual elite from their homes in the thick of the night, torn from their families and thrown into the torture chambers and finally to the execution squads of this merciless regime and if you feel, gentlemen, that I am re-sorting to the idiom of cheap journalism"—his head swung up to look at us—"in order to get your sympathy, it is not the case. These people, the most enlightened intellects be-hind science and industry and education, are indeed being taken from their homes and tortured and finally shot to death, as we sit here now. My brother is one of them."

The silence hit us in the face and then I heard someone say "Oh, Jesus," under his breath.

"I'm sorry." Jarrow, Secretary of State.

"But what is more important," Qiao said quickly, "is that whereas the uprising of 1989 slammed the door on our hopes of democracy in the People's Republic of China, the recent flare-up of dissension has locked and barred it and drawn chains across it that we shall not, I think, see broken asunder in our lifetime." He took his glasses off and wiped them, and I noticed the edge of his eyelids glistening. "Unless of course we can succeed in what I shall propose."

I had questions but couldn't ask them. Were these tears for his brother or for China? How much had his personal tragedy pushed him into betrayal and defection, into bring-

27

ing us down here tonight to listen to him? Hyde would know. He knew the whole thing: he'd probably been at the conference at No. 10 with Qiao, because the Bureau is responsible directly to the Prime Minister. He'd known enough, at least, to set up the mission and select me for the field and get me down here tonight, privy to information that would rock Beijing if it got out: *I need hardly say, gentlemen, that the most extreme discretion must be used by all those present*, yes indeed.

Qiao was using his handkerchief again; I didn't think it was really a cold; it was because of the cable he'd had, the signal to the embassy in Portland Place: *Regret to inform Your Excellency that your brother has been arrested and his whereabouts are not at present known*, or words to that effect. It could have been only hours ago when he'd heard it, perhaps even less.

"There is one man," he said, "who has so far escaped the firing squad. His name is Dr. Xingyu Baibing, our most renowned astrophysicist and the most popular intellectual in the country, since his outspoken criticism of the present regime has brought it home to the people and especially to his fellow intellectuals that oppression by the ruling clique and corruption within it do not necessarily have to be endured for all time. This man became a popular figure in 1987, when he was ousted from the Communist Party for making speeches on behalf of democracy and inciting student rebellion. His standing with both the Chinese intellectuals and the people in the street is comparable with that of Lech Walesa in Poland. Today Dr. Xingyu has been branded by the Communists as a traitor and—I quote—among the scum of the nation. He is accused of committing crimes of counterrevolutionary propaganda and instigation, and his immediate arrest has been ordered."

The young counselor, sitting next to him, unzipped the heavy briefcase and brought out some papers, but Qiao motioned them away. "The night before last, Dr. Xingyu sought refuge inside the British embassy in Beijing, and he is there now as a guest of the British government and under its protection."

Reflected in the windows opposite I saw Hyde turn his head to look at me. I didn't look back. I watched Qiao. In his last few words he'd focused the whole thing for us, like a zoom lens moving in.

"We should not, of course, expect that the Communists in Beijing will necessarily respect international laws designed to protect foreign embassies. We should remember the sacking of the U.S. embassy in Tehran, and the torching of the British embassy in Beijing itself by Mao's Red Guards. The safety of Dr. Xingyu cannot be guaranteed, since it is in inverse proportion to his importance to the democracy movement. He endangers the regime by his very existence, and the British government is under great pressure by the Chinese, as you can imagine, to turn its guest out of the embassy into the hands of the militia now waiting outside the gates." He glanced across at Jarrow, the Secretary of State.

"That, yes, is the position," Jarrow said. "Her Majesty's Government is of course resisting the belligerent demands of the Chinese and will continue to do so." He looked as weary as Qiao and his counselor, or maybe it was the dim yellowish lighting; but for the last two nights he would have been in late and exhaustive sessions with Thatcher and her advisers. "I should tell you, however, that we are working out a plan on the highest diplomatic levels to obtain an undertaking from the Chinese that if we were to release Dr. Xingyu from our embassy—that's not quite the word, of course, since he's a guest and not a prisoner—if Dr. Xingyu were to leave the embassy at his own request, he would be allowed free passage to the airport." He passed a hand over his eyes, squeezing them shut for a moment. "The exchange has been going on pretty intensely, of course, and the good ambassador and I have not had too much sleep—nor indeed has the Prime Minister. On the one hand, my government is trying to persuade the Chinese that since we intend to continue our hospitality to Dr. Xingyu for as long as he wishes—for years, if it comes to that—it might be better for them to throw him out of the country and into exile, where he couldn't do much harm. On the other hand, they're very keen to get him under their control and brainwash him and push him in front of the television cameras to confess his sins and declare himself reformed, putting him through, politically speaking, a frontal lobotomy and rendering him harmless to the regime. From our side, we are of course offering certain trade concessions to give our argument a little weight. Look," he said to Barstow, "do you think those chaps outside could rustle up some tea?"

That was 3:30 A.M.

It had got smoky in here by now and the MI6 man had gone along the coach pulling the little windows open. Most of us had got through our first cup of tea and were on the second one: the police outside had brought a whole urn, piping hot, with a boxful of plastic cups.

The Chinese ambassador was talking about the People's Liberation Army.

"There is a schism in the military that reflects the political scene in Beijing. There are bones of contention among the commanders and their troops. As you know, some of the armies surrounding the capital in 1989 showed sympathy for the students in Tiananmen Square, and many officers were shot for refusing to fire on the people. At least fifteen generals are still in prison awaiting courts-martial. In the uprising of last week there was, as you know, no military action called upon, though a readiness alert went out to all commanders in the vicinity of Beijing. While the old guard is still loyal to the Communist Party, the young and educated officers now rising from the ranks are impatient for reforms that would turn the PLA into a modern, more professional military machine, with new weapons and new technologies that the United States and other Western countries would be prepared to offer them, once a democratic government was in power."

Light flashed from the tunnel as the welder used his jet. The plainclothes police on the platform stood at ease with their hands behind them, not moving about very much. Smoke curled from Jarrow's cigarette, fanning out under the ceiling lamps. The MI6 man got himself another cup of tea from the urn and went back to his seat. I didn't think it was likely that anything that could be said in the stale confines of this railway coach buried deep underground in London could have the power to change the lives of a billion people on the far side of the planet.

Dead wrong.

"I will put it simply for you," Ambassador Qiao said. "Despite the present unrest among the People's Liberation Army, and despite the growing sympathy of many of its generals for the intellectuals in their underground fight for democracy, I do not believe that any spontaneous military action could be expected in defiance of the government in Beijing. We cannot hope for armed support for any future uprising, based solely on the sympathy of certain generals. But I do believe that given new inspiration, given a leader who could offer himself to the people and lend them his power as a figurehead, we could indeed incite the armed counterrevolution that is needed to bring down the Communist regime." He paused, I think to make sure he was getting our attention. "Dr. Xingyu Baibing could give us that power, if he could leave your embassy unmolested by the security forces."

I saw Hyde turn his head slightly toward me again, reflected in the window. Objective for the mission, yes, Xingyu.

"I should tell you, gentlemen," Qiao said, "that my decision to defect was not an impulse. I became disgusted in June 1989, when the ghost of Mao rose and brought brutality and bloodshed back into the streets. Since then, I have made it my business to establish contacts and relationships in Beijing that would be called treasonable, and for which I should be shot. Among those contacts is a certain general of the People's Liberation Army. He is now prepared and waiting, with his armored division, to support the armed rebellion that could be effected under the leadership of Dr. Xingyu, who is also waiting—for the freedom in which to act."

He got out his handkerchief again, this time to wipe his face. He was talking about inciting a coup that could bring his country out of stagnation and despair and into the light of freedom and its fruits; world acceptance, world trade, and an honorable place in the community of nations; and on a personal level, perhaps, he was talking of the hope that there would be time to save his brother.

"After all," he said in mock innocence, "we shall only be following the wisdom of the late Chairman Mao himself, who said that power lies in the mouth of a gun. If you, gentlemen, can vouchsafe the freedom of Dr. Xingyu Baibing, we shall have that gun in our hands."

Qiao left ahead of us, his counselor with him, clutching his big briefcase. Hyde and I stopped for a few minutes to talk to the MI6 man; then we took the elevator to street level and walked into the open air and the wail of police sirens, and stood there with the flash of the colored lights in our eyes and our breath clouding in the chill of the morning as we looked down at the little Chinese ambassador spread-eagled on the pavement with his glasses smashed and his blood trickling across the edge of the curb.

Chapter 3

Pepperidge

S he was very thin, and faded-looking, still pretty, though, perhaps had been stunning, once, with her large eyes and her cheekbones. She sat decoratively on the worn settee, her thin legs trying, I believed, to cover the patch of cretonne where the cat had sharpened its claws, where perhaps it always did.

"Would you like some tea?"

"No," I said, "thank you. I haven't much time."

"He won't be long now," she said.

"Supposing I go and meet him?"

"You could try. But I don't know whether he's gone to the grocer's or the post office, and they're in different directions." She smiled ruefully at the contrariness of life.

"I see."

The cat was on a windowsill by a pot of geraniums, its fur mangy, their leaves yellowed. It spreads everywhere, if you let it, or can't stop it, through the body and into the house, through the house. They'd told me she had cancer.

"It's so cold," she said in her pretty voice, "so early, this year, isn't it?"

"Yes. We could get a white Christmas, though."

There must be a kind of terrible relief, I thought, in actually knowing you didn't have long, in knowing that it wasn't worth the effort of trying to fight it off, in having time to get ready, and tidy all the drawers, instead of taking your fear with you to a rendezvous with potential death as I did,

33

time after time, carrying it for years like putrefying baggage.

"... last year, didn't we?"

"I'm sorry?"

"I said we had a little snow last year, didn't we, for Christmas?"

"Yes, that's right," I said, "I remember."

What would her brother give her for Christmas? A posy for her grave? We tend, as I'm sure you've noticed, to be a trifle morbid when we're waiting to go out.

"What's she called, your cat?"

"Smoky. It's actually a he." Another little smile.

"He's very handsome," I said. I like cats myself; I always think of them as female, I suppose because of their grace and their mysteriousness.

"If you haven't got long," she said, "you could go and stand outside, to watch for him. Then you could go and meet him."

"All right."

But he was coming down the narrow little path between the patches of brownish grass when I went out there.

"Hello," he said. "You were quicker than I'd bargained for." I'd phoned him from the Bureau. "I had to get some things for Gladys."

"That's all right." I took one of the brown paper bags and we went back into the house.

Pepperidge had only directed me once in the field in Singapore; he'd conned me into it at the Brass Lamp, making me think he was a burned-out spook, too far gone to take it on himself. He'd been very good, before that, as a shadow, first-class at covert infiltration, knew how to kill with discretion when it was necessary; then he'd come in and managed the Asian desk for a while. He'd been a good DIF, getting me through the Singapore thing without any fuss and doing most of it from London, through the signals mast at Cheltenham, before he'd come out to the field and brought that bastard Loman with him. But Loman had done well too, handled me well, give him his due.

"How are things going?" I asked Pepperidge.

"Oh," he said cheerfully, "we soldier on, you know. Did they tell you about her, then?"

"Yes."

He nodded, picking up a spanner, looking at it. We were out in the little toolshed at the back, where she couldn't hear us; not that she'd pass anything on, I was sure; it was just our natural habit to drift somewhere out of earshot, wherever we were. "She hasn't got anyone else, you see. Poor old George went—oh, it must be five or six years ago now. I'm all she's got left." He gave a dry laugh, watching me with his yellow eyes in the half-light of the shed, the shadow of his rather ragged mustache hiding most of his mouth. "Been mending the lawn mower," he said, putting the spanner down, "though the grass is pretty well dead."

The word dropped into the silence like a stone into a pond, irretrievably, and I saw the slight tightening of the skin across his sharp cheekbones; then it was over. "Know anything about lawn mowers?"

"You have to push them along, don't you?"

"Only if you can't wheedle out of it. They got the fidgets again, have they?"

"Yes."

"Anything to do with the Chinese ambassador?"

It had been on the nine-o'clock news.

"I can't really tell you anything," I said, "because they've thrown a blackout across it. All I really came for was to find out if you'd be interested in taking it on."

"Directing you?"

"Yes."

In a moment he said, "It was nice of you to bring her flowers."

She'd put them straight into a vase, and shown them to him when we'd come back. "She's a pretty woman," I said.

"I suppose she is." He was thinking about what I'd been saying, about the mission.

"She ought to get married again," I told him.

35

"Why not? Why not. . . ." He brushed some dry grass cuttings off the edge of the worn bench. "No one else phoned me, I suppose you know that? Only you."

"Hyde was going to, but I said I wanted to come here on my own, see how things were, sound you out."

"That was kind." He stared through the little cracked window, where there was a piece of paper sticking: *Get blades ground.* "Hyde's going to run it?"

"Yes."

"He pick me?"

"No. He asked me who I wanted."

"You couldn't get Ferris?" The gray October light touched his face at an angle from the window; he wasn't all that old, perhaps forty, but the skin had shriveled into fine lines across his cheeks, like a balloon almost deflated. He'd been out East a lot.

"Ferris hasn't got Chinese," I said. But he knew that I must have tried for Ferris and couldn't get him. "It's very big, this one. Very big indeed."

"Or they wouldn't have asked for you."

"I was available. It wouldn't keep us out there too long, so Hyde said. A matter of days, all going well."

"Days?" He turned his head to look at me. "Sounds pretty concentrated."

"That's why MI6 wouldn't touch it."

"They were approached first?"

"Yes. The thing is, we're talking about looking after someone out there, and he's going to be right in the spotlight. We might have to do things they can't." The Bureau doesn't officially exist, but the other services are expected to keep their house clean, not get into anything wet. They're specifically public servants, whereas you could call us, I suppose, a maverick force, answerable only to the PM.

"Looking after someone," Pepperidge said, puckering his thin mouth. "There's already one down, isn't there?"

"Yes."

He meant the Chinese ambassador. They'd come in very

early, the opposition, though not early enough: the meeting we'd had would provide the blueprint for the whole mission. My guess was that Qiao hadn't been discreet since the uprising of '89, when he'd become "disgusted." It couldn't have been easy for him to hide it, in the confines of his embassy in London. Or perhaps he'd talked to his brother, and his brother had been put under the screws out there, and Beijing intelligence had signaled their agents here in London: *Get Qiao.*

"The other chap came through, though," Pepperidge said, "didn't he?"

Hou Jing, the little counselor. "They said his briefcase saved him. There was a lot of stuff in it."

"Close shot?" He was still watching me.

"Passing car."

"There were some policemen killed, it said on the—"

"Three. It was an assault rifle."

"Those bloody things. I suppose there wasn't anything like a bit of kevlar in that briefcase, was there?"

"I thought of that too."

In this trade we are steeped, as I told you, in subterfuge. Hou Jing could have worked as a spotter.

Pepperidge looked through the window again, and got a piece of rag and wiped some of the grime off, but most of it was outside in the air, fog pressing down from a steel-gray sky. "Let's go in," he said, "and talk to Gladys."

She was in the kitchen, scraping at the bottom of a burned saucepan, her thin body leaning against the sink; I would imagine she got tired easily.

"You go," she said, when Pepperidge put it to her—we were in the sitting room now, where the cat was arched like a drawn bow with its claws on the settee and its haunches flat on the carpet. "I'll be perfectly all right here," she said. "*Don't*, Smoky! I've got friends who come in, Doris and Marjorie." She didn't ask how long he was talking about, I think in case it was a long time and she'd feel scared and we'd see it.

"It's only for a few days," her brother said quickly.

"Oh," relieved, "then what's all the fuss?" A pretty smile, radiating life.

"If you go out, Glad, I don't want you walking any farther than Tesco's."

"All right."

"And don't carry anything too heavy. Doris has got her car."

"I've never heard such a fuss! Now off you go, for goodness sake." She picked up the cat and held it while she came to the front door with us. "It was so nice of you to bring the flowers." The smile of a young girl, shy and vulnerable. I couldn't take her hand because of the cat, so I kissed her cheek and we went out, Pepperidge and I, and got into the Lamborghini.

"Nice hot cuppa, love?"

"Please."

She looked at me from under the heavy false lashes. "Do you good."

She mopped the plastic table top and limped off to the tea urn with her arthritic hip. You think your nerves aren't showing, but Daisy will catch the vibrations.

Pepperidge had been put on a plane for Hong Kong an hour ago and I'd been cleared and briefed and there was nothing to do now, nowhere to go while I waited, as the light lowered in the basement window, the winter seeping into the room like a cold shadow, dimming the light bulbs, bringing a chill to the air. They'd overdone the thermostat thing when Hyde had sent his instructions, and now this bloody place was as cold as the grave.

"There you are, love."

"Thank you, Daisy."

"What about a nice buttered bun?"

"All right."

For something to do. I sat with my hands around the cup of tea to warm them. Anyone forming the actual intention of putting this stuff into his body would be clean off his rocker: it's jet-black and there's enough caffeine in it to blast the back end off a bulldog. What we really come down here for is to escape the madhouse going quietly on upstairs along those bleak and dimly lighted corridors and behind the doors of those unnamed and unnumbered rooms, with signals coming in from the mast at Cheltenham and traffic going out from Codes and Cyphers, the whole giddy circus engaged in the sinister task of dealing with lies and secrets, subversion and betrayal, in the name of the need to know.

"There you are, duck."

Margarine, not butter, but what can you do? What they budget for in this place is to buy loyalty, to put a price on trust, to replace a car full of bullet holes at some far frontier post, to arrange, when things go wrong, for funerals, to fork out a widow's pension.

"I put it in the microwave for you."

Standing over me with her bright ginger wig like a fire in the gloom and her rouged cheeks burning with the warmth of motherly love.

"Good old Daise."

We come here for escape and the comfort of this woman's saintly presence as she limps from table to table and back to her huge steaming urn, our very own blowsy and overblown Mother Teresa, garbed in her stained and sluttish apron and dispensing not only her black undrinkable tea and her stale uneatable buns but also the sweet anodyne of compassion that we need so badly when we crawl back from a mission with the rattle of shot or the scream of a dying man still echoing in the far reaches of the mind, or when we sit here with our hands around a cup while our fate hangs in the balance like a rope in the wind, as those bastards upstairs turn the signals round and peck at the computers and shuffle softly from room to room in their worn suede shoes and finally decide which one of us should be picked for the mission that's just come onto the board, which one of us shall be sent out to worm our way through the dark serpentine shafts of the labyrinth to seek the enemy and overcome him, pre-mission nerves, I trust you will understand and perhaps even excuse, this is just a touch of the willies.

"You'll need to get that dressing changed every three days, until they say you can leave it off."

Clearance, medical section. I'd said yes, I understood.

"And you need to take a gram of C and two hundred and fifty milligrams of calcium in this form, the citrate, every day."

"Why?"

"You're just back, aren't you, and going out again?"

"Yes."

"That's putting a strain on the adrenals." She gave me the small plastic box. "Don't forget."

I'd got a map of Hong Kong and a plan of the airport from Travel but I hadn't studied them yet and didn't want to: nothing was certain; they might not be able to con the Chinese into giving Dr. Xingyu free passage out of the embassy, or any one of a dozen scenarios could come up and we'd have to abort this one while the shadow executive was still trying to get his teeth into this bloody bun.

I kicked the chair back and went out of the Caff and up the stairs and along the corridor to the room at the end and found a slack-bodied woman in a drooping twinset peering into a filing cabinet through a pair of steel-rimmed glasses that were surely thick enough to be bulletproof.

"The buns," I said. This was what they grandly called Administration Services. "Those bloody *buns* down there."

She looked around and stared. "Buns?"

A girl came through the doorway and took a look at my face and scuttled for cover behind a pile of papers. "Those *buns* down there in the Caff," I said, "are nothing more than resuscitated crud left over from Oliver Twist's workhouse. Have you ever—"

"If you wish to make a complaint, you'll have to fill in the appropriate form in triplicate. We can't—"

"You expect us to go out there and shove our heads right into the cannon's mouth and when we're lucky enough to come back the best you can give us is crud." I looked at the mousy-faced girl. "What's your name?"

"Gertrude, sir."

"Little Gertrude, do something for me. Fill out the appropriate form in triplicate with my complaint, which you can put down as attempted food poisoning, and drop it into my message box for me to sign."

I went along to see Holmes and blow his head off for nothing at all, which is what friends are for, but he wasn't in, so I looked in at Signals and saw a very sticky endgame going with Croder himself manning the board for *Flamingo* and Holmes watching the score as the stuff came in from Nigeria. Two other boards were open, the fourth was dark, and the last one was lit up but blank except for the word *Bamboo* chalked at the top, code name for the mission. That would be mine, and I stood for a moment looking at it with a feeling of time warp going through me, as if I could already see the future, the board filling with status reports as Pepperidge sent them in from the field, with routine information or requests for help; and I wondered how far down the board we'd manage to go before something flew at me from the dark or a wheel came off or I ran into a dead end with nowhere else to run, and Pepperidge would have to send the last signal: *Shadow down.*

The adrenals, yes, a strain on the adrenals, so let us quietly close the door of the signals room and go back to the Caff and drink some tea and pop some calcium and inform Daisy that one fine day she might well achieve a certain tawdry stardom in this bloody place for being able to offer its hard-pressed denizens some eatable buns.

Ten minutes later my beeper went and I used a phone and they told me Hyde wanted to see me for final briefing, and I knew they weren't going to abort this one: the mission had started running.

* * *

"Pepperidge," Hyde told me, "will be in Hong Kong by the morning. That was a good choice you made," swinging his large head to watch me obliquely, "with Pepperidge. He's very fine indeed with his signals and of course he's got a great deal of regard for the way you work."

"I didn't know."

"He said it was an honor. I'm sending you out tonight, is that all right?"

"Whenever."

"You'll stop over in Bombay to meet someone. The situation is this. The Foreign Office together with the PM has managed to complete a workable deal with Premier Li Peng, assuring him that we are willing to keep Dr. Xingyu Baibing in our care at the embassy out there for as long as he wishes, which could of course be years, during which time our relations with China would remain distinctly cool. We have made it clear that a guarantee from Beijing that Dr. Xingyu could move safely from the U.K. embassy to the airport would in turn bring our guarantee that normal trade could be resumed between the two countries."

"Xingyu's going straight to Hong Kong?"

"Straight there."

"When?"

"Within a few days. They'll give us a specific date and time when they're ready—they're making the concession, not us. That part, actually, was comparatively easy. The difficult part was to persuade them that we're not aware that the moment Dr. Xingyu lands in Hong Kong he's to be snatched by Chinese agents and sent straight back to Beijing for brainwashing."

He poked his tongue into his cheek and waited.

"Why can't Xingyu be met by a platoon of Hong Kong police and taken into hiding?"

"I'm not sure," Hyde said, "whether anyone's made an estimate of the percentage of the Hong Kong police force who are active agents for Beijing, but I would put it rather high. Xingyu would be walking right into the tiger's mouth. We can trust, you see," his large flat hand hitting the desk, "no one. No one at all. We also have to relax their agents at the very critical time when Dr. Xingyu lands at the airport, by letting it seem that we have not the slightest idea that he's up for snatching. We shan't even be sending anyone from the British High Commission as a formal courtesy. The *major* requirement is to play this operation in very low key."

"What happens to the clerk?"

"He'll melt away at the right time. I'll go into that for you; then you must tell me how you think you're going to get Dr. Xingyu clear."

"Few questions first."

"Of course."

It was after seven in the evening, and the sounds of the traffic outside had changed, coming off the rush-hour high with not so many buses now, more taxis honking as people started out for the evening. It calmed me, I think, a little, to hear the steady beating of the city's pulse, something for me to remember, a touchstone, when I was out there in the cold.

"What are we going to do," I asked Hyde, "about the media? They'll be jamming the airport and they'll get in my way."

"No, we thought about that, so the FO made the kind suggestion to Beijing that Dr. Xingyu should be smuggled in a plain van from the embassy to the airport and put onto the last night flight, strictly incognito and with a briefed cabin crew. This would avoid, we suggested, unwanted publicity that would make it seem that in allowing Dr. Xingyu his freedom, Beijing had lost the game. It was meant to look like another concession and they went for it."

There'd been some good thinking, and it reassured me a little. "Where do you want me to take him?"

"Out of Hong Kong." One of the phones rang and he pressed the off switch. "There's no way you could safely keep him there, even if he wanted to stay—the place is infested with mainland agents. Beijing has grabbed at this deal because it's pretty well their only chance of getting their hands on Dr. Xingyu again, and when he lands in Hong Kong they'll have their own people there in force. And when you take him over they're going to ransack the island and at the same time they're going to put every point of exit under close and immediate observation. That," he said with his hand dropping onto the desk again, "is the objective for the mission. Not just to take this man into your safekeeping at the airport, but to get him out of Hong Kong."

"Where to?"

That bloody shark bite had started itching.

"Wherever he wants to go—subject to our good counsel."

It was on the left forearm, and the smell of the antiseptic was getting on my nerves.

"Are you sending pictures of me to the U.K. embassy for Xingyu to look at?"

"We faxed them out there as soon as you accepted the mission. Dr. Xingyu's instructions will be that once he recognizes you at Hong Kong airport he'll do exactly as you tell him. His life, he realizes, will be in your hands, because if they can't snatch him back they'll go for a kill."

He poked his cheek again; that was getting on my nerves too, like the shark bite. Everything was getting on my nerves, and it was going to be like this until I reached the field. Part of it was because of the kill they'd already made, early this morning.

"Ambassador Qiao," I said. "What's the analysis?"

Hyde got up and went to a window, shoving his huge hands into his pockets. His voice bounced off the glass. "It's too early for a complete analysis, of course. It's been impossible to ask any questions in his embassy here, even by phone. The diplomatic card is that Her Majesty's Government deeply regrets the affair, but the language was couched to make it perfectly clear that the assassination was none of our doing and they'd better not try to accuse us. It's fairly obvious that Qiao hadn't been able to hide what he called his disgust with his government, and when his brother surfaced as a resurgent last week they added things together and ordered a wet affair, before Qiao could try defecting. They were of course too late."

"He could have been followed," I said, "to the tube station last night."

"Despite the precautions, yes." He half-turned his head. "The Foreign Office set up that rendezvous, together with the Yard. We'd have done it differently."

"All those police." I got out of my chair, too, feeling restless.

"All those police, yes. But what could we do? The FO had called us in. It was their field."

"Hou Jing," I said. The little embassy counselor with the briefcase. "Where's he now?"

"In the country. He seems terribly cut up, but he's being rather carefully questioned, of course."

There was a black rectangular clock on the desk, with a disk you could turn through the international time zones. Here in London it was 7:14. "Was Hou Jing's briefcase actually hit?" I asked Hyde.

"At an angle. It was in fact shot out of his hands."

In a moment I said, "I don't want to be blown before I'm even clear of London."

Hyde moved his head, tilting it upward, his eyes remaining on my face. "We shall make it our business," he said, "to ensure that nobody gets at Hou Jing. Until you complete your mission, he will remain under protective house arrest."

I left it at that because most of it was paranoia and I didn't want it to show. I felt drawn to the clock again because time was running down, my time in London.

At 7:20 we sat down again and I told him how I was going to take over Dr. Xingyu at the airport and put him in a safe house until we could get him out of Hong Kong. The safe house was for Pepperidge to set up when the time came. It took me twenty minutes and Hyde said he liked it and told me I'd get the people I wanted at the scene.

"You'll be flying to Bombay," he said, "via Cairo, where you won't leave the aircraft. We've made a rendezvous for you with a man named Sojourner."

"He's Bureau?"

"No. He's been around the U.K. embassies for quite a few years and he's been a first secretary in Beijing for the past eighteen months. He's made contacts there, some of them underground—it's the way he likes to work. One of his contacts is the People's Liberation Army general who's pledged to support Dr. Xingyu." He didn't tell me the general's name. He wasn't telling me a lot of things; all he wanted me to have in my head when I went out there were the absolute essentials. The less I knew, the less anyone could get out of me if I ran into a trap and couldn't reach the capsule in time.

"What is Sojourner's job?"

"He's the coordinator. He'll put everything together at ground zero, as you'll hear when you meet him. Let me say that he's extremely capable and we have every confidence in him."

"What's his intelligence background?" I would have been happier if Sojourner had been Bureau, not an itinerant diplomat.

"He has no actual intelligence background, but in point of fact it was he who suggested this whole scenario to the late Ambassador Qiao, in essence, following clandestine approaches to the army general. You may trust Sojourner. You may trust him completely."

There wasn't anything I could say. I had to trust all of them completely: the Head of Bureau, Chief of Signals, London Control, my director in the field, and whoever was manning the signals board if *Bamboo* began running hot.

7:46 on the black clock and I looked away. "How many people have you got lined up to replace me if I go down?"

In a moment Hyde said heavily, "I don't understand."

"Oh for God's sake." Showing my nerves; too late to take it back.

"I would certainly have told you," Hyde said, "earlier in your briefing, if I intended to put anyone else into the field. We—"

"Look, I'm just one man, and you're talking about bringing down a government. It's—"

"You don't feel confident?"

"Of course I feel confident, but why not put ten people into the field, a protective cadre with Xingyu in the middle?"

"As they did with Guzhenko?"

It stopped me dead in my tracks, as it was meant to do. Five years ago the Bureau had tried to bring Guzhenko across to the West, an invaluable double agent with his head stuffed with ultrasensitive information, and it had to be done extremely fast because he'd been blown and our people had picked him up from the half-submerged wreck of a dredger on the Volga where he'd run for cover. Portland had been London Control for the mission and he'd sent out six men and a support group backing them up, and one of the six had been caught and took a capsule in time and the next one had run out on the operation when the KGB had closed in and two others were shot in a rearguard action and the support group had scattered because Guzhenko was exposed and targeted and there was nothing they could do, *nothing*, and the trap was shut and Guzhenko was taken back to Moscow and thrown into a psychiatric ward and came out five weeks later with his head as empty as a coconut husk and half the files in our Moscow desk blown through the ceiling.

I said: "Point taken."

"Good. I run things differently."

7:51.

"Yes. No more questions."

Hyde came to the door with me. "There's an enormous weight of responsibility," he said, "on all of us. The destiny of a billion people, if one were to put it vulgarly, is at stake. But don't let that discountenance you. This is a case of softly, softly, catchy monkey—in other words we play this very low-key."

I saw Holmes for a minute and picked up my briefing and the prepacked suitcase on my way out of the building and the time on the round oak-framed clock in the hall showed 8:02, and that was the time they would note on the signals board for *Bamboo*, after the date and the chalked entry: *Executive dispatched*.

Chapter 4

Incense

They circled continuously over the dead.

"And how is London?"

"Cold."

Here in Bombay the evening was mild, a little humid.

"I miss London."

We were on a veranda overlooking a courtyard full of frescoes and eroded statuettes and frangipanis, with only a boy in sight, white-robed, watching.

"Not everything, of course," Sojourner said, "happens in London. One has to peregrinate."

They were black against the sky, images cut from black crepe and thrown to the azure heights above the Parsee Towers of Silence on Malabar Hill, where they dived and rose and circled in the lowering light. They worried me.

"One can hardly stay all one's life in one place," Sojourner said, "even London."

I was becoming interested in seeing how long he could keep talking without actually saying anything. But he wasn't just trying to make small talk at our first meeting. He was, I thought, assessing me very carefully, watching for gestures, alert to the tone of voice.

I didn't answer, and he listened to that too.

"You flew straight out?" he asked me.

"Yes."

"And shall you be flying straight to Hong Kong?"

"I don't know."

It was the first time he'd looked at me directly. Up to now he'd been like a headmaster questioning a schoolboy, studying his nails, eyes averted, stripping the boy of his identity, listening as if to a liar. But now Sojourner looked up, but couldn't make contact: I was watching the boy down there, slender in the white robe, his eyes jeweled in the shadows as he stared up at the veranda. He hadn't been in the courtyard when I'd arrived, but had come through the crumbling stone archway soon afterward.

Sojourner looked away from me, and down at the boy. *"Door wo ja-'o', Patil. Chalah ja-'o',"* he called.

The boy slipped through the shadows, not glancing back.

"You don't know?" Sojourner asked me. About flying straight to Hong Kong.

"No."

I looked upward again. They worried me, those bloody birds. In the five towers the dead would be lying on stone slabs in three concentric circles, the men on the outside, then the women, with the children in the middle. They would be picked clean before dark.

"I see," Sojourner said, and left it at that. The implication was that he would certainly find out, and I wished him luck. *You may trust Sojourner. You may trust him completely.* Hyde. But I make my own rules in the field.

There wasn't anything to dislike, particularly, about Sojourner, except perhaps for the rather cloying cologne he used, or the slender grace of the boy in the robe. To look at he was unremarkable, a smooth well-shaven face, heavy thick-lensed glasses, decent enough suit, a lawyer, to look at, or a scientist, one of the brilliant younger men searching cleverly through the subatomic particles for the Nobel Prize. And I disliked, of course, his arrogance, because arrogance is a dangerous trait in the netherworld of subterfuge where an inflated ego can prove fatal. But I suppose it was understandable in this man, because Hyde had said the whole operation was his idea in the beginning, and he'd naturally feel he was running the show.

"Ba-ai-ra," he called, and our server came, moving quietly through the gap in the shutters, smelling faintly of body oils. *"Hum kuche order kerna cha-ha-thi hy."*

"Sahib."

"What do you think?" Sojourner asked me. "They do curries well here, of course, or do you prefer something European?"

I said I'd have whatever he was having, and we watched the last of the sated vultures drift away from the hill to the trees below as the light lowered.

Later the server touched the wicks in the brass openwork lamps with the flame of a Bic lighter, and as the darkness was pressed back, Sojourner began talking, wanting to show me, I think, how well versed he was in the world's affairs, perhaps even trying to make me see that I could trust him, because of his openness.

"The idea is not actually to save China," he said, "but to save Hong Kong, as you have probably realized. China is very resilient, and if all those people are content to live with a bowl of rice and a bicycle all their lives then it's their right to choose, and they've chosen the form of government they want, in the broader sense. We are committed, nevertheless, you and I and certain others, to bringing about a form of government that only a few thousand of them want, and with the grace of God we shall see that they get it. But that's not the real focus. The real focus is Hong Kong."

Below the veranda, people moved through the courtyard, mostly in white tunics and saris, their sandals scuffing across the cobblestones. I wasn't worried about the people in the courtyard; I'd checked the environment with the strictest attention on my way here from the airport, and the only danger was if Sojourner hadn't also covered his tracks. I assumed he would have.

"There are of course great opportunities for trade between China and the West. Ten years ago the trade figures were in the region of two billion U.S. dollars, and it's now five times bigger. But what these bright-eyed and bushy-tailed captains of industry don't realize is that a trade boom *fifty* times that big would come into being given a democratic government in China. But no one had time to squeeze the present government out of Beijing with a quick and effective stranglehold of sanctions and embargoes in '89. It would have been easy enough—the top people had already begun transferring massive amounts of cash into Swiss and Hong Kong bank accounts as soon as the uprising started, and they had a Chinese Air Force transport plane standing by in Beijing with an escort of MiG fighters to get them out of the country. Success for the democracy movement was *that* close, but big business had its nose stuck fast in the bookkeeping. Is the patatchi all right?"

I said it was very nice.

Some kind of argument had started down there on the far side of the archway; a man in a rumpled white suit was apparently trying to get into the hotel. Sojourner watched for a moment and then lost interest.

"But in Hong Kong it was different," he said. "It couldn't apply sanctions, as the West could have done. Moreover, it was told by Beijing that any real signs of support for the democratic movement would deny it the continuance of a capitalist economy after the takeover in 1997. But there were things it *could* do, by virtue of its unique political and economic position. Politically, it can do pretty well what it likes, since it's responsible to no one—it is not, for instance, a world leader required to set a shining example in everything it does. Economically it has great power and many friends among the giant corporations." As the twilight bled from the sky the lamps along the verandah held back the dark, but shadows came close, and I could no longer see Sojourner's eyes: his thick horn-rimmed glasses had become a mask, showing only reflections. "Hong Kong also has enough cold cash," he said quietly, "to buy up the People's Republic of China, and that is why we are here now."

He looked down into the courtyard again. Someone had called a policeman, but the man in the rumpled white suit was still protesting, pointing up at the two-story hotel. I had thoughts again about security. I was also having new thoughts, of course, about Sojourner. He was a great deal more than just a coordinator.

"What's happening?" I asked him.

"The man says his wife is in the hotel, and he wants her to come home. Presumably he means with the money, though he doesn't understand that she has to finish what she's doing before she can be paid. When I say to 'buy up' the People's Republic of China," turning his masked face to watch me again, "I mean of course to pay for the ousting of the doddering octogenarian clique at present in power and for the installation of a young and enlightened intellectual administration eager to embrace the capitalist way of life." He was leaning toward me a little now, I believed, though in the shifting shadows it could have been an illusion. But what I was quite certain about, as I went on listening, was that he wasn't talking so freely to me in order to give me information, but in order to celebrate his own ingenuity. "In ten years from now," he said softly, "Beijing will still be the capital of China, and Hong Kong will be its flourishing commercial center, closely comparable, if you will, with Washington and New York."

He waited until the server had taken away the plates. "Some fruit? Some preserves?"

"Not for me," I said.

"*Main kuche phal pasen karta hoo,*" he told the man, "*sha-aid ek a-am.*"

A bell had begun tolling from a temple some way off, its bright-edged sound cutting through the softness of the voices in the street beyond the archway, and the scuffing of sandals and shoes.

"It amuses me," Sojourner said, "to think that the remarkable changes about to take place in China—if you'll forgive the understatement—will have been initiated by the aforementioned doddering clique of octogenarians at present in power. It was they, after all, who announced in the *People's*

Daily in 1989 that 'not engaging in activities to overthrow the Chinese government was a precondition for allowing Hong Kong to retain its capitalist system following its adoption.' Warning enough, don't you think? Mr. Szeto Wah put it rather well when he said, 'The force of the wind tests the strength of the grass.' *That* was when it happened. *That* was when Hong Kong realized that in a few years from now it could become either an impoverished little island with the rubble of abandoned commerce littering the streets, or the economic hub of a new world power. You must have realized this yourself; you saw the papers like everyone else, and read between the lines. It was there for all to see, but no one *did* anything. Now we are to do something, and within a few days. You must surely feel . . . *excited* to be playing a part in all this."

"I do my job," I said.

He dipped a glance across the courtyard. "You do your job. Well, that's all we ask of you." Then he was watching me again in the gloom. "And what have you been told, specifically, to do?"

"I've been told, specifically, to do what you require of me."

He let it go, but it worried me. If he'd had any experience in intelligence he would have known he shouldn't ask me questions like that. The only confidence I had in this man was based on Hyde's telling me I could trust him. It wasn't enough.

In a moment Sojourner said, "When the time is right, you will be put into contact with a certain general of the People's Liberation Army, through his aides. This general was one of those who refused to have his troops fire on the civilian population—one of the few, in fact, who recognize that they are members of the *People's* Army. Others of like mind were shot for refusing to attack the students in 1989, and three, to my certain knowledge, preempted retribution by taking their own lives when they refused orders to use arms against unarmed civilians. It was my good fortune," he said carefully, "to have been in personal touch with our particular general a little time before the uprising of last week. Sensing the color of his inclinations, I made one or two trips to Hong Kong, where some of my friends have access to the top executive officers of the big American, Japanese, and Hong Kong corporations. Then I went back to the general. Have you ever played chess, by any chance?"

"Do it all the time."

"Then you'll understand my gratification that I was fortuitously in the right place on the board, at the right time, with the right people."

"And were offered the right money."

The light flashed across his glasses as he looked down quickly, interlacing his fingers and putting his hands palm down onto the tablecloth. It had sounded rude, I suppose, but I wanted to know where this man's loyalties lay. It was important, because if money were his only incentive it could be dangerous, and I'd have to signal London and tell them I was dropping the mission if they couldn't find another coordinator. I didn't expect Sojourner to be an altruist, but he'd have to show at least a degree of personal commitment to the Bureau, and to me. Mercenaries can change sides at the drop of a doubloon.

In a moment he raised his head. "Are you looking for a cut?"

"Not really."

"You don't imagine I'm sticking my neck out for the sake of a few million Chinese peasants, I hope."

I noticed he'd forgotten his studied manner of speech, and knew it was his guard coming down. This too was worrying: I hadn't said much to provoke him. How would he stand up to Chinese intelligence, if they asked any questions?

"The price you put on your services," I told him, "doesn't concern me, though I imagine it's in the region of ten or twenty million U.S. dollars, which is very nice. What concerns me is whether you might at some time sell yourself to the opposite camp for a higher figure and leave me swinging in the wind."

"They couldn't possibly afford it," he said. I think it was meant to be a joke. "But surely your desk officer told you I could be trusted?"

"He may have."

He turned his head, and I saw that the boy Patil had come back into the courtyard. He was leaning against the wall under a lamp, watching the veranda.

"So what are you going to do about it?" Sojourner asked me.

"Take a few precautions."

In a moment, "Precautions."

"Don't worry, you won't notice them."

"I've often considered," leaning back now, needing more distance, "that you people think rather—oh, I don't know—rather boyishly. Cloaks and daggers and so on."

"Have you now."

"But I'd expected you to be like this. It doesn't disturb me."

"Jolly good show. But it disturbs me a bit that you might have been followed here tonight, and that sitting in your company I might be at risk, and that Patil down there might be working as an informer. Boyish, I know, but it happens. I can show you the scars."

He didn't answer for a while, and as I sat there among the restless shadows and the oil lamps flickered to the movement of the moist night air I felt a sense of foreboding. Beyond the courtyard the night pressed down across the city, the few visible stars half lost in the haze. Voices out there in the street sounded hushed now, and I thought I heard the fluting of a snake charmer near the marketplace. The smell of incense came from the dining room through the doors behind us, sweet and heavy and oppressive. It wasn't a case of nerves, this: I was out of London and halfway to the field, and the jitters had gone. I was reacting, on a level of the psyche infinitely more sophisticated than the nerves, to vibrations in the moist and perfumed night, a trembling of the spirit's gossamer web.

"I think," Sojourner said at last, "that you exaggerate the circumstances. For someone as experienced as I'm told you are, this isn't a very dangerous operation." Clasping his hands, spreading the fingers, "No one is likely to get killed."

"Ambassador Qiao probably thought the same."

He looked down again, not knowing he didn't have to, not knowing I couldn't see his eyes behind the glasses. "In all probability," he said, "the poor chap was marked down by Beijing." Looking up at me suddenly, "He had a brother, you know, mixed up in the events of last week, and they arrested him. Talked too much, wouldn't you say, about Qiao?"

Instant chill.

The poor chap had been totally false, totally out of character, and he'd looked up like that so suddenly, almost jerking his head as he realized he'd have to face me if it were to ring true, this thing about Qiao; and when he threw in the placatory *wouldn't you say?* I didn't have any doubts left, none at all. I've lied myself so often in the field, lied to save my life, and I know how difficult it is to do well.

And there was the other thing, when we'd first met this evening—*How is London? . . . I miss London. . . . Not everything happens, of course, in London. One has to peregrinate. . . .*

"I'm sure you're right," I said.

Signal to Control: *I believe Sojourner was in London and either killed Ambassador Qiao or arranged it.*

"And after all," he was saying, "it suits our purpose rather well, don't you feel? One grieves, of course, but what if Qiao had been got at by the people on his staff at the embassy, and grilled? We wouldn't have had any operation left."

I said, "That's true."

He seemed satisfied, and looked away again, down into the courtyard, and gave a slight nod. The boy in the white robe came away from the wall and into the hotel.

"The purpose of our meeting," Sojourner said in a moment, "was to become acquainted." He was back to his mannered speech patterns, feeling relieved, reassured that his lies about Qiao's death had appeared to stand up. "And I think we've accomplished that." He pulled a folded sheet of paper from his pocket and straightened it out. "You've had your instructions from your desk officer and I've told you that you'll be in contact eventually with 'our' general through his aides. They'll tell you precisely when we need Dr. Xingyu flown back into Beijing, and that will be your responsibility. It might help you to know that we don't anticipate any major problem, once the general's task force has moved into the Great Hall of the People and placed the Chinese leader under restraint. That will be arranged to take place at a time when he is due to appear on nationwide television in order to vilify the intellectuals for their insurrection last week. Instead of doing that, he will be obliged to make the following brief announcement, at gunpoint—though the viewers will not of course see the gun." He tilted the sheet of paper to catch the light. "'A military detachment has this evening moved into Tiananmen Square to establish control there while certain negotiations proceed between my government and a spokesman for those intellectuals seeking reform. I ask the people to remain calm. There must be no demonstrations and no disorder in the streets that might cause bloodshed. You will be informed as the situation becomes clarified. Meanwhile I will repeat: there must be no provocation offered the security forces. Calm must prevail.' "

He folded the paper and put it away. "Do you have any questions?"

"It's going to need careful timing."

"Very careful timing, yes. We need senior leader Deng Xiaoping, Premier Li Peng, and Communist Party chief Jiang Zemin together in the Great Hall of the People at the same time as our general moves his tanks into the square and Dr. Xingyu Baibing is brought forward under close protective escort to take over from Deng Xiaoping in front of the TV cameras. But I envision no difficulty. It's a matter of efficient coordination."

"Do I fly Xingyu into Beijing?" I'd been briefed on this but I wanted Sojourner to think I didn't know. I wanted him to think I knew as little as possible.

"No. You'll hand him over to a special military escort that will land at whatever location you designate to pick him up. He'll be met at Beijing by a stronger contingent, which will escort him to the Great Hall of the People."

"Understood."

I asked him a few more questions and then he put some notes on the bill the server had left and we got up and went through the main dining room to the hall.

"Just a word," Sojourner said, and lowered his voice. "You'll only make things difficult for yourself if you don't decide to trust me. Your people have checked me out quite thoroughly, as you must know. I wish you a pleasant night."

It was not quite eleven and I took a turn in the courtyard for a while and then went upstairs to my room. I had the key in the door when the screams came and I took the passage at a run and heard where they were coming from and found the door locked and broke it open and saw Sojourner writhing on the floor half erect and the naked and terrified boy flattened against the wall and on the bed the cobra with its black hood spread.

Chapter 5

Messiah

The rain was hitting the deck in a deluge as I dropped onto the flooded boards from the jetty and went below and saw Pepperidge sitting there watching me.

"Traffic?"

"Solid."

"Hong Kong for you."

I shook water off my raincoat. "It took forty minutes, so I'll want an hour and a half when I leave here." Xingyu was landing at 9:12 tonight from Beijing and it was now 6:31. "Has anything changed?"

"No." Pepperidge got up and helped me off with my coat. "There's no rush."

He said it to relax me, part of his job.

"How's Gladys?"

"Fine. Spot of tea?"

I said no. I wanted an empty bladder by the time I was back at the airport to meet the objective. "Are they lined up?"

"Yes."

That was one of the things I liked about him as a director in the field. Others—Cone, Fane, that bastard Loman—would have said "Of course," meaning that I shouldn't have asked, should have trusted them to line up the people, get everything ready. But I didn't trust *anyone*. It can be fatal, if anything goes wrong or the mission starts running hot. You can—

"Have a pew." He touched my arm. "It's a piece of cake."

Showing my nerves. The thing was, I'd spent the time on the flight from Bombay going over the whole thing and I'd worked it out that when the action started at Kaitak airport I was going to take exactly nine seconds to do what I had to do. *Nine seconds.*

"I had to go through Rangoon," I told Pepperidge. "Nothing but bloody delays."

"Thought you were cutting it fine, but here you are and you've lots of time. Bit of shuteye?"

"No. I had seven hours, slept in." I hadn't planned to sleep on the plane: you don't hit the same delta waves.

"Food?"

"I'm okay."

"Calcium?"

"I forgot." He got a glass of milk from the fridge while I opened my flight bag and found the stuff.

"Feel like debriefing?"

"Go ahead. Did you get my cable?"

"Yes." He went to the end of the cabin and sat down by the phone and I joined him there. All I'd put in the cable from Bombay was *Contact down*. It couldn't mean anything else. I suppose it must have shaken him. Sojourner had been pivotal to the mission and if we couldn't find another co-ordinator the mission was dead in the water.

I watched him at the telephone, his yellow eyes shadowed by the cowl of the lamp, its light etching the mass of fine lines on his face, making it look like crumpled tissue paper. The scrambler was as big as the telephone itself, and he'd switched that on first and then dialed. I didn't know how he was sending this stuff but there were plenty of ways: he could go through Government House in Hong Kong to the Secret Services communications mast in Cheltenham and on to London, or direct to the mast or direct to London—it would depend on the degree of urgency. When he'd got my cable today he would have hit London direct.

"He's in very good shape," he was saying, "and we'll

debrief on Bombay before he leaves for the rendezvous. Everything is in order." He filled in the weather conditions and the state of the roads locally and put the phone down. It hadn't been a conversation, just a one-way report for the signals room in London, and Holmes or someone else would pick up a piece of chalk from the ledge at the bottom of the board for *Bamboo* and fill in the spaces: *Exec. arr. base 18:31 HK. Rdv. DIF. Action ready.*

Pepperidge got his pad and looked across the little teak-wood table at me and I told him what had happened at the hotel. He used the fastest shorthand I'd seen, not noting everything, just the main points. Most DIF's use tapes but there's always a risk of their getting wiped out by interference in transit, and Pepperidge doesn't like that.

"The boy didn't put the snake into the bed?"

"No. He was terrified."

"Was he a trap?"

"He could have been."

"How long did you stay there?"

"I got out straightaway, because I was obviously at risk. Other people came along—they'd heard the screaming too. I got my bag and kept clear and then followed the ambulance to the hospital, then peeled off and phoned the emergency room. I think it was a king cobra, the bloody thing was huge."

"No tags anywhere."

"I checked, believe me." I'd spent the evening with a man who'd been already targeted and I'd watched him dying.

"Sojourner didn't seem worried, anxious, beforehand?"

"No. Perfectly confident. But I wasn't certain I was ready to stay in the mission unless London would agree to replace him." I was picking my words carefully: this would go down on record at the Bureau. "I wasn't with him very long, but he came across to me as a mercenary, and therefore unreliable, possibly dangerous." I gave him the details of the conversation. "In fact I think he might have either killed Ambassador Qiao outside the tube station or had him killed."

Pepperidge held his pencil still for an instant, and then went on. "Why?"

"To keep him quiet. He was a risk to us, I grant that."

"Yes."

He made some more notes and then we began going over the action for tonight. It took half an hour and I began checking the time: I would leave here for the airport at 7:40, in twenty minutes from now. The adrenaline had started and the mouth was drying a little. I felt all right about things, felt perfectly sure I could do what had to be done; it was just that very narrow gap in the timing, just nine seconds to go in and get out and take Xingyu with me.

"You'll bring him here," Pepperidge said, recapping, "unless for some reason you're prevented. We'll keep him here until he decides where he wants to go; then we'll get him out of Hong Kong. There'll be a makeup artist coming here as soon as I signal for him; he's standing by now. Name's Koichi. He works for the Tokyo Film Corporation and lends his services to the Tokyo police now and then for their undercover people. I—"

"He's not Bureau?"

"He was one of our sleepers in Tokyo until he got too busy being successful; it seems he's a genius." He caught my expression. "He is vouched for by Bureau One himself, and I shall be here to look after things."

"You're staying?" I asked him.

In a moment, "If you've no objections."

I had to think. Once I'd got Xingyu under my wing we'd be in a red sector, and wherever we moved we'd take it with us, bring it to this boat. *Beijing has grabbed at this deal*—Hyde, in Final Briefing—*because it's pretty well their only chance of getting their hands on Dr. Xingyu again, and when he lands in Hong Kong they'll have their own people there in force. And when you take him over they're going to ransack the island and at the same time they're going to put every point of exit under close and immediate observation.*

"You'll be a bit close to things," I told Pepperidge, "on this boat."

In any mission the DIF is there to nurture the shadow executive, get his signals out and bring him London's instructions, support and liaise and comfort him, if necessary feed him, if necessary get him out of the action when a wheel comes off. But he works from his own secure base, usually a hotel, not hidden but simply unrecognized for what he is. And the executive is to make contact only when it's safe, when he's clear of the opposition and not, in other words, a danger, a contaminant. For every director who goes home there can be a dozen shadows out there hanging on the wire because the nature of their work entails risk and the director's does not.

"If it worries you . . ." Pepperidge said, and waited, his eyes on me.

I gave it some more thought and said, "Stay on the boat, then, but when Xingyu and I leave here we'll be on our own."

"Of course." He put his notepad away and got up, rummaging in a zipped bag. "It's going to help me, you see, if I can meet Xingyu and get to know him a little. I shall be better informed, more useful to you later. I brought this for you," holding out a kevlar vest.

"Instructions?"

"No," he said, "I won't insist on it."

"Those things worry me."

I believe that if you think you'll be bitten by a dog, you'll be bitten by a dog, though there's more to it than that. There's logic too: you'll behave differently when the heat's on, take unnecessary risks because you think you're protected, and besides, any professional is going to shoot for the head if he means to kill.

"I'm sure you won't need it," Pepperidge said, and stuffed it back into the bag.

There was a whistling in the air, threading its sound through the pelting of the rain on the roof of the cabin, a big jet lowering overhead on its approach path to Kaitak. We were southeast of there across the water, in Chai Wan Bay.

I looked at my watch again. I would be leaving in nine minutes.

"Synchronize?" Pepperidge said.

"Yes."

The mouth still dry, everything settling now, becoming quiet in the mind as the ego accepted the inevitability of things, the understanding that it was too late to turn back, the feeling of being carried slowly by the force of one's own decision to the eye of the storm.

This degree of gooseflesh surprised me a bit, but I suppose it was partly because there'd been three dead before I'd even reached the field.

I gave Pepperidge the cable that London had sent to my hotel in Bombay: *Mary and children arrive 9:12 PM on 11th, very much hope you can meet them. Barbara.*

He put it away. "Anything else?"

Bombay hotel bill, air tickets from London to Hong Kong, a postcard I'd bought in Rangoon to look like a tourist. He put those away too. Everything in my wallet now identified me as a resident of Hong Kong: banks, credit cards, driving license; and London had given me shoes made in Kowloon and Hong Kong labels in my clothes.

"That's all," I said.

"Then I won't keep you." He picked up the phone and dialed and I got my soaked raincoat and put it on. "You're in place?" he said into the phone, and listened for a moment and then put the receiver down and followed me as far as the deck and the pouring rain.

"Piece of cake," he said.

I said that's right and went over the side onto the jetty.

I counted twenty of them.

Flight 206 was running late, with its arrival on the screen showing a twelve-minute delay: 9:24. I had asked about it at the check-in, and they'd said there'd been head winds.

At least twenty of them, possibly more: you can't always be sure. They were professionals, all of them, not just standing around in the gate area but keeping themselves busy, buying postcards, sitting with a paper and a cup of coffee, talking to children, ruffling their heads. I recognized them by their physique—compact, muscled, athletic—and by the way they glanced across people's faces, their eyes never resting, never showing interest, never glancing at one another. I recognized them by their shoes, which were rubber-soled, like mine, not leather, and by the way they sat, and stood, and walked, not because the difference between their way of doing it and the way ordinary people did it was very great, but because there was in fact a difference, a slight one, and because I'd watched people like these in a hundred airports, in a thousand streets, and knew them for my own kind.

Twenty, then, at least, and there'd be more of them in the main hall and at the baggage claim and outside the terminal, professionals too but with less training or less natural aptitude, mobsters, if you like, dispersed throughout the environment to make a rush at any time if they were needed, piling themselves like fire ants on the flames if something went wrong.

I'd been on the move since I'd come into the gate area, pacing from one end to the other in my soft gray cap and glasses to establish the image, checking my watch now and then because the flight was late and I was getting impatient. I walked with a soldierly pace, shoulders back and hands behind me, an umbrella tucked under one arm, a copy of the *Hong Kong Times* folded into a pocket and one end sticking out.

The helicopter to Macao will depart in ten minutes. Passengers must prepare to board immediately.

I could also see the two Chinese agents who would personally greet and escort Dr. Xingyu Baibing on arrival. They were the only two men in the contingent standing together and talking to each other; they were also immaculate in blue serge suits with lots of linen showing, their smart shoes polished right down to the rubber soles. I didn't know what their cover story was; they might say they were plainclothesmen from the Hong Kong Police Department, sent here to escort Dr. Xingyu through the terminal in case he were recognized, in case the press might pester him; they would show him their official identity. Or they might say they were representatives of the Hong Kong Democracy for China Association, who would be honored to entertain him during his stay. Whatever they said, he would accept it. Those were his instructions.

Hyde had done a great deal of work, as I'd realized in Final Briefing, liaising by telephone with the British embassy in Beijing and four of the Bureau's sleepers who had gone into the embassy on routine errands. Xingyu had been shown photographs of me and given a detailed description; he'd listened to a tape of my voice. He'd been told precisely what he should do at every stage from his arrival at Gate 7 to taking his seat in the car outside: the car that I would be driving. He'd been put through an exhaustive rehearsal, using a plan of Hong Kong airport and photographs of the outside of the terminal alongside the baggage claim area. He'd been told what he must do if anything went wrong, if I or any of my three support people made a mistake.

That mustn't happen, because if it happened, Dr. Xingyu Baibing would be kept overnight as a guest of the Kuo Chi Ching Pao Chu, the Chinese Intelligence Service, and given a shot of diazepam or one of the other benzodiazepine derivatives and taken back on the first morning flight to Beijing and put into a psychiatric ward for a few weeks and then propped up in front of the television cameras, *I was wrong,* declares hero of Chinese democratic movement in dramatic appearance on TV, *I now realize that only through our resolute faith in the principles of Communism can we construct the future.*

This we must circumvent.

Japan Airlines Flight 343 to Tokyo will depart from Gate 2 in ten minutes from now at 9:34.

I took another stroll the length of the gate area and heard

the faint roar of reversed engines from the main runway and tucked my umbrella more firmly under my arm and walked back as far as the telephones, standing within a few feet of a group of women in black silk with colored beads in their hair and a travel agent holding a board marked *Criterion* and a pretty girl with calm eyes and wavy hair and a blue plaid rug over her legs in the wheelchair. No one was moving about anymore. The flashing red lamp on the top of the 747's cabin lit the windows as the jet slowed to the passenger tunnel, its thin whistle cutting through the walls.

The timing was accurate: it had touched down at exactly 9:24, as scheduled by its adjusted ETA on the screen. It was a good portent; now that we'd got the head-winds thing over, the rest of the evening would go smoothly.

I suppose Pepperidge had watched this flight a few minutes ago, lowering across Chai Wan Bay and his little boat, and now he would possibly be praying. Does Pepperidge pray?

We didn't move, any of us. We had friends to greet, wives, husbands, children, business associates, and Dr. Xingyu Baibing. *Accord him*, Hyde had told me in London, *appropriate honors while he is in your care. To the brave and desperate Chinese, he is the anointed one, the messiah.*

He was to be the last one off the plane, as agreed between London and Beijing when the deal had been struck; this was in case there were any photographers in the gate area who might recognize him.

The passengers began coming through.

Certain amount of sweat on the skin, and the mouth drying again. I slowed my breathing, brought it under conscious control.

People laughing as they went by, some of them stopping to hug, a little bunch of flowers falling, for a moment unnoticed.

Pepperidge, waiting on his boat. *Piece of cake.*

A flutter of Chinese schoolgirls in blue uniforms and prim velour hats, their laughter reminding one of bird calls. A thin beak-nosed Englishman in a crumpled tweed hat, just off the grouse moors, *"Hello, Bessie old thing!"*

Pepperidge waiting on his boat, and in the signals room in Whitehall the kind of silence that always falls at a time like this, when the executive out there in the field has reached the phase when he will either do it right or blow the mission off the board.

They'd seen the flowers now, the little bunch of flowers, and someone was picking it up, *"Oh darling, thank you, how terrible of me but I was so excited to see you."*

Then the line of people began thinning, and there were gaps, and a young Chinese came through carrying some kind of stringed instrument made of bamboo, then a lost-looking woman with tired eyes and too much lipstick and no one to meet her, and at last a short man in an overcoat and dark glasses.

The messiah.

Chapter 6

Flashpoint

The baggage claim area was crowded: Flight 206 had been at least three-quarters full and the KCCPC contingent had moved down here and taken up station around the walls, watching the carousel but not looking terribly like passengers, though it didn't matter: no one would notice.

As soon as I'd seen the two Chinese escorts go up to Xingyu Baibing and show him their identity cards I'd gone into the toilet and left my coat and cap and umbrella and newspaper in one of the cubicles and then joined the passengers. The bags hadn't started coming through yet; I stood well back from the carousel, six or seven feet away from Xingyu Baibing. He hadn't seen me yet, hadn't looked around for me. Those were his instructions.

One of my support people was in place near the exit doors to the pavement outside the terminal. He was a signaler, that was all.

The two Chinese escorts were keeping close to Dr. Xingyu, though not crowding him. They weren't expecting him to make a run for it; he'd convinced them that he believed they were friends. He didn't look like a messiah; he was short and wore an overcoat that sagged at the bottom; his shoes one could call serviceable. The only thing about him you might notice was that his hands were big for such a short man; they hung at his sides. He talked to the two men, nodding sometimes, giving a little bow as they presumably paid him a compliment. They hadn't told him they were

police officers; they were behaving much more like representatives from the Hong Kong Democracy for China Association, courteous to him, deferential. I found it refreshing
to watch intelligence agents so sophisticated.

The first bag came through the chute and flopped onto
the carousel.

I felt very good now. There wasn't one of the KCCPC
people in the place who wouldn't have shot me dead with
a silenced gun if they'd known who I was, why I was here.
The odds against me were massive in terms of numbers, but
I liked that; it honed the edge of things for me, brought me
to the state of mind where I could work at my best, going
into that strange mental zone where action becomes automatic, unimpeded by conscious thought.

You'll need more than nine seconds.

Not really.

You must have timed it wrong. You'll need much—

Shuddup.

But these people are professionals, trained to kill—

I said *shuddup.*

Bloody little organism, always sniveling when it thinks it
can smell trouble.

"I get that for you?"

An American, helping someone. A cardboard box with
string around it came out of the chute, one side split open.
I watched for my bag.

Xingyu had been asked to pack two bags, one of his own
containing junk supplied by the British embassy and one for
me, also containing junk but with a distinctive multicolored
stripe running lengthwise, so that I could recognise it easily
on the carousel. It hadn't come around yet; nor had Xingyu's.
I moved a little closer to him; both bags should come onto
the carousel at about the same time, since he would have
checked them in together.

They were speaking in Mandarin, he and his escorts, and
he gave another little bow. Then I saw the bag with the stripes
drop out of the chute and onto the carousel and I moved

forward, passing Xingyu, watching the bag, checking the name on the tag, *V. W. Locke*, and grabbing the handle, swinging the bag across the side of the carousel and turning to face Xingyu as I made my way past him, giving him time to study me while I looked past and beyond him, edging my way through the crowd.

His instructions had been to the effect that the man who picked up that particular bag would be the agent from London, and that agent would take care of him from that point onward.

The man over there by the exit door hadn't moved. He was waiting for Xingyu to get his own bag off the carousel. It hadn't come around yet, and I held back, letting a woman go past me, one of those with the pretty beads in her hair. Then I saw Xingyu move, nodding, and one of the escort people got a bag off the carousel and I turned my head and saw the man at the exit doors go outside and signal for the Jaguar.

The timing was rather more critical now: we were moving toward the flashpoint, toward the start of the nine-second phase. With a crowd this size it was easier, in a way, because of all the movement and the confusion; on the other hand I would have preferred a clearer path because I had to stay close to Xingyu now and keep up the same pace toward the doors.

I was into the zone by this time: the light seemed a degree brighter, and images, edges, outlines were sharper; they were talking, to my ear, more loudly now, Xingyu and his two escorts.

They went through the doors ahead of me. I had the bag in my hand. It was still raining outside, and people came across the roadway with umbrellas open, some of them with folded newspapers over their heads; there was a dog, yelping with excitement, soaked, shaking itself, and I heard a woman saying *Frou-Frou* to it, its name I suppose, you remember the little things as the time telescopes, moving you forward, perhaps because only the little things are unexpected, whereas the major components of the action are already familiar from the exhaustive mental rehearsal that's been going on for hours, days, *Frou-Frou*, she said, laughing because the dog was so excited about the rain, it was a Mercedes SL 20.

It was standing immediately outside against the curb. A Chinese in chauffeur's uniform was waiting with the rear passenger's door held open for Dr. Xingyu Baibing. Another Mercedes was standing immediately behind with two men sitting inside. Behind the second Mercedes was the black Jaguar XJ6, the car I'd brought here, the one the man inside the doors of the terminal had signaled for a minute ago, a minute and a half. A man was at the wheel. He was Bureau. These Jags are lively; in Hong Kong you can hire cars like that from Exclusive Rental; you can even get a Rolls if you give them enough time. I put my bag down next to some others and stood waiting.

Stood waiting for a few seconds, for the few seconds that were left before flashpoint, looking to my left for whoever it was that was meant to pick me up, though no one was meant to pick me up, we weren't going to do it like that. There were two green-uniformed policemen, one of them fifty feet away, the other closer but at the far end of the pedestrian crossing. That had been expected.

We had foreseen in Final Briefing that the permutations were countless: Chinese Intelligence could have sent only one escort to meet Dr. Xingyu, or three, or four; there could have been two men waiting with the Mercedes, or three, and more than two men sitting in the one parked behind it; there could have been fifty KCCPC people in the background, instead of the twenty or so that I'd counted, so forth. But the reality was containable; we could manage this.

Dr. Xingyu was getting into the rear of the Mercedes, the chauffeur still holding the door open for him. One of the escorts was taking the bag across the pavement to wait by the boot of the car. The chauffeur slammed the door and came to the rear and opened the lid of the boot. The escort started to swing the bag inside.

We had also decided in London that if the KCCPC contingent were to fire weapons they wouldn't do it during the flashpoint period because there would be policemen here, and other people, innocent people, some of them children, and from the negotiations between Prime Minister Thatcher, the Foreign Office, and the Chinese government, it had been made clear that both sides wanted to proceed in very low profile with Dr. Xingyu's arrival in Hong Kong, and gunfire in a public place under the eye of the police could bring disastrous repercussions politically. If there were to be weapons fired it would happen later, when perhaps there might seem a chance for the KCCPC agents to keep Dr. Xingyu under their control, or failing that, to kill him.

But the hairs were lifted a little on my arms: I could feel the gooseflesh, and my scalp was shrinking.

I brought this for you.

Holding out the kevlar vest.

Instructions?

No, I won't insist on it.

Those things worry me.

But the nerves were still touchy because my body was exposed and vulnerable; and it sometimes happens that when action starts suddenly, someone panics. But don't imagine I had any regrets. I didn't have any conscious fear of a shot exploding in the flesh at this point; the nerves were just reacting to the primitive brainstem awareness of danger, of potential death.

The man was swinging the bag into the boot of the Mercedes, and I watched him. The scene was still, frozen, because flashpoint was very close now. The brass locks of the bag glinted in the light, and I saw that a thread was hanging loose at one corner where the seam had started to split; I don't think I could have seen a detail as small as that from this distance in the ordinary way, but my vision was brilliantly clear as I watched the bag making its arc across the edge of the boot as the man swung it.

For all of us, time is variable; it expands and contracts

according to what we are doing. Nine seconds, in one sense, isn't long, when one has to do what I was here to do; in another sense it could seem—seemed, now, to me—very long indeed, dangerously, fatally long, because I was exposed and alone here against these considerable forces, alone except for the man sitting along there at the wheel of the black Jaguar; but his instructions were to do nothing at all to help me, only to wait.

One of the policemen blew his whistle as a hotel shuttle bus slowed and tried to move into a gap too short for it; the driver throttled up again.

The rain was steady, a gray steel curtain with diamonds sprinkled in it.

I was standing next to one of Dr. Xingyu's escorts, turned away from him, not looking at him, looking through the rain now, as if waiting to cross the roadway; he didn't have any interest in me: there were other people around, other passengers. I would see to him first, then the man who was swinging the bag into the trunk, then the chauffeur, who had gone back to sit at the wheel of the Mercedes.

The rain had the sound of steel brushes stroking a snare drum softly in the night.

Flashpoint as the bag dropped onto the floor of the boot and I used the right arm from the elbow to keep the strike short and visually discreet and felt the softness of the flesh covering the escort's vagus nerve against my wristbone and saw his hands coming up too late to protect himself. I didn't worry about his hands because his pulse would have begun slowing now and venous dilation would be drawing blood from his brain. His legs were buckling as the second man straightened up from dropping the bag into the boot and I used a knee against his sacral plexus hard enough to incapacitate and pulled him out of the way and slammed the boot shut and went to the side of the car and opened the driving door and worked on the chauffeur's thyroid cartilage, taking my time because he was surprised and hadn't even moved his hands and couldn't move them now because of the numbing effect of the squeeze. I used my other hand to drag him off the seat and onto the streaming roadway and got in and slammed the door and started up and checked the nearside mirror and used a light foot but even then got wheelspin as I took the Mercedes away and saw the black Jaguar pull out immediately and then swing back to block off the Mercedes behind me as it started up and tried to follow. The police whistles were blowing and I'd expected that but I didn't know why the woman over there was screaming and holding her face, perhaps just because there were three people lying on the roadway in the pouring rain and they surely must be ill or something.

I turned my head and told Dr. Xingyu to get down low on the back seat in case there was any shooting and he did that. I'd reached the airport road by the time a dark green Volvo flashed me from behind and came past and slowed and pulled into the curb ahead of me. The driver got out and took over the Mercedes and I put Xingyu into the front of the Volvo with me and when I was sure we were clean and clear I used the car phone and told Pepperidge we'd got him.

Chapter 7
Headlights

I pushed the needle into his hip and aspirated and didn't get any blood, started squeezing the plunger.

"All right," Pepperidge said, "what about the next one, the man who was putting the bag into the boot?"

He was making notes, shorthand, sitting at the end of the bench that ran the length of the cabin.

"Still," I told Xingyu. "Keep perfectly still." He hadn't got a lot of patience, we'd found. "Knee to the coccyx," I told Pepperidge. "The sacral plexus would have been affected, where most of the major nerves go from the spine to the hips and the legs. He went down straight away." I pulled the needle out of Xingyu's muscle and rubbed it for a bit.

Pepperidge: "What's his future?"

It's a new thing they've started to ask for in London: when we're debriefed after any kind of action we're expected to give details. It's all in the book in Norfolk but it's meant to inspire the rookies when they're told exactly what was done in a real situation.

"His life's not in danger," I said. "He'll need some spinal surgery, that's all. He'll walk again."

Dr. Xingyu pulled up his black woollen slacks and did the buttons.

"Thank you."

"Don't mention it." Saliva in my mouth, I'm queasy about needles but it had been no good asking Pepperidge to do it because I was going to be tied to Xingyu right through the mission and he needed it twice a day, 300 Insuno intramuscular, just my luck. I took the syringe over to the little copper sink and filled it with water.

"The chauffeur?"

"I used a *Chin Na* grip on the thyroid cartilage to give him enough pain to stop him thinking of anything else, and then pulled him out of the car and dropped him on the roadway." I took the syringe out to the flooded afterdeck and dropped it over the side and came back. "Just to give him enough pain, though, that's important, because you can kill like that if you do it too hard. They should understand that. I didn't need to kill anyone."

Xingyu was putting the bottle of insulin away in the pocket of his sheepskin coat. Pepperidge finished writing and didn't look up as he said: "They ran over his head. Not your fault."

In a minute I said, "Oh, *Christ*."

"Don't have it on your mind, but I had to tell you. They were in too much of a hurry trying to follow you."

Explained, then, why that woman had screamed when I drove away: I'd wondered. Three down already, and we were learning fast: *Bamboo* was hungry.

"I took *trouble*," I said.

"Of course you did. You're always fastidious."

I sat down on the opposite bench, feeling cold, and Dr. Xingyu looked at me and then at Pepperidge and said, "So what will you do with me now?"

Tone of total cynicism, almost hostility. He was sitting very upright, his big hands on his lap, his feet together and his head lifted, sitting very still, like something to be shot at. Pepperidge came around the end of the teakwood table and sat facing the Chinese, resting his hands in front of him with the fingers spread open, a symbolic posture, I suppose, to mean he wasn't hiding anything.

"Dr. Xingyu, you were told at our embassy in Beijing, as politely as possible, that you were becoming an embarrassment to the United Kingdom in our efforts to reestablish

normal relationships with your government, and we therefore offered to ensure your freedom if you chose to leave the
embassy. You were—"

"I can take care of my own freedom now. This is Hong
Kong." His eyes narrowed, his tone sharp.

"You're at liberty, Dr. Xingyu, to leave this boat on
your own and go wherever you wish, but before morning
you'd find yourself back in Beijing, and no longer free. If
you'll—"

"I do not think that. And I do not like all this—this
subterfuge. It is not necessary. And a man has been killed,
you say. That is terrible. *Terrible.*"

He is known for his extreme openness—Hyde, in Final Briefing—*and his compassion. You may find him difficult, therefore, to
control.* There'd certainly been no subterfuge, I knew from
the papers, in his opposition to the Communist Party in
Beijing: he'd told them exactly what he thought of their fail-
ure to protect the welfare of the people.

"Dr. Xingyu"—Pepperidge, his yellow eyes holding the
other man's steadily across the table—"you have a brilliant
mind. You must use it now as you've never used it before,
because the future of the Chinese people depends on it."

Xingyu stood up so quickly that he knocked his head
against a beam, but didn't flinch. "I can only help my people if I am with them in Beijing. I should not have come
here. I—"

"Since you're here, Doctor, I would ask you to do me the
courtesy of hearing what I have to tell you."

Xingyu stared him back for a moment and then dropped
his head and sat down. "Excuse me."

It was his wife, I think, who was most on his mind: he'd
talked about her in the car on our way from the airport. She'd
been meant to join him at the U.K. embassy as soon as she
could get there. *I would not have gone there myself, you see, if
I had thought she could not come. It was a terrible mistake.* His
wife and his friends, most of them fellow professors at the
university, most of them now under arrest and inside Bambu

Qiao Prison. *Many of the cells have no doors or windows*, he'd told me, *there is only a trapdoor in the ceiling, and you cannot stand upright, the ceiling is too low.*

"You are more than excused, Dr. Xingyu." Pepperidge was looking down, not wanting the Chinese to find his eyes on him when he raised his head again. "You've got a lot to worry about, I know that. Now, I can't tell you as much as I'd like to, because if the KCCPC find you and take you back to Beijing by force, we don't want you to have any information about us that they might try to extract from you. But if all goes well, we might be able to send you back to Beijing to greet the leaders of a new and democratic government. This—"

"It would take years. *Years*."

"If you were ready to cooperate with us, Dr. Xingyu, it might take only a few days."

"That is out of the question! You do not realize—"

"Dr. Xingyu. You must be prepared to listen to me."

It took another ten minutes for him to get the message across and he didn't tell Xingyu any more about the setup for *Bamboo* than he had to know, which was simply that when he went back to Beijing it could be to help his people work out the structuring of a new China. What he did tell him in great detail was more to the point.

"You mustn't think, then, Doctor, that you're in any way our captive, or under any kind of duress. You can part company with us at any time you like—but I want you to understand that my government has put a very great deal of work into this operation, at the highest level, and we don't feel that a person of your intelligence would allow an impulse to destroy our efforts on your behalf, and incidentally on the behalf of the People's Republic of China."

Pepperidge has a quiet voice, and when he's talking about something important he measures his tone to catch your thoughts up in its rhythm; this is why Xingyu Baibing was listening carefully now, and not interrupting as he'd done before. I watched him as he listened, because it was necessary to get an idea of his character, the cut of his jib; later it would help me, and help him, and perhaps save his life, or mine.

"We cannot expect from you," Pepperidge went on, "any assurance, at this stage, that you won't decide to leave the protection we offer you and go it alone." A beat, while he considered whether Xingyu's grasp of idiom was adequate. "To leave our protection and rely on your own resources."

Headlights.

"But I'd like your assurance, at least, that you'll give us warning if at any time you feel you must go back to Beijing, which will always be a temptation for you." He waited, watching Xingyu, his eyes a degree more open, alerted: he'd seen the headlights too, through the cabin windows.

"I tried twice to leave the embassy," Xingyu said, hunched forward a little now, his hands clasped and the fingers working, the whispering of their dry skin audible below the beat of the rain on the cabin roof. "I tried twice."

"That's what I'm talking about," Pepperidge said. "You're worried about your wife. But I want you to understand, you see, that if you put your trust in us, you may hope to be back with your wife much sooner, perhaps in a matter of days."

Silence for a moment, then the big dry hands flew apart. "You talk of a few *days*. But they have a *stranglehold* now, the Party. A stranglehold on the *people*, through the *army*."

The headlights weren't moving now; they'd swept their beam through the rain, silvering the images out there on the quay, and now the beam rested and only the rain moved, slanting through it.

I looked at Pepperidge. "Did you order anyone in?" I meant support.

"No."

I watched the headlights again.

"You must put your trust, you see, in whatever we tell you." Pepperidge waited for it to sink in. "That isn't easy, but it's got to be done. We know much, much more than you do, Dr. Xingyu, about this operation." He leaned forward across the table, and his voice was quieter still. "You remember what they did to the Berlin Wall. We're going to do something like that in China."

I looked at Xingyu. It had got his attention. Behind him on the varnished timbers the gloss darkened as the headlights went out.

"Don't worry," Pepperidge told me.

It practically amounted to instructions. The executive in the field had brought the objective under protection but the mission was only three days old and there'd been three people killed and we still had to get this man out of Hong Kong and into deep shelter and the risk was extremely high, and the above-mentioned executive was ready to get his nerve endings into an uproar at the sight of a pair of headlights, point taken, don't worry, just as you say, there are fifty boats tied up here and their owners come down to the quay by car and at night of course they have to switch their headlights on.

"I'm not worrying."

"That's good."

But he'd noticed them, the headlights. I'd seen the reaction in his eyes.

"I do not think you realize," Xingyu was saying, "the power of the people you have to deal with."

"We realize it very well." Pepperidge leaned back again, away from the good doctor, and told him that we had our powers too, told him that the planning of this operation had been made by some of the most brilliant men in British intelligence, laid it on a bit thick, I thought, but we'd got to convince the little bugger somehow, listened to Pepperidge, I listened to Pepperidge while the blood from the ambassador crept its way to the curb and the snake spread its hood and the wheel went across the skull with the sound, I suppose, of a cracking coconut, a coconut splitting open, listened to Pepperidge and watched another car come down to the quay and the ghost-white shape of a jet go sloping down to Kaitak with the strobes making white hazy explosions through the rain while he went on talking, Pepperidge, and at last got an undertaking from Xingyu, for what it was worth.

"Then I will give you warning, if I decide to go back to Beijing. I will give you warning."

Pepperidge slid his rump along the bench to the far end and stood up. "Calls for a spot of tea, I'd say, what about you chaps?" Filling the kettle, plugging it in, it had been a lot of work getting even that much out of the Chinese. "So we'll be leaving Hong Kong some time tomorrow, can't say exactly when, but the thing is, we'd rather like to put you on a plane for London, naturally, and look after you there while events develop in Beijing. Would that suit?"

"London?"

He seemed surprised, Xingyu, though I couldn't think why: it was the obvious place to keep him holed up, a nice long way from the People's Republic of China and the merry boys of the Kuo Chi Ching Pao Chu with their little trapdoors in the ceiling, a safe haven, I would have thought, London, placed under honorable house arrest in one of the discreet Mayfair flats where even one young bobby would be enough to keep people away.

"That's right," Pepperidge said, and dropped two Earl Grey teabags into the pot. "Just for a few days."

"No," the feet planted together, the hands resting squarely on the black-trousered knees. "I want to go to Tibet."

The rain drummed on the cabin roof like a light rattle of shots.

Tibet.

This bodes ill, my friend, this bodes ill indeed.

A car door slammed, somewhere along the quay.

"A few sardines?"

"No," Xingyu said.

Pepperidge held the tin aslant under the small reproduction binnacle lamp, peering at the trademark. "*Crown Prince. Rich in Natural Fish Oil, No Salt Added.* They're very good."

"I wish to eat nothing."

I don't think Xingyu was sulking, although he was just sitting there hunched up with his forearms on the table now, the big hands open, empty, empty of hope for the wife and the friends he believed he'd deserted, and that was it, not sulking but despairing, because Pepperidge hadn't sounded too charmed by the idea of putting this man back into China, which getting him to Tibet would mean.

"We couldn't take you through Kathmandu," Pepperidge had told him, "because there wouldn't be time to make the trip by road from there to Lhasa. That *is* where you meant, isn't it, when you said Tibet? You meant Lhasa?"

"Yes. I have friends there."

"The thing is, we'd have to fly you in, because that's all we'd have time for, and that means we'd have to go Hong Kong to Beijing to Chengdu to Gonggar. As far as I know there's no Air China flight direct from Hong Kong to Chengdu without going through Beijing, which is out of the question. Sorry. You've asked for the impossible."

"I wish to go to Lhasa. I will be safe there."

That was an hour ago and Pepperidge had compromised and signaled London through the scrambler and told them the situation. They said they'd confer with Bureau One and send his instructions. We were still waiting.

I hadn't heard any footsteps after the car door had slammed out there on the quay. I would have liked to hear footsteps going from the car to one of the boats. I didn't want to think that a car had arrived and doused its lights and was just standing there with people inside, people watching. I'd come away clean from the airport thing and switched to the Volvo and the chances that anyone had seen the switch and followed me here were strictly slight but you can't, you know, you can't entirely ignore the nerves because it's not always paranoia, it's sometimes a warning of danger culled from the observations of the subconscious, and if you don't give it at least a bit of attention you can shorten your life without even trying.

Pepperidge had told me the procedure: if anyone came near this boat, Xingyu would be bundled quietly into the head and I would go to the sleeping quarters behind the curtains and Pepperidge would stay where he was with his .37 magnum on his knees under the table.

But it shouldn't come to that. This thing about Tibet had caught me unawares, that was all. Xingyu had turned out so unpredictable and we couldn't trust him: he must know we couldn't fly him to Lhasa without going through Beijing and that might be what he'd got on his mind—trying to jolly us into getting him back to Beijing so that he could give us the slip there and leave the plane and rush off to join his friends in Bambu Qiao Prison.

"What you must realize"—Pepperidge stirred his tea and watched Xingyu, watched him with no great affection—"is that we have to consider the timing of this operation. Our deadline, as I have told you, is in three days from now. In three days we expect to be able to fly you into Beijing with impunity, a very different Beijing from the one you have just left. We—"

"You have not told me why it is to be in three days, why it is not ten, or twenty. You tell me little."

"That is essential, for your own safety. I have told you that, also."

Patience on a monument.

Hyde had briefed me about the deadline: three days would bring us to the 17th, and that was when Premier Li Peng was going to make a party address and launch a ferocious attack against the intellectuals. It was on that day that we had to get Dr. Xingyu Baibing readied for the TV cameras instead. It was information that I'd had to be given as the executive for the mission but it couldn't be given to Xingyu because those three days were going to expose us to the entire force of Chinese Intelligence and Security and I had a capsule to pop if I had to and Xingyu didn't.

"I have also told you," Pepperidge said, "that if we—"

The phone was ringing and he answered it.

London. You will on no account take the subject into Tibet, so forth, good old Bureau One.

But Pepperidge was speaking in Japanese, and in less than half a minute he rang off.

"I have also told you, Dr. Xingyu, that if we are prepared to expose ourselves to very great danger on your behalf, we expect you to give us as little trouble as possible." He gave it time to get through. "That was the man who is coming to design the mask you'll be wearing when you leave this boat. His name is Koichi, and he'll be here later tonight to take the matrix."

"I shall wear a mask?"

"You see—" a wistful smile—"I tell you as much as I can."

"I shall wear no mask."

"Without one," Pepperidge said gently, "you will never leave Hong Kong a free man, I can assure you." The telephone began ringing again and he picked it up.

"Yes?" He reached for his signals pad, and I slid it along the table to him. This, yes, was London.

Headlights swung through the rain again, their beams glancing across the long narrow ports and sparking on the polished binnacle lamp.

"Very much so." Pepperidge. "He argues that the last place the Chinese will expect him to go is back into China— a point which I concede—and that he would only be fifteen hundred miles from Beijing when we're ready to fly him there. He has very reliable friends in a monastery in Lhasa, with—as Tibetan monks—a deep hatred of the Chinese." He listened again.

A point which I concede. I think he threw that in to let London know that if they finally instructed us to take the subject into Tibet then we would do that, however dangerous. We have our pride, my good friend, we have our principles.

A car door slamming outside on the quay. Two. Most of the boats tied up here were cruisers, and I suppose the owners were coming back from the town after dinner there. That would be natural.

While Pepperidge was on the phone I watched Xingyu again, ready to glance away if he looked up. He'd put his hands into his coat pockets now, and his face looked cold, pinched. I'd have put him at no more than forty, forty-two, and the lines in his face were of strain, I believed, the long strain of living in a country that he called his own, but a country where his worst enemies were the people who governed it, *ruled* would be a better word, ruled with the unanswerable power of the gun. And the strain, more recently, of becoming separated from his wife. I could have felt compassion for him, as I had before, except that he was now trying to drive us straight into a trap if he insisted on going to Tibet and London approved.

"... check out the possibilities," Pepperidge was saying; he'd been on the phone ten minutes now, listening more than talking, and I hadn't been able to tell which way things were going. I wished, quite honestly, that he'd get it over, so that I could know the worst, or preferably not the worst.

"Understood," he said and rang off and went straight to the telephone directory and began riffling through the pages, not looking at me, carefully not looking around as he sat perched on the end of the bench with his thin legs drawn up and his shoulders hunched a little, as if against the rain outside, or against the cloud no bigger than a man's hand that had been gathering in here while he'd talked to London.

He picked up the phone and started talking again, this time in Mandarin, to a woman I think, his tone gentle, even more gentle than usual, giving her the names *Hong Kong* and *Chengdu* and *Gonggar*, which was the airport for Lhasa. I didn't understand the rest.

Xingyu was listening attentively, his head turned.

I watched Pepperidge too, his hunched shoulders, head bent over the telephone, and had the eerie feeling that I was watching him from the future, looking back on him from some other time and some other place and remembering how it was when everything had become fixed in our affairs, locking us in with our karma, and this feeling persisted when he put the phone down and turned around and said to Xing-yu, "It would be out of the question, as I told you, to take you on any flight that would go via Beijing, but I've found that Air China has a new charter service through Chengdu direct, and according to my instructions we shall be taking you into Tibet."

Chapter 8

Mask

Koichi opened one end of the big plastic bag and lowered it over Xingyu Baibing's shoulders with his head sticking out of the hole.

"Please excuse! Not polite to put gentleman in garbage bag! You have had cast taken before?"

"No."

Xingyu was sitting upright in a deck chair under one of the binnacle lamps. Koichi had tried talking to him in Chinese when he'd come aboard, but either he wasn't fluent or the good doctor wished us all in hell and wasn't ready to exchange any courtesies. *I shall wear no mask*, he'd told Pepperidge.

"You have sometimes claustrophobia?"

"No."

"Good! Sit still, please." He pulled a bald cap over Xingyu's head and drew the hairline across it with a felt pen and used the spirit-gum. Then he smeared Vaseline along his eyebrows and lashes and began mixing the alginate in a bowl. I'd seen this done before at Norfolk as a demonstration, not by this man but by the master himself, Robert Schiffer.

I was now watching the operation again, and very carefully, because I might have to put this thing on Xingyu myself, when he flew into Beijing.

Pepperidge was on the telephone again, talking in Chinese, presumably booking our seats on the charter flights; he would leave before us on an earlier flight to set up the

91

safe house and a base for himself in Lhasa. When Xingyu had been using the head before the Japanese had come aboard, Pepperidge had told me, "I spoke to Bureau One personally, and we agreed that the subject would be psychologically more manageable in Tibet—closer to his wife and friends—than if we took him to London. The point was made that we should let him feel endangered, just as they are, with the KCCPC hunting him down. What do you think?"

"I think you're right. He won't feel quite so much that he's left his people in the lurch." But it took some saying. I didn't, quite frankly, fancy Tibet.

"Exactly. I don't believe, actually, that we would have stood much chance of getting him on a plane for London. I think he would've slipped us and tried to get back to Beijing."

"I didn't expect him to be so bloody tricky. Now we know how he feels about his wife I'm surprised he ever agreed to coming out here to Hong Kong in the first place."

Pepperidge had touched my arm. "It was the only way he could get out of the embassy, and he wanted to get out of there to be with his wife. Hong Kong was the only place the Chinese would agree to, for obvious reasons." The only place outside China that was saturated with their security agents. "We've got to consider the man he is, and make allowances. He's always been ready to defy his government openly and in public, and here we are trying to smuggle him through a security tunnel and he doesn't like that, doesn't like subterfuge, anonymity."

It had been an apology, in a way. Pepperidge and Bureau One had agreed to push me through the mission right under the nose of the KCCPC, and I hadn't got a choice: these were instructions.

"Still, please. Keep still!"

Xingyu Baibing had started jerking his head around, trying to say something. The alginate was covering the whole of his face now, and I suppose he was feeling stifled.

"You say you do not have claustrophobia! Now I do this

for you, and you breathe better!" The timer went off and Koichi reached around to the table and reset it.

From what I've seen at Norfolk it's not much of a joke: the stuff has got to be pushed right into the corners of the eyes and under the lashes. It wouldn't have made Xingyu feel any better to know what the Japanese was actually doing: he was making a death mask.

"As soon as you possibly can." Pepperidge was on the phone to someone else now, in English. "I want to leave here in the morning, no later than oh eight hundred. My flight's at nine-oh-five."

Visas. Passports and visas. There must have been a hitch somewhere, because the Bureau forgers in Hong Kong who service our Far East sector would have got their instructions direct from London days ago.

"I'll pick mine up on my way to the airport. You'll bring theirs when you bring the car."

Don't worry, he'd told me, but he wasn't trusting the Volvo out there. There was almost no chance that anyone had seen us switch cars on our way here from the airport, but if there were a chance in a thousand he wasn't taking it.

"Are all the bags ready?"

One for Xingyu, one for me, the clothes secondhand and worn a little, Hong Kong labels on them, the luggage tags already fixed, the initials on the bags matching our cover names. The only thing Xingyu would take from here would be the insulin and the needles.

"At whatever time," Pepperidge said and rang off.

"Must wait now," Koichi told us, and his smile was a fraction weary. To do that job really well is exacting. "Ten minutes, maybe fifteen." When he left here he'd be working most of the night to produce a flexible prosthetic from the negative and have it ready by morning.

"What about a drink?" Pepperidge asked him.

"Not yet. When finished, then some *sake*!" He touched the alginate here and there, his fingers as sensitive as a blind man's. "Will make you look older, you understand, maybe ten year older. Depressing! But then—" He picked at the alginate, dropping a fleck of the stuff into the bowl. "But then when you take off, young again! Very cheerful then!"

It was nearly midnight when he peeled off the negative and studied the inside, holding it to the light, turning it, nodding and frowning; then the big grin came again. "It is good. Will be good mask, finally!"

Pepperidge switched off the cabin lamps for a moment and Koichi slipped through the door and vanished into the rain. Xingyu went into the galley and washed his face, snorting and making a lot of fuss. "You are taking a great deal of trouble," he said as he used a towel, "to protect me from the security forces, and you say you are in favor of a democracy in my country. But what possible interest could the British have in the fate of China?"

"We're traders," Pepperidge told him, "and China's a huge country, with a lot of potential profit for the West."

"I see. You have no actual sympathy for the Chinese people and their predicament."

"But of course. I would happily go to Beijing and lead your people to freedom, but my government believes that you can do it rather more effectively."

Koichi was back before seven in the morning and fitted the mask and brought out his mirror for Xingyu and I had a feeling of slipped focus, putting myself in the place of the Chinese and getting a sense of what was going through his mind, because that wasn't his face in the mirror, nothing like it, an older man's, unrecognizable. All I could see of Dr. Xingyu Baibing were his eyes, and they were frightened. I suppose he'd already begun to feel a certain loss of identity since he'd run through the doors of the British embassy a week ago and asked for asylum, to be sequestered among aliens and cut off from his wife and his friends, and now he was on foreign soil and staring into a mirror at a face he'd never seen before. He wasn't, after all, an intelligence agent; he was an astrophysicist.

"It's good," Pepperidge said. "It's good, Koichi."

"Yes. Am satisfied. *Sake* now." Huge grin. "No, is joke, I go home now." To Xingyu: "When you leave here?"

"Eight tomorrow," Pepperidge said. "Eight in the morning."

"I will come here half past seven, to fit mask again." He peeled it off, and I noticed Xingyu grab at the mirror again and stare into it, and the fright go out of his eyes. Koichi laid the mask gently into a white cardboard box and went to the door of the cabin. "Go home now." A formal bow to Xingyu—"Thank you"—and one for us—"Thank you,"—and he was gone.

The rain had stopped, and through the doorway I could see white mist clouding across the water of the bay and the bristling masts of the marina, half lost in the haze, their pennants hanging limp. In the stillness of the morning a voice sounded, a long way off, and the slam of a hatch cover.

Pepperidge briefed us a little before eight o'clock. "This is the way it goes. I shall take the nine-oh-five charter flight this morning to Chengdu and change planes there for Lhasa." He was sitting at the table, with two manila envelopes in front of him. A courier had come to the boat in the night, leaving some papers with Pepperidge and three worn leather suitcases near the door. "In Lhasa I shall go to the monastery you've indicated and tell them you're coming. I'll then go to my hotel. You will take the same flight the next day, keeping your distance from each other as strangers. If the flights are on schedule there's a twenty-five-minute stop in Chengdu and you'll change planes, but remember that flights are often overbooked, unavailable, or canceled because of bad weather. The airport for Lhasa—Gonggar, ninety-five kilometers from the city—is notorious for strong winds, and the CAAC will only allow flights when conditions are perfect."

He briefed us on customs, immigration, boarding requirements, and slid one envelope across the table to Xingyu and the other to me. "Everything you need is there." He was making less eye contact than usual this morning and was, I thought, a little reserved, distant, and it occurred to me that while I felt that he and Bureau One had agreed to push me through the mission under the nose of the KCCPC and had left me with no choice, it couldn't have been easy for them. If a wheel came off and we crashed, Pepperidge would have to answer to Shepley, and Shepley to the head of state, and just incidentally a nation of one billion people would have to go on living under the boot of a decadent clique until they were ready to risk more bloodshed in the streets.

"You should also know," Pepperidge said, "that the charter flights out of Hong Kong were of course fully booked, and we had to buy three cancellations, and if any of the airline computers get things mixed up, the passengers you're replacing are a Mr. Brian Outhwaite and a Mr. Yan Hanwu. Everything was done correctly, so you have to insist that those are indeed your seats."

It's standard Bureau practice when a flight's booked solid: you send in a contact who picks the shabbiest-looking passenger in the waiting area and makes him an offer he's not liable to refuse for rescheduling his flight and leaving a seat available.

"That's all," Pepperidge said. "Questions?"

"Any support?"

He looked at me briefly. "None on the first flight, one at the airport in Chengdu. That's all"—a shrug—"we'll need."

Because if the Chinese secret police got on to us for any reason we'd just have to argue things out in the interrogation cell. Pepperidge could send in a dozen people in support and there wouldn't be anything they could do because the KCCPC wasn't just a private opposition unit in the field: it *controlled* the field, sharp-eyed and gun at the hip. We were going through the bamboo curtain, and the only reason for putting a man into Chengdu airport was to have him report to London if he saw us being hustled into a van.

"Signals?"

"Through Cheltenham," his yellow eyes on me again, "but all you'll have is a telephone booth. Have you made many calls in China?"

No signals line, then, no contacts, no couriers, nothing, just that one man in Chengdu with a watching brief. Xingyu Baibing was the most wanted man in China and that was where I was taking him and we couldn't risk anyone else getting near him because they'd know where he was, and if they were picked up and put under the light they could break and speak and we'd crash.

It was the way I'd always wanted to work: no support in the field, no contacts, no cutouts, no one who could get in my way. I'd argued the toss about it time and again with Loman, Croder, Shepley, trying to make them see that I could work best when I worked solo. This time I'd got what I wanted.

And felt lonely.

"I lock up?"

"Yes," Pepperidge said. "Drop the key into the letterbox on the jetty."

"No more questions."

He looked at Xingyu, who was sitting at the table with his head in his hands.

"Dr. Xingyu?"

He looked up. "What? No. I have no questions."

Perhaps it was partly the diabetes that was making him so depressed. Did diabetes make people depressed? I didn't know, didn't think so. All I knew was that it was going to be a long day, and a long night.

Pepperidge looked at his watch and got up and let his eyes rest on me for a moment and then got the attaché case with his name tag on it and opened the door of the cabin, going out and looking around him.

"Smells nice," he said, "after the rain. It's going to be a fine day."

* * *

"She is very attractive."

This was at noon. We'd got through four hours together, mostly in silence, with the tension in Xingyu filling the cabin.

"You have seen photographs of her?"

I said I had.

"She is very attractive, yes?"

"Very."

"And she is quite a little younger than I am, as you know, if you have seen her photograph. I am a lucky man."

I didn't say anything. He wanted to think aloud, not talk to anyone. But it was true: the press photographs I'd seen of his wife showed that she was very attractive, with a brilliant smile in some of the shots, and younger than Xingyu, but, from her description, as brave, marching with him in the streets, sharing the contempt hurled at him in the government-controlled media nationwide, an intellectual, Xingyu Chen, a professor in economics.

"I wish to telephone to Beijing."

This was soon after three in the afternoon. He'd lapsed silent for hours, doing something with papers, foolscap sheets he'd found in a drawer of the small writing desk near the galley, filling them with Chinese script and mathematical hieroglyphs and formulae. But now he wished to telephone to Beijing.

I told him no.

"I must know how she is," he said, and his eyes behind his heavy horn-rimmed glasses were hard, obstinate. "I must know that she is not being victimized. Victimized because of me. Because of *me*."

Told him he couldn't telephone. He knew that already; Pepperidge had told him enough times. Perhaps he thought I'd be softer to work on, couldn't read faces very well.

"I wish to telephone a friend, a very close friend, the dean of my department at the university. He will know what is happening to my wife. They will not trace the call, you must realize that."

Water slapped the beam of the boat as another vessel left the quay, spreading a wake. Light dappled the bulkhead from the ports on the other side, from the sunlit sea.

"No," I said, "they wouldn't trace the call, but your friend would be excited to hear from you, and would be very quick to tell your other friends, and when one of the plainclothes Armed People's Police on the campus picked it up, your friends would be arrested. Is that what you want?"

It took another hour to get him to see what his situation was really like, to think more like an intelligence agent than a physicist, more like the most wanted man in China, to understand that just by picking up the telephone over there he could send his best friends into the interrogation rooms in Bambu Qiao Prison.

Perhaps he managed to get a different perspective on himself, I don't know; I hoped so, because he could let us take him through this mission as an exercise in clandestine intelligence work or he could drag us through the labyrinth with death and destruction grinning from the dark at every turn.

"Have you a wife?"

Back to that, to his pretty Chen.

"No."

"If you had a wife—" He reached for his worn black wallet and began opening it, then shut it again and put it away, remembering there was no photograph of her there anymore, because Pepperidge had cleared out the whole contents and sent them to London through our courier line for safekeeping. "If you had a wife like mine, you would know what I mean."

Said I was sure I would.

The next thing he wanted was a newspaper, and I was surprised he hadn't asked for one before; perhaps in the claustrophobic atmosphere of the boat he was forgetting the facilities of the outside world. I didn't refuse him this time: Pepperidge had briefed me privately that within the stifling confines of the mission I was to allow Xingyu as much freedom and as much information as I could, to build his trust in me and keep him from going crazy.

I used the phone and told the contact what I wanted and fifteen minutes later a car stopped and there were footsteps and a knock on the cabin door, three long, two short, three long, and I opened it and took the copy of the *South China Morning Post* and gave it to Xingyu. He went through the first two pages and passed them to me, not saying anything, just prodding a finger at a half-column report on the second page.

XINGYU BAIBING SENT INTO EXILE. As the result of an agreement reached between the People's Republic of China and Great Britain, Dr. Xingyu Baibing, formerly Professor of Astrophysics at Beijing University and a notorious agitator, has been released from the British embassy here, where he fled to evade arrest after fomenting dissension among his colleagues in the faculty. This concession on the part of the People's Republic was granted in order to preserve the positive relationship between the two nations.

Should Dr. Xingyu choose to return to Beijing of his own free will, his present status as an exile in disgrace would be reviewed, a source close to Premier Li Peng has revealed, but he would face a rigorous inquiry as to his actions before fleeing to the British embassy. Certain other intellectuals, several of them friends of the exiled scientist, have been placed under arrest and will be invited to explain their part in the unrest of the past two weeks and to volunteer information on the role played particularly by Dr. Xingyu Baibing, so that the truth may be brought to light in the interests of the people.

The rest of the report was a summary of Xingyu's repeated attempts to interrupt the steady progress of socialism in the People's Republic, and ended with praise for Premier Li Peng's magnanimous gesture to Great Britain in relieving her of the embarrassment that inevitably followed her misguided decision to offer sanctuary to a notorious troublemaker whose continuing presence in her embassy could only have exacerbated her predicament.

Photograph of Xingyu, carefully chosen from hundreds

of others, that had caught him with an expression on his face that could be seen as fearful, hunted.

I'd asked for the English-language *Morning Post* because it would give Xingyu an indication of Beijing's attitude toward him and his present position. The *Hong Kong Times* would have slanted the report in sympathy with Xingyu and would have used a different picture. What worried me was that the *Post* hadn't mentioned Xingyu's wife, hadn't reported her feelings about losing her husband to the West, a traitor to his people, so forth. I would have expected it to do that, to turn the screw.

Lying in my bunk, hours later, my eyes open and watching the play of light on the overhead from boats moving in the bay, I went on worrying about it, about the obviously deliberate omission of any reference to Xingyu's wife, certain that it was designed to set him up in some way, designed as a trap, went on worrying instead of sleeping, as the boat moved gently to the waves coming in from the bay and the lights played on the varnished timbers and the sound came of Xingyu's quiet sobbing in the dark.

Chapter 9

Chengdu

"**H**ave you been there before?"

"Where?"

"To Lhasa?"

"Yes," I said.

"Why did you go?"

"To meditate."

"Ah. I saw the Dalai Lama, once."

I didn't say anything.

"He is beatific. Beatific."

The wheels went down with a thump and the cabin shuddered.

"He radiates good. You can see it, like an aura."

I think the Hong Kong Chinese chew more gum than the Americans. Everyone, I'm sure you've noticed, does more American things than the Americans do.

"He personifies the second coming of Christ, I truly believe."

Or he would, I suppose, if he weren't a Buddhist. I saw Xingyu scratching at his face again. He was sitting five rows back from the flight deck. I was in a rear seat, from which I could watch everyone.

"You don't talk much."

"I've got toothache," I said.

"Ah. You should suck cloves."

The aircraft settled into the approach. Buildings below us now, a waste ground of buildings, block after block of apartment houses, factories, their smoke clouding like stirred mud across the bare winter trees of the apple orchards to the west.

Chengdu.

I had expected trouble going through Hong Kong airport, because that had been where the objective for *Bamboo* was to have been completed: to get Dr. Xingyu Baibing out of Hong Kong. There was a new objective now: to get him into Tibet and under cover and protect him until he was needed in Beijing. But I'd still expected trouble going through the airport, because the mask might not have been good enough, or my own blue woolen cap and glasses might not have been enough to change my image. That image hadn't been in view for more than a minute outside the terminal where I'd made the snatch on Xingyu, but someone might have remembered it.

But there had been no trouble in Hong Kong.

The Chinese stewardess came down the aisle checking seat belts, her face lit with a china-doll smile.

The trouble came in Chengdu.

"You may find itching," Koichi had said, Koichi the Japanese. "Sometimes find itching, under mask. But do not scratch. Must think of something else." Huge grin. "Think of very fine Chinese dinner, very good sizzling rice and everything."

There was no grass down there below us, no trees, nothing but stones, asphalt, bricks, rooftops, with a tangled web of electric cables spread across the streets to power the trams.

I would have liked to go forward and tell Xingyu not to scratch, to think of very good sizzling rice. In a few minutes we'd be going through immigration and customs checks, and the mask had to go on looking perfect. But I couldn't leave my seat now.

It was going to be more difficult, of course, to get through Chengdu than out of Hong Kong. In Hong Kong there'd been a strong cadre of KCCPC agents on the watch; in Chengdu there would be more, simply because this was a major Chinese airport and passengers from Hong Kong would be coming, in effect, from the West.

"Do you speak Chinese?"

"Not very much."

"Then I will try to buy some cloves for you."

Scratching again, Xingyu. He must be mad.

The cabin leveled off and we bumped three times and then the brakes came on and there was some Chinese coming from the speakers and then some English.

All passengers must remain in their seats with their seat belts fastened until the aircraft comes to a stop. For your information, CAAC Flight 304 will depart from Chengdu at 12:25 P.M., in thirty-five minutes from now. Your guide will escort you to the gate.

I got into the aisle without wasting any time and reached the queue at the immigration desk with Xingyu ahead of me in plain sight. The terminal was huge, bleak, echoing, built on Soviet lines, and there were upward of a hundred people here in uniform with peaked caps, most of them standing at the line of desks and farther out near the walls and the exit doors; they formed what amounted to a living barricade, a potential trap, and it was now that I looked at Xingyu standing there under the immigration sign and thought for the first time that there wasn't a hope in hell of getting him through this massive array of police and onto the flight for Tibet, not a hope in hell.

He'd blow it, the whole thing. He wasn't an experienced agent, not even an agent at all; he might know the chemical composition of Jupiter but he wouldn't know what to say when they asked him what his reason was for going to Tibet. He'd remember what we'd told him to say, of course, that he wanted to study the language, but it wouldn't be the truth, and he'd been used to shouting the truth from the rooftops all his life, it was in his character, in his bones, and he was going to tell these peak-capped robots his precise reasons for going to Tibet, he was going there to implement the overthrow of the Communist Party in Beijing and let freedom ring throughout the land, so forth, while I stood here listening to the orders for the police to close in and take him away, milling around him like a pack of starving dogs that had found a bone.

Nothing you can do now, it's too late. Just stand here and wait for it, stand here and wait.

Sound of Bedlam, like bloody Bedlam in this place because there was no carpeting, no acoustic ceiling, only the peeling paint of the walls and the scarred concrete floor and the vast dirt-filmed windows throwing the echoes across and across the hall, with somewhere the tinny sound of music from the loudspeaker system or someone's radio, a Chinese singing a Bing Crosby song, "I'm in the Mood for Love," a hilarious thought, a hilarious thought, my good friend, in a place where any kind of love had long since fled, or died, like a butterfly caught in a machine.

"George, are you going on with the rest of us?"

"Look, for God's sake don't give them any lip, you'll drop us all in the shit."

"Where's Jimmy, then? He said he'd be here."

The United Kingdom contingent, not from Hong Kong, doing the Tibet trip, a change of pace from Majorca.

"Show them *everything*, mate, don't try any tricks."

"Everything all right?" A face close to mine suddenly, the voice very quiet, the eyes looking nowhere.

"Tell him," I said, "to stop scratching his face."

He turned away and wandered about again, passing close to Xingyu ahead of me in the queue and then moving away, standing at a distance, looking around him for some lost sheep according to his cover, *Aurora Travel* on the red plastic disk pinned to his lapel, the man from the Bureau, sent here to signal London that he'd seen the shadow executive and the subject land safely at Chengdu and present themselves to immigration, or of course to report that the subject had in point of fact been smothered suddenly in a scrum of policemen and hustled into a van outside, it would depend, wouldn't it, on what the most-wanted man in the People's Republic of China said to the smartly uniformed officer behind the desk, on how he said it, and on whether he was going to stop scratching his face until he tore a hole in the mask and *finis*, all fall down, he must be out of his mind.

"Marjorie's not coming." Scared blue eyes.

"But she was on the plane."

"She's not coming with us. She wants to go back to Hong Kong."

The queue shuffled forward again. Dr. Xingyu Baibing was the next in line at the desk. Not, perhaps, out of his mind, no, in the sense that he didn't realize the danger, just being driven out of his mind by the itching under the mask, itching can do that, yes.

"What on earth for?"

"She says she can't get her mind off what they did that time in Tianen—Tia—you know, that square."

"God, that was ages ago. Tell her—"

"She says she's frightened of them. She's never been in China before."

"Tell her she's all right with us. I can't leave—"

"She's being sick in the lavatory."

"Then for God's sake go and help her. Tell her the plane goes in ten minutes."

Shuffled forward again, and Xingyu got his papers out, clumsily, dropping one of them, picking it up—*would they notice the blood hadn't gone to his face after he'd bent down like that?*—showing them the papers now while the man over there with the Aurora Travel badge swept his eyes across the crowd and didn't let them stop at Xingyu. One of the policemen took a step forward, a step toward the desk, stretching his legs, perhaps, but his eyes were watching the desk, watching the little man there from the shadow under the peak of his cap, the shadow thrown by the bleak neon lights that hung from the iron rods under the ceiling while the noise went on, the din of so many voices, of so many people trapped in here like cattle in a slaughterhouse but we must not, must we, let our imagination get out of hand, we must not be sick in the lavatory.

"Joyce, who's going to take her back to Hong Kong, then, if we can't stop her going?" '

"Could ask Harry."

"God, not Harry."

"She's not in the mood for anything like that."

"Harry wouldn't care."

Presenting his papers, our little messiah, the only hope for a billion people out there in the rice fields and the factories and the universities, living their daily lives in the shadow of the tanks. The only hope.

Shepley must have had a brainstorm when he'd set this thing up, instructing us to take a man like Xingyu through three airports, Hong Kong and Chengdu and Gonggar, under the eyes of the Kuo Chi Ching Pao Chu, gone clean out of his mind, and not much better ourselves, Pepperidge and I, we should have rehearsed this poor little bugger, told him what it was going to be like when he landed back inside his beloved country, what they would ask him at the immigration desk, what he should tell them, rehearsed him until he could have gone through this checkpoint word-perfect, but in fact we couldn't, I suppose, have done that to him, he would have told us we were playing spies, being melodramatic, knew his galaxies, didn't know his codes, no go, my good friend, it's going to be no go, because the officer at the desk is beckoning the man over there, the plainclothes supervisor, and he is going over to the desk, his steps measured.

"What's holding us up?"

"I don't know."

"Look, go and help Kate with Marjorie. I'll keep your place."

"You can't do that here. You—"

"Wait a minute. Excuse me, but do you mind if my friend just went to the toilet?"

"*Shén mē shì?*"

"My friend here, oh God, he doesn't—"

"Let me help. *Zhèiweì nǔshì xiang qù chèshuǒ, rámhòu huídaò queue.*"

"*Xíng.*"

"He says that's fine."

"Oh, I'm much obliged. Go on, Doris, get her back here so I can talk to her, for God's sake. We're going to miss that plane."

The air cold in here, with the harsh reek of the factory smoke creeping in under the doors, the lights clouded, some of the tubes flickering, some of them dark, they don't run a good ship here, my friend, they do not run a good ship, their methods are crude and their thinking is proscribed, conditioned, and they will throw him into the van like a common criminal while I go on shuffling forward like a puppet, not daring to leave the queue and follow him, follow them, hoping to do something miraculous and get him away, get him to ground, not daring to do anything except shuffle forward and go through the charade and get out of here, because this was no place for miracles.

Get out of here and signal London, let the hand pick up the piece of chalk and change the board. *Executive reports subject lost to KCCPC, Chengdu airport, 12:16 l.t.*

The man from the Bureau was watching the desk, his dead stare fixed now. I couldn't see much of Xingyu because he was shorter than the three girls in front of me and they were moving around, anxious for Marjorie.

I watched the man over there instead: we had, in this instant, established signals. He would swing his head and look at me when anything important happened there under the immigration board, under the flickering lights, would let a smile touch his mouth if all were well, or leave his stare on me and move his head to and fro by the smallest degree if all were not well, if the trap slammed shut, *finito.*

"She's got no need to be frightened of them, for God's sake, they're only *people*. It's just the air trip getting to her stomach, that's all."

"This is all we needed."

"It's what we've got. We'll muddle through somehow, we're British."

The stink of the smoke in here was enough to make anyone sick, it wasn't the air trip, but you're wrong, my little love, you're wrong, you know, there is every need to be frightened of these people, there is every need. They are only people, yes, but they are the people with the tanks.

Movement suddenly at the desk as the officer got to his feet and another one came up and the plainclothes supervisor nodded and turned away and the man from the Bureau swung his head and looked at me with his mouth relaxed and I saw Dr. Xingyu Baibing leave the desk and pick up his bag and walk slowly away, folding his papers and putting them into the pocket of his sheepskin coat. I went forward and passed through the checkpoint and then customs and joined our charter group.

"How is your toothache?"

"Much better."

But he was reading a newspaper.

CAAC Charter Flight No. 4401 to Gonggar will depart from Gate 6 at 12:15. All passengers must report to Gate 6 for embarcation.

They were already lined up, windbreakers and sheepskin jackets and woolen hats and skiing gloves or red hands rubbing together, heavy boots, combat boots, a whole line of boots with the people tethered by them to the littered concrete, swaying in the stream of cold filthy air from the ventilators, all of them except Xingyu Baibing.

He was reading a newspaper, standing near the poster on the wall, *Mitsubishi*, holding the paper quite still and concentrating on a certain page, a certain column, and as I walked over to him I knew I'd blown *Bamboo*.

I shouldn't have let him buy a paper.

They hadn't set a trap for him here in Chengdu, specifically. They'd set a trap for him *everywhere*, wherever he

110

might go, once he'd got out of Hong Kong. They'd been prepared even for the impossible, that somehow, despite their agents there, he'd get clear of Hong Kong, and they'd set a supertrap that couldn't fail.

He was in it now and it had sprung.

"We're boarding," I said, as if nothing had changed, as if by one chance in a thousand I was wrong.

He looked at me, his eyes smoldering, the newspaper trembling between his hands.

Passengers for Flight No. 4401 for Gonggar are now boarding. All passengers for Gonggar must report immediately to Gate 6 for departure.

Xingyu pushed the newspaper toward me.

"Read."

Top of page two.

WIFE OF DISSIDENT IN PRISON. Dr. Xingyu Chen, wife of the exiled scientist Xingyu Baibing, who left the People's Republic yesterday in disgrace, was arrested late last night in their apartment in Beijing and taken to Bambu Qiao Prison, where she is now undergoing intensive interrogation, in the hope that she can be persuaded to inform the authorities on the whereabouts of certain friends and colleagues also wanted for questioning, and to offer information particularly on her husband's subversive activities at the university.

Though nothing official has been announced, a source requesting anonymity has declared that if the exiled dissident Xingyu Baibing were to return voluntarily to Beijing for interrogation, his wife would in all likelihood be released immediately.

I folded the paper.

Xingyu stood facing me.

"I must go to Beijing."

"No," I said, "you can't do that."

"You cannot stop me."

Chapter 10

Su-May

She came floating toward me, big eyes in a small pinched face, her body swathed in the folds of a hooded fur jacket too big for her, the hide torn and patched and stained, floating toward me looking rather like an Eskimo child, though she wasn't a child, more like a grown-up china doll.

"They have asked me to assist them," she said.

I tried to relax, and she stopped floating. On our way from Gonggar to the city the tour guide had told us that at eleven thousand feet we might hallucinate sometimes; there was oxygen available, he said, at most of the hotels.

"Assist them?"

I didn't know why it was anything to do with me that they'd asked her to assist them, the people in uniform behind the long cluttered counter, Chinese Public Security officers, one of them watching me steadily, would have worried me if it weren't for the fact that he'd never seen me before, hadn't been outside the airport in Hong Kong when we'd done the Xingyu thing. On the other hand I wasn't totally at ease: they'd picked me up in a military jeep and brought me here for questioning and my passport and visa and Alien Travel Permit were spread all over the counter and the PSB officer would certainly recognize me again if we crossed paths.

"With your case," she said.

I hadn't got a case. I'd left it in my cell at the monastery with Xingyu looking after it.

"I see," I said.

She meant my *case,* of course, criminal charges, so forth. I suppose if the Bureau knew I'd got arrested within an hour of entering Lhasa on a strictly zero-zero clandestine operation they'd call me in straight away, wouldn't blame them. But that wasn't all I'd done since we'd flown out of Chengdu, it was not all, my good friend, that I had done. But I don't want to think about that now, I want to listen to this little china doll and find out if I can rescue anything from the wreckage.

Xingyu is safe.

Yes, concentrate on that. He is safe and among friends at the monastery and you can say, if you want to be charitable, that I've completed the mission, the objective of which was to get Dr. Xingyu Baibing out of Hong Kong. But we remember, don't we, that *Bamboo* has a new objective now: I have to get him back into Beijing when the time is right, and I'm not sure how I can do that if these people throw me into jail.

I think she was waiting for me to say something.

"What exactly is my case?"

"You were out of bounds."

"Ah. I didn't know."

In fact when the military jeep had pulled up and the soldier had shouted something to me above the noise of the engine I'd thought he was offering me a lift.

I told her this.

The throttle had got stuck, I suppose, with the engine roaring like that; or he was having to keep it running somehow with the windchill at minus forty degrees. She was telling them what I'd said, in very fast Mandarin, her tiny porcelain teeth flashing their way through the syllables. Mandarin has got something like four hundred syllables and they've all got several tones and if you don't get them exactly right you might as well speak Dutch, it's a real bitch.

"They say there are signs posted."

"I don't read Chinese."

"There are signs in English: *Military road. Out of bounds.*"

114

"I didn't see anything in the kind of English anyone would recognize."

"I must not tell them that."

"I know."

I'd said it to find out which side she was on, though it already seemed fairly clear: she was one of a dozen or so people in here lined up along the counter with their papers or arguing with their hands, Chinese, Tibetans, Nepalis, Muslims, Kashmiris, a couple of round-eyes, tourists, traders, yak herders, women with braided hair, men with high boots and sashes and daggers, all of them wrapped in shawls and hides and furs against the cold outside. In here it was close to eighty, with two enormous yak-dung stoves burning, smoking the place out. I assumed they'd all been hauled in on some kind of charge: this was a PSB office, where the people on the other side of the counter in Beijing and Shanghai and Chengdu had got their clubs out on that June night and gone to work. There would be a basement under this place, underground cells.

"What will you tell them, then?" I asked the girl.

"It is difficult. You were on a military road. But I think perhaps that if you made profuse apologies, they might listen. Especially if you behave contritely."

One of the officers pushed a flap open at the end of the counter and beckoned a man through and took him to one of the doors at the back, with two other officers closing in. Everyone stopped talking while this happened, then the noise started up again.

"Then of course I apologize," began using my hands, "I apologize profusely," shooting the officer looks of penitence, "and I shall certainly make sure I read the signs in the future."

He didn't turn to look at the girl as she translated, but went on looking at me. He'd been seventeen, once, seventeen, eighteen, top of his class and fond of sports, taken his mum and dad out sometimes, given them a treat, told them he wanted to go into something he could be proud of, something that'd make them proud of him, say the police force, and this afternoon he was standing here with the gun and the truncheon on his belt and hoping for the chance of pushing the flap open at the end there and throwing me into a cell and beating me up if I wouldn't answer questions.

This wasn't Beijing, this was the Holy City, but last year there'd been troops brought in by the thousand to quell the uprising, and more monasteries burned and more corpses dumped into military trucks and taken away for mass burial in the gaping earth with the bulldozers standing by.

"He says it is not enough."

I hadn't thought it would be.

"Then I'd be happy to pay a fine."

I meant it to sound naive, to let them know I didn't really understand the gravity of the charge. The least I was going to get away with was a night in the cells, and that was no big deal in itself, but it meant that I would become more familiar to them over the hours, more recognizable. That could be fatal, later, for me or for Xingyu Baibing or both.

The girl turned back to me and went on speaking in Chinese and corrected herself. "Yes, you must pay a fine of fifty yen and write a confession."

"That's very generous."

"You have money to pay?"

I got my wallet and put down a ¥ 100 note and she pushed it across the worn, paint-chipped counter. The young officer looked at it as if it were a piece of yak dung but in a moment pushed my passport and the other stuff over to me and I put them away.

"You will receive fifty yen change," the girl said. "Now we will go over there."

Rickety desk, one of the dozen in here, with a cheap ballpoint tied to a nail with a bit of dirty string, some kind of stool to sit on, though I didn't trust it.

"Write, please." She pointed to the block of schoolroom paper and took her hand away quickly when she noticed it was trembling. "In transgressing the laws of this city, I have shamed my ancestors." The ballpoint ripped a gash in the gray thin paper and she tore off the sheet and I started again. "Certain roads here are strictly out of bounds, and they are adequately provided with signs to this effect, in Chinese, English, and French. In failing to take notice of the signs, I am guilty of a grave lack of attention."

The door banged open and someone came in with a chicken underneath each arm and one of them let out a piercing squawk and flew into the air and sent a streak of white droppings across the counter and one of the PSB men shouted and someone else caught the poor bloody bird by one wing and bashed it against the wall.

"My ancestors are disturbed in their honorable sleep by my fall from grace on this sorry occasion, and my esteem in their eyes has grievously diminished."

The pen dried up and she got me another one from the next desk, pulling the looped string carefully off the nail in a show of deep respect for PSB property in case she was being watched.

"Finally, I wish—"

"Are you cold?"

Her eyes widened as she looked up at me. "It is not cold in here."

Then it was fear, making her hands shake. It was also in her eyes, fear of committing even the tiniest breach of protocol, damaging their bit of string, interrupting the written confessional by normal conversation. She looked down at the pad.

"Write, please, and do not interrupt. Finally, I wish to apologize sincerely for the trouble I have caused the officers of the Public Service Bureau, and vow that such a transgression will not occur again."

They were pushing the man with the chickens out of the door and a gust of freezing air blew in again. A wind had got up soon after we'd landed in Gonggar today.

"Do you wish to add anything?" the girl asked me.

My late Aunt Ermyntrude would also be shocked clean

out of her celestial corsets by my lamentable fall from grace, but we'd better not put that, we had better, my good friend, not put anything like that, I am simply feeling a touch light-hearted, you'll understand, because they're going to settle for fifty yen and this bit of bullshit and I could well have got their goat in some trivial way and finished up in the basement chained to the wall. Far better to take all possible notice of my little Eskimo here and walk on eggshells.

"I'd like to thank them for their leniency," I told her.

"No. They might decide to double the fine, one must understand. Please sign what you have written."

She tore it carefully off the pad and took it over to the counter, and we had to wait until they'd dealt with a youth in a smart leather jacket and sunglasses, chewing gum as if he were starving while he showed his papers and they told him to take off his sunglasses and he didn't want to and they snatched them off for him and flung them across the floor. Then the girl went forward and read my confession in Chinese while the PSB man watched me the whole time and I looked penitent and hoped to God we'd got it right, because I'd got quite enough worries already with Xingyu Baibing sitting up there in his cell on the top floor of the monastery, sitting there like a time bomb because there'd been nothing else I could have done, *there'd been nothing*.

The PSB man put out his hand and the girl gave him the sheet of paper and he scanned it for long enough to make it look as if he could read a bit of English and then tore it in half and jerked his head toward the door.

"We can go," she told me.

"Do you know this place well?"

"This restaurant?"

"Lhasa."

"Yes. I have been here often. I am an air stewardess with CAAC." She looked down quickly, perhaps because in the torn, patched coat that was too big for her she knew she looked more like a vagrant.

"When are you flying out?" I didn't imagine she was flying anywhere but I wanted to keep her talking. The minute we'd left the PSB office she'd told me she'd show me a cheap place to eat and when we'd got here she'd asked if we could sit together and I realized she was starving and hadn't any money.

"I won't be flying out for a time," she said. They'd brought up some bowls of noodles and meat dumplings, and she was using her chopsticks busily.

"You've got friends in Lhasa?"

"Yes." She looked up at me, then down again. "I cannot impose upon friends."

I began listening between the lines, because that was the way she communicated. I'd seen she was starving and I knew that when we left here I'd be paying the bill and when she told me she'd got friends here I'd wondered why they weren't looking after her and she'd told me: she couldn't impose. But she'd helped me with the confession thing and I was in her debt and here we were in this place with smoke creeping out of the seams in the pipe above the stove in the corner and condensation trickling down the windows and the dogs under the table snarling and scuffling in competition for any scraps that might fall.

"What's your name?"

"Su-May Wang," she said, putting it the Western way round. "What is yours?"

"Victor Locke. I'm just here for a few days. Are you on holdover, or what?"

I didn't like asking direct questions, but there wasn't much time: I had to find the Barkhor Hotel and report to Pepperidge and then get back to the monastery before ten o'clock because of the curfew, and I needed to know exactly how useful this girl could be, exactly how well she knew the town, because I'd found that the local laws and restrictions were like booby traps and I couldn't afford to be run into another PSB office: they'd throw me into the cells for a week next time just to make me pay attention.

"No," Su-May said, "I am not on holdover." She stopped eating and for the first time looked at me steadily in the eyes, and her question was clear enough: could she trust me? Then she bent her head again over the bowl of food. "Things are bad," she said, "in China. You are a tourist?"

"Yes."

"What do you think of things in China?"

"I think they're tragic."

"The bloodshed that time in Tiananmen?"

"And the crackdown that's been going on ever since."

She finished her bowl. "Would you like some more *tukpa*?"

"Very much." I got the man over and she ordered in slow, careful Tibetan, then turned back to me. "The British are on our side?"

"On the side of the people. You don't imagine we'd support the primitive thugs you've got in your government, I hope."

"Trade went on," she said evenly, "between the British and those primitive thugs. Nothing has changed."

"I realize that. It was disgusting. We're like any other people—we don't always agree with what our government does. What's he asking for?" There was a young boy waving his hand in front of my face.

"A pen. Don't give him one." She said a sharp word or two in Tibetan and he moved on. "My father is missing," she said in a moment.

A man in an ancient fur hat was watching me from the next table, but I didn't think there was any problem: round-eyes get watched quite a bit in the backwaters of the Orient. There wasn't any question of checking the environment in this place: it was like a flypaper, with as many people in here for warmth as for the food. I'd done a lot of routine checking on the flight into Gonggar and on the CAAC bus into Lhasa and we'd been absolutely clean, Xingyu and I, and no one would have got on to me here in the city, no one clandestine. But I began looking around me now for anyone who looked as if he could understand English, because she'd started saying things that were potentially dangerous.

"Missing from home?"

"Yes. And from his university. That is why I am worried, as you have noticed. That is why I am here."

"You're missing too."

"Yes." She was looking me in the eyes again, losing her unwillingness to trust me. "He disappeared a week ago, when the wave of arrests began. He left a note for me, saying I must not worry. They are hunting for him now. He is quite an important man, an important dissident." A shrug. "Of course, there are many. There are thousands."

We stopped talking when the man brought the food she'd ordered, and waited until he'd gone. I asked her why she'd come to Tibet.

"It was the next flight on my schedule. They use relatives, you see, as hostages. It is a well-established practice. They want my father in prison, or perhaps executed, and they would have me arrested on some pretext—anything will suffice, one must understand, suspicion is enough—and then they would have reported it in the media, to bring my father out of hiding to take my place."

I must go to Beijing. Xingyu, staring at me in the bleak light of the airport at Chengdu. *You cannot stop me.*

"You simply got off the plane here," I said, "and didn't go back?"

"Yes. Others have done this. Many of us have brothers, sisters who are students, or parents who teach. Some of my friends have gone to Hong Kong, and stayed there. But if they are picked up and sent back, they will be accused of fleeing the country, of evading their responsibilities as citizens. I am perhaps safer here. I have not fled my country."

Then what she was saying, what she was feeling bore down on her suddenly, and her eyes took the weight of it, the life going out of them. It's difficult to tell the age of an Oriental: she had looked, until this moment, no more than twenty, with her clear luminous eyes and her flawless skin, though she was probably more than that; now she had grown suddenly old, though her skin hadn't changed; the only expression was in her eyes, and they looked out on a frightening world with the despair of middle age, when for so many things, for so many people, it has become too late.

My father is missing. They would have arrested me. I have not fled my country. Not the burden of the years but of being a young woman in China in this year of such little grace.

"Your mother?"

She looked down and began eating, but from habit. "They do not agree. My mother is against his activities, his protests."

If they arrested her mother, then, he'd be unlikely to come out of hiding. "Where are you from, Su-May?"

"Beijing. That is where the worst happens, the worst of it all. For me, I am worried now because my father will find out I am missing too, and he may believe I have been arrested. They might even lie, and report it in the media that I have been arrested. But from here, from Lhasa, it is difficult for me to get a message to him, saying I am safe. There are people I could write to, but it is dangerous to send letters. Many are opened. Telephones are monitored. They catch many that way."

She looked up as a beggar came and crouched by the table, an empty tin bowl cupped in his hands, his eyes hollowed and demanding, not imploring, as he attacked our indifference. "Give him nothing," she told me, "or we shall have dozens here." She waved him away. "They have come from remote places to the Holy City, and have no money left." She shrugged. "I am the same. But they have come here to pray. I have come here" on a rueful breath "maybe it is the same thing."

Dark was coming slowly against the windows, and more people were arriving, packing against the bar counter shoulder to shoulder. Two PSB officers came in, their guns silhouetted on their hips, their eyes hidden by the shadow of their caps, and I caught a look on the face of Su-May as she saw them, not fright, something like disgust, as if she'd seen something obscene. They moved between the tables, and the people pressed back to give them room—again, it seemed to me, not from fear or in deference, but as if wanting to distance themselves from lepers. Beijing, she'd said, was where the worst had happened, but the people of Lhasa would disagree, seeing as they had the sky black with the smoke of burning monasteries, hearing as they had the crackle of bullets and the cries of grief.

I waited until the two officers had left. "If you like, Su-May, I can get a message to your father in Beijing, telling him you're safe."

She dismissed it. "You are a tourist."

"I can do it," I said, "if you like."

She brought her hands to her face suddenly, knocking her bowl and spilling some food. "How?"

"With great discretion."

"But how?" She held her face, staring at me from over her spread fingers.

"By word of mouth."

In a moment—"You are not a tourist, then." A tone of suspicion. Tourists were harmless, a gaggle of gawpers pointing at things strange to them, finding most of them funny. I was not one of them, if I could get a message to her father. I must be something else, not what I seemed, and therefore suspect.

"Yes," I said, "I'm a tourist, but I've got friends in Beijing. Close friends. Think about it, and let me know if you want me to help."

"But how would you tell them?" Her hands came away from her face and she leaned across the stained bare-wood table. "You must not use the telephone, or—"

"There's someone leaving here for Beijing tomorrow, by the morning flight from Gonggar. I would tell him."

She closed her eyes slowly, compressing her mouth, praying for patience, I think. In a moment, her eyes coming open with nothing in them but fright, "You do not understand how *dangerous* this is. You are just a tourist. People speak. People betray, sometimes without intention. One must understand, my country is full of spies, informers. One does not any longer know one's friends, trust one's friends— it is like in Nazi Germany, a child will give away his parents to the police, because he has been indoctrinated. My country is full of fear." She didn't look away, but she hesitated. "Do you know what they asked me to do, the PSB men? They asked me to follow you when you left there, and see where you went, and go back and report. I said my mother was very sick, so I had no time to help them. This is how it is, in my—"

"Why are they interested in me?"

"Simply because you are from the West, and might be a journalist. They are most afraid of foreign journalists, be- cause Lhasa is always on the point of rebellion, like most cities now in China, and they don't want the news to get out. All they can do is expel the journalists in time, and that is almost as bad, an admission that something will happen that must not be seen." Hesitation again, and then, "Your friend, what does he do?"

Another man came with a tin bowl, already with scraps of food in it, to show how generous others had been, his hands thinned to the bone under the skin, his face whittled by want.

"*Zǒukaī!*" she said, "*Zǒukaī!*" He went off, his bowl clang- ing against the corner of the table.

I think she was afraid of being overheard, more than anything; she couldn't leave it alone, this thing about getting word to her father. I said, "My friend is a Chinese, a lawyer. He knows as much as you do about the danger of indiscre- tion."

In point of fact the message would go to her father through the mast at Cheltenham and the signals board in London to the British embassy at Beijing and then to one of our sleepers or agents-in-place.

"Why should you help me?" Her hands had gone to her

face again, as if she wanted to hide as best she could from whatever treachery there might be in me.

"In the West," I said, "we hear the news from China and we feel great sympathy for the people. It's not often we can really do something to help, and it's a chance for me. I'll be envied, when I go home."

Not untrue. Harry, the man who looks after things at my flat, had gone out and got drunk after he'd watched the Tiananmen Square thing on the screen that night in June; he can't stand seeing things in cages, told me he'd screamed his head off the first time his mum took him to a zoo.

"You will be envied?" I don't think she believed it, but wanted to, because her eyes were suddenly wet. "It is difficult for us to understand that we have friends outside our country. We feel alone, and isolated. So when you say you will help me like this, it—"

Then she couldn't stop the tears, and tugged the edges of her mangy fur hood across her face and sat there with her long eyes squeezed shut and her body rocking backward and forward in its shapeless coat while one of those bloody dogs under the table bit my ankle and I gave it a smart kick and got a yelp.

The boy came around again with the teapot and I showed him some money and he peeled off a couple of notes and went away, not even glancing at the girl, I suppose because it wasn't unusual for women to weep in this ravaged city.

"I do not feel well, one must understand," Su-May said at last, "it is the high-altitude sickness. Have you felt any symptoms?"

"Bit light-headed sometimes." Our tour guide had warned us on the bus ride from the airport, the best thing was to rest up for the first two or three days, take it easy, and if anyone had any blood-pressure or chest problems he shouldn't have come here at all, this place was a killer, so forth, he wasn't joking.

"One must take it seriously," Su-May said, refusing to talk any more about the other thing, lost her pride, crying like that, lost face. "One must be very careful."

"So they tell me," I said. "Now write down the name and address of your father's friend, the one we have to contact, and give it to me."

For a moment she pretended not to know what I was talking about, and then found a bit of paper and went over to the counter for a pen and came back and wrote, looking up at me only once with her eyes deep and with an expression in them that clearly said, *If you betray me, I shall lose my trust at last in all humankind,* then bent her head again and finished writing and gave me the scrap of paper.

Professor Hu Zhibo, The Faculty, Department of Economics, Beijing University.

"And can he get the message to your father?"

"Yes."

"And the message is that you are safe and well, nothing else?"

In a moment, "And that I love him."

"All right. You can—"

"Perhaps I should put the name of the place where I am staying, in Lhasa?"

"No."

We want nothing in your heads, the executives in training are told at Norfolk, *that we wouldn't want anyone to get out.*

"I am grateful," she said with quiet formality.

"Little enough to do." She'd have a bad time, tonight, not getting to sleep because of the thoughts flying at her in the dark that I wasn't what I seemed, that she'd been out of her mind to trust me; but there wasn't anything I could do about that: the most fervent protestations of good faith are the most suspect.

We drank the rest of our tea and went out into the freezing wind and through the streets to her broken-down guesthouse near the market, and I left her there and found a streetlight and got out the CAAC map. Pepperidge had left the name of his hotel in code for me at the monastery, with a cross-street bearing, and I walked on again with my head

126

down against the wind, not looking forward to seeing him, not looking forward to it at all, because I was going to tell him what I'd had to do at Chengdu airport to stop Xingyu from going back to Beijing, and Pepperidge would realize what it was going to do to the mission, if London didn't abort it straight away and call us in.

Chapter 11

Tea

"I left him in charge of a monk."

"Will that be all right?" Pepperidge asked.

He meant was I certain that Xingyu Baibing would still be there when I went back, that he wouldn't be got at, that he wouldn't decide to leave the monastery of his own free will.

"Yes," I said. "Security's the best we can hope for, and we've reached an agreement."

Slight understatement.

"Well done. Spot of tea?"

"Not just now."

"If you haven't got a hot shower where you are, come along here." He was squatting in a cowhide chair with his long legs drawn up and his heels on the edge of the seat, watching me with his pale yellow eyes and taking everything in.

This was the Barkhor Hotel, Chinese, not Tibetan, no sign of luxury but he didn't want that; all he wanted was a telephone and there was one here.

"Feel all right?" he asked me.

"First-class."

"Altitude's not a problem?"

"I've hallucinated a couple of times, that's all. Wouldn't want to do much running yet."

"Won't have to."

He wanted to sound reassuring. In our language, running doesn't mean just around the park.

"You'll need your pad," I told him.

"Debriefing?"

"Call it that." I went across to the narrow bed and sat with my back against the wall. "Mind?"

"Of course not. Rest all you can."

I wasn't quite sure where I should start, so I looked around the room while he got his pad, cracks in the wall-plaster, the Cantonese rug worn to a hole in the middle, some kind of bleached burlap for the curtains, not totally opaque—I could see a streetlight in the distance—picture of Premier Li Peng over the bamboo chest of drawers, shot of three pretty Chinese girls being photographed against the gates of the Forbidden City, cockroach moving in fits and starts along the bottom of the wall, telephone on the bed table, with its plastic chipped and the cable in knots, was *that* our lifeline to London?

He was waiting, Pepperidge.

"All right," I said, "but you won't like it much. Just before we got on the plane in Chengdu this morning, Xingyu bought a newspaper, and there was a trap in it."

"I saw it," Pepperidge said.

"Did you?" For some odd reason it made me feel a bit better. "Well, he read that part and told me he was going straight back to Beijing."

"And you told him he couldn't."

Your director in the field doesn't normally jolly you along like this; you're meant to give it to him straight and he just shorthands it or puts it on tape and *then* he starts asking the questions. But Pepperidge is a kind man, and he knew I was going to tell him something quite appalling—*but you won't like it much*—and he was just helping me along, more than you'd get from that bastard Loman.

"Yes," I said, "I told him he couldn't."

You cannot stop me.

Facing me under the bleak tube lights, the blast of cold air from the ventilators sending a corner of the newspaper fluttering between his hands.

"That is a *trap*," I'd told him, "don't you know that?" He went on staring at me, hadn't heard of traps in newspapers, thought I must mean something else. "Your wife's not in danger—they just want you to think she is, to get you back there. Try and *understand*."

"How do you *know* that?"

"It's an old trick, that's all. They're just working on your emotions. If you—"

"You cannot say that! You cannot give me any *guarantee* that my wife is safe!" He shook the paper, pushing it against me. "It could be true, don't *you* understand? *No one* is safe in Beijing!"

I heard the girl at the gate talking to the tour guide, raising her sharp thin voice, we were going to be late, so forth.

I got the paper out of Xingyu's hands and folded it, bunching the bloody thing up and throwing it into the big oil drum against the pillar and standing close to him, talking quietly, holding his arm, looking into his masked face and moving into his mind with my own, just as they'd done, the people in Beijing. "Dr. Xingyu, you're playing into their hands, and if you go back now your wife won't see you again, not the man you are now, not when they've finished with you. All we're asking of you is three days, and in three days you can go back to Beijing, do you understand? You've got—"

"Look, if you're coming with us"—tour guide—"it's now or never, come on!"

"I am not going with you," Xingyu said and turned away and began walking and I caught him up. "When we land in Gonggar you can phone your wife, then you'll—"

"You say three days—why three days?"

"It's all the time we need. You—"

"To do what? I know nothing of what you are trying to

do, *nothing*. I am going back to Beijing."

Tour guide shouting now—*"You'd better phone my office, okay? Tell them what happened!"*

The need to make a decision came right up against my face and I stopped walking and thought about it, thought about *everything*, all the options, all their permutations, and finally faced the stark fact that if Dr. Xingyu Baibing got as far as the check-in counter across there and booked to Beijing we were finished and there was only *one* way I could try stopping him.

Caught up with him again and said, "If you knew our plans for you, you wouldn't want to go back to Beijing."

"That is possible. If I knew. But I do not know."

Standing together in the unearthly light of this place, attracting God knew what attention from the police and the plainclothes PSB agents among the crowd, with *Bamboo* ticking to doomsday on the big round clock.

"So I told him."

Pepperidge didn't react.

"How much?"

"Most of it. The army division and everything."

"When did you tell him?"

"There wasn't time at the airport. I just gave him my word that if he caught our plane I'd answer any questions he wanted to ask."

He sat very still, Pepperidge, the pad on his knee and the ballpoint sticking out from his thin wrinkled fingers, his eyes looking down, and in a moment he said gently, "Well, there's always something that can be done."

He should have blown my head off.

I felt very tired suddenly, as if I'd been climbing a real bitch of a mountain and got to the top, felt I could let go at last, flop out, because I'd told him now, I'd got it over, very tired indeed, suddenly, or perhaps it was the AMS the tour guide had warned us about, acute mountain sickness, exactly, the one I'd just been climbing, I'm sure you see my little joke.

"What else could I have done?"

Sounded angry, didn't have the gentleness of this bloody saint, didn't have the kind of philosophy that was going to get us through this one if anything could.

"Not much," he said.

Well yes, I could have gone on arguing the toss with Xingyu until the plane had left, taken him to a hotel and called London, not having Pepperidge's number in Lhasa yet, called London and told them the situation and asked for instructions, let *them* take this one on their back, or I could have told Xingyu to phone his wife or a trusted friend, anyone in Beijing who could have told him there was nothing in fact to worry about, his wife was only under house arrest with no interrogation going on, but it might not have worked all that well because the pretty Xingyu Chen could indeed be in Qiao Bambu under a five-hundred-watt lamp bulb and it would have been someone else who'd answered the telephone, a colonel of the KCCPC who'd been stationed in their apartment to wait for this very call.

Or I could have simply tried to *muscle* him onto the plane for Gonggar, a center knuckle on the nerves here and there to get his attention, to show him I was serious, but of course he could well have reacted, started an uproar, and they would have closed in rather smartly, the chaps in their peaked caps, and *finis*, my good friend, *finito*.

"The alternative," I said, "would have been to try keeping the man hanging around Chengdu scratching his mask off while I tried phoning London or tried getting some news from Beijing, and—"

"You don't have to explain."

So I shut up. He'd thought out all the alternatives for himself in five seconds flat. But I hadn't been trying to tell my director in the field how to suck eggs; I'd wanted him to know that I'd seen what the alternatives were and seen that they weren't worth using. But he would know that too.

I closed my eyes and let the whole thing ride, because I was going to need my strength. Someone, my gentle DIF or my Control in London or Bureau One himself, would have to work out what to do next, and their instructions could be frightening.

It had seemed so easy, almost a model exercise. The shadow executive was to take charge of a distinguished dissident from Beijing at Hong Kong airport and keep him discreetly sequestered for a day or two and then send him back to the capital when all was ready. The distinguished dissident would not of course be informed of the main operation, would know nothing of the People's Liberation Army general who would contain Tiananmen Square with his tanks while Dr. Xingyu Baibing, the hero of the hour, went before the television cameras in the Great Hall of the People and offered to lead his country out of the shadow of Communism and into the light of democracy.

Things were different now. He'd picked up the paper.

Plopping sound, like a silenced shot. I let my lids open a degree and saw Pepperidge had pulled the cork out of his big thermos flask.

"A drop now," I said.

"Do you good. Rest a lot, drink a lot."

"Yes." Rest, drink, but do not be merry, my masters, 'tis not the hour.

If he hadn't done that, Xingyu, if he hadn't picked up the paper, there would have been no mission-breaker, no ultimate risk of something happening that could blow the whole enterprise. Even if Xingyu were killed in some kind of unexpected action he could be replaced by someone in front of the television cameras, a disciple of the messiah who could still do the job at a pinch. Even if they blew us, the KCCPC, blew Pepperidge or me or both, we would pop our capsules to protect security and London could replace us and the operation could still proceed. If Xingyu were captured and sent back to Beijing and brainwashed it could *still* proceed, because the army general would still make his move and Xingyu's replacement would still do his job, at a pinch.

But now we had a mission-breaker. We would have to

go on from here in the face of the ultimate risk.

"Cheers." Pepperidge gave me a mug of tea.

"Cheers," I said.

And the ultimate risk was buried like a bomb inside the head of Dr. Xingyu Baibing himself. He knew *everything* now, because I'd had to tell him, and if they got at him tomorrow or the next day and put him under implemented interrogation he'd blow every phase of *Bamboo* like a firecracker, and within the hour the PLA general in Beijing would be arrested and shot and his division ordered out of the capital and when Xingyu was finally propped in front of the cameras like a ventriloquist's doll they'd wind him up at the back and he'd say he'd been wrong after all, he'd say that the people had mistaken their way along the road to socialist salvation, tempted by foreign blandishments, he'd say they must hold high the torch and keep the faith, while all over the city and across the nation a hush would fall, and hope for the future would limp away like the beggar at my table in the café, his tin bowl empty.

Pepperidge sipped his tea. "I shan't inform London."

I sat up straighter. "You've got to."

"I see no reason."

"This is major. You can't just go it alone."

"I don't see," he said slowly, "that London could have instructed you to do anything else at Chengdu, other than what you did. I think you took the only way out, and it must have shaken you to do it. I can only commend your decision."

He was going right out of his way this time. But it wasn't just charity. We were going to have to keep the mission on track if we could, and the director in the field didn't want to run a shadow executive who was living on the edge of his nerves because he'd made an ultrasensitive move without asking London's permission.

"Few things you should know," he said, "before we make up our minds what we're going to do. I've been in signals with London quite a bit since I got here, picked up some of the gossip. The Bombay police found a body in a canal last night, been garotted, head half off but with the face still there and papers intact in his wallet, five snake bites on him. It was Sojourner."

"*Sojourner*? I thought that thing had killed him."

"No. Two of our people were flown out from London to dig up the facts. Apparently Sojourner was released from the intensive-care unit twenty-four hours after he went in there, and a friend of his fetched him from the hospital. He was reported as being 'still weak, but ambulatory,' and his friend—a Hindu—declared he would look after Sojourner with great care."

"How old was the friend?"

"I asked that, too, because of what you'd told me. He was an adult, not the boy. Of course, it wasn't necessarily that man who killed him, though it looks like it. They're trying to put everything together." He brought the thermos over and sat on the edge of the bed. "Top you up? The only thing that worries us, of course, is that he might have been interrogated, during the time when he was escorted from the hospital and the time he was killed. For the moment London is assuming that Sojourner's assassin didn't get it right the first time and simply had to finish him off. Snake venom's uncertain in its effect, depends on body weight and general constitution. Whatever they find, I'll let you know."

"If he *was* interrogated," I said, "and they got *everything* out of him . . ."

"Let's not think about it. On the more positive side," getting up and fetching a news clipping from his briefcase, "when Dr. Xingyu was at our embassy in Beijing they asked him if he'd got any photographs of himself taken abroad, and he came up with this one, among others."

Head-and-shoulders shot, saying cheese, against the background of Big Ben, unmistakable. Caption: *Dr. Xingyu Baibing, released yesterday from the British embassy in Beijing, in London for talks with the Foreign Office.*

"Any chance they'll swallow it?"

"Not much. The first place Beijing would expect him to

go is of course London, and of course they would have posted a very large contingent of their people at Heathrow to watch for him. But who knows, they might fall for the snapshot."

He took another sip of tea and sat looking down into the mug, perhaps waiting for me to say something, though I didn't think so. He'd been going over the Chengdu thing while he was talking, and had now reached, I believed, a decision. I had an idea of what it was going to be, and I hoped I was wrong, hoped to God I was wrong.

Sand hit the windows as the gusts came whipping into the streets from the plateau. I found I was watching the telephone with its chipped plastic and its tangled cord, and either Pepperidge noticed this or there was one of those little flashes of telepathy that we become used to, when the mission begins to take shape and our nerves follow the same rhythm and our minds touch and drift away again but not far.

"I would phone London, of course, if you wanted me to."

In a moment I said, "Have you got the answer?"

Swinging his head to look at me. "I think so."

"And you're ready to go ahead with it?"

"Not really the question." He looked down again. "It's whether *you* will be ready to go ahead with it."

Sand on the window, coming in waves across the rock desert out there in the night, eroding the town by infinitesimal degrees, reminding me how impermanent life was, how fragile.

I said, "Try me."

He got off the bed, taking his mug and putting it down carefully on top of the chest of drawers with its patchy varnish, one brass handle missing.

"The only *added* risk," he said, "that we now face is Dr. Xingyu himself. For as long as he stays uncompromised, we shall have no trouble." It's one of the precious euphemisms those sniveling scribes at the Bureau think up to soften reality: in this case, for the opposition to 'compromise' Dr. Xingyu Baibing they would throw him into an interrogation room and squeeze out every bit of information he'd got in his head while the radio was turned up to full volume to cover the noise. "If he were found and seized and interrogated," Pepperidge went on, "all would of course be lost, and there wouldn't be anything we could do about it. After all, Sojourner possessed the same information that you—" tiniest hesitation—"that Dr. Xingyu has now become privy to. The only difference is that we believed Sojourner was safe from any attention, whereas Dr. Xingyu is being actively sought throughout the world. We should have protected Sojourner, and didn't, but at least we know we must protect Dr. Xingyu, if necessary to the point of death."

I sat with my hands around my mug of tea to warm them. The ancient electric heater set into the wall was keeping the room just this side of freezing.

He didn't mean mine, my death. The shadow executive doesn't necessarily expect to return from a mission; that much is a given—it's in our contract. *And it is understood by all parties concerned that in inclement circumstances the life of the undersigned may become forfeit despite any or all efforts that will if possible be made to protect him.*

We've lived with that one from the beginning, and never pay it much attention. People get killed in bullfights, in marital strife, on the road. What frightened me was that Pepperidge meant *Xingyu's* death, not mine.

"I don't want," I told him, "to make guesses."

"No, quite."

If you think I was giving him a hard time, my good friend, you are in error. I wanted to be *absolutely* sure of what my director in the field would give me for instructions, because in the heat of action I might forget what was said, or what was meant.

Pepperidge took a step or two, his thin body stocky-looking in his padded windbreaker, his raw, knuckly hands tucked under his arms, his eyes resting nowhere.

"Quite. Well, let me ask you this. Do you think there's

any chance of persuading Dr. Xingyu to carry a capsule? If you explained the need?"

I didn't even have to think about it. "No."

"Understandable, quite, devoted to his wife and all that. Just thought I'd ask, because you've been with him longer than I have." He turned away, taking another step, so that his voice reached me indirectly, echoing softly off the walls above the moaning of the wind outside. "So what it comes down to is this. I need to know whether, in order to protect the mission, you yourself would be prepared to take his life."

Chapter 12

Cockroach

He looked like a Buddha sitting there.

I didn't know if he'd seen me; he didn't give any sign.

There was a three-quarter moon outside; it had lit my way, no more than a patch of light through the haze of the flying sand but enough to show me the road, rutted by carts, up the long hill to the monastery. It shone through the oblong gaps in the walls here that once may have been windows, and through the broken timbers bracing the roof, its light leaning between the pillars, some of them rearing at an angle: the whole top floor had shifted, by the look of it, during the fire. There were ladders everywhere, most of them broken, hanging from their top rungs from the floor beams; the one I'd just climbed was the only one still usable—I'd checked for that, earlier, when we'd come here.

He sat very still, the moonlight touching on his scalp, turning his red robes to black, conjuring a spark of luminosity in the shadow of his face, a tiny jewel from this distance, his eye. So he was watching me.

This place was a catacomb, its spaces tunneling through massive timbers, its perspectives broken by frozen cascades of plaster blackened in the fire, by doors hanging from a single hinge, with cells making hollows darker than the walls, and galleries running as far as the light allowed the eye to follow. The smell of the fire was still here, acrid in the mouth.

The wind shrieked, rising to a gust and dying again,

141

keening, and sand drifted through the beams of moonlight as if through the timbers of a wrecked galleon. I'd made no sound coming here, climbing from the main hall of the monastery: I wanted to know how good this monk would be as Xingyu's guard; but there was enough noise going on already, from falling debris and the shifting of joists and roof beams as the wind shook the building. Perhaps he'd seen me in any case from the distance, as I'd climbed the ladder.

He hadn't moved, but since his eyes were open I knew he wasn't meditating or in prayer, but I gave a bow to make sure I wasn't disturbing him, and he returned it, getting to his feet when I neared him, a gold tooth gleaming as he greeted me with his palms touching lightly together. He was a *gelong*, fully ordained.

"He sleeps," he whispered to me.

"I won't disturb him. Did he ask for anything?"

"For paper, to write. And must buy drug."

"What drug?" He couldn't mean insulin.

"For the sickness that he has."

"For his diabetes? He needs more insulin?"

"Yes."

"You mean there's none left?"

"Must buy tomorrow, he say."

He could have warned me, Xingyu, for God's sake, that he was getting low.

"All right," I said.

"Peace be with you," the monk whispered. We exchanged bows, and he moved along the gallery, a rufous shadow in his robes, picking his way across the gapped timbers to the ladder.

He'd been upset, Xingyu, by the fuss in Hong Kong, the airport snatch and the mask and having to go back through the terminal for the flight to Chengdu; it could have made him forget he was running low on insulin. But that might be his way, to forget things, and I'd have to watch it: he could be living half his life on the edge of the galaxies, the absentminded-professor syndrome, it could be dangerous,

could be dangerous *now*—how easy would it be to get hold
of insulin in a place like Lhasa?

I opened the door of the cell as carefully as I could, but
the wooden hinge still creaked. It wasn't a cell exactly,
though Jiang, the abbot, had called it that; it had once been
three or four cells, but the shifting of the building during the
fire had brought down some of the flimsy plaster walls, and
we had the luxury of space here, you could call it a guest
room, almost, a royal suite, with glass in every window and
straw on the floorboards, a pipe from a cistern on the roof
bringing water to the metal trough in the corner where the
midday sun thawed the ice and you turned the tap on with
a wrench. It had been used, Jiang had told me, to accommodate a visiting dignitary on a secret mission for His Holiness during the 1959 rebellion; hence the glass in the
windows and the water basin, and of course the unlikelihood
of our ever being found here on the fifth floor of a ruined
hulk.

I couldn't tell if Xingyu were awake, as I opened my
sleeping bag. He didn't speak, or even stir, as far as I could
tell with the noise the wind was making, and I found myself
worrying, as I believe young mothers do, whether my precious charge was sleeping quietly or lying there in the silence
of untimely death: the insulin thing was on my mind, and I
didn't know how fast a coma could set in, with a change of
diet.

I lay on my side, with dust sometimes settling on my face
and making the skin itch as the wind fretted at the cracks in
the ceiling, worrying also that I had crept in here to lie in
the dark beside this man, his watchful guardian and defender
of his faith, but if things went terribly wrong, his executioner.

So what it comes down to is this—Pepperidge—*I need to
know whether, in order to protect the mission, you yourself would
be prepared to take his life.*

I hadn't said anything.

Sand blowing across the window. Took another step,
Pepperidge, head down, looking at the floor. "Let me spell

out the situation for you. Memory is fallible. The situation I'm talking about is one in which for some reason Dr. Xingyu were found and seized and you were unable to save him, but were able to take his life before it was too late, before there was any time for the KCCPC to put him under interrogation. I hope that's clear."

"Yes."

It wasn't likely that a situation like that would come up: it was more liable to be one thing or another—either I'd succeed in protecting Xingyu and bringing him safely to the plane for Beijing, or something would go wrong and the KCCPC would infiltrate our operation and catch Xingyu and break him and send him to Beijing for the puppet show. But I could think of a hundred situations, a thousand, where I could be *right* in the middle of a last-ditch action to save the protégé and indeed have the option of seeing him taken away or protecting the mission by taking his life. The most obvious scenario would be that we were *both* found and seized and taken for interrogation, giving me the chance of seeing to Xingyu somewhere along the way and then popping my capsule. We were both replaceable, and *Bamboo* could survive.

Seeing to Xingyu, oh for Christ's sake who's just been bitching about the use of precious euphemisms, *killing* him, yes, *killing* Xingyu, I take your point.

"You didn't draw a gun," Pepperidge asked me, "this time out?"

"I never do."

We're given one or two options on our way through Clearance, draw a weapon if we feel like it, draw a capsule; but I don't like guns; the hands are quieter and I prefer going in close.

"I know," Pepperidge said, "but I just wondered, you know, this time. In the kind of situation we're talking about you might not get a chance of staying near him, near enough. Question of distance, timing, chance of pulling off a shot."

My hands had gone cold around the mug; the tea was cold, my spirit was cold, and I got off the bed and put the thing down on the chest of drawers and told him, "You can't insist. You cannot *insist*."

Touching my arm, "Of course not. I've just got to sound you out, you see, find some sort of compromise. Got to remember, though, haven't we, that there's rather more at stake than the disinclination of one single executive to take a life. There's the future, isn't there, of China and Hong Kong."

Beginning to feel light-headed, you've got to avoid stress, the guide had told us, or you'll make things worse, the altitude sickness, take it easy, walking, I was walking about now, Pepperidge moving over by the wall to give me room, that *bloody* cockroach crawling along the wainscoting, looking for a way out, felt like, I felt like putting my foot on the thing, Ferris would have done that, he loves doing that, he's always looking for beetles to tread on, makes me sick because where do you stop, putting my foot on a cockroach, on Xingyu, said, I said—

"They must have provided for an accident, in their original planning in London, an accident to Xingyu, I mean, they—"

"Oh, yes." His voice gentle, reasonable. He knew I was looking for a way out and he wasn't going to let me have one. He couldn't. "There are several known dissidents in Beijing available, top intellectuals much admired by the people. London would certainly have gone to one of them, through the embassy, and put things to him."

"You think someone's been *briefed* to take Xingyu's place, if he gets killed?"

"We can be certain. Most of the planning was made by Bureau One, with Sojourner as his adviser. But we don't want to see Dr. Xingyu as in any way . . . expendable. We would *hope*, if anything happened to him, that his replacement could rally the people under the protection of the tanks, but we are *certain* that Dr. Xingyu could do it. He is our highest priority. But if there were any risk of his exposing the mission..."

Walking about, I walked about, cold all over now, deathly cold, logical thought not coming easily but it didn't take a lot of working out, Xingyu Baibing was the messiah, with the future of all those people in his hands, but also with a bomb in his head they were asking me to detonate if he became a danger to them.

Pepperidge, watching me, the naked bulb in the ceiling reflected in his yellow eyes, waiting for me to understand that I hadn't got a chance. The objective for *Bamboo* was to protect Xingyu Baibing, but that objective would automatically be overridden—if something went wrong—by the highest priority of all: to protect the mission itself.

This hadn't been part of the planning, specifically; it had been built into the very bones of the Bureau in its conception, a commandment carved in stone: *Protect the mission.*

In the end I said, "No gun."

"Very well." He had to accept that much and he knew it. I've got my commandments too. "But you accept the need to avoid any risk to the mission?"

Said yes.

I had said yes.

Lying here in the padded sleeping bag with the dust settling onto my face, making it itch, lying not far from him, from the messiah, watchful guardian and defender of his faith, but if things went wrong, the implement of his crucifixion.

Blood on the floor.

I was sitting against the wall on a slatted bench, head down, chin on my hands, looking across at the counter sometimes and then looking down, ill, depressed, abandoned to my fate, appropriate cover for a place like this.

Streaks of blood across the floor, he'd been brought in a minute ago, a young Khampa horseman, I would have said, in his brigand's garb, they ride as if into the teeth of hell and sometimes come a cropper. A woman in a stained white smock came with a mop and bucket, shaking her motherly head. There were a dozen people in here, most of them at the counter, some with an arm in a sling, one carrying an infant with its face red with rage, its cries piercing. The monk was at the other end, at the dispensary.

His name was Bian. The abbot had assigned him to me, telling me that he would do what I wanted better than anyone, more discreetly. I'd been surprised at first how ready the abbot had been to help me, but Xingyu had explained things: the monastery, like a hundred others, had been half destroyed by the Chinese forces in 1959, and the monks were still painstakingly restoring it; their hate for the Chinese had burned on when the fire was put out, and they would help anyone who could free Tibet and leave them in peace.

Yelling the place down, the infant, as the mother shuffled forward in the queue. Bian, the monk, was talking to someone now across the counter, a man in a white coat, the dispenser, giving him the prescription. It had become grubby in Xingyu's wallet and had been much handled, and I'd improved on that, making a smudge across his name that had left it unreadable.

This was simply an exercise in caution. Quite apart from the world-media photograph of Dr. Xingyu Baibing in London, the Chinese weren't likely to suspect that he was already back on the mainland. *It's the last place they'd expect me to go,* he'd told me on the boat in Hong Kong, and that was why Pepperidge and London had agreed to let him come to Lhasa. But I'd asked Bian to buy the insulin for me to cover the thousandth chance that we were wrong, or that one of the KCCPC agents who'd seen me making the snatch at Hong Kong airport was now here in Lhasa, and that they suspected I was still looking after him. So this was just routine, straight out of the book.

"I shall require another injection," Xingyu had told me, "by noon."

He hadn't apologized for the trouble involved, hadn't realized there was a risk, however slight. He'd been squatting on the floor when I'd left him, writing busily, some kind of diary perhaps, that he'd have to leave behind him when we made our final move; if so, the abbot would look after it for him.

The monk, Bian, was nodding, putting money on the counter, hitching the red robe higher on his shoulder, taking a packet from the dispenser, coming away.

I left the clinic five minutes after him and cut him off in a narrow street behind one of the temples, deserted except for a huddle of mendicants sheltering from the wind.

"I did not bring it," Bian told me.

"The insulin?"

"This is aspirin. I bought it in case I was watched. The dispenser said he would give me insulin but warned me, saying he had orders to report it."

Mother of God.

"To report *any* sale of insulin?"

"Yes." He looked along the street, then back to me, the stubble on his face catching the light from the flat gray sky where the sun made a hazy disk, his eyes watering in the freezing wind. "He was a Tibetan, and was sorry, but said he would lose his license, perhaps be arrested for disobedience."

Perhaps I was just paranoid, losing my grip. There could be other explanations. "Bian," I said, "how many places are there in Lhasa where you can get insulin?"

"Very few. Very few places."

So they wouldn't have to put a standing watch all over the town, the KCCPC, though of course if they had to, they would do that. They'd got limitless manpower.

Put a final question, to see if it was just paranoia: let *him* tell *me*. "Bian, can you think why they would watch for anyone asking for insulin?"

He seemed a little surprised. "I would think because they know our guest has need."

Had need. *And was somewhere in Lhasa.*

He stood there, Bian, holding the small brown-paper packet of aspirin and some money, the change; he watched me with pain in his eyes: it was perhaps his 'guest's' karma to be found and taken away. The wind whipped at his worn soiled robes.

"Where else," I asked him, "could I find insulin? Not the hospital or the clinics—would an apothecary stock it?"

"Perhaps. I will try—"

"No."

It was too dangerous now; it needed professional handling. I asked him for the prescription and told him to offer the money at one of the altars at the monastery and add the aspirin to their medical supplies; then I walked with my back to the wind and sat on a broken bench in a little park and worked on things and came up with the essentials: that unless there were diabetic on the run the KCCPC either knew or suspected that Xingyu Baibing was here in Lhasa and were closing in; that it would take time to signal Pepperidge because the telephones here weren't very good and you had to go through an operator and I didn't know Mandarin or Tibetan; and that Xingyu had *got* to have insulin before noon and there was only one way I could get it for him and the risk was appalling.

Chapter 13

Apothecary

The snakes were alive, I think.

It doesn't need saying, surely, that in any mission, whatever the objective, whatever the target, the one primordial requirement is to stay clear of the opposition, particularly if the opposition is not a private cell but the entire security network of the host country: police, secret police, civil and military intelligence. The one primordial requirement is to stay clear of them and get back across the frontier with a whole skin and the documents or the tapes or the defector or the blown spook who's going to die out there if you don't, die out there or finish up under the five-hundred-watt bulb without a capsule and blowing the roof off London.

They weren't moving. They were just a lot of colored spirals curving around the inside of the big glass jar, their little black eyes open, but that didn't mean anything, we go on watching life after death, don't we, until someone closes the lids. But in any case I was disgusted, I can't *stand* those bloody things.

The apothecary peered at the grubby bit of paper. The light was bad.

Of course there are times when we can't for some reason stay clear of the opposition and then all we can do is to pop it and protect the mission or get clear again, bloodied but unbowed, so forth. Then there's a third situation that comes up sometimes but thank God not very often: it's where the only way to keep the mission going and hope to survive and

151

reach the objective is to set yourself up as a target and wait for them to shoot and that was what I was doing now.

One of them was moving, its small head dropping and swinging around inside the jar with the black forked tongue flickering, and I looked away, the flesh creeping, they've got no bloody *feet* anywhere, those things, all they can do is *writhe*.

"Insulin," the old man nodded, peering at the bit of paper.

"Yes," I said.

The decorated canopy crackled above the shopfront in the wind, and the man behind me fell prone again onto the flat of his hands, facing toward the temple farther along. A dog sniffed at his rags.

I'd tried two other apothecaries but at the first one the girl had just looked at the prescription for a long time and finally shaken her head and flashed all her gold teeth and at the second one the man had said in quite good English that he was disappointed at not being able to oblige me but that I should try the one around the corner, toward the Barkhor plaza. I was there now.

There were other things, apart from the snakes: rows of bottles and bowls of herbs and a huge dried starfish and an armadillo; but there was a shelf of phials and flagons with typed labels, and a small poster with *Bayer* at the top. I'd been trying apothecaries in the hope of making a deal; they owned their own places and could break the rules if they wanted to, and I put the price of their wanting to at about one hundred yen.

The old man was raising his head slowly, looking up from the prescription and bringing his eyes to focus directly on mine with his face close; and in his eyes there was a warning. Then their focus shifted, and it was quite clear that he was looking behind me, through me, at something else.

I said softly, "Police?"

He nodded, pleased that I'd understood. "If sell you this, must tell them. It is order." Below his bald pate his brows made furrows, as many as the armadillo's. "Perhaps better you leave now."

I heard the man outside fall flat on his hands again in obeisance to the gods of the temple; he'd moved another few yards. I could hear other sounds, mostly voices from the people at the vegetable stalls opposite, and the rumbling of ironbound wheels and the dragging of harness. The dog that had sniffed at the pilgrim's rags now sniffed at my combat boots. Farther along the street there were prayer bells ringing, tuneless but with a steady rhythm. I listened carefully, analyzing the environment, because in a moment I was going to cross the line and present myself to the opposition, because I had no choice.

"I must have the insulin," I told the apothecary. "It's urgent." He watched me steadily, his eyes bright with intelligence, but it was obviously beyond him to understand me. "It doesn't matter," I told him, "about the police."

There was no point in pushing money at him as a bribe. In the last few minutes I'd come to know him well enough; he was an apothecary, a man of high standing in his community, a man, by his art, of great responsibility, and if he decided not to report me to the police he would do it as a point of honor, the police being the enemy here; his goodwill would not be for sale.

"You understand," he asked me, his eyes grave, "you understand what is the truth of this thing?"

"Yes. But the police are not looking for me. I shall have no trouble."

He lifted his hands, their skin like crumpled silk, and let them fall gracefully. "Ah. Then it is good."

It was a long time, minutes, before he'd filled in the form, peering again at the prescription. "And the name? The name is not clear."

"Xiao Dejian," I said, and spelled it for him. He wrote it down, using a pen with ink the color of blood. Then I gave him some money and he gave me change and I took the flat packet of ampoules and returned his bow and walked through the strange leaden light of the morning, hearing the sudden shout and ignoring it because it was only in my mind, the nerves shimmering in the system with a feeling of cold light and the scalp drawn tight, because I had staked the whole of the mission on one throw, on the logical assumption that if the KCCPC were watching the clinics and the apothecaries for anyone buying insulin they wouldn't make an arrest but would simply follow.

They were not clods in the Kuo Chi Ching Pao Chu. A cloddish intelligence service would have given orders to have me arrested and thrown into a cell and interrogated, but these people knew how long the odds are against getting information out of a trained agent; it's not an exact science, and you can beat a man into the kind of stupor where he himself wouldn't know the truth from a lie, or you can push him beyond the point when he can tell you anything at all.

They thought or they knew that Dr. Xingyu Baibing was in Lhasa, and the odds were better that I could lead them to him now.

Why did they think, or how did they know? I must find out.

Perhaps he would tell me, the short, squat-bodied Chinese who was walking behind me on the bright curved surface of the copper samovar, fifty paces, I would have said, behind me, allowing for the reduction in size of everything reflected there, a cup of tea, how nice, but I haven't the time just now, warming their hands, the little group around the stall, warming their hands on the cups as the tea came gushing from the spout, hanging back a little now, he was hanging back, because here the street was clearer and if I looked around he'd stand out and I might notice him, he was good at the rudiments of urban tracking and that made things safer by a degree because a trained tag is predictable and his movements would be unsurprising. I could do with that.

I could do with anything in point of fact that I could get in the way of advantages, because he would carry what those Americans so delightfully call a "piece" and it would be heavy-caliber, big enough to drop me from a distance if I looked like getting away. It was probable too that he'd been here on the roof of the world a bit longer than I had and had got used to the atmospheric pressure and would be able to run more effectively, to outrun me if he had to, through the leaden light of the forenoon.

There's a case to be made for calling us cocky, you must understand, we the brave soldiery of the thrice-accursed Sacred Bull that runs us across the board like pawns until at last the paint wears thin and the glue cracks and the head comes off and they throw us away, for calling us cocky, yes, as we work our way through the labyrinth, meeting so often face to face with our grinning fate that we lose much of our fear and become irrational in the heat of crisis, and this, my good friend, was a crisis, because the executive had moved deliberately into the surveillance field of the opposition and attracted its attention and the opposition was not some maverick terrorist cell with no claim to expertise or efficiency but the multifaceted and highly competent intelligence service of the People's Republic of China, and as I walked across the packed dirt of the next street to my right my feet felt sticky on the web.

He was keeping pace, moving across the window of a bathhouse, neat in his new parka, his head turned to the side a little in case I looked back, cocky, yes, in a crisis, and this has often been our undoing, the head comes off, you understand, and they throw us away; but this was a two-edged thing, because if we couldn't allow ourselves the choice of deadly options and face the matter head-on we'd never get anywhere, would we, all we'd do is sit there in the park with a drip on our nose and a plaid rug on our knees feeding the bloody pigeons, turned again, I turned again, working my way to the edge of town through the leaden light of the forenoon.

There'd been no other choice, let's face it. That improvident diabetic up there in the monastery, that crass idiot, the messiah, my precious protégé, needed the stuff in my pocket before he started slipping into a coma, and I couldn't have asked Pepperidge for help because the director in the field can have no part of the action; his job is to hole up in his ivory tower and liase with London, report to the signals board on the progress of the mission and request instructions, to protect, nurture, and advise his executive, certainly, but not on the streets, in harm's way, because if a wheel comes off he provides a kind of black box for the Bureau, slipping away from the field and leaving the blood and the smoke behind him and taking plane for Londinium and a debriefing room, there to explain what happened, why we crashed, so that our little mistakes can go down in the records and those poor little buggers in training at Norfolk can be duly warned: *Here is a case, you see, where the executive began believing himself to be invulnerable, and overestimated his talents.* Got cocky, yes.

Yet it was logic that drove me through these streets and I won't have it otherwise: that man *had* to have his medication and there was *no one* else who could get it for him—I'd already put that monk in hazard without meaning to—and there'd been *no way* I could have bought it in time without walking straight into the trap, won't have it otherwise, I tell you, I don't care what you think.

Things were not, though, going to be pretty.

I was walking a bit faster now, giving him the picture, glancing around sometimes to see if anyone were watching, my steps more purposeful, man with a mission, yea, verily, a huge black yak coming the other way, pulling a cartload of dried dung, whites of its eyes, breath clouding on the air, one hoof split and bound with a metal ring, the driver chanting, head lifted to the sky, lost in his own world, I could have run now, using the yak and the cart for cover and taking whatever doorway or alley I could find, running flat out and gaining enough ground to get me clear before he could catch up; but there'd be no future in that: he could have dropped me with a shot or cut across the terrain and intercepted me, his lungs better than mine, more used to the altitude, and in any case it would only have confirmed to his agency that they were right: Xingyu Baibing was indeed in Lhasa and must now be hunted down.

Also I had a rendezvous: this he must assume.

Walls of a temple garden, huge cracks in it, weeds growing, a pair of timbered gates, one hanging from a rusty hinge, the other decorated with dried leaves in an intricate design, embodying prayer, presumably, or homage to the Lord Buddha, so I went in there, it seemed appropriate, went in there to keep the rendezvous.

It was mostly a ruin.

The main doors had been chained at some time but one of the hasps had been jimmied away from the woodwork and now the doors hung open. Human excrement on the worn stone steps, pages torn from a pulp magazine, a cracked boot lying on its side in a corner and the white bones of a skeleton glowing in the half-light inside the doorway, a dog's, with one leg missing.

Smell of stale incense, or perhaps a fire, a torching of aromatic timber: this could be one of a hundred temples ransacked and ravaged by the angels of Chairman Mao. It was cold in here, silent, smelling of a grave, with feeble light from the aureoles along the gallery pooling on the floor, playing on dead leaves and the carcass of a rat.

Suddenly a face in front of mine as I moved into the shadows, the shock hitting the nerves and the adrenaline hot in the blood, a face with the gold leaf peeling away from the dry cracked wood underneath, the eye sockets brooding in meditation, the hands folded across the gross belly two inches below the navel, I didn't stop, didn't hesitate, because the scenario required confidence here: I was meant to know my way, I was bringing the insulin to Dr. Xingyu Baibing, for it was here that he was hidden.

Scream of a bird and the echoes played it back from the domed ceiling, a flurry of wings and a spattering and then silence again until I moved forward, my boots grating across the chipped tiles, there was a door here.

I pushed it open and it swung back, hitting the wall before

I could stop it, darkness now, blindness across the eyes, and a silence so deep that even my breath echoed until I controlled it and went forward again, swinging the door shut but not with a bang, because any noise in this place could attract attention and we wouldn't want that, Dr. Xingyu Baibing and I.

"I've got it," I said, we must not ham it, must not actually say *insulin*.

"You were late," at the back of the throat. "I need it now."

Then I waited against the wall behind the door.

I was relying on his pride.

This was a kind of inner chamber, I suppose, but it might have another door, to the outside, either locked or chained or able to be opened. There could be fixtures in here, lamps, candle sconces, Buddhas, perhaps, unless they'd been saved from the torching; by the acoustics it was a small place with a flat ceiling, not domed; there was not a photon of light here. It smelled of damp rot, with a mortuary sharpness that caught at the throat: there might be a cadaver here, neither rat's nor dog's this time, and not bared to the bone, the flesh still stirring to the feast of maggots, but we are being morbid, perhaps, the nerves producing a little video show for the imagination to work on, worried now, I was worried because I was relying on his pride and that could be a mistake.

From far away the tolling of a bell, perhaps in requiem, we are not, are we, feeling too cheerful just now, less than sanguine, because he might not, lacking pride, decide to push the door open and come in with his gun to catch us unawares, Dr. Xingyu Baibing and I, and make the arrest and herd us to the nearest Public Security Bureau, promotion assured, the man who caught the infamous dissident, subject of a worldwide search. He might decide instead to play it safe and leave us here, sure of our staying at least long enough for him to fetch help in case we were armed.

I didn't want that to happen. I'd pushed the mission into a new phase by making contact with the opposition, with the intelligence service of the host country, and I wanted it to stay like that, and control the outcome if I could. There were—

No, he hadn't gone.

The door had a metal lever, and he was pushing it down, and with great care, by infinite degrees, and sweat came on my skin immediately and the pulse went up and I steadied the breathing, we are engaged, my good friend, we shall have our reckoning, he and I.

They would have been interested in this, the people sitting there at the signals board in far Londinium; it would have broken the ennui for them. There'd been a flurry of excitement I suppose when Pepperidge had put it through the mast at Cheltenham, *Executive undertakes to ensure silence of subject if protection of mission necessitates*, but since then they'd been sitting on their hands.

That was last night. Mr. Shepley, Bureau One. *Nothing since?*

No, sir.

Then where the hell is he? Hyde, my Control, less patient than the King of Kings, less able to control his nerves.

The lever on the door was still moving.

It would have got them going, wouldn't it, if they'd known the score. Holmes would pick up the chalk and look at the big digital clock and punch the international time-zone button and note Tibetan local and fill in the rest of the line, *Red One, DIF on open circuit.*

And they'd start walking about, not looking at one another, because *Red One* is perhaps rather theatrical shorthand for a situation in which either the executive's life or the security of the entire mission is in extreme hazard, which can simply mean that the poor bastard out there is stuck on a frozen roof two hundred feet above the street with the lights of the chopper fingering the buildings one by one or spread-eagled facedown with a boot on his neck and a gun in his spine and the stink of exhaust gas from the unmarked van in his lungs or reeling in the chair under the light and praying for the ill-judged blow that will bring him what he can't bring himself because they found the capsule on him and he's got promises to keep before he sleeps and he can't take much more before he breaks them, not much more of this.

There was light on the wall now, a thin pale sliver of light that ran like a vertical crack on the plaster, and across it was his shadow.

There was nothing to be done yet. Things would take their course. I don't like guns and I never use one, as you know, but that's not to say that I don't respect them, for they can summon the death-bringer.

DIF on open circuit is more technical, and simply means that the director in the field can put his signal straight through to the speaker system at the board, taking automatic priority over all other traffic. It can make things tricky if there are two Red Ones in operation from two different missions but that doesn't happen often.

The crack of light was widening.

Shall we raise him, sir?

The DIF?

Yes.

Not yet. It's Pepperidge.

Don't call us, we'll call you: despite his gentle manners, Pepperidge has more nervous stamina than most, and doesn't shoot till he sees the whites of their eyes.

What I didn't like was that the hinges of the door were on the left, looking from the other side, from the side where he was standing now, and I was right-handed, and the choice was unaccommodating: either I'd have to use my left hand or move my whole body into his vision field before I could use my right. Either decision could be lethal.

As I'd thought, this place wasn't very big. The light coming through the doorway was faint, but I could see the opposite wall now, and it was close. There wasn't anything to see on the floor so far except chips of plaster and broken tiles, no cadaver despite this smell of decay, no remains of some starving pilgrim who'd crawled in here to sleep and dream no more, nothing, either, like a fallen joist or a broken pane of glass that would do for a weapon.

I could hear him breathing.

He wasn't going to rush it. I didn't expect him to: he'd be well trained, a professional. We could have a whole armory in here, Dr. Xingyu Baibing and I.

The hinges of the door hadn't made any sound when I'd opened it and later closed it, but that could have been because I'd swung it fairly fast. He was moving it much more slowly now, and that could make it creak, and if it did *that* I would expect him to use his shoulder and smash the door back before we could find our guns, my insubstantial companion and I, because we might be somewhere off this chamber where we couldn't see the light but could hear the door.

This would be in his mind, as it was in my own. Our heads at this stage were probably eighteen inches apart with the door between them, each the vessel of a quiet blaze of consciousness as the synapses fired in their billions and the nerves at the extremities of our bodies recorded the pressure of the floor underfoot and the tactile impression of the air on my face and the trigger under his finger and our cortices processed the data and reacted accordingly. I had been as close as this before to a fellow creature whose presence could bring my death, but it's not something you get used to, because every time can be the last and you know that.

The strip of faint light widened on the wall, and his shadow took on bulk. His head was defined now and I could see his right elbow but not the gun: that would be held in front of him.

I could smell him now.

Danger came close—he could smell *me*.

Nothing, there was nothing to do but wait, and it wasn't easy but it had got to be done because I couldn't leave him alive and I'd have to see more of his body before I could take him down—I was badly positioned because of the left-hand-right-hand thing.

It wouldn't be long now. You can't stand as close as this

to someone and not become aware of him, and this man's senses would have started picking up the signals by this time, the almost soundless exchange of air by the lungs, the barely discernible rise in temperature as the heat radiated from the skin, and above all else the vibration of the aura itself beyond the reach of the senses but within the field of the subconscious where the alarm would be raised and the nerves galvanized and—*he fired the gun and the shock smashed at the walls.*

Chapter 14

Trotter

"*Qíngkuàng yánzhòng ma?*"
"*Bù hěn yánzhòng. Tóu zhuàng le yi xìa.*"
Water splashing.
"He says it's nothing serious. Bit of concussion."
I think I said that's good or something.
The Chinese went on squeezing the sponge over the side of my scalp, water splashing into the bowl. It didn't hurt, couldn't feel anything, water very cold, that was all.
"Are there any snakes?"
"What was that?"
"Snakes?" Then I said, "No, don't worry."
"Feel all right, my dear fellow?"
He was a big man, bright teeth in a black beard, very good sheepskin coat, jeep full of rocks, rocks and picks and a spade, rope, things like that, told me he'd been getting samples from the high plateau, told me his name was Trotter, taught Oriental languages at Oxford.
"Feel fine," I said.
He'd brought me to a street clinic, Chinese scrolls hanging all over the place, pictures of roots, leaves, herbs, the front part, where he'd brought me inside, Trotter, front part rather like the apothecary's place, that was why I'd asked about the snakes, can't stand those bloody things.
"... coming through next week, overland from Kathmandu, although I don't think she was terribly keen," another quick laugh from deep in the chest, talking, now I

163

thought back a bit, about his wife. "She doesn't trust the CAAC, even though I told her it's the safest airline in the world, never flies in bad weather. This man's extremely good, don't worry, best in Lhasa, none of your Western medicine here. . . ."

Tuned him out, had to think, but not easy, kept seeing the flash.

I would say he'd fired so as to light up the little chamber and see where I was. I'd got a glimpse of him, his eyes very wide, not afraid, very alert, needing to know things, just as I did, then he'd brought the gun up and I'd gone for him.

Dark again, totally dark after the flash, place stinking of cordite, I found his right arm by feeling for it, you can say feeling for it but I mean we were spinning together trying to find the killing point, or at least I was, he seemed more interested in breaking clear so that he could threaten me from a distance with the gun and of course I didn't want that.

Strong smell of sweat from both of us: the adrenaline was pouring into our systems and the muscles were charged, I found his gun hand and extended *ki* and tried for a *kotegaeshi* but he was very strong and I felt the gun turning toward me, into me, and that was frightening because he'd be selective, shooting to maim, to incapacitate, to put me out but keep me alive and get me to an interrogation cell and ask me where Xingyu Baibing was.

I didn't want that either. We draw the capsule but we're not going to use it if we can make a killing first, it's not just a gesture, you know, we're not a league of bloody gentlemen, *fired again* and the sound crashed and I wasn't certain if he'd made a hit, you don't always feel a bullet going in when the organism's functioning at this pitch because the endorphins move in immediately on the pain, *fired again* and I couldn't afford this so I used the flash and saw his throat exposed and made a half-fist and drove deep and he fell and dragged me down with him and my head hit the edge of the open door.

He didn't move again. I got his parka off and put mine

on him and took his papers, shut the door after me, hit the wall once or twice before I found the steps and went down them, the sky reeling overhead.

There'd been a horse and cart and I was trying to get the driver to take me on board when the jeep had come past and Trotter had seen the blood on my head and put his brakes on.

The stuff was stinging, whatever he was putting on the wound.

"All right, my dear fellow?"

He was watching me attentively. I said fine, yes, the stuff smelled like alcohol, suppose it was some kind of antiseptic.

"Tā shūo tā juede tǐnghaǒ, li zhěn mē rènwei?"

"Tā búhuì you da wèntí. Haǐbá zhèmē gāo, tóu shòu shāng dōuhuì yūnde. Ta shìbúshì shuaǐle yi xià?"

"If you feel," Trotter said cheerfully, "sort of ga-ga, don't worry about it. The altitude makes things worse than they really are. What happened, did you fall?"

"Yes. Fell on my head. Time is it?"

"I'm sorry?"

"What time is it?" My watch had got smashed.

The man, the doctor man, helped me sit up and the whole place spun, the scrolls whirling around, "Steady as you go," Trotter was saying, "steady as you go, my dear fellow."

Their hands on me, felt grateful, good of them.

"Time?"

"What?" Trotter took out a heavy gold pocket watch. "It's twenty past eleven."

"I need a taxi."

I stood up and Trotter's huge hands were supporting me again, he was like an amiable black-bearded bear, "Look, you mustn't—"

"Taxi," I said, and managed to find my wallet. "Ask him how much I owe, will you?" My head was clearing now, by necessity: I had to reach Xingyu Baibing by noon and we were running it close because I couldn't take the taxi all the way, I'd have to get him to drop me off half a mile short at a different monastery, the hills were full of them, some where tourists could go. I got out a ¥ 100 note. "Is this enough?"

"Look, you can't go anywhere on your own like this. You need—"

"Appointment," I said, "extremely important, I've got an appointment."

He studied me, worried. "He doesn't need money; he's a friend of mine. Now let me take you to your hotel—which one, the Lhasa?"

"Several places," I said, "I've got several places to go. I can't keep you hanging about." I put the ¥ 100 note away. "Will you thank him for me, then? I'm most grateful to you."

He followed me out and said, "Hop on board, then. There's a taxi up by the post office."

It was a broken-down Austin smothered in dust, and Trotter helped me into it. "I don't know whether you're intrepid," he said, "or foolhardy." Laugh booming, gave me his card. "If ever you need a friend . . . in the meantime for God's sake look after yourself."

Thanked him for everything and slammed the door and slumped back against the torn vinyl seat.

"Where go?"

"Telephone."

He twisted around to look at me, a wizened face wrapped in scarves. "Number One Guest House?"

"No. I want to make a telephone call."

"*Rei*. Telephone at Number One Guest House, not far."

"Good."

The light kept flashing so I shut my eyes but it went on doing it. He drove on the horn, this man, and one of the rear tires kept hitting the crumpled wing, what shall I say, how shall I tell it, the light fluttering on and off, it wasn't, probably, so much the actual concussion but the stress of things in the temple, you don't imagine, I hope, that we operate like bloody robots, do you, with no feelings?

He answered on the second ring.

"Yes?"

I spoke in French; it's less understood here than English. "There's a body," I said, "in one of the abandoned temples at the edge of the town. One of the opposition, but I put my coat on him and took his papers. If you can get someone to go along there and bury it, there won't be so much of a fuss." I gave him the directions. "How long will it take you to make the call?"

Some people came into the guest house, dropping baggage.

"Sixty seconds."

"I'll call you back."

I leaned with one finger on the contact: there were three hikers, round-eyes, crowding me, one with dark glasses on and his face peeled raw by the ultraviolet. Then I got the operator again and asked for the Barkhor Hotel.

At first they said there was no one of that name there and I told them I'd just been talking to him and they wanted me to spell it and we were running it so *very* close to the noon deadline.

"Yes?"

"Can they do it?" I asked Pepperidge.

"They'll try."

"All right, and then I'll need an rdv, say about fourteen hundred. Where?"

"You tell me."

The only place I knew was the one I'd been to with Su-May Wang, so I told him where it was. I didn't want to go to his hotel more often than I had to; it's always dangerous to establish patterns.

"I'll be there," he said. He sounded relaxed, quietly cheerful, though he must be working out the signal to London: any kind of major action had to go on the board, and this involved a death, the fourth for *Bamboo*.

"For now," I told him, "you need this: they were watching every source of insulin in Lhasa, and this man tagged me, so it looks as if they either suspect or know that the subject is here in the town."

Short silence; it had rocked him, of course. "How did that happen?"

"I think I know. But we'll talk about it later. I've got to go now."

"Fourteen hundred," he said and rang off and I went out to the taxi.

"Where go?"

Told him north, I'd show him the way, got out some money, quite a lot. "Go very quick, understand?"

The apothecary had given me a dozen new needles, 23-gauge one-inch Becton Dickinsons, and I pulled one off the strip and fitted it to the syringe.

"You feel all right?"

"Yes," Xingyu said. "But I was worried."

"I got delayed." Drew five cubic centimeters out of the ampoule, pressed out the air. I didn't tell him he could have saved his worries if he'd just let me know he was out of insulin a bit sooner. Dabbed with the alcohol swab.

"You do not look well," he said.

"Touch of indigestion." Pulled the plunger, got no blood, put pressure on it.

Everything had become very clear, sensitive. Head was throbbing and I was still out of breath from climbing the ladder, but even in the light from the dirty windows things had a sharp outline and I could hear one of the monks chanting three floors below and could feel the plunger hit bottom before I pulled the needle out. Mental clarity was back too, heightened, the dance of conscious thought quick and colored.

Put the plastic sheath back on the needle and dropped it into the waste box, pressed the cap on the syringe, everything orderly, the blood singing quietly through the veins, the beat of the heart strong and steady, vital signs, the vital signs that had come so close to getting cut off down there in the temple, and this was it, what it meant, this feeling of heightened awareness, I've had it before, it comes as a revelation when you realize that life is going on and not without you as you thought it must, were certain it would, the reek of cordite in the lungs and the crash of the last shot still roaring in the brain, the certainty of oblivion in the next breath and then the reprieve. It leaves you exalted for a little time, touched with grace.

I put the box in the corner of the cell, underneath the pile of hides that Jiang had given us for extra warmth at night. "You know where it is," I told Xingyu. "If I'm absent at any time, remember where the stuff is, and do it yourself."

Exalted, touched with grace, but touched also with the guilt that comes when the struggle has been to the death, though we mustn't put it too dramatically, must we, but that was what it had been today, and the loser loses all, lying there in the dark with a rat's carcass his fellow traveler to the shades of Lethe, I can never take a life without adding it to the little wooden crosses in the shadows of the mind, of the memory, I'm never free of them, never shall be.

"What is that smell?" Xingyu Baibing asked me.

"Antiseptic. Where did you put your mask?"

He finished buckling his belt and went across to a part of the wall where the plaster had broken away and left a hole that he'd covered with a bit of loose timber.

"In here."

He stood with his arms hanging by his sides, head turned to look at me, something in his eyes asking for my approval, and I was moved and it caught me unawares, moved by his attempt to play the *espion*, hiding things away, making my life easier.

"A good place," I said. "I'd never think to look there."

"I washed it."

"And dried it completely?"

"Yes. The Japanese gave instructions."

I went and sat down, my back against the wall. "We need to talk, Dr. Xingyu."

"Very well."

He squatted on the floor with his legs drawn up, the light

catching his glasses as he looked at me. The chanting rose from below, many voices now, surrealistic in this great shadowed ruin, the voicing of lost souls.

"In the town," I said, "I found out that the KCCPC suspect that you're here in Lhasa." I didn't tell him that when the body was found in the temple they'd know for certain. But it might not happen before we flew this man to Beijing. "Can you think why?"

He went on watching me for a time, and then looked down.

"I mentioned it," he said.

I didn't say anything for a moment. My tone would have to be perfectly normal when I spoke again, with no anger in it, no frustration. He was an astrophysicist, not an intelligence agent; he was also a man, by reputation, to say what was on his mind, even to the chiefs of government.

"When did you mention it?"

"When I was in the British embassy in Beijing."

It had been the only answer I could think of, when I'd known they were watching the sources for insulin, the KCCPC. I was certain we'd reached the airport at Gonggar clean, and that we hadn't been followed, Xingyu and I, into the town: I'd checked thoroughly for surveillance. I'd even thought that one of the Chinese agents who'd seen the snatch outside the terminal in Hong Kong might have recognized me when we went through there later, on our way out to Chengdu; but if that had happened they'd have seized Xingyu on the spot. They hadn't known. We'd pulled it off, Pepperidge and I, we'd got Xingyu Baibing through a whole regiment of the KCCPC and into Lhasa, clean. But he'd brought his own seed of destruction with him, like a bacillus in the blood.

"You told someone you might come here, if the Chinese allowed you to leave the embassy?"

It was easier for him if I gave him questions, easier than having to tell me direct. He knew now what he'd done.

"Yes."

"Who was it? Who did you tell?"

"One of the embassy staff. I think his name was Fellows."

A first secretary: they'd given me a list of people at the embassy when I'd gone through Clearance. Fellows was down as totally reliable; they all were, except for two counselors, Murray and Sleight, whose backgrounds were less well documented.

"Fellows," I said, "didn't give you away. Was there anyone else there at the time?"

He took a little while. "Yes. We were in the cafeteria." Spreading his hands, "I was just talking, that was all."

And hadn't known that when you're talking about something sensitive you've got to make *bloody* sure you know who you're talking to and that there's nobody else around. He wasn't an *espion*, that was the trouble with this man, he wasn't one of us; he was just a normal human being with a brilliant reputation in science instead of secret intelligence and that was why he'd walked straight into the trap in Chengdu and I'd had to get him out again by giving him *Bamboo*, chapter and verse, filling his head with stuff that was going to blow us all into Christendom if they found him and put him under the light, and that was why he'd brought those KCCPC agents into Lhasa on our track, a whole cadre of them, specialists, assigned specifically to hunt him down and throw him into a cell and get all that stuff out of his head, *finis*, *finito*.

"You were 'just talking,'" I said.

I hadn't meant to say it, hadn't meant it to sound like that; I was furious, that was all. No excuse.

"But of *course*." He'd raised his voice.

"Never mind, let it go. It wasn't Fellows, but someone else must have overheard it and passed it on, maybe not even seeing the danger. It's too late now, so don't worry about it. But you've—"

"How do you know the KCCPC think I am in Lhasa? How do you *know* that?"

Gray light flashing across his glasses as he bent forward

171

toward me. Furious too, furious with *me*, for Christ's sake.

"I told you, don't worry. The thing—"

"But you do not answer my question. You wish to accuse me of doing something wrong, but you will not answer my question. That is *unjust*."

Characteristic of the man: he'd ranted and raved about injustice to the Chinese government until they'd chased him into the embassy.

"Dr. Xingyu, the important thing for you to remember—"

"My question! My *question*!"

"*Keep* your voice down, for God's sake, don't you realize—"

"Answer my question," hissing it out now, "and tell me why you think the KCCPC—"

"Because they were watching every single place where you can buy insulin—doesn't *that* answer your question?"

I came away from the wall and got on my knees to face him, close as I could, to stop him raising his voice again.

"How do you *know* they were watching?"

Patience, God give me patience. "Because one of them followed me."

"Perhaps you *believed* he was following you. You are always suspicious, because you are an intelligence officer, and you therefore believe—"

"Dr. Xingyu," I leaned closer, "I was followed by a KCCPC agent and I led him into cover and when he tried to shoot me I killed him with my bare hands. *Now* will you understand that we are not playing games?"

In a moment—"You killed him?"

"Yes."

"That is terrible."

"Taking a life is always terrible, yes, but if this man had overpowered me I would have been taken to a cell and tortured until I told them where you are, and they would have come here for you. *Now* will you understand why we have to do things that are sometimes terrible? You must get a *perspective* on this."

He said nothing.

I sat kneeling, as he was. We faced each other in the gray light from the windows, looking, I suppose, like two monks at their prayers.

In a moment I said, "Your life is in danger, Dr. Xingyu, every minute. You *must* understand that. My government has committed me to protect you and defend you until you can go back to Beijing in a few days and lead your people toward the new democratic government that is their most fervent dream, and if you can bring perspective to bear, you'll see that the death of one junior officer of an organization that is the most ruthless enemy of the people was necessary. Terrible, but necessary."

After a time he raised his head and looked at me. "I am not very helpful to you, am I?"

"You're not trained in the field, that's all."

"I am not used to violence."

"Not personally, no. But you can remember the violence in Tiananmen Square. Those are the people you have to fight. You have a reputation for being among the first to man the barricades, and you've got to understand that you're there again now—*these* are the barricades."

In a moment, "Yes. I understand that."

"Good. You must also understand that when the KCCPC agent who followed me is reported missing, it's going to look as if someone in fact bought some insulin, and managed to silence the agent. Have you ever used a gun?"

"What for?"

"Have you ever fired a gun, on a practice range?"

"Of course not."

His back had straightened. He was indignant.

"Now that you know your life is in danger here, every minute, would you be prepared to fire a gun in your own defense?"

He looked from side to side, into the shadows, confused, hunted. "No. Of course not!"

"All right. Don't worry about it. But—"

"Did you imagine I would be capable of such a thing?"

"No."

"Then why did you suggest it?"

"Because at this moment, Dr. Xingyu, I'm looking for miracles."

Stiffly, "I am afraid I cannot help you."

In Beijing, if we could ever get him there, he would climb onto the rostrums and face the people and throw them miracles until they were dizzy with them, but here in the burned-out hulk of the monastery he could offer them none, not even the pressure of his finger on a trigger to defend his life, the life of their messiah.

I understood that. I understood. But I could have used a miracle myself; it would have lightened the load.

"Forget I mentioned it, Dr. Xingyu. But you've got to do something for me. It would have been far less difficult, as you know, to have taken you out of Hong Kong to safe territory, where your government has no jurisdiction. But you asked us to bring you to Lhasa and we took your point and we agreed. You had friends here, you said. Now this is what you've got to do for me. You've got to trust no one. *No one.* You must talk to no one, even if you're alone with him, even if it's the abbot himself, or the monk who guards you while I'm away, Bian, *especially* him, because it's natural that you should want to talk to him—you're not used to being alone, with no companionship."

They were chanting still, below, and a bell had started tolling, the huge bell that I'd seen in the garden behind here, its mouth two or three feet across with a beam as big as a tree trunk slung on ropes to strike it with, and as its rhythmic booming sounded through the great hollows of this place it made me afraid, I'm not sure why, perhaps it was just the vibration stirring in my body, in my bones, or perhaps it had the semblance of a clock, its beat inexorable as it measured the seconds, bringing us closer to what was to come.

Fatigue, surely. Fatigue and the altitude and the head wound, everything adding up as I knelt there swaying in front of him, in front of Dr. Xingyu Baibing.

Yes, I knew him once. We were trying to get him back into Beijing, but they ran us too close . . .

The great bell boomed in my bones.

Finally he said, "I will talk to no one."

"No one. Trust no one."

"I understand."

"Do that for me."

"I will do it for you." Like a litany, kneeling together.

"Because at any time now," I told him, "they're liable to start hunting for you, now they know you're in Lhasa. They've got hundreds of men they can use. They can search every building, beat every bush." I was swaying again, and made an effort to straighten up. "But I can keep you hidden, Dr. Xingyu. I've had extensive training and a lot of experience. I can make it extremely difficult for them ever to find you. With luck, impossible."

The great bell booming.

"But I can't do anything for you," I said, "if you take risks, if you put us both in danger by talking. Some of the monks in this place don't even know that you're here: the abbot assured me of that. Only a few know. So don't talk to anyone. Don't trust anyone, whoever he is."

"I understand."

The great bell booming in my bones.

I wonder if he does, if he does.

In my bones.

Chapter 15

Drunk

"**W**e couldn't do anything," Pepperidge said. "The police were already there."

My skin crawled.

"What time was that?"

"My chap got there just before noon." He took another spoonful of soup.

"He was fast," I said.

"Adequate."

"New to the field?"

"Oh no. Been here a year."

"English?"

"Chinese. How are you feeling?"

"Bit skewed, still. Listen, when you debriefed him, did he say how long he thought the police had been there when he turned up?"

"He said not long. They hadn't brought the body out."

"How long did he stay?"

"A good hour. He was in a Jeifang, made out—"

"What's that?"

"Sorry—truck, big as a dinosaur, always breaking down, so it was good enough cover, he had the bonnet up, got some spanners out."

"He's Bureau?"

"Yes. Reports to Hong Kong." His yellow eyes were on me suddenly. "You're active, are you?"

"Call it eighty percent." He hadn't been satisfied when

177

I'd told him I was a bit skewed. I shouldn't have done that, got to play by the book, and the book says the shadow executive has to give his director in the field his *exact* condition when asked for. All right, say eighty percent. Fully active would mean I was fit enough to do anything at all, nothing barred, run a mile flat out or swim submerged or deal with any sort of attack and defeat it and get clear. I couldn't do that, not as I felt now: the head was still a degree dizzy and I could feel the effect of the altitude in the lungs.

"Look," I said, "they couldn't have got onto it that fast, I mean from their end." They couldn't in other words have put down that agent as missing and started a search for him and found him at the temple: there hadn't been time. "Someone must have heard the shots and reported it."

Pepperidge was quiet for a moment. The inference was there all right and it gave me the creeps: if anyone had heard those shots could have seen me leaving the temple soon afterward, and given the police my description.

"Possibly," Pepperidge said at least.

Two people came in, peasants, slamming the door, and it reached my nerves. "It's not very good," I said, "is it?"

"Not very." Spooned some soup. *"Nil desperandum."*

Easy to say. The KCCPC had suspected that Xingyu Baibing was here in Lhasa because he'd blown it at the embassy in Beijing, and now they'd found that body it wouldn't be long before they identified it even though I'd made a gesture and changed coats and taken his papers, and they'd check their assignment roster and find that the agent posted on watch at the apothecary's wasn't there anymore and that'd be all they'd need.

"How did you do it?" Pepperidge asked me. "The agent?"

This was for Norfolk, for the new recruits. "I broke the thyroid cartilage with a half-fist, immediate internal hemorrhage."

"He had a gun?"

"Yes."

"And he fired it."

"Yes." He could smell the cordite on me.

"How much light was there?"

"Not much. Practically dark."

Tell those poor bloody children at Norfolk to try *that* one against a loaded gun and they'd get their brains blown out. Don't do as I do, so forth.

"How did you get here?" Pepperidge asked me.

"There was a tourist bus at the monastery down the road, just starting back."

He thought about that. "Who was running it?"

"Couple of Australians. There weren't any Chinese," I said, "on board."

"Good-o." He finished his soup and pushed the plate away and said, "I've been in signals with London, as you can imagine." Because of the temple thing. "They asked me what I thought our chances are now." His yellow eyes on me.

"Chances of what, specifically?"

"Of protecting the subject."

"What did you tell them?"

Head on one side, "What would you have told them?"

I gave it a minute, not the time for making a wild guess. "I'd have said our chances are fifty-fifty."

He looked away. "You're that sanguine?"

"I'm not a bloody amateur at this kind of thing."

"No offense, of course. But you see, you're operating on foreign soil with the police, the public security forces, the intelligence services, and the military already searching for the man you're assigned to protect. On top of that, this town is under martial law and there's a curfew." His fingers drummed softly on the bare-wood table. "I don't think your chances are fifty-fifty."

"Tough shit."

"I understand how you feel."

"So what did you tell them?"

"I told them that in my considered opinion our position is close to untenable."

If he'd been Loman or Fane I'd have walked out and gone underground and taken Xingyu with me. But this man I could respect, and he wasn't getting cold feet; he was seeing things as they were, or as he thought they were.

"Most of the situations in most of the missions we're given are untenable, for Christ's sake. It's part of the job, you know that."

He leaned closer, tracing the edges of the stains on the tabletop with a finger. "There's so much stacked, you see, on this one. We have to play for safety, can't go taking risks. We—"

"So what did they say?"

His finger tracing the stains, "Your instructions are to get the subject to Beijing as soon as possible, without waiting for the deadline."

Bloody dog sniffing around my feet and I kicked out and got a yelp. "*Shepley* said that?"

"Hyde. But of course it would have come from Bureau One."

"They're out of their bloody minds."

"At first glance, perhaps. But they have a point."

Door slammed again, they wanted a bit of rubber or something on that *door*, stop it *banging* all the time, got on your nerves. "They're not out here in the field," I said. "They're five thousand miles away in London looking at a chessboard, what the hell are you talking about?"

"I don't think," he said, "that they're asking the impossible."

The thing was to keep my voice down, keep control, but it wasn't easy. "The whole of this operation's built on timing and coordination. He can't go into Beijing until they're ready for him there, until the tanks have taken control and they can meet him at the airport and escort him to Tiananmen Square. You know that. And now London's pushing the panic button and telling me to go pitching into a precipitate last-ditch *sauve qui peut* that's going to cut right across *Bamboo* and blow it to hell."

He waited for a while, looking past me at the people in here, fingers drumming softly on the bare stained wood, giving me time to listen again to what I'd just said, test it out perhaps, perhaps reassess.

It didn't work. Let the defense rest. *Bloody* London.

His eyes came back to rest on mine, and his voice was gentle.

"The overall timing is important, yes, but not to us. We are *local*. Our bailiwick is *here*. All we're being asked to do is to get the subject out of Lhasa and into Beijing, and the only difference is that they want us to do it now, instead of later."

Head throbbing, wouldn't leave me alone. That worried me, because it wasn't the injury so much, it was the stress, and if the executive was starting to lose his cool at this stage of the mission then God help us all.

The door opened again and I tensed, waiting for the bang.

"I don't see anything precipitate here," Pepperidge said. "Right or wrong—and I think I'm right—I've reported that our position here is nearly untenable, and London is simply changing procedure to protect the mission. When we started out, we believed that Beijing was too hot for our subject, so we brought him here—the last place, as he told us, where they'd expect him to be. Now things have changed. Lhasa has got too hot for him, and the last place they're going to look for him is in Beijing. We've got plenty of people there, and they'll keep him underground till everything else is ready." He leaned forward, touching my arm. "There's no real problem, you see."

It's difficult.

Someone over there was getting drunk, a round-eye, hitting the table, shouting something in English, something about bloody travel agents.

It's difficult for me, always has been, to give London

credit. It's not because they don't deserve any: they're not stupid, in fact they're brilliant, or I wouldn't work for them. The trouble I have with London is a lot of my own making, you know that, if you've known me long, although they've certainly got habits that can drive you straight up the wall, and people, of course, people like that bastard Loman with his cufflinks and his polished shoes and his pedantic bloody speech, enough to send you—but you note how easily I can get carried away, about London.

"Come and see the marvels of the Holy City on the Roof of the World," the man over there was shouting, "and all I've seen so far is a lot of burned-out fucking monasteries and yak shit wherever you go, stinking the fucking place out!"

Hitting the table, red-faced, woolen hat with a bright green pom-pom on it, while two other men tried to shut him up.

No, the thing with London is that they control me. I signed for it, fair enough, but it's not easy to live with. I don't like it when a signal hits the board from the field and Croder or Shepley picks up the executive like a bloody pawn and puts him down on another square, when in point of fact the said executive can be working his way through a mine-field in the dark with a pack of war-trained dogs on his tracks or cooped up in a plain van with a gun trained on him while he tries to get at his capsule before they put him under the light—I've been in *both* situations and a dozen like them, not a dozen, dear God, a hundred, and you get to resent those people back there in Whitehall, the red-tabs ensconced comfortably behind the firing line, doing their daily stint and going home to a nice hot shower while you're lying out there in a cellar in Zagreb with four days' filth on you and blood in your shoe. You get to *resent*—

"Invigorating mountain air, they told us, Christ, you can't even fucking *breathe!*"

You should try those people in London, my good friend, then you'd have some real yak shit to chew on.

"They're right," I told Pepperidge.

He leaned back, letting his breath out.

"I was hoping you'd see."

"It's the only thing we can do. If we can do it."

"But of course. *Carpe diem*." Seize the day, quite so. "The mask is still in safekeeping?"

"Yes."

"And you can fit it on for him?"

"Yes."

"Then we shouldn't have any trouble. How is he?"

"Bearing up. I'm treating him as gently as I can."

Head on one side—"In what way?"

"He's so bloody innocent. I had to know what had brought the KCCPC on our track, and I found out. He'd told someone at the embassy that he wanted to go to Lhasa if he could get out of there. I think he was overheard."

His fingers began drumming again. In a moment, "Possibly. But I got a signal early this morning. Our people in Bombay have taken a good look at Sojourner's body. He'd been tortured."

In a moment I asked him, "Between the time he was taken out of the hospital and the time he was killed?"

"Right. Not before the snake bit him. So it could have been that. Sojourner had talked to the subject at the embassy, of course."

"Oh, my God."

"Not happy, is it? But let's not see demons—"

"Sojourner could have blown the whole thing. *Bamboo*."

A brief shrug. "Possibly. London doesn't think so."

"Why not?"

"Because our sleepers in Beijing have reported no movement at all among the army generals and their garrisons. If the Chinese government had got wind of things, they'd have taken our general away from his command and shot him. He is alive and well."

"Is that all we're relying on?"

A wintry smile. "We rely on anything we can get. But it

stands up, you know. They wouldn't have let the subject leave the embassy if Sojourner had been broken."

It wasn't easy. I'd never known a mission to be so dogged, step after step, by the threat of destruction. Ambassador Qiao, in London, blown and killed; Sojourner, in Bombay, blown and killed; and the very man we were protecting, the subject, the messiah, treating the whole thing as if those thugs in power in Beijing were a league of gentlemen. *He knew bloody well they weren't.*

"He's such a *saint*," I said, "and he thinks everyone else is the same. He—"

"The subject?"

"What? Yes. He—"

Crash as the man over there knocked a metal bowl off the table, shouting his head off, and another gust of freezing air came through the door as one of the staff went trotting outside. The talk had died down in here; these people were unused to drunkenness: all you could get in here was *chang*.

"He thought it was all right," I said, "to talk about coming to Lhasa, he fell straight into their trap at Chengdu, and he didn't believe I'd been followed this morning—I had to spell it out. I've warned him not to talk to any of the monks, but he hasn't got any idea of even normal discretion. And he's got the whole thing in his head, you know that, the whole mission."

Pepperidge sat with the collar of his sheepskin coat turned up against the draft from the door, fingers restless on the rough tabletop, the dregs congealing in his soup bowl.

"Then we must simply be careful," he said, "and you know how to do that."

He was quiet again for a while; I assumed he'd started working out the future, the immediate future for the mission. Anytime now I was going to get his instructions, and I didn't feel ready for them: I wasn't fully active, wouldn't be able to take on anything really critical and be certain of coming through.

"You got a lift here," Pepperidge said, "on a tour bus. You still don't want a car?"

"No."

We'd been over it before, in my first briefing here. In a big modern city the executive has got to have a car because it gives him transport, cover, protection, a mobile base, and a weapon, but in a place like Lhasa a car was too noticeable, and if I'd used one it would have established a dangerous travel pattern to the monastery and back.

"Very well." Pepperidge leaned forward again and folded his hands on the table. "We're safe for the moment in thinking that while the subject is instantly recognizable without the mask on, the KCCPC are not looking for *you*. This gives us the edge we need: you're still operational at street level."

Argot. The opposite of street level is going to ground, losing yourself, burying yourself. "Unless someone saw me at the temple," I said. I didn't think anyone had, just wanted to make the point.

"What are the chances?" He watched me with his yellow eyes, trusting me not to lie.

"How do I know, for Christ's sake? Anyone could have seen me go in there, or come out."

Not precisely a lie. Call it an exaggeration, playing it safe, playing it *too* safe, because I didn't want any action, I was still healing, uncertain of my strength if there were demands made on it, out there at street level.

"I think," Pepperidge said, "the chances are slight. But I won't push you."

I looked away. We were getting awfully close to the unthinkable. *Signal for Bureau One, his eyes only. Executive's injury has left him less than fully active. Suggest bringing replacement to stand by.*

The unthinkable.

"Push me," I said. "Push me as hard as you need to."

"Perhaps, then, a compromise. Take every chance you can find of normal cover. Don't reinforce the image."

Show my face, in other words, as little as possible. That was all right.

"What I'll do," Pepperidge said, "is bring in the Jeifang. The truck. I'll use the same man, Chong."

"The man you sent to the temple?"

"Yes." He got out a scrap of paper and a ballpoint. "The Jeifang is green. Most of them are, in Lhasa. This is the number plate. He'll be at the rendezvous after dark, at twenty hundred hours, and he'll take you and the subject to Gong-gar, where you'll sleep for the night, in the truck. The CAAC plane normally leaves between ten hundred and ten-thirty in the morning. I want you to fit the mask on the subject and see him as far as the departure gate, but don't keep close; you'll be there simply in case of any trouble. Then you'll go back to the truck. He'll be met in Beijing and taken off the street immediately."

"Chong stays with the truck?"

"Yes."

"What's his cover, if we're stopped?"

"*I'm going to ask for my fucking money back! They can't do this to me.*"

Bottle smashing, then very quiet. I suppose the man on the staff had gone darting out just now to fetch the police.

"Chong's cover," Pepperidge said, "is just what it looks like: he's the driver for a transport company."

"Will he be armed?"

"No." Pepperidge watched me thoughtfully. "Do you want him armed?"

"No."

Then the door opened again and Su-May came in and caught sight of me by chance and edged her way between the tables and passed close to us, whispering, "*You shouldn't be in here—the police are looking for you,*" and I saw them in the doorway, fur hats, red stars, holstered guns.

Chapter 16

Shiatsu

S kull of a dog.

"How do you know?"

Freezing in here. The window was open.

"I have to report back there," she said, "twice every day."

The Public Service Bureau, where she'd helped me this morning.

Skull of a dog on the wall. Narrow bed in a corner and a few bits of rough wood furniture and one or two oil lamps, the window-blind with a bracket loose at one end, hanging at an angle, no telephone need I tell you, cut off, I was cut off from my director in the field, cut off from London and going to ground, I would *have* to go to ground, lose myself, bury myself, don't think about it, Dr. Xingyu Baibing stuck up there on the third floor of a monastery and the man who was meant to get him to the airport stuck in a tenth-rate hotel and freezing to death while the police scoured the town for him, think about anything but that.

"Why?"

Why did she have to report back to the PSB station twice a day? She didn't volunteer very much; I had to keep asking questions.

"I broke the curfew last night." Her teeth were chattering. She was freezing too, or frightened, or both.

"So you have to report back? Can't we shut the window?"

She went across to it, but it was stuck and I helped her. She'd had trouble with the stove by the look of it, the front

187

was raised and there was ash on the floor, the cheap linoleum had burned patches, why, I suppose, she'd had to leave the window open, smoke, *stank* in here, it wasn't wood smoke, it was yak dung, having to make an effort, I was having to make an effort to think straight, get things in order, because the mission was like a sinking ship now, rolling in midocean in the dark, the decks awash and wallowing and the stern down, sliding to the cold vast bosom of the deep, must get perspective, yes.

"You are not well," Su-May said.

"So what happened, when you reported back?"

"The officer who dealt with you this morning was still there. He asked me about you."

She went across to the stove and got some dung out of a torn brown-paper bag.

"What did he ask?"

"If I knew where you were staying. I said no." She lit some paper and put the stuff on top and began blowing it.

"Why did they want to know where I was staying?" I suppose it was just her way, didn't talk much.

"They are looking for a man who was seen near a temple. They say someone was found dead there, an agent of the KCCPC."

I moved nearer the stove. It wasn't giving out any heat yet but there was a flame to watch. "What did you tell them, about me?"

"I told them we parted," she said, "as soon as we left the PSB station. I said I had not seen you since then." She was squatting by the stove, the box of matches still in her hand, her eyes lifted to watch me with the question in them quite clear: *Did you kill him?*

"What else did they ask? What else did they say? Give it to me all at once, will you, everything you can think of."

She looked down, ashamed: I'd criticized her. "They said that I should look out for you wherever I went, and tell them immediately if I saw you again," the small flame growing in the stove, its yellow light reflected in the sheen of her thick black hair, the matches still in her long ivory fingers, forgotten, "I told them I would look out for you, and tell them if I saw you. What else could I say?"

I got down beside her, sat on the gritty linoleum, standing made me tired, *you are not well,* she'd said, did I look that bad? "There was nothing else," I said, "you could tell them. When you came into the café, you didn't expect to see me there?"

"Of course not." She brought her head up and looked at me. "If I had known you were in the café I would have gone there sooner, to warn you."

"Thank you."

"There is hot water here, for the shower." She put the matches down on the plank of wood fixed to the wall with bent wire supports, a shelf. Other things on the shelf: incense, a torn glove, a half-burned votive candle on a spike in a rusty bowl. "Not really hot," a shy smile, put on, acted, because that too was shameful: she was my host and could offer me hospitality but it wasn't as it should be, not really hot. "But it is not cold, either. Please use the shower, if you wish."

Do not think it strange, my good friend: in Lhasa in wintertime a shower that is not freezing cold is a luxury beyond all the perfumes of Araby, and I probably smelled, most people here did, lived in their clothes, and I'd soaked these with sweat in the temple when he'd come for me. Her invitation must be counted as grand hospitality.

"I'd like that," I told her. She got up quickly and I said, "Su-May, do you think the PSB officers followed you away from the station?"

She looked confused.

"Would you know," I asked her, "if anyone were following you?"

"I have never thought of it."

"Don't worry about it."

They could have followed her, or they could have passed

my description on to the police, for what it was worth. The police had come into the café, but that had been because of the drunk.

She'd gone straight to an empty table and sat down facing me, holding her eyes on me, a warning in them.

"I'm going to fucking sue them!" On his feet now, swaying between two friends, a woman trying to quiet him.

Pepperidge watching me: he'd caught her whisper.

I had said: "I'll be at the small hotel two blocks from here, in Xingfu Donglu; it's called the Sichuan. Get Chong to pick me up there at eighteen hundred hours. Tell him to wait outside."

"Understood."

"You the police? I want to talk to you! I've been ripped off by a bloody travel agency!"

I passed close to her table. "Can I go to your hotel?"

"Of course."

Through the back way past the toilets and stacked crates and some bicycles and a hen in a cage, slipping on broken eggs and finding the door and the yard and the alley; she came behind me but vanished soon afterward and got there before I did, to the hotel. We weren't tagged, didn't have to lose anyone.

It was the only place I could go, the only rendezvous I could give Pepperidge for Chong, and if I walked any farther than two or three blocks I'd run into a police patrol.

"Towel not very big," Su-May said, dissembling. CAAC insignia.

I took it into the shower, a cramped corner of the bathroom lined with sheets of plastic, flakes of plaster from the ceiling embedded in the grime on the floor, a streak of rust down the wall under the tap, but the water was warm as she'd promised, and as I stood under the thin sputtering jets I was conscious of the benison not only of the healing water but of the grace of womanhood that had offered me this much comfort at a time when I badly needed it, more in point of fact than comfort, a kind of sanity regained, a renewal of the heart, the means, even, by which I could conceivably do what I had to do, after all. When dark came it would be easier; the dark has so often been my shelter, the ultimate safe house when all other doors are shut.

I found my clothes and Su-May said, "Leave your coat off. I will give you *shiatsu*." She'd pulled the bed away from the corner so that she could move around it. "Cold now, but you will soon be warm."

There were hours before dark came, and I lay down and she began working on me.

"You're an air hostess, an interpreter, and you practice *shiatsu*. You're very accomplished."

"I have license as therapist. Must understand, many people in China do two or three different jobs if they can, to afford anywhere nice to live, nice food. I earned more than my father, and he is university professor." Her fingers moved over the *tsubo* points. "Tell me when there is pain."

"All right. The message will have reached him by now, the one I told you I'd send."

Her hands paused. "So quick?"

"By telephone."

"From here?"

She meant from Lhasa. It worried her. "From here to London," I said, "and from there to Beijing." I'd asked Pepperidge, told him she'd been helpful to me at the PSB station.

My eyes were closed, but I felt her attention in the stillness of her hands. If I could reach Beijing so easily, who was I, what other powers did I have? "Thank you," she said at last. "It means very much to me. My father will have worried about me; I vanished from out of his life when I came here. Now there is the message." She cupped her hands against my face for a moment, very gently, then went on with her work. "Please relax. Your muscles are so tight everywhere." In a moment: "It hurts just there?"

"Yes."

"Very well." She worked on the *tsubo* point, and warmth flowed, and hope flowed with it. I would have, yes, to go to ground, but the Jeifang, the big green truck, would offer me safety, and there might still be a last chance of getting Xingyu to the airport, some time in the night.

"And there," I said.

"Very well. Your head is in pain, because of this?"

"Bit sore, yes. I tripped and fell, hit the edge of a door."

Even the partial truth is uttered seldom in our trade; I felt saintly.

The dung in the stove was glowing now; I could see it at the edges of my lids. It seemed less freezing in here, because of the stove and her hands and what they were doing to me, easing away some of the fear that always dogs the footsteps of a creature that knows it's hunted.

"You have pain also in your heart," she said.

"No."

"I do not mean in your heart, exactly. In your spirit. There is a ghost there."

Immediate gooseflesh: I felt the hairs lifting on my arms. It's always haunted me, this business of taking a life in the course of a mission. It's not at all to do with guilt: the man in the temple would have taken mine if it had suited him. It's that the closeness to death, your own or another's, brings you to the edge of the unknown, where quantum forces play among the infinite reaches of the universe, and souls drift like leaves on the cosmic wind, seeking their new incarnation. It awes me, in a word, but then of course there's the physical thing, the sweat and the muscle burn and the mechanics of force and leverage as one body tears the life out of another, there's that too, and it leaves a taste in the mouth, and in the heart a feeling of despair. *Post mortem*, also, *animal triste est*.

I said to her, "I've got quite a few ghosts. One more won't hurt."

Her hands moved over me, tracing the meridians, and in the stove a pocket of trapped air popped.

"Did you kill him?"

"That thing," I said, "on the wall. What is it?" The skull

of the dog, set in a pattern of straw and colored wool. Bloody thing had been worrying me ever since I'd come into the room.

"It is a spirit trap. When enough bad spirits have been caught in it, someone will take it down for burning."

"How will they know when it's full?"

"I think they just leave it for a time, knowing what it will do."

Spiritual Airwick, traps bad karma, replace as necessary, so forth. I'd given her an answer, in any case, by not answering; she knew anyway: she could feel his ghost in my spirit.

"Why a *dog*?"

"Because they are sacred. Please turn over, and relax more if you can."

"Did you go into that café for something to eat?"

"Yes." Her fingers moved along my spine, seeking the knotted *tsubo* points, pressing.

"You're still hungry, then."

"No. It was for comfort. The world is very frightening."

In a moment I said, "It won't be long before they change the regime in Beijing, and then your father's going to be safe, and a hero. It happened all over Europe."

"Yes, I very much hope. But until it is real, I am frightened. If the Public Service Bureau here in Lhasa finds my name in the records and sees who my father is, they will send me straight to Beijing, and use me as a hostage to bring him from hiding. So I am afraid every hour, every minute. Hurt here?"

"No."

"Here?"

"Yes."

Her finger pressed, kneading. Against my closed lids the light was fading over the minutes; before long now it would be dark, and I would have a cloak for my clandestine purposes.

"There's nowhere else," I asked her, "that you can stay? Where they can't find you?"

She pressed again, and a nerve flared. "I have one or two friends in Lhasa, yes, but I cannot go to them. It would mean danger for them. I know some other people, but not well. They might turn me over to the police; it happens a lot. Everyone is frightened. Everyone."

"It won't last long," I said. "The leaders are old, and the people are enraged."

I turned my wrist and looked at my new watch, a cheap digital thing, the best I could find; I'd bought it from a stall on my way to the café. The time now was 5:41, and we lacked nineteen minutes to the rendezvous.

"The people are enraged," Su-May said, "yes, but the soldiers have the guns. It is always the same." She worked in silence for a time, and I watched the shadows darken across the floor, and heard the sounds from the street below diminishing; a man shouted and a dog yelped; bells had begun tolling, two, then three, then many, their carillon summoning the night.

"That is all," Su-May said, and took her hands away. I didn't move for a minute or two; my whole body was tingling.

"You're gifted," I said. "I feel well again."

"I am glad."

I got off the bed and found my coat. "How much do I owe you?"

"Nothing. I earn a little here and there, translating for the tourists, acting as a guide." In the shadowed room the expression in her long dark eyes was hidden. "What happened in the temple has great value for us, for the Chinese people. We rejoice in the downfall of even one of the enemy." The glow from the stove touched her face on one side, bringing a spark of light into her eye. "You are going now?"

"Yes."

"But where? You are like me; everywhere is dangerous for you."

A siren had started up somewhere, its undulating sound threading through the tolling of the bells.

"If the police are looking for me," I said, "I can't stay here." I wanted to check my watch again, but couldn't now; I didn't want her to know I had any kind of appointment. The rendezvous must be close, but the timing wasn't critical. Chong was Bureau, Pepperidge had said; I could therefore expect routine procedures from him: if I weren't down there in the street at 1800 hours he'd wait for me or make circuits.

Su-May moved closer to me in the shadows. I think she wanted to say something important; I could feel it. The siren was louder, coming toward the building.

"Think of a friend," I said, "someone you can trust, and shelter there. It might not be for long."

In a moment she put her hand on my arm. "It is difficult. Everything is very difficult for me to understand. There are things I would like to tell you, but I cannot." I waited, not interrupting. There was no warmth from her hand on my arm; she was still cold, still frightened. Then she said quietly, "You must be careful. When you go down to the street, make sure you are not followed."

That was the important thing, I suppose, that I'd felt she'd wanted to say.

"By the police?"

"No. By anyone."

"I'll be careful," I said, and took her hand from my arm and kissed it and went out and down the stairs and waited in the hallway until the siren's howling had died to a moan. Through one of the windows I could see the vehicle was an ambulance; it had stopped some fifty yards along the street, and people were gathering to watch. There was one minute to go, but when I walked into the street the huge green Jeifang was already waiting there higher up with its engine running, facing away from the scene of the accident and out of sight from the hotel windows, and I crossed over and the door of the cab came open and I climbed inside and we started off. There wouldn't be anyone following us: he'd be in the ambulance by now.

Chapter 17

Chong

*I*t looked all right until we got as far north from the town as the No. 4 truck depot along Jeifang Beilu, I mean the vehicle we were in was good cover and Pepperidge had protected the rendezvous and I was looking forward to telling Xingyu Baibing we were going to get him to the airport and fly him into Beijing tomorrow—he'd be seeing his wife sooner than he'd expected—but as we approached the crossroad where Daqing Lu runs east-west we saw red lights flashing in the dark and Chong said it was a police roadblock and put his foot on the brakes.

"They're not police," I said. "They're military." I could see the vehicles had camouflage paint on them, as the lights of the traffic swept across their sides.

"Yes," Chong said. "Soldiers."

There was snow blowing on the wind; there'd been a few flakes in the town when we'd left there ten minutes ago.

Most of the traffic was coming the other way, from the north; the soldiers weren't stopping it; against the dark background of the hills we could see lighted batons waving the stuff through: jeeps, a tourist bus, horse-drawn wagons. Another big green Jeifang overtook us from the south, from the town, and came to a stop behind the traffic piling up against the barrier, a couple of hundred yards from where we were standing.

"What are they looking for?"

Chong sat with his thin shoulders hunched over the

wheel, a big moth-eaten fur hat dwarfing his small face, his jaws working on some chewing gum. "They're always looking for something."

"Can we go north any other way?"

"We could turn back and get onto Linkuo Lu."

"Then where?"

"North again as far as the Sky Burial Grounds, then west, then north again on the road we are on now."

"How long would that take?"

"Maybe forty-five minutes."

"Let's do it."

"Okay."

"Turn your lights off before—" But he'd hit the switch already and looked at me and away again and made a U-turn and switched the lights on and throttled up, some heavy metal clanking in the rear of the truck.

"What are we carrying?"

"Mining gear." He'd learned his English in the States, or from an American. "I'm on contract."

"What's your cover story for this run?"

"Oh, I sometimes work late."

"Do you know what we're going to do?"

He looked at me briefly again. "Pick him up, take him to the airport at Gonggar."

We rumbled through the night.

It is difficult. Everything is very difficult for me to understand. There are things I would like to tell you, but I cannot. Her long eyes shadowed.

What things?

You must be careful. When you go down to the street, make sure you are not followed.

Why had she said I could go to her hotel when she'd known there'd be surveillance on it from the street?

By the police?

No. By anyone.

Who?

The snow slanted across the windshield, whitening from the dark across the headlight beams. When we turned again I asked Chong if we were now on Linkou Lu, the road to the north he'd talked about.

"Yeah. Maybe another thirty minutes now."

I wound the window down an inch and the freezing air blew in, but it was better than the exhaust gas seeping up through the floorboards.

"You know you've got a leak in the exhaust on this thing?"

"Sure. Leaks everywhere."

Head was aching again because of the bumps when we went across potholes; everything rattled and bounced, the windshield, the seat, the floorboards, the brains inside my skull.

I would ask Pepperidge to get a coverage on her from London; her father was a university professor and she was an employee of the Civil Aviation Administration of China with a license to practice *shiatsu*, and all those things would be in the official records. London could get one of our sleepers in Beijing to raise everything there was on her background; if we ran into trouble it might be useful: I could get some idea of where her loyalties lay, what value she might have for the mission, what dangers she might pose. But of course if we could get Xingyu to Beijing tomorrow it wouldn't matter a damn, nothing would, mission completed, so forth.

"Shit," Chong said.

Red lights flashing, a mile ahead of us to the north.

"Are they at the crossroad?"

"Yeah."

"We should turn west there, then north again?"

"Yeah." He braked and ran the big truck onto the rough ground at the side of the road and doused his lights.

"Have you seen military blocks like this before?"

"You bet."

"I mean at two adjacent crossroads?"

"Not so much. Thing is, when they block every goddam highway, means they're probably in a ring right around the town."

Traffic was coming past us from the north, running into the screen of snow and breaking it up, sending it into eddies as the wind took it again.

"This snow. Is it going to settle?"

"Guess not. The ground's too dry. It'll maybe pile up into drifts against the scree, that's all. It's too cold for it to keep on coming down." He moved his gum to the other side of his mouth. "We go back?"

A ring around the town, Jesus, it wouldn't matter where we went, we'd run into a block. In a minute I asked him, "If I weren't with you, would you have any trouble getting through?"

He thought about it. "I can't answer that. I mean sure, in the ordinary way, maybe I'd get through okay, my cover's watertight, I've got my contract I can show them, this is one of my regular routes and everything, but see, it depends what they're looking for, what they want, they can just say, look, I don't give a damn if you're the king of Siam, you just turn around and get your ass back down that highway. With these people you can't make any predictions."

"Switch this bloody engine off, will you?" I got the window down as far as it would go, blast of cold air but at least it was fresh. Snow blew against the side of my face, and I put a gloved hand up. The wind hit the truck, rocking it on its springs. I didn't know, suddenly, what we were doing here: with a ring of military checkpoints set up around the town there wasn't a chance of reaching the monastery and bringing Xingyu Baibing back through an armed blockade.

Your instructions are to get the subject to Beijing as soon as possible.

Pepperidge.

No go.

"Chong, was there a phone anywhere along the road we've just come up, any building we could phone from?"

"Guess not."

"Are you sure?"

"Yeah."

He was probably right. The only buildings I'd seen were sheds, barns, ruined temples.

"Then where is the *nearest* phone?"

"Way back down there on Dongfeng Lu, the Telecommunications Office."

Thirty minutes away. We don't often feel like asking for instructions at the highest level from London when we're stuck in the field with the odds stacked and the chances thin because we know the situation and the environment better than they do; but tonight I thought there was a case for putting a signal through, phoning Pepperidge: *We're cut off by roadblocks set up by the military and there's very little chance of bringing this thing off until at least the morning, if then, so please signal London and see what they say.*

I knew of course what Croder would say.

Follow your instructions.

His small pointed teeth nibbling at the words like a rat with a corncob, one hand stroking the metal claw that he used for the other, his black eyes watching for your reaction, ready to catch any sign of hesitation, of weakness, ready to pull you off the mission and throw you out of London and into Norfolk for refresher training, *executive replaced*, stroking the metal claw, ready to bury it into your guts if you were found wanting, *follow your instructions*, oh, the bastard, *follow your instructions.*

"Chong, can we make any kind of detour?"

"Mean get past the block?"

"Yes."

He began chewing faster. "Jeez, I dunno." I waited for him to run it through his head. "Thing is, sure, we could try, yeah, but we couldn't use our lights. They'd see us, I mean they'd see we weren't on any kind of a regular highway. Be on a pretty rough surface west of here, but of course this baby can handle what you might call inclement terrain, so high off the ground. Sure, we could try it. That what you want to do?"

"Yes." He started the engine. "But take an angle," I told him, "go south about half a mile if the ground's all right, then stay parallel with the east-west road."

"You got it."

I think he was pleased, in his quiet way, hadn't wanted to give up and go back. "Chong, have you ever been in trouble?"

Argot for intensive action: getting out of a trap, battling unequal odds, running a frontier under fire, things like that.

"What kind of trouble?"

He didn't work in London, wasn't used to the idiom. "Say, breaking out of an interrogation cell and leaving dead."

"Oh, right, yeah, couple of times." He turned his small head to look at me. "I tote a capsule."

"I just wanted to know what your status is."

"We get into trouble tonight," he said, "I aim to kick any asses around I can find." Working his gum. "Call me reliable."

He looked ahead and put the big truck at a slope of shale and gunned up. With the lights off we couldn't always make out what was ahead of us; the moon was a hazy crescent high and beyond the flying snow.

Pepperidge would not of course have given me an amateur. It was nerves, that was all: I'd never worked with this man Chong and if those people up there at the roadblock caught the outline of this truck they'd come and ask questions. The snow made a light screen but this thing was as big as an elephant.

"Can we work our way south a bit more?"

"Guess not. There's ravines down there, not big ones but we get a wheel jammed and we could break the axle."

Crash of metal from behind us as we took a bump, skewing across loose stones and swinging back.

"Take it slower," I told Chong.

"You got it. But sometimes, see, you got to take a run at

a slope or you don't have enough momentum."

"Keep the sound down as best you can."

"Yes, sir." He fished in a pocket. "Care for some gum?"

"Not just now."

He spat out of the window and peeled the packet. "Saves my nails. You worked in Beijing?"

"No."

"I was born there. Mom and Dad fighting like cats when I left school so I shipped out on a freighter to San Francisco, five or six years there, got involved with a private detective agency and took in most of the cities across the States, did a few things for the CIA kind of under the table, then I shipped out again to London, got into a very interesting situation getting a Nicaraguan vice-consul out of a hostage deal at the embassy in Gloucester Road—that time I was still on the unofficial payroll of the CIA, but it brought me in touch with your outfit. They wanted someone like me in Beijing, bilingual native with a little experience in what they called the 'clandestine arts'—those guys kill me—so I said okay."

The wheels began spinning again across loose shale and he played with the steering and got us straight. "Then you know what happened? I found I was Chinese again, and see, I had a kind of advantage in Beijing—I could sink right down into the daily life and look out from there with what you could call Western eyes and see what was really going on, and at first it didn't bother me too much—this was in Mao's time but I learned to live with it because I was in your outfit now, sending stuff in to London, and they were very pleased." He slowed the truck and we rolled carefully down a slope with the brake shoes moaning in the drums. "Then something happened that kind of changed things. I had a sister, see, and she had a kid, couple of years old, good husband, I liked him, still do, works in a coal mine, and then they made a law you couldn't have more than one kid, keep the population down, and she made a mistake and had another one and they towed her and a lot of other women naked behind a truck through the streets as punishment, and that was what really changed things for me, see." He turned to look at me. "That really changed things. I told my director I wanted different work, where I could get at these people with my bare hands, you know, the police and the PSB and the KCCPC and the military, any son of a fucking gun I could get near, so I could practice my clandestine arts, you understand me?"

The slope leveled out and he gunned the engine again. "You wanted to know my status, and now you do."

His big fur hat bobbed as we took the bumps, his thin body coming right off the seat over the bad ones, his small gloved hands playing on the thick rim of the wheel. I didn't say anything, but it reassured me, what he'd said; if we got into anything sticky on this trip I wouldn't have to carry him.

Sometimes the moon came out as the wind took the snow and cut swatches through it, letting the light reach the ground.

"What happened at the rendezvous, Chong?"

He caught the truck as it skewed again over the stones. "I guess it was more or less routine. Your DIF sent a guy along to see if the hotel had any surveillance on it, and it did. So we took it from there."

It's in the book, under the heading of Protecting the Rendezvous. There are fifty ways of doing that but tonight Pepperidge had chosen this one because it had suited the situation: there were people in the street and the Jeifang had a big profile and I had to climb into it without anyone paying attention and in any case the peep had got to be removed so that he couldn't tag me, so our man had worked out the timing and ten or fifteen minutes before the rendezvous he'd dropped the peep with a discreet nerve strike and then made a show of helping him as he lay on the ground, told someone to call an ambulance, this man was having a heart attack, and by the time the ambulance was on the scene everyone in the street was watching the action while I got into the truck farther along.

"Is he going to follow up?" I asked Chong.

"Your DIF?"

"Yes."

"Sure, told me he would. We need all the info we can get, right?"

Right. Who the peep was, who was running him: the man who'd dropped him would stay close.

There was an inch of snow on the window on my side and I let it down an inch again and saw the red lights still flashing up there to the north, behind us a little now. We'd been going for fifteen minutes but this was virgin rock without even a wagon track and our average speed wasn't much more than walking pace.

"Snow's easing," Chong said.

"Yes."

We didn't want that. The light from the three-quarter moon was brighter now across the ground, throwing shadows. It made the going easier but the truck would stand out more against the lights of the town to the south.

"Chong."

He turned his head.

"What's your cover story for driving overland like this?"

"I'm looking for the new mining site. The research crews have just set up camp, there's no road made yet."

"What are they going to mine?"

"They're not sure yet—it's just an assay. They're going to drill a hundred meters down and take samples. The geologists say there should be copper in this region."

"That's your full story?"

He looked at me. "You think anyone in the People's Liberation Army's going to question it?"

"Possibly."

"Tell you something. What the average soldier in the PLA has got in his head is rice."

I let it go. It shouldn't come to that; if they were going to see us they'd have seen us by now.

The snow had almost stopped; isolated flakes drifted,

black against the sky and turning white as they settled on the dark green of the truck. The shadows were sharp now, and rocks stood out, their flint surfaces glinting in the light.

"Chong. Where are you going to put him?"

"I got crates back there, one of them empty. He can breathe okay, gaps where the lid goes. We can pile a whole lot of drilling gear on top, see. He'll be snug as a bug in there, got a blanket and some cushions, nothing too good for that guy."

A front wheel caught a loose rock and threw it upward and it banged on the underside of the truck like a gunshot. Reaction from the nerves and it worried me. The effects of the *shiatsu* had worn off a little, or it was simply that I was standing back in my mind and seeing the whole thing in perspective from overhead: the truck, small from that distance, crawling across the dark terrain a mile and a half from the group of army vehicles and the flashing red lights, a mouse creeping across the floor under the nose of a cat, not a pleasant simile, no, uncomfortable, unnerving.

"You weren't there," Chong asked me, "in Beijing, that time?"

The time of Tiananmen. It was how they all spoke of it these days, as "that time."

"No."

"I was there."

The rocks glinted, their chipped facets reflecting the light as the shadows sharpened.

"You know what the worst thing about it was, in Tiananmen Square?"

Said no.

The rocks glinting ahead of us, bright now, too bright, the shadows too black, too sharp. I turned my head.

"The worst thing, the way I remember it—"

"Chong," I said, "they've seen us."

Headlights in the dark.

Chapter 18

Flower

"Your papers say you're a tourist."

"Yes."

"Then what are you doing in this truck?"

"I'm a geologist. I'm interested in minerals."

"But how did you come to be in this truck?"

"I met this man in a bar. He's going to show me the mining camp. They're going to drill for minerals."

"Okay," Chong said, "that'll stand up. Like I say, they got their gourds full of rice."

He didn't sound nervous.

Headlights bouncing over the rocks. They were too bright for us to see what kind of vehicle it was, but it must be small, bouncing like that, perhaps a military jeep.

"Is there a gun in this truck?"

Chong looked at me. He wasn't chewing any faster than usual. I liked that. "I guess not," he said. "It's instant jail, they find one on anybody in this town. We need a gun?"

"No."

"You carry one?"

"No."

He lifted his gloved hands off the rim of the wheel and dropped them again. "Got these."

If there'd been a gun in the truck I would have told him to throw it across the scree, out of sight.

The beams of the headlights swung away, sweeping the black shale and sending the shadows jumping like choppy

207

water, then coming around in a half-circle and lining us up dead ahead and closing in, blinding us through the windshield. He didn't trust us, hadn't just come up alongside.

Above and between the headlight beams there was movement and a glint of metal, something quite long, perhaps an assault rifle.

"Don xìa chē!"

"He says we have to get out," Chong said.

The shale was gritty underfoot. We stood by the doors, one on each side of the truck.

"Jǔ qǐ shǒu laí!"

Chong raised his hands and I did the same.

He'd switched off his engine when we'd seen the headlights; the engine of the jeep was still running. Nothing happened for a while. The soldier was watching us, standing in the middle of the jeep, the light bouncing off the rocks and the front of the big Jeifang and glinting on his gun. Then he dropped onto the ground and came toward us, the shale scattering under his combat boots. He said something to me, his voice barking, and I looked at Chong.

"Tā bú huì zhōngwén," Chong said.

Telling him I didn't speak Chinese. The man concentrated on Chong, talking to him, getting answers. Then Chong took his coat off and the soldier frisked him, kicked at his leggings, stood back, then came over to me. Chong started to follow him but the man swung around and shouted, and Chong stood still.

I took off my parka and dropped it onto the ground. The soldier frisked me, keeping the muzzle of the assault rifle lodged against my stomach. Then he stood back. He wasn't a young recruit. I'd say he was over thirty, looked experienced, seasoned, with a strong squat body under a heavy military coat, insignia on the sleeve, perhaps a sergeant.

The exhaust gas from the jeep drifted on the air. The snow had stopped, and there would be moonlight across the ground here when the glare from the jeep had gone. The night was still, the temperature below freezing. I could feel the heat from the huge radiator of the truck, smell the tires, the diesel oil in the tank. Sound would carry well on a night like this, cold and with no wind now. A man would get nowhere, in stealth, over this kind of ground.

Not of course that either Chong or I would have any chance of using stealth, of getting anywhere; I was just analyzing incoming data: visual, acoustic, tactile, olfactory, because at some time we would have to make an attempt to get away from this man, this soldier, this strong-bodied sergeant in his warm greatcoat, who was eyeing me from underneath the red star on his cap as if I were something he'd found on a rubbish dump.

I didn't like him.

"Chong. Tell him I want to put my coat on."

Translation.

"He says you can. He wants to know all about you. I give him the story you told me, okay?"

"Yes."

Gooseflesh. It was too late to do anything if Chong hadn't tested this man to make sure he didn't understand English. But he must have done that. I was to expect, if we remember, professional procedures from anyone Pepperidge would send in. The director in the field, one of his caliber, can ask for blind faith from his executive, sometimes, many times, where the difference between life and death is on the cards.

I put my parka back on while the sergeant watched me; then he walked over to Chong, not turning his back on me, walking sideways a little, keeping me within the periphery of his vision field where the eye detects only movement. He held the big gun level, aimed at Chong's diaphragm, and they began talking.

It wasn't conversation. The sergeant had this guttural bark, loud and unpleasant to the ear. His squat body jerked forward sometimes from the waist, to put emphasis on what he was saying. Chong looked relaxed, arms hanging, head angled forward by a degree—I liked that too: he wasn't on the defensive, had the confidence of a man who can do no wrong.

"*Tā zaì zè chēli gànsháo?*"

Why was I with him in the truck, perhaps, if I were a tourist.

"*Tā shìgè dìzhìxuéjīa. Duì kuàng chǎn yǒu xìngqù.*"

I am not normally worried by guns, for several reasons. They're often held by amateurs, who don't know they should keep their distance when they're using them as a threat, and then it's only a matter of how fast you can move before they can fire. A gun also allows false confidence, and that can be fatal, has been, in my own experience, fatal to those who have held a gun on me. So normally they don't worry me, except that I don't like the bang they make: I am by nature a quiet soul.

This man, though, worried me, with his gun. He wasn't an amateur, and even with a thing this size he was keeping his distance. There was no question of whether Chong or I could move fast enough to make a strike before he could fire. Nor was the gun giving him any feeling of false confidence. He was a professional soldier, trained in the armory and at the butts, trained to man a roadblock and conduct an interrogation of enemy prisoners.

We got these. Chong, lifting his hands off the steering wheel, dropping them back. But our hands weren't going to be enough. I would have liked to know what was in his mind, Chong's, as we stood here in the blinding light. He nursed a hate for these people, the people in uniform who took orders from the overlords, who themselves had thought fit to turn women into cattle and drive them naked behind trucks through the streets; but I could only hope that he could control it, his hate, and not let it reach flashpoint and tempt him to rush the gun.

He wouldn't of course do it without thinking: he wasn't mad. But he might let the idea simmer, might watch for a chance. That could be fatal. He might watch for a chance and see it suddenly and take it and get it wrong and go flying back with his feet coming off the ground and the smoke curling out of that thing and the echoes banging their way among the rocks and the people up there at the roadblock turning their heads, *go and see what's happening with the sergeant down there,* fatal, not just for Chong but for *Bamboo,* and for Dr. Xingyu Baibing, and for me.

I'd have to speak to him, to Chong, if I could. *You will not make a move. I repeat: you will not make a move. That is an order.* There exists, within the structure of command laid out by the Bureau, a form of ranking that is designed not with any kind of military pecking order in mind, but the concept of safety. It is safer, when a shadow executive is in the field with other people—support, couriers, contacts, sleepers— for this ranking to be recognized and observed, so that everyone knows where he is and what he can do and above all who calls the shots.

"Dào chēhòumìan qù!"

In any given situation it's the executive who calls the shots, and if this man Chong had been trained in Bureau lore and mores he would know this, and observe them.

"We got to walk to the rear of the truck, okay? He didn't go for our stories. He says you must be a journalist."

Merde.

I said: "Don't do anything."

He didn't answer. I didn't expect him to. Any kind of exchange between us would sound like connivance, and the sergeant would be onto it straight away, *no talking,* so forth, and that would make things more difficult for us. It was all we had left to save ourselves with, if we could: communication.

More shouting.

"C'mon over here. He wants us side by side."

I walked past the big radiator, feeling its heat on the side of my face.

We couldn't do anything with heat.

"Not too close, okay?"

I stopped, turning my back to the light, and heard the sergeant's boots crunching across the shale away from us. He was getting into the jeep. It occurred to me that it could suddenly be over, that he'd positioned us close together in the beams of the headlights so that he could pump out a dozen or so shells from the assault gun and then drive away, *they tried to sell me some kind of story about being geologists but I think they were just a couple of underground revolutionaries and we're better off without people like that, send someone to take the truck in to the barracks, leave them where they are,* because that was the way of life in the People's Republic of China now, you wave a placard with the word *Democracy* on it and they'll shoot you dead, you kneel on a prayer mat and they'll burn your monastery from under you, these are the dark ages in a totalitarian country and if you try to run counter to the requirements of the state then the state will require you to be shot, so it is written, so it shall come to pass—

"*Zhòu!*"

"Walk," Chong said.

The engine of the jeep was throttled up a little, and there was more shouting.

"We keep in front of the headlights."

Began walking, the jeep behind us, its tires crunching across the ground.

"Chong. Don't do anything."

"You got it."

"If I think there's anything we can do, I'll give you time."

More shouting.

"Keep in front of the headlights."

The jeep was turning in a curve and we moved with it, our shadows going ahead of us, reaching into the darkness beyond the range of the headlight beams.

"Sure, okay, you'll give me time."

The spread of light turned in a half-circle and we turned with it, walking, the four of us, two men and two shadow men, across the roof of the world.

We couldn't do anything with shadows.

The truck came into view again and we approached it from the rear, and there was another shout.

"Halt," Chong said.

Boots rang on metal, then a third shadow moved in as the sergeant walked into the light.

Orders.

"You stay right where you are, okay?"

Chong went forward to the tailboard and hit the pins clear of the posts and it swung down, banging against the stops.

The sergeant walked past us at a distance of fifteen feet with the gun trained on us; then he climbed the side of the truck and sat on the roof of the cab facing the rear. High on the big truck, he was above the full glare of the beams.

He barked an order, and Chong pulled himself up to the bed of the truck and stood there, waiting, his back to me now, his shadow beside the sergeant's legs on the rear of the cab.

"Là shi xie shénme?" Pointing.

Chong looked down, then up at the sergeant again. *What are those?* Something like that. *They're drilling rods.*

"La xiene?"

Chong began shifting the equipment, dragging the steel bars to one side, heaving a canvas bag off the floor and dumping it out of the way. The sergeant sat with the big gun sloping downward, keeping us both covered.

Some of the equipment was light: short steel rods, five-pound hammers, a set of levers with a strap around them. Chong pulled them aside, stacking them out of the way. I watched him. They would make good weapons.

We couldn't do anything with weapons.

There were three crates, and that was what the sergeant was interested in. He barked more orders, and Chong snapped the fasteners open and lifted a lid. In the first crate there were instruments of some sort; I couldn't see into the crates from where I stood because the bed of the truck was more or less at eye level, but Chong was taking a few things out, holding them up. In the second crate there was camping gear for the drilling crew: billy cans, butane stoves, a frying pan, blankets. Chong dropped them back into the crate and swung the lid down.

I knew now.

The exhaust gas came clouding through the wash of light, giving it a bluish tint, and sometimes the engine's note faltered and picked up again, perhaps because of impurities in the fuel, or a loose spark-plug lead. My shadow stood against the tailboard of the truck, stark, sharp-edged at this distance.

I knew now what the soldier was looking for, what they were all looking for, the soldiers up there manning the roadblock, the soldiers manning the roadblocks in a huge circle right around the city of Lhasa.

Chong worked on the fasteners of the third crate and swung the lid open.

"Lǎer shì shénme?"

Chong pulled out a blanket, then a cushion, then another one.

I got crates back there, one of them empty. He'll be snug as a bug in there, got a blanket and some cushions, nothing too good for that guy.

A lot of questions now from the sergeant, and answers from Chong.

"Wei shénme chúle zhè xie dōngxī wai zhè xiāngzhi shì kōngde?"

"Lìng yīge xiāngzhi mei kòng."

"Yǒu hěng dūo kòng. Dǎ kai xiāngzhi."

Chong went to the first crate, the one with the drilling gear, and opened it.

"Bú shi laige xiāngzhī. Shì dì èr gè."

Chong let the lid fall and went to the second crate and opened it. I think the sergeant had asked why there were only a blanket and a few cushions in the last crate and Chong had said there wasn't room in the other ones, but it didn't matter very much what construction I was putting on things because the sergeant was standing upright suddenly.

"*Hěnghào!*"

Excitement in his voice, triumph in his whole attitude. He hadn't found the man he was looking for, the man they were all looking for, but he believed he might have found a potential hiding place for a hunted man in transit, if one were needed.

He wouldn't be sure. Chong might have told him that the empty crate was for the ore samples they'd be bringing back, and that the blanket and cushions had been thrown in there for the drilling crew as an afterthought, but the search the army had mounted tonight from here to the Lhasa River was for Dr. Xingyu Baibing, the notorious dissident, and that was all this sergeant had got on his mind.

"*Hìa chè!*"

Chong came across the tailboard and dropped to the ground, his eyes passing across mine with some kind of message that I couldn't interpret. He looked calm, still, and I wondered whether he'd been interrogated before; when I'd asked him earlier if he'd seen any action he'd said sure, a couple of times, but that didn't tell me much. He might have fought some kind of rearguard operation or got clear of an intelligence trap but that kind of experience wouldn't help him now. The sergeant would keep that assault rifle trained on us until we were back in the cab of the Jeifang and he'd be behind us all the way to the roadblock. Then we would be interrogated, and by professionals.

There wouldn't be any kind of rearguard action we could fight and we weren't going to get out of this trap because there wasn't anything we could do about it now. We couldn't do anything with heat or with shadows or with weapons and I'd stopped grasping at straws in my mind and started thinking ahead, and all I could see ahead of us was an interrogation cell and their eyes in the shadow of their peaked caps and the instruments, whatever instruments they would use. These people had refined the art of torture over thousands of years, but there still wouldn't be anything more effective than a sharpened twig of bamboo under the eyelids or the nails.

I tote a capsule.

Quite possibly, but a capsule isn't the answer to everything. If the opposition think you're a high-level intelligence officer they'll search you for a capsule and if they find it you're finished, but even if they don't make a search you've got to reach the bloody thing and pop it and break the shell before they can move in, and there's something else: you can put a man through Norfolk and throw every psychologist in the place at his head and pass him out with a Suffix-8 after his name in the ultraclassified records as a man who is confidently expected to use a capsule if the circumstances dictate the necessity and that is of course a quote, my good friend, it is a direct quote from the book of rules, don't you think it's charming, I mean as a euphemism, meaning as it does that he is confidently expected, this man, this doomed and beleaguered spook, to use his capsule because he believes— and undertakes in his contract to uphold and implement the belief—that his life has less importance than his duty, that he recognizes the highest priority of them all in this circumscribed and exacting trade: to protect the mission.

"Dǎkaī chē dǎngbǎn!"

Chong moved to the tailboard of the truck.

Yet even then, the capsule trick isn't foolproof. You may well have passed out of intensive training—intensive? But I joke, my good friend, it's ruthless, merciless, murderous— you may well have passed out with the exotic Suffix-8 after your name and it may be that the opposition has failed to search you for a capsule, but there will be the moment of decision-making, and that will vary from one man to another, will vary even within each individual according to his personal disposition as he sits under the blinding light with his inquisitors, for you cannot always decide exactly *when* you will no longer be able to stand this, no longer be able to allow them to do this to you *as the sharpened twig of bamboo is thrust again*, no longer be able to shut off your mind to what is happening and shift into theta waves, *is thrust again and deeper now, deeper*, you cannot always decide how long it will be before the instant arrives when you know you would prefer death, and then of course it's too late to get at your capsule.

So you have to compromise.

Chong heaved at the tailboard. He wasn't a strong man, too thin, too light. But he was winning: he'd got it to shoulder level. The sergeant watched him struggling.

You have to compromise. You leave it as late as you can, and then decide. You go into the cell and look around and see what they've got for you, how serious they are, how professional, and you look at the people who are going to work on you, and make a decision. If they look as if they're prepared to take things to the limit and you don't feel within you at this particular moment the ability, the spiritual, almost supernatural ability to go through *anything*, anything at *all*, then you go as fast as you can for the capsule and crack it with your teeth, *finito*.

"*Là shì shénme?*"

Sergeant shouting.

I knew my capabilities, what they would be when we arrived in the interrogation cell. But I didn't know what his would be, Chong's, and it worried me because he knew where Xingyu Baibing was, and that would be their only question.

"*Là shì shénme?*"

The sergeant had moved to the tailboard. I couldn't quite see what was happening because Chong's body was in the way, but I think he'd tried to hide something, push it among the other stuff in the truck, and the sergeant had seen him, wanted to know what it was.

"*Ná guòlaí geǐ wǒ!*"

Chong gave it to him, some kind of wallet, and the sergeant opened it, holding it in the glare of the jeep's head-lights, and I was close enough to see a wad, two wads of Chinese banknotes with elastic bands around them.

"Zhè yònglaí gàn shénmede?"

"Xùnlìan gōngrén de gōngzhī."

Wages, for the drilling crew? There wasn't any drilling crew.

They were ¥ 100 banknotes, if both wads were the same. It looked as if there were two lots of perhaps fifty. At a rough guess, the equivalent of £1,000 sterling. The sergeant was looking at them, looking at Chong. Chong was saying nothing. The engine of the jeep throbbed steadily in the background; the exhaust gas clouded blue in the headlight beams.

It's on record that the pay of a sergeant in the People's Liberation Army runs at about ¥ 200 a month. This one was looking at twenty months' pay.

"Nì xǐang huìlùo wǒ?"

"Dāngràn búshì."

Asking Chong, perhaps, if he were trying to bribe him. But he couldn't be. There wouldn't be any price on the honor and prestige of this man if he could find the archenemy of the People's Republic of China, Xingyu Baibing. Chong would know that.

"Hěnghǎo!" The sergeant pushed the wallet inside his greatcoat and went on talking, and when he'd finished Chong turned to me.

"Okay, he says we have to stay right where we are. When he's back in the jeep we have to get into the cab of the truck and head for the roadblock up there. He follows us. Christ sake don't make any kind of move, okay? He's mad at me." He turned back to the sergeant and gave him a careful bow.

The sergeant began walking backward to the jeep, keeping the assault rifle at the hip.

"Like I was saying," Chong said, "you know the worst thing, for me about Tiananmen? They turned the lights out before they started the massacre. Don't you think that was obscene?"

The sergeant swung his assault rifle into the jeep and

Chong took his glove off and put a hand into his pocket and there was a dull flash and the sergeant bloomed like a huge crimson flower in the night.

"Don't you think that was obscene," Chong said, "turning the lights out?"

Chapter 19

Bells

Something brushed my foot, a rat, I think.

I stood still, just inside the doorway. It was as far as I had got. I watched the two great beams of timber, above my head and to my right. There was a gap there, where the balustrade along the second floor had broken away. The movement had been there, just now. I had seen it when I had come in.

They were everywhere, the rats. You heard them squeaking. It was winter, and they were desperate for shelter all over the town, desperate for food.

The movement had been just there, in the gap along the balustrade, or what I'd thought was movement. This was the door the abbot had shown me earlier. I could come in this way without disturbing the monks: I'd told him it was important to me, not to disturb them in their prayers, their daily life, and in part it was true. But he understood. It mattered more to me that I wasn't seen coming or going.

The moon was high in the south, its light slanting in rays through the breaks in the timber where the roof on that side had been destroyed; the rays were gray, substantial, like a milkiness in water, because of the incense they burned in here, and the yak-butter lamps with their smoky wicks. I was used to the smell of this place; it was pungent, a presence; it only faded after I'd been back here for an hour or so.

Dpal ldan mgon po . . .

It was close on midnight, a time, I suppose, for the last prayers of the day. The chanting was not loud; it came from the big hall on the east side of the monastery, where the huge gilded Buddha sat, brought here from a gutted temple after the uprising, the abbot had told me.

Po spyan hdren na a . . .

Small bells rang at intervals. The chanting and the bells didn't worry me; the whole ruin was already alive with sound: in the intense heat of the sunshine during the day the timbers swelled, and at night cooled; their straining was as familiar and as particular to this place as its smell, and I was used to it. It was a kind of silence, and unfamiliar sounds would alert me.

Movement again and I caught it but not in time to identify it before it was gone. I kept still, waiting for minutes, then took a step across the earth floor, sighting again from a new angle. At this point hallucination began, the eyes becoming jaded by the unchanging view, the mind presenting phantasmagoria for them to look at. I let them close and stood for minutes on end, clearing the images.

Perhaps it had been the same kind of illusion when I'd come in, the movement I'd seen, thought I'd seen. Or possibly there were owls here. It was time to go forward, find the first ladder and climb. Xingyu Baibing was in danger here now; the police and the PSB had called in the military to help in the search and they'd set up roadblocks everywhere and soon they'd be beating on every door in the town, searching every building, house, hotel, temple, monastery.

Chong was waiting outside with the big Jeifang.

It had taken three hours to get here, moving overland and keeping clear of the roads and their intersections, coming up against terrain that wouldn't allow even the big truck across it, turning back a mile and going north again, keeping a watch on the lights flashing far in the distance.

"Little thing I learned from the CIA."

We'd been bumping and rattling for nearly two hours since we'd left the jeep, over rocks that split under the weight of the front wheels and sent bright slivers flying through the moonlight. I was waiting for a tire to blow.

"How to make them?"

"Yes." The little remote-control bombs. "They were designed for automobiles and planes, but I've used them a few times on people. They're good. I call them people-boomers. I got a few bigger ones stashed away, building boomers. You need any, you tell me."

He'd driven the military jeep half a mile and run it into a ravine deep enough to hide it from level sight. They'd see it all right from a chopper in the morning but we couldn't do anything about that; all we wanted was enough time to get to the monastery and take Xingyu Baibing to a new hideout. There was no hope of getting him to the airport now.

We'd left the sergeant to the birds.

"He'll be picked to the bone inside of two hours from first light," Chong said when he got back into the truck. "There's a sky-burial site a couple of kilometers from here, that direction. The birds know where to come. Then, get a wind, the rest should be covered in silt, but the military are going to look for the bastard anyway, once they find the jeep." He peeled some chewing gum. "Did me a whole lot of good, you know? Drop in the ocean, sure, but I got a real kick out of looking at all that red in the moonlight, head coming off—did you see the head coming off? Kind of making a personal statement, lighting one little lamp in Tiananmen, you know the trouble with guys, I mean guys as distinct from gals? They're so fucking romantic. Glory of war, all that shit."

I let him go on talking as we drove the big Jeifang north; he didn't want any answers, any questions. I was getting to know him; underneath the easy manner there was rage burning, in the name of Tiananmen.

"We got enough gas," he said after a while, "for maybe another fifty kilometers, this kind of ground, if the tires hold out, got two spares. Got food, I brought some army rations, canned stuff, last awhile, the two of you."

Xingyu and myself. Chong would make his way back and report to Pepperidge and provide liaison.

I put my feet on the top of the dashboard to ease the muscles, head was all right, wasn't throbbing so much now in spite of the bouncing around. A crack had started in the windshield; this wasn't shatterproof glass. The whole truck was taking a beating and that couldn't last forever, perhaps not even for fifty kilometers.

"What are the chances," I asked Chong, "of finding somewhere for him between here and the airport?" He knew the region better than I did, and I could be missing something.

He turned to look at me. "We don't have any. We don't have any chances. Go south with him on board, we're just putting him into their hands."

"North, then," I said, "within fifty kilometers, what have we got?"

"Few farms. Few more monasteries, up in the hills. Yak herds, nomad camps, couple of mining sites."

"They'll check all those. The military."

"Bet your ass they will. They got choppers, go where they like, put troops down and beat the bushes." A front wheel hit a rock and something smashed, I think a headlamp.

"*Shit.*"

I asked him if there were caves.

"Caves? You bet. Few hundred."

"How big?"

He half-turned on the seat, interested. "All sizes, I guess, but there'd be plenty with enough room for just two people, no crowding, you know? Some of them big as a ballroom. Sure, you could do that for a couple of days, maybe more if you had to."

I thought about it. The objective for *Bamboo* was to fly Xingyu Baibing into Beijing, assuming the coordinator replacing Sojourner had managed to take over without any delay. But we couldn't do that now. All we could do was keep Xingyu underground, keep him from being flushed out and sent to Beijing and brainwashed and pushed in front of the cameras, the return of the prodigal son, penitent, re-formed, an example to others who thought fit to impede the onward struggle for socialism.

"That's the plan?"

Chong was watching me, taking snatched glances away from the moonlit rocks ahead.

"There's nothing else," I said, "we can do."

"Okay. Have to do it tonight, use the dark. That sun comes up, we're going to see a sky full of choppers looking for that fucking sergeant."

That had been an hour ago, and now he was waiting outside the monastery with the truck. It didn't need two of us to fetch Xingyu Baibing.

Thugs rje hdul dang dbang . . .

I crossed the earth floor and climbed the ladder. If there had been movement, if it hadn't been an errant flicker of hallucination, I would find out what it was at close range. The ladder had a tilt to the left, and I put my feet on the other side, testing the rungs. This was the ladder the monks used, Bian the guard and his replacement; they brought water from the reservoir, and food, and changed the sanitary bucket. It was a good strong ladder, and the tilt didn't worry me. It was something else that worried me.

I stopped climbing and let the data come in, the chanting and the bells and the moonlight and the scent of the incense and the lamps, the feel of the rough wood under my hands, while the primitive brainstem signaled the nerves, opening the pupils by a degree, stimulating the olfactory sensors, tuning the tympanic membranes to sweep the environment for unfamiliar sounds, sensitizing the tactile nodes of the fingers and palms, returning me to the ancient status of the animal in the wild seeking the means for survival, the skin crawling now and the hairs lifting on the scalp because of the scent I'd detected, strange and sweet and unfamiliar here, perhaps dangerous.

I couldn't identify it, couldn't find the key, the association

225

with other things, other environments where I'd smelled this scent before. I waited, standing still on the ladder, and let the mind range on its own, taking slow deep breaths to present the stimulus. Nothing came. Nothing came and I climbed again, watching the long gallery on the second floor, watching the gap where the timbers had fallen during the fire, watching for movement.

Ldan na . . . Dpal ldan mgon po . . .

My boot scraped a splinter from a rung of the ladder and I heard it fall, because it was silent here in this huge derelict place, with a silence beyond the chanting and the bells and the creak of the beams as the cold contracted them, a silence in which all I could consciously hear were unfamiliar, un-expected sounds, the animal brainstem tuned to them, and this was good, this was as it should be, the senses taut, alert beyond the norm; but I was not reassured. There was still something else, other than the strange sweet unfamiliar scent, that was causing the gooseflesh, lifting the hair on the scalp.

Screech of a night bird somewhere and I felt the sweat springing, saw lights for an instant leaping against the dark as the nerves were fired.

I stopped moving, absorbed the shock, climbed again. Still something else, but I was beginning to know that its source wasn't physical, sensory. Information was shimmer-ing at a level of awareness beyond the conscious, as subtle as the trembling of a web, and it was bringing fear into my spirit, bringing desolation.

But let us not, my good friend, lend ourselves over-much to the imagination: the organism is under stress, and prey to fancy. Let us rather climb to the gallery and find things out.

You know it's true. It's not just your imagination.

Yes, but what can I do about it, for God's sake?

The ladder gave a little when I reached the top; one of the rawhide straps had worked loose, but no matter, I was safe enough, I was on the gallery and this was where the movement was, the one I had seen from below. It was a colored rag, hanging across a strut of timber and moving very slightly in a draft of air; it must have dropped from the floor above, and caught across the rough woodwork. I hadn't noticed it the last time I'd come; perhaps it hadn't been there.

Po spyan hdren na a . . .

Faint now, the voices below, the muted tinkling of the bells. What were they praying for down there where the great gold Buddha sat with his fat stomach and his enigmatic smile? For peace on earth and goodwill to all men? For a brave new China and the blessings of democracy? For the sergeant down there across the trackless wastes, or perhaps for Dr. Xingyu Baibing, the new messiah? Let them pray for him, above all pray for him.

Screech of that bloody bird, enough to scare the wits out of you as they say, I suppose it was one of those that wheeled and dived across the burial site that Chong had spoken of, as I'd seen them doing in Bombay, and there's a euphemism for you, sky-burial, a pretty thought but what it means when you get down to it is that you leave your dear ones out there under the sky and those bloody birds come down and pick at them, taking chunks of flesh in their great hooked beaks and flying off with them, plundering the dead I would rather call it, the flesh tearing under the talons—nor is it the time, though, to be morbid, no, I take your point, standing here on the gallery with the sweat seeping along the skin and the hackles raised and the fear of Christ in me because of that strange sweet smell and the intelligence that informed my spirit that something had gone wrong here in the monastery tonight, horribly wrong.

Chapter 20

Dawn

"The subject has been seized."

I waited, giving him time.

In a moment: "Is he still alive?"

"I don't know. They killed the monk on guard."

Waited again. Pepperidge would want to put the questions in order of their priority and I left it to him. He'd have to signal London as soon as I'd rung off, and they'd want the precise facts. The mission had crashed and I didn't know what they would do, put another one together with a standby executive, fly people in from Hong Kong, call out everyone they'd got in Lhasa, sleepers, supports, agents-in-place, God only knew what they would do, if there was anything they could do at all.

"When would you say it happened?"

There was a lot of crackle on the line but that was normal for this place. "I can't say for certain. One of the monks said he thought he heard something like a shout, not long before we got there. Call it between twenty-three-thirty and midnight."

Chong watched me from the cab of the truck. He'd broken the lock on the gates of the depot to get me inside to the phone and then brought the truck up to block off the entrance. His face looked smaller than ever at the window of the cab, cold, pinched, his eyes watchful, pain in them, it hadn't been his fault but it had bruised him: he'd been called in by Pepperidge to support a major operation and the subject

229

had been Dr. Xingyu Baibing, the messiah, and he'd only been with the mission a matter of hours before it had crashed, and on the long nerve-racking trip south across that appalling terrain he'd been terse, brooding, banging his fists on the rim of the big wheel and shouting above the din of the truck, cursing in Chinese, cursing or praying, I didn't know which, then falling quiet for an hour, two hours, finally finding his center and talking normally, the rage and frustration buried again behind the easy, American-style manner.

He watched me from the cab, turning sometimes to check the street. In the sky behind him, to the east, a crack of saffron light lay across the horizon. Neither of us had eaten, slept, washed for the past twelve hours, rations in the truck but we couldn't touch them, no appetite for anything but the rancor in the soul to chew on.

"Was there any sign," Pepperidge asked me, "that he wasn't taken alive? That he was killed?"

I thought back. It didn't look as if there'd been a struggle. Bian, the monk, was lying on his back staring into the moonlight, his prayer beads lying half across his face; I would think that another monk or someone in a monk's robes had brought food or water to the third floor and surprised him, killing him silently and going in to Xingyu's cell.

Told him these facts, Pepperidge, these assumptions.

"There would have been a second man?"

"Possibly."

A second man who'd climbed the ladder as soon as Bian had been dealt with, in case it needed physical force to take Xingyu. But I thought I knew now what that strange sweet smell had been in the monastery: chloroform.

"Were his things missing?"

"Yes." The diary, the technical papers, the flight bag, insulin kit. "But they didn't find the thing that Koichi made." The mask. "I brought that away."

"And you'll keep it with you."

"Yes."

Hell was he talking about, there was only one man in

this world the mask would fit and he was gone and it looked unlikely we'd ever see him again.

"You told the abbot?"

"Yes."

Brought them away from their prayers, the abbot and the interpreter, committing a sacrilege I've no doubt, their sandals scuffing on the earth floor, their robes sickly with the smell of incense, the abbot's eyes wide as I told him, his hands going at once to his beads.

"*Nǐ kěndìn Bian shǐle?*"

The interpreter looked at me. "You are sure that Bian is dead?"

"Yes. I'm sorry."

"*Xīngyu xīanshēn, tā meí shǐ?*"

"I don't know. They came for him, but I doubt if it was to kill him later."

The abbot spoke to the interpreter, who turned and called two other monks away from their prayers; they passed us with shock in their eyes, their robes flying as they hurried across the main floor to the ladder in the corner.

In a moment I said, "Your Holiness, I imagine there are monks here who joined you not so long ago, people you don't know very well as yet. Do you think anyone like that could have betrayed Dr. Xingyu?"

For an instant he looked appalled, then said through the interpreter: "Only four of us knew about our guest. Only four."

The abbot himself, the interpreter, Bian, and the monk who'd shared guard duty with him.

"The man who helped Bian," I said, "did you know him well?"

"But of course. It was a great responsibility I gave him."

I left it at that, didn't ask if this man might have talked to anyone else here. It wouldn't have been easy for those who knew about this eminent guest of theirs to keep silent. This was a small sect, and the messiah was in their house.

I told Pepperidge this much, and then for a moment there

was nothing on the line but crackling. Then he said, "That could have been what happened, yes. People talked, someone chose to betray him. But they didn't go to the police."

"No." Xingyu hadn't been taken by the police, the PSB, the KCCPC, or the military, or there would have been jeeps raising the dust outside this place and shouting and the tramp of boots and Xingyu would have been hustled away with his wrists bound and his feet dragging, the abbot too, for summary trial and execution. "It wasn't the police," I said, "who took him, or anyone official. It was a private cell."

And this was the worst of it. I hadn't told Chong on the way south in the night; he was support, not executive; his job was to provide manpower, pass information, liaise with the director in the field, protect the shadow, blow up sergeants. Support people must be told even less than the executives because they're more vulnerable, more in danger of capture and interrogation.

I wouldn't have told him in any case; he was frustrated enough as it was. But this was what we faced now: we hadn't just got the police and the Public Service Bureau and Chinese Intelligence and the People's Liberation Army to deal with. Somewhere in Lhasa, in the streets, behind the walls, behind the doors, in the shadows, there was a private cell operating, professional, effective, and with powerful political backing, or they wouldn't have targeted a man like Xingyu Baibing, and this was the worst of it because the forces of vast organizations like the police and the military have got the advantage in numbers and equipment and information resources and it's often difficult to keep out of their way, but at least you know where they are and what they look like, you can see them coming.

A private cell is different. You can be standing next to a man in a bar or a hotel or an airport and not know that you're in hazard, not know that your mission has been infiltrated and that you'll crash it if you're lucky or be found dead by morning if you're not.

A private cell can work in the dark, in silence and in

stealth. Its power to destroy the opposition is not paraded, like that of a rattlesnake, but shrouded, like that of the black widow.

We were the opposition.

"Do you think"—Pepperidge on the line—"that someone is just trying to make some money?"

Xingyu would have a price on his head, a big one.

"No. The people who took him were professionals, not mercenaries, not terrorists." It had been done with great expertise: they'd not only succeeded in finding Xingyu Baibing but they'd gone into a monastery full of monks and got out again with the man they wanted, killing silently and disturbing no one.

Chong was getting out of his cab, looking along the road, looking at me, his gloved hands palm down, pressing the air, *don't worry, just keep a low profile, stay where you are, don't come into the street.*

I'd told him I'd gone to ground, but going to ground doesn't necessarily mean you've got to bury yourself in a cellar, though it might come to that if it's the only way to survive the field and finally get out and go home; it normally means you've got to keep off the streets if you can, stay away from hotels and taxis and airports, watch for the police every minute you're exposed and be ready to duck and run and wait things out if they see you. It's a status we loathe and fear because it can only get more dangerous as time goes by.

They knew my name at the Public Service Bureau: they'd checked my papers there and they'd asked Su-May Wang if she knew where I was. The police would have been alerted as a routine procedure and I'd given my passport and visa to Pepperidge in the café because if I were stopped on the street I couldn't show them, would have to say I'd lost them and then try to get clear before they took me along to the station for an inquiry: you cannot, in a town where martial law obtains, go without papers.

Pressing his hands down, Chong, *everything's under control,* his breath clouding on the raw morning air as the light in the east took on more color, pouring gold along the horizon.

"Do they want the subject," Pepperidge asked, "or what he's got in his head?"

Not after facts now, simply tapping me for what he could get, for what I could give him, because London would ask these questions and he'd need answers. "If all they'd wanted was information," I said, "they'd have gone for me, not him." Information on *Bamboo,* the information I'd been forced to give Xingyu to keep him from running home to Beijing.

"So what do they want him for?"

I had to think, but it wasn't easy, the cold was like a clamp, numbing the body, numbing the brain, not cold so much as fatigue, been a hard day last night. "They want him," I said, "for bargaining, perhaps. As a hostage." There were a whole lot of possible scenarios with Xingyu Baibing as the catalyst, brought forward to bring political pressure, a guarantee, a bargaining chip, a martyr to foment reaction. We'd planned to use him ourselves to bring the weight of the people against the Chinese government.

"They can't do anything with him here."

"No. They'll have to take him to Beijing."

"But they can't do that." His voice kept fading, coming back. "Any more than we could have, now that he's being actively sought." In a moment, "What is your situation?"

"Ground. Chong's still in support." I told him about the roadblocks, the sergeant.

"Can you still use the truck?"

"Yes." The sergeant wouldn't have seen it distinctly enough from the roadblock to identify it as a green Jeifang, and the most he would've said to anyone would have been that there was a vehicle on the move down there, he'd go and check it out.

"If they were searching *vehicles,*" Pepperidge said, "it couldn't have been a coincidence. Someone must have told them you were going to take him on board." A beat. "They're very close, aren't they?"

I didn't say anything. I'd thought about that before but it hadn't got me anywhere, simply confirmed that we had a private cell dogging my shadow, infiltrating *Bamboo*, driving me to ground.

"I'll have to signal," Pepperidge said, "of course." The line crackled, and I waited. Chong came through the gates, standing inside, his back to me, stamping his feet, gloved hands rammed into the pockets of his coat. An engine was rumbling and I watched the gates; they were heavy timber, with gaps at the hinged ends, a gap in the middle. "I will relay," Pepperidge's voice came again, "what you've told me. They'll want to know what your plans are."

That had been the reason for the silence on the line: he'd been thinking out how to put it, because this was going to be rough.

In a moment I said, "To find the subject?"

It was an army vehicle, a camouflaged personnel carrier; I watched it through the gaps in the gates, past Chong's motionless figure. It was loaded, the carrier, with Chinese troops in battle dress. It was going slowly, toward the center of the city.

"Yes," Pepperidge said, "your plans are to find the subject, of course. But London will ask for details."

Either they were coming down from the intersections in the north, the roadblocks, or they were moving into the town from an outlying base, to begin a house-to-house search for Xingyu Baibing.

"Tell London they can't have any details," I said into the phone.

The carrier had stopped, not far from the big green Jeifang, and Chong turned and stood facing me now, his mouth working on the chewing gum, his eyes blanked off. We'd agreed, on our way south through the night, that we would go on using the truck as our base, at least for the first hour or two of the day, that it wasn't a risk, wouldn't call attention. There were hundreds of these things in the city and around it and along the roads to Chengdu, Golmud, Kathmandu, most of them painted green like this one. The only man who could have recognized it as ours was dead.

But perhaps we were wrong, because boots were hitting the ground as men dropped from the carrier. Or their city-wide search was going to start here, at the truck depot.

"It's like this, you see"—Pepperidge—"I've got every confidence in you, and I think you've got as good a chance as anyone of bringing this thing home, even now."

The mission. As good a chance of bringing it home as any other executive they might fly out here to take over and do what he could to go in cold and try pulling something else out of the wreckage.

"The only point," I said, "in getting someone else out here would be that he could work at street level." Unknown to the police and the PSB, unknown to the private cell.

Boots on the road outside. I watched the gates. The engine of the personnel carrier was still running; it hadn't moved on.

"What they'll say"—Pepperidge—"is that while I have total confidence in you, they cannot share it. Unless you can give me any idea of where you plan to go from here, they may well instruct me to send you out of the field."

He hadn't liked saying that. He would have done anything not to say it.

"I quite understand."

Best I could do, put him out of his misery, take it like a man, so forth, as I watched the gates and saw them coming over to them, three soldiers.

Chong didn't move. He was standing twenty feet away, between me and the gates, facing them now, perfectly still. There were trucks standing in the depot, a dozen or more, most of them big Jeifangs, adequate cover. On the far side was a low wall, and that was the way I would have to go. And this is the problem of going to ground: you can be forced at any minute to run, and keep on running. There's no base anymore that you can work from, no stability; the sands are shifting all the time under your feet.

You can see their point, can't you, in London, quite understand.

Shivering in the first pale light of the new day, shivering under the warm padded coat, the one I'd taken from the man in the temple, first his life and then his coat, uncivil of me, I will admit, shivering despite its warmth as the soldiers came to the gates and started banging on them.

"*Dǎ kaī!*"

Chong didn't move, shouted back at them—"*Zhèr haì meí rén!*"

Pepperidge: "I can only obey their instructions, of course." London's. "If they—" he broke off— "was that someone shouting?"

"Yes."

"Are you pressed?"

"Not really."

"*Tāmén shénmé shíhòu daò?*"

Crackling on the line. "Who is shouting?"

"Chong. He's all right, but I might have to ring off. If I do, I'll get through to you again from somewhere else."

In a moment, "Don't leave anything too late."

Chong hadn't moved. "*Jǐu dǐan!*" Shouting at them.

He would give me time, I knew that. If they started forcing the gates he'd turn and give me the signal and we'd separate, make our own way out, if they didn't start shooting first.

"Look," I said, "they can't get him out of Lhasa. He's still here somewhere. I'm going to find him."

Soldiers banging at the gates.

Chong standing perfectly still, shouting at them.

"*Líhai zhěr ba. Jǐu dǐun huǐlaí!*"

Pepperidge on the line, worried by the noise. "I'd be happier if you'd ring off and look after things there."

"He's still in this town," I said, "and I'm going to find him. Tell them that. Tell them to give me a bit more time. A few hours."

Banging at the gates.

"That's all I'm asking. A few hours."

Chapter 21

Dog

Chong hit the brakes and the big truck lurched to a stop.

"What did you tell them?"

"Jesus," he said, "we've done a kilometer in thirty minutes down this goddam road." We were blocked off by a yak wagon, couldn't overtake. "I told them nobody was at the depot yet, they'd have to come back."

"They didn't argue?"

He rested his hand on the huge vibrating gear lever, the engine rumbling. "Sure they argued. But their heads are full of rice."

One of the yaks was lying slumped in the shafts. "What's the problem?"

"It's died. Everything dies, wait long enough." He kicked the clutch and hit the gear lever and we moved off again. "We going anywhere special?" He was still furious, his throat tight when he spoke. "We going to find where they took him, maybe?"

I watched the road ahead.

"Eventually."

This was the road south into the town, Linkuo Lu, where the temple was, where I'd taken the coat from the man. Grit blew in through the cracks of the doors; there was a wind getting up. Eventually, yes, of course, we would find where they'd taken Dr. Xingyu Baibing, and we would bring him back under our protection, but meanwhile they would not

239

be very happy in London, there would be no dancing in the streets.

Subject seized, location unknown. PLA sergeant deceased.

Croder at the signals board, his black basilisk eyes watching the man with the piece of chalk as the stuff came in from Pepperidge, Hyde standing there poking his tongue in his cheek, the whole place very quiet as they listened to his voice, the calm and gentle voice of my director in the field as it reached them through the government communications mast in Cheltenham and the unscrambler in Codes and Cyphers three floors above.

Subject is expected to reveal critical information with or without duress. His captors believed to be private cell, repeat, private cell operating in the field.

There's a bell, in Lloyd's of London, the *Lutine* bell, since that is the name of the vessel it was salvaged from, and they ring it whenever news comes that a ship has gone down, and there is a silence afterward. It's rather like that in the signals room, when news comes of the kind that Pepperidge had given them now, that the mission had foundered.

Executive to ground and inactive.

The two major items of course were that the subject was expected to "reveal critical information"—to blow *Bamboo*—and that the executive had gone to ground and was inactive, which meant that he must be wanted by the police and security forces of the host country and could no longer operate at street level, and that he had no further ability to advance or even protect the mission.

"Who's this bastard?" Chong said.

Man waving.

The signal reporting a deceased PLA sergeant in the field was obligatory: any "terminal incident" must be noted in the records. But it also told London Control that there was now a hue and cry going on as a result, with the military searching earnestly for the assassin.

"Pull up," I told Chong.

The report that a private cell had entered the field was

of critical importance, but with the mission crashed and the executive incapable of further action there wasn't much that London could do about it.

"You say pull up?"

"Yes."

Not quite incapable: that is a mortuary word, suggestive of worms and the silence of the tomb. Pressed, harassed, beleaguered, what you will.

The man who had been waving came to the side of the cab as the truck ground to a stop with the brake drums moaning. His Beijing jeep was standing at the roadside.

"*Kěyì dā nǐde bìan chē ma?*"

"Chong, what's he saying?"

Stink of diesel gas seeping through the floorboards. I wound the window down.

"Wants a lift."

"We'll give him one."

Chong looked at me. "He a friend?"

As distinct from foe, trade argot.

"Yes."

"*Shang che.*"

As the man came around the front of the truck I said, "Chong. You don't speak English."

"Gotcha."

I pushed the door open and shifted over to make room and the man came aboard, hauling himself up by the big iron handgrip, expensive duffel jacket, heavy black beard, an energetic, barrel-shaped body, dropping onto the seat beside me, pulling the door shut with a noise like a bomb.

"*Xiexie.*"

"That's all right," I said.

"Ah." Peering at me, then—"Well, well! You're getting a lift too?"

"Yes."

I had sunglasses on; otherwise he would have recognized me sooner, even with the two-day stubble. A lot of people wore sunglasses here without attracting attention; the ultraviolet was intense at this altitude: this was cataract country.

"Trotter," the man said. "How is the head?"

"Much better, thanks of course to you."

"My dear fellow, I'm glad it turned out all right." In a moment "That bloody jeep always gives trouble about here— I do this road every day. Grit in the carburetor, I dare say, an occupational hazard for every vehicle in Lhasa, but the thing is they never renew the air filters at the rental place."

He sounded, I thought, a degree too talkative.

"That's a shame," I said.

Chong shifted the huge gear lever again. For a truck as big as a dinosaur there wasn't much room in the cab. I felt Trotter moving closer to me.

Very quietly, under his breath, "This chap speak English?"

"No."

"Ah." Gloved hands a little restless on his knees, fingers tapping. "I don't know if you're aware of it, my dear fellow, but the police are looking for you. Locke, isn't it?"

"Yes. How do you know?"

"I'm sort of local here, on and off, come here to dig as often as I can. Police know me well, and they sometimes haul me in whenever there's a problem with a round-eye, ask me if I know anything and so on." In a moment, "From what I gather there was an agent of the KCCPC found dead in a temple yesterday." A beat. "The one where I picked you up. It appears someone described you." He turned his face toward me. "I can assure you it was not I."

Chong hit the brakes again as a tour bus cut things close past a horse and cart, and we put our hands on the dashboard.

"Bíe dǎng dào!"

I hadn't given Trotter any kind of an answer.

"Look," he said, "in the first place I told them I didn't know anything about you, obviously. It wouldn't be wise for me to refuse to help those buggers when I can, because they turn a blind eye if I'm still on the road after a curfew, back late from a dig, that sort of thing. But they get damned little out of me, I can assure you."

Buildings were coming up as we passed the nomad camp ground, the big Telecommunications Office in the distance: we'd been making better time. I hadn't said anything.

"In the second place," his deep voice muted, "I'm not the slightest bit interested in your affairs, but if by chance you happen to have dispatched an agent of the KCCPC then I'm delighted, between you and me. You're *certain*, are you, that this chap doesn't understand English?"

"Certain."

"Well and good, because this is tricky territory, as I imagine you realize. Never know who you're talking to"—his gloved hand on my knee for an instant—"I mean the Chinese. So the thing is, since the police are after you, it might be a good idea to make yourself scarce, don't you agree?"

"It sounds logical."

"*Ni yào kǒuxiāngtáng ma?*" Chong, holding out his packet of Wrigley's.

Trotter shook his head. "*Bù, xièxie nǐ.* It's not easy," he said, "in a place like this, to make oneself scarce, with martial law and everything. Of course, the entire populace hates and detests the authorities, but one or two are so scared of reprisals that they'll give anyone away, even their friends, even their relatives." We reached for the dashboard again as Chong used the brakes for the first traffic lights, the drums moaning. "What I would like to tell you, my dear fellow, is that if you need a good place—a *safe* place—to sort of lie low till things blow over, I'd be delighted to assist." He leaned forward, looking past me at Chong. "*Máfán nǐng, kěyǐ ràng wo zài xiàyitíao jīe xià chē ma?*"

"*Kěyǐ.*"

"I gave you my card, I believe?"

"Yes."

"Phone me at any time, my dear fellow. At *any* time. I know a *safe* place, if you're really stuck—not the hotel, of course, it's just a tiny apartment in the native quarter. Dear God, the whole town used to be the native quarter, but now the Chinese are taking over, it's appalling. The sooner they get that gang of cutthroats out of power in Beijing the happier I shall be, not to mention my good friends the intellectuals." He looked at Chong again. *"Wǒ qían nǐ shénme ma?"*

"Bù. Heng huānyíng nǐ dā wǒ de chē."

"Nǐ zhēnshì gè rè xīn rén." He braced himself as the truck slowed. The big black beard close to my ear—"Please remember, Mr. Locke, that you can count on me, for the aforesaid reasons. I have a feeling you are hardly a friend of those bastards in Beijing, which makes you one of mine."

He used a fist on the door handle and dropped onto the street, looking up at me with his dark eyes serious. "You know where to find me." Swung the door shut with a bang.

Across the road was a red-and-white sign in Chinese and English: Truck Rental.

Chong gunned up and got into second gear. "You know that guy?"

"Slightly."

"British?"

"Yes. How many people," I asked him, "have we got in the field?"

"Maybe a dozen in support, some of them sleepers, got a short courier line to the airport, longer one to Kathmandu, then we can use—"

"All right, I want a two-way radio with a ten-kilometer range and fresh batteries. I want another one delivered to our DIF with the frequencies synchronized." He slowed for traffic lights, and I gave him a rendezvous. "I also want a different truck—what are those brown things with the rounded front?"

"Called a Dongfeng, sure, I can rent one of those."

"How long will it take to get what I need?"

"How soon do you want it?"

"Fast as you can."

He worked at his gum. "Gimme an hour, okay?"

I switched to receive. "Hear you."

"I've had no response yet."

There wouldn't have been time. With the signals board in the state it was, they'd have to call in Bureau One, the all-highest, and he'd have to confer with Croder and possibly that bastard Loman and decide which way to go, leave me out here in the hope that I could make another move or call me in and replace me.

"Did you tell them I'm asking for a few hours more?"

"Of course. But I assume nothing has changed."

He waited.

You cannot lie. You can lie to every single human being you meet in the field, you can lie like a trooper, like Satan himself, because your life will often depend on it, and that is understood. But the shadow executive cannot lie to his director, because he is his link to London, to Control, and to the signals board and the mission screens in the computer room and finally to the decision-making process that is the crux and fulcrum of the entire operation. That too is understood.

"No," I said into the radio. "Nothing has changed."

Someone else came through the doorway across the street, a man wrapped in rags with some kind of basket on his back. I watched him until he was out of sight past the vegetable stall. I was sitting in the truck, the new one, the Dengfeng, bloody thing reeking of yak dung.

"But at least we are now in constant touch," Pepperidge said.

That was like him: he'll always find the remnant of a silver lining in the darkest reaches of despair and bring it into the light.

Said yes.

"Location?"

It would be very dangerous to give it to him: there was no scrambler on these things. "I can't do that."

"*Very well. I had a signal,*" he said, "*through Beijing, an hour ago. The deadline has been moved up a little.*"

Mother of God.

The briefing was that Premier Li Peng was due to address the Chinese nation on television from the Great Hall of the People at ten o'clock on the morning of the 15th, and that was the governing factor that fixed the timing of *Bamboo*: the premier was to be removed by force from his desk and Dr. Xingyu Baibing installed in his place. The briefing had noted that if the deadline couldn't be met, we wouldn't get another chance for months: Premier Li wasn't scheduled to speak again until the spring.

I asked Pepperidge: "By how much?"

"*The speech was going to be made at ten hundred hours on the fifteenth, as you know. It's now down for eighteen hundred hours the previous evening, which means that the bomber will have to pick him up at Gonggar at three tomorrow afternoon, instead of midnight.*" Short silence. "*Bit rough, I know.*"

I watched the doorway.

Nine hours.

"What's London telling the coordinator?"

"*In what way?*"

I think he knew, but didn't want to get it wrong. This was sensitive ground. "Is the coordinator being told that the subject is now missing? That we can't have him ready for the rendezvous at Gonggar in any case?"

In a moment, "*No.*"

A gust of wind rocked the truck, blew dust along the street. "When will they tell him?"

"*I think they'll leave it to the last possible moment. There's not much to lose, after all. The bomber's scheduled to leave Beijing at fifteen hundred hours Beijing time, thirteen hundred hours Lhasa. If we can't make the rdv, all we have to do is put through a signal for them to cancel the flight, five minutes before takeoff. It gives us a slight edge, if there's anything we can do in the meantime.*"

Meant find Xingyu.

"All right," I said.

In a moment, "Have you any plans?"

"I'm going to follow up whatever I can find." Couldn't tell him what I'd asked Chong to do for me; we weren't scrambled. But I think he knew what I was going to do. I think he knew.

"*Very well.*" A note of cheerfulness, I wished he wouldn't do that, it was like whistling at a funeral.

Meant to be kind, he meant to be kind, God knew how this man had got through all the missions he had—*major* operations, three of them Classification One to my knowledge, global scale—with this much humanity, this much compassion. Simply because, perhaps, he could preserve enough heart in his executive to keep him running on, give him the feeling he wasn't alone, take enough tension out of his nerves to let him see a chance he might otherwise miss, and muster the strength to take it.

Miracles do not always come easily, do not burst upon us with the holy light of revelation; they must sometimes be conjured from the sickly flame of despair, the hands held close to keep the draft away and the gaze steadfast, bringing to bear upon the matter the grace of faith, until through the dark of disaffection the small flame thrives, leaping at last to burn with a light that holds the very soul in thrall, by which I mean, my good friend, that one must not go limping home, must one, when all is wretchedness, no, one must sit here in this stinking truck and watch the doorway over there, not for an instant taking the eyes away, in case there is a last chance, however thin, of conjuring that little flame within the hands, and there she is.

Su-May.

She was alone, coming through the doorway of the little broken-down hotel, first looking to her right and then to her left in the way they do, the amateurs, when they want to take care they are not watched, making her way past the vegetable stall, a small figure bundled against the freezing wind, soon to be lost among the blade-edged shadows of noon.

Hit the button—"Breaking, stay open, out."

She was at a table in the far corner.

I could only just about see her: large luminous eyes set in a small pale face above the fur collar of her parka; something had gone wrong, I suppose, with one of the stoves in here, the café was thick with smoke. This was a bigger place than the one I'd gone to before with little Su-May and later Pepperidge; it was crowded, people hungry in the middle of the day. My stomach was empty but I hungered not, had ordered tea. Fear doth not prick the appetite, and Lord, I was afraid.

The oil lamps flickered against the walls like warning beacons across a foggy sea, and dark figures moved through the smoke, servers, customers, beggars, and monks; dogs darted between their feet and under the rickety bamboo tables and out again, seeking scraps for their hallowed stomachs.

They are sacred, she had told me, little Su-May, believed by some to be the reincarnation of departed monks, I think she'd said, believed by some but not by me, kicked at one of the little buggers and felt it connect, they'll start gnawing on your bloody ankle if you don't watch out, sitting with my hands around the cup of tea, nursing my nerves.

Because it had come to this. When a mission has crashed and the opposition has gained the field and there is nothing you can do, almost nothing, we will correct that, almost nothing you can do, there is always a last desperate ploy that you can consider using, and it has never failed. It will give you access again, a way in through the wreckage, and if you get it right you will once more confront the enemy, and with luck and the blessing of every saint in Christendom you may even, finally, prevail.

Men moved like shadows in this ghostly place, women

too, I suppose, though it was difficult to tell because most of them were swathed in robes or skins or coats and big fur hats, the drab plumage of their winter hibernation here on the bleak roof of the world. Someone was coughing his heart up in the drifting smoke, and a door was banged open behind me to let some of it out.

There were no mirrors in here.

It's not in the book, the ploy I was talking about, even though it has never failed. You'd think a thing like that would be a dead ringer for the *Manual of Procedures*, which is the Bible rewritten for the shadow executives of the Bureau, and I've tried to get it put in, but their lordships of the hierarchy won't have it, and the best I can do is spell it out for the neophyte spooks whenever I give an instruction class between missions at Norfolk.

She had been sitting alone, but now a man was joining her at the table, his black leather outfit gleaming in the shadows as the light from the oil lamps caught it. He looked young, athletic; he was an Oriental. I didn't think I'd seen him before, though I might have—no one in this smoke was easy to recognize. I hadn't known she'd come here to keep a rendezvous, but I'd thought it possible, by the way she'd checked the street outside the hotel, right and left, in the way they do, the amateurs, the unfortunates in this life who pass too close to the machinery, sometimes with the thought in mind of monetary gain or the perverse excitement of betrayal, sometimes just by accident—as in her case, I believed, little Su-May's—passing too close to the subtle and delicate machinery of international intelligence, fine as the web of that black widow we talked of, you and I, the machinery of subterfuge and treachery, deceit and untimely death.

They were talking, she and the young athletic-looking Oriental, their heads close. She hadn't seen me: I knew this. She would have reacted, would react if she saw me.

They won't allow it in the book, their lordships of the hierarchy, because although this last desperate ploy has never failed, it is deadly. It is lethal. It has killed.

At first I'd thought she was all she'd seemed to be, little Su-May, a refugee from the continuing oppression in Beijing, afraid for her father. Then I'd thought—had known—she was something more than that, perhaps working for the private cell that had moved into the field—not, certainly, working for the police or Chinese Intelligence: she was totally untrained. Then I'd assumed that she had, yes, simply passed too close to the machinery, to become caught up, her loyalties compromised, fragmented, so that she was grateful to me for the message I'd sent to her father, impressed that I'd killed an agent of the KCCPC, the arch enemy, had protected me from the police in the café—*perhaps on instructions*—but had been working against me for the private cell and even then had become torn both ways and finally had warned me.

You must be careful. When you go down to the street, make sure you are not followed.

By the police?

No. By anyone.

All I knew of her now was that she might provide me with the only link there was to the opposition, to whatever agent or cell she was working for, and could conceivably lead me to Xingyu Baibing.

The man in black leather could have been one of the people who had gone into the monastery last night and seized Xingyu and killed the guard. I could be within touching distance of the subject, the messiah.

It was all that sustained me, this thought, all right, this *straw* I was clutching at. Without it, nothing could have made me leave the truck and follow this woman here through the bright streets of noon, totally unable to know if I myself had picked up a tag among the people of this place in their robes and skins and coats and big fur hats, their disguise if you will, because that's what it amounted to, totally unable to know if I had been followed here and were being watched at this moment through the drifting smoke.

No mirrors, and a door wide open behind me, does that

tell you anything? Normal security measures had gone to the dogs: I'd used no cover on my way here, hadn't even looked back, had walked into this place alone instead of waiting for other people to camouflage the image through the doorway, had sat down at a table in the middle of the room, my back to the door, breaking every single bloody rule in the book, chapter and verse, because *that* is what the ploy demands before it can work for you.

I took another swallow of tea; it was thin, bitter, sharp with tannin, but hot, scalding still from the big black insulated jug they carried from one table to the next; it warmed my hands, burned them, as I sat here with the skin crawling and the nerves flickering along their pathways like liquid fire, a lone spook cut off now from all support, contact, and communication, sitting here like a rabbit on a firing range, divorced from the mission, sequestered in a location unknown to my director in the field, offering myself body and soul to the opposition in the hope that all could be reversed as the hours mounted slowly through the day, to allow me at last a chance, however small, of finding him, Xingyu, Dr. Xingyu Baibing, and of bringing him to safety.

You know what it is, the ploy.

She was standing up suddenly, Su-May, at the far table in the corner, still talking to the man in black leather, looking down at him, one hand resting on the tabletop, a bag of some kind slung from her shoulder.

You know what it is, my good friend, if you've soldiered with me before: it is a matter of *getting in their way*. If you cannot find them, let them find you. Let them see you, let them come for you, let them trap you, and if it becomes necessary let them do the most dangerous thing of all—let them *take* you.

Voilà.

Jason did it in Sri Lanka and got away with it, brought home the product. Tomlin did it in Costa Rica, got in and got out and left a chief of police hanging from his feet in a brothel. Cartwright did it in Tokyo, took on their *mafiosi* and got a British national home and followed on with a smashed hip and his nerves like a bombed piano—but they were the success stories, the ones we pass around in the Caff between missions to remind ourselves how good we are at this game, how successful, how intrepid, as an antidote to the fear of going out again. There are also the others, the other stories, which are not passed around in the Caff—Brockley tried the get-in-their-way thing in Athens and the colonels had him shot at dawn; Fairchild tried it in Calcutta and went out wearing a garotte; Myers tried it in Damascus and lasted three days and died mad, I was there in the signals room when the DIF reported through a drug runner's radio: *executive seized, believed under torture, am pulling out.*

So that is the way it is, it sometimes works and then you're in spooks' heaven and hallowed be thy name around the tea-slopped tables in the Caff, but it very often doesn't work and you can end up in the scuppers of some stinking hulk with your throat cut or spread-eagled on a trash heap with their heavy bone-white beaks picking at the still-warm flesh, I don't mean, I do not mean to sound discouraging, my good friend, but that, as I say, is the way it is, we must keep our fingers crossed and from the depths of the timorous soul pluck up a prayer that this time it will work for us. She had taken a step, had turned for a final word, hitching the shoulder strap higher, the cloth bag swinging; now she had turned again and was coming between the tables, coughing in the smoke, and I angled my head to make sure she'd recognize me and she slowed at once, almost tripping, then went on past my table without looking at me again, her voice just loud enough for me to catch.

"You are in great danger."

Swallowed some more tea, didn't actually need telling of course but she'd meant well, could have saved me as she'd done before in the other place, went out, she went out through the wide-open doorway into the street.

He stayed ten minutes, the young Oriental in black leather, then put some money down and left the table, moving along the bar on the far side without coming anywhere near me, though the path Su-May had taken was the more direct. So I had made contact, and must follow up.

Put five yen on the table, the generosity of a man with nothing to lose, got up and went to the door and found the smoke drifting into the sunlit street and some policemen pulling up in a jeep, it looked in fact as if the whole place was on fire, turned my face away and followed the man in black.

He wouldn't carry a gun; the police were fussy here, pick you up on the spot and search you and he'd know that. But he was a senior belt, by his walk, and that was far more dangerous. And he wouldn't be alone: he was walking alone toward the marketplace but there would be others not far away; this was already a mobile trap they'd got me in—it hadn't, you see, failed; it never does.

They wouldn't like it in London.

Executive in immediate contact with opposition and fully compromised.

It's the way they say things on the signal boards and I suppose it works, as a kind of shorthand. They wouldn't know, of course, for a while; they'd have to wait until I'd surfaced and reported my new position to Pepperidge, or had not of course reported at all, because of the bone-white-beaks thing they so charmingly call sky-burial.

How does it feel to have the left eye plucked from the socket and carried aloft, and then the right, carried aloft by those great black wings and digested in the airy pathways of their going, the eyes and the tongue and the genitals and then the whole thing buried in the sky with only the skeleton left down there, grinning at its fate, how does it feel? But we must not be morbid, we must keep on walking, keep up a steady pace and not bump into any monks, they're everywhere, there must surely be redemption for this doomed spook in a place so holy, turning to the right, into an alleyway, the man in black leather, and I followed him.

The sun beat down from a brazen sky and the smells

from an apothecary's stall were rich and strange as I passed through them; they grind the bones of tigers here, and bottle the ashes of snakes and sea horses, a different smell, you will acknowledge, than your good old milk of magnesia.

I walked into the alleyway and in a moment they followed, the others, but simply kept station, not crowding me, and I felt pleased, as well as frightened, horribly frightened, pleased that even though I might never get out of this alive at least I had decided to make a final effort and get in their way, not for his sake, Xingyu's, not for the future of the Chinese people or the stock market in Hong Kong but of course from pride, the stinking pride of the professional, that and vanity, the constant itch to take on dangerous things to prove not that I can do them but won't die in the doing, that personal and very special game of hide-and-seek you play in the shadows, so that when the grim reaper comes you can take him by surprise and with his own dread scythe cut him asunder.

There were stray dogs here in the alley, mangy and hollow-flanked, their eyes milky, and one of them, dirty white with brown patches, backed off from me as I went down on my knees and stayed like that for a moment and then fell prostrate like the monks I'd seen, the dog coming close now and sniffing at me as I wondered if I were facing the east as I should be, prone on the ground like this.

Chapter 22

Mad

Naked, she was more slender than I'd imagined.

It had been the clothes she'd worn, thick and padded against the cold, that had made her look almost dumpy, in spite of her small face. Sitting like this in the soft light of the lamp she had the stillness of an ivory figurine, one arm resting across her raised knee, her dark eyes watching me and her mouth pensive, her throat shadowed, flawless, a tuft of silken black hair curling from her armpit, her small breasts high on her chest, their nipples erect in the center of their large ocher-colored areolas. She hadn't spoken since we'd come in here.

For a time I just let my eyes take in the beauty of her face, her body, and then I began feeling restless because it wasn't enough, and I put my hand on her sharp, delicate shoulder blade and she came against me at once, but I couldn't see her so clearly now because they'd taken one of my eyes, the shadows of their great wings falling across her body, and then I was sightless, and my tongue flared and they began tearing at my genitals and I think I called out, though there wasn't any pain, just a feeling of surprise that I knew what it was like now, to be buried in the sky.

"*Ta kuai xingle.*"

Indefinable scents in the air, and colored lights drifting against the walls, casting rainbows across the huge gold man.

"*Yào wǒ qù jao tā ma?*"

No, colored lights not drifting anywhere, it was when

255

I'd turned my head; the lights weren't moving.

"*Shi.*"

The huge gold man sat very still. I'd seen one as big as this before, in the monastery. They were all over the place, all sizes.

"Water."

I heard sandals scuffing across the floor, opened my eyes again—the lids had closed without my knowing it—saw the head and shoulders of a man going through a doorway, I must be lying on my back.

"Here."

A face near me, creased into fine lines, a dark mole on the temple just above the eye, reflections throwing light across it, reflections from the glass of water.

A stray thought, quick as a spark—he'd known I would be thirsty: the water had been here. He wasn't the man who'd gone through the arched doorway.

"Thank you."

"Drink."

Yes, thirsty.

"Where's the dog?"

He frowned, shaking his head, tugging his robes tighter around his thin body. Perhaps he didn't know about the dog, the dirty white one with the brown patch.

"Feel pain?"

"What? No." I finished the water and he took the glass away, putting it down on something hard, perhaps marble: this was a temple, and the colored light came from a window high in the arched roof.

No pain, but felt heavy, weighed down, when I moved, when I tried to sit up, couldn't manage it.

Someone was coming.

Tried again to sit up and the big man came across the room and got me gently by the arms and gave a heave—

"Let me help you, my dear fellow."

White teeth in a thick black beard, dark intelligent eyes,

couldn't think of his name for the moment, things a bit hazy still, sitting on the ledge now, a kind of plinth where they'd kept altar bowls and prayer wheels, they'd been moved onto the floor to make room for the blankets, for me, this was a temple, got it now, Trotter, yes.

"Oh," I said, "hello."

"This is Dr. Chen." Trotter turned to him. "What do you think, Doctor?"

"He is all right soon. Is the altitude sickness, that is all."

"There you are," Trotter said, "nothing to worry about, rest up a bit, right as rain." He looked around and brought a teakwood stool over and sat on it facing me. "But tell me how you feel."

Tone hearty, voice coming from a barrel. I'd noticed how strong he'd felt when he pulled me upright, formidably strong.

"I feel," I said, "like anyone else would feel when someone's drugged his fucking tea."

I'd meant to follow them to their base so that I'd know where it was, but this place could be anywhere; there were a thousand temples like this one all over Lhasa.

Trotter said, "Sorry about that, yes." His tone had changed, dropping the false bonhomie. "Time was of the essence, you understand. I needed you here."

The colored light was fading now; dusk would soon be down. I'd been out cold for five or six hours: we were running it terribly close. All I could hear were distant sounds, some dogs fighting, the chanting of monks, the rumble of a cart, prayer bells, no modern traffic, no trucks. This temple was on the outskirts of town.

"I see." I tilted forward and got onto my feet, nearly fell but he caught me, used some kind of cologne. We stood like that for a bit, dancing in a sinister way, sinister because this man was so strong and even if I'd been in good condition I wasn't sure I could have reached his nerves before he threw me against the wall.

"Take it easy," he said, and when he thought I could stand on my own he took his hands away. "Doing rather well."

Stray shred of incoming data: he wanted me on my feet, not sitting down anymore.

"Thank you," I said. Jumping to conclusions could be misleading, possibly dangerous. He'd probably killed Bian, the monk, or had him killed, but that didn't make him a barbarian, in this trade. If I got a chance of playing him I might do well to play him like an English gentleman, in deep with some kind of spook faction; he didn't seem deranged but he could be neurotic, psychotic, a latter-day Philby, and he was certainly running a professional cell.

"Want to walk about?" he asked me.

"Yes."

Took a few steps, felt the motor nerves stirring, the balance mechanism making frantic adjustments and then getting it right until I could walk from one wall to the other, looking at my watch when I turned, didn't want him to know how very important it was that I should get it all back, a clear head and usable muscles, reasonable strength, enough to overwhelm if I could be quick and get in there for the major paralysis strikes. Dr. Chen wouldn't give me any trouble unless he had a gun under his robes and I didn't think so, he looked so very old, so very wise, could be perfectly genuine, a doctor turned monk or a monk turned doctor, his services available to anyone in need of them, to a man like Trotter, who would be generous, pay him well. But I didn't count on it; those people running China were old, too, and murderous.

A lot of thinking to do but I'd got one thing now: it didn't make any difference to Trotter whether I could walk from one wall to the other; he wanted my *head* clear, because he'd brought me here to talk, so we needed to get the circulation going again, get blood to the brain and the liver, deal with the lingering effects of the drug.

That was all right: I wanted my head clear too and it was

no good making out I was still groggy, there wasn't time.

"The military," I said, "have they been here?"

"Yes. They searched the place late yesterday. They won't disturb us."

I kept walking, throwing in the odd word or two when I was facing him because I had to see his reactions if he let any get through. "Were you in Bombay?"

"Yes. I hate to seem uncivil, but I need answers from you, not the other way round."

Facing him—"Did you kill Sojourner?"

No reaction.

"Did you have that snake put in his bed?"

"Of course not. That was the work of a jealous lover."

"But you got him out of the hospital, sucked his brains dry, killed him, had him killed?"

With studied patience, "As I have said, the questions are for me to ask, not for you. But first of all there are a few things you need to be told. It will help us both." I heard Dr. Chen moving behind me but not with any stealth: his sandals flapped. A spark came into each of Trotter's eyes as a lamp was lit. "The operation I am running is precisely similar to yours, Mr. Locke. My avowed intention is to get Dr. Xingyu Baibing out of Lhasa and into Beijing, so that he can go in front of the cameras at eighteen hundred hours tomorrow. We—"

"You've got him here?"

"Yes. He's perfectly well, and we're giving him his injections as prescribed."

"You killed the monk? Had him killed?"

I just wanted to know his style.

"It was an accident, I'm afraid. Those were not my instructions. There was a struggle." He shrugged. "These things happen when there is a great deal at stake, but believe me, I feel badly about him—he was nothing more than a holy man doing what he believed was right. Exercise a little, if you want to. Just a little—don't overdo it."

I swung my arms, up on the toes and down again. When

I'd looked at my watch a few minutes ago it had been 5:46. Eleven minutes, now, give or take forty-five seconds. I began worrying, because I wanted to know things from this man, everything I could, before we were interrupted. And I wanted my strength back, as much of it as possible.

"You also need to know," Trotter said, "that I have not only been keeping pace with your operation, but protecting it."

Keeping pace since Bombay, since he'd had Sojourner worked over, since *Bamboo* had been blown, oh Jesus, long before we knew it, the shadow executive, his director in the field and London Control, let them put *that* on the signals board.

In the chill of this place with its marble and stone and hard surfaces I began feeling the outbreak of sweat. This English gentleman with his style and his manners was not only formidably strong, he was formidably intelligent. It had crossed my mind that he could have been sent to Bombay by some other branch of the Secret Service, but he hadn't used a word of the language, and that's always the dead giveaway.

I would have said he was from Beijing, not London.

"Protecting my operation," I asked him, "in what way?"

"Oh, keeping a watching brief, that's all. I told Wang Su-May to look after you, and I got you away from the temple out there where you killed that KCCPC agent, got your head fixed up, offered you sanctuary, nothing major, but helpful, I hope you feel. Try a few knee bends, what do you say?"

"My head's clear enough now."

"Oh, good. Well the crux of it is, Locke, that I can't any longer protect you. That much is obvious."

"Not to worry."

He was left-handed; I'd noticed that before. If I could do anything at all I'd have to go in on his right side; he hadn't turned his back to me since he'd come in here. He wasn't Secret Service—"operation," not "mission," "sanctuary," not "safe house"—but he was nevertheless a professional, not to be underestimated—I could go in on his right side or anywhere else but I could get myself killed if I got it wrong.

Nothing could be relied on. It wanted ten minutes, now, to six o'clock, but nothing could be relied on, and those ten minutes could give me the last chance I'd get.

"Let me," Trotter said, "put it briefly for you." His thick arms hung easily, and this too I noticed. "You need perspective. Your operation is very big, and it's sponsored by H.M. Government and its intentions are to secure the future of the Chinese Republic and incidentally to save Hong Kong. Now I take that very seriously, of course. But try to understand that I am now in a position to take over—that I *have* to take over—if those aims are to be achieved." His massive head on one side—"Trust me."

Dr. Chen moved and I turned my head to keep him in the periphery of my vision field. "Look," I told Trotter, "time is of the essence for me too, and I've got to go now."

To see what he'd say.

"I'm afraid I can't let you."

Tone softer, no smile now. The Chinese was lighting another lamp, that was all.

"I'm afraid you've got to."

The double doors were heavy, twenty-five feet away. I couldn't see any other exit although there were some broken-down screens leaning in a corner, could be a door there. But if I got that far, got outside, there would be people of his there and they'd be trained killers, because that was the kind of cell this man was running.

"If I let you go," Trotter said quietly, "you'd get yourself arrested within the hour. The police are looking for you and the military are going through this town systematically, work it out for yourself." He took a step toward me. "You know what the PSB agents are like—they'd flay you alive until you told them *all* they wanted to know, and you'd give me away and they'd come for me too and they'd have me shot for harboring a criminal. You know this. You *know* this."

Dogs still fighting over something out there, and the

sound of a truck now. The light in the stained-glass window had died to an ember's glow. Eight minutes, seven, more like seven.

"You worry too much, Trotter."

Slight reaction for the first time: he didn't like being made light of. Just a flicker, deep in his eyes. Perhaps I could work on that, unbalance him emotionally, enough to give me an edge.

"I was born," he said, "in China. I spent my first ten years there, first with a nanny and then a tutor, at a British consulate. Then England, of course, prep, public, Oxford, but my first country is China, and my love for its people is deep and abiding."

Getting down to basics: here was his soul.

The altar bowls were heavy brass, small enough to use in one hand, big enough to use as a curved blade and to kill, given the necessary force to split the skull. There was nothing else—I'd have to break the screens up before I could make a weapon. The best chance would be to work on his nerves with the bare knuckles, use science, not bloody bric-à-brac, the sweat springing on the flanks now, time running out, five minutes, less.

"When did you hear I'd got something going?" I asked him.

Head on one side. "Sojourner was indiscreet. So you see, I'm prepared to do a lot for China. That's why I'm here now, to take over your operation. And be assured—" his huge hand rose in a gesture of avowal—"be assured that I shall see our friend safely in Beijing according to plan."

I thought I'd better put it on the line, because I needed to know exactly what I was up against. "If I let you leave here with him, I mean supposing I trusted you to see things through, where would I stand?"

The heavy brows lifted, I think he was surprised, thought I already knew the answer to that one. "You can't use this as your sanctuary forever. You'll have to show yourself in the streets, tomorrow or the next day. You're a risk, you see.

You'd expose me as soon as those buggers in the PSB got down to the questions." A little shrug—"and I can't afford that. It could destroy my plans for him, for us all." Another step closer. "There would be nothing *personal*, you must understand. It's a question of expedience."

These things happen when there is a great deal at stake, but believe me, I feel badly about him—he was nothing more than a holy man doing what he believed was right.

I heard myself asking a strange question, those bloody birds on my mind, I suppose.

"Would I be given burial?"

Chapter 23

Needle

"**B**urial? Only if you insisted, and if we had time."

"A dead body's going to attract attention."

Trotter was within six feet of me now, still not close enough.

"But it couldn't be made to talk. Forgive me for putting it like that. I have great admiration for you, and if things had turned out better you would have completed your operation and our friend would have reached Beijing under your aegis, and I personally would have been mightily pleased." He took another step closer, perhaps because Chen was here, and understood English, and this was an intimate matter we were talking of now, Trotter and I, my death at his hands, directly or otherwise. "I can only hope it's a consolation for you to know that your goal will be reached, nevertheless."

This worried me too: he wasn't putting it on, wasn't enjoying this. He meant what he was saying, that he would have to kill me to keep me quiet, crudely put, if you like, but that was the crux of the matter. And he'd feel genuine reluctance, genuine sorrow, and it worried me because it gave him a deadly credibility.

I needed to know more; the organism was clamoring for information: my eyes were measuring the distance between us and the height of the carotid artery on the right side of his neck and noting that his left foot was slightly in front of his right and would spin him effectively out of reach if he were faster than I when I moved; my ears were sifting the aural data available: street sounds and the moan of the wind gusts through the cracks in the wall, alert for anything that could give me clues to the environment outside; but it was my mind that was desperate for information on a level far more subtle, and it could only get it from the mind of the man in front of me.

"Why did you take him by force like that from the monastery, get a man killed to do it? Why didn't you contact me instead, as soon as you started thinking I couldn't get him to Beijing, and ask me to hand him over?"

A smile of disbelief. "You would have agreed?"

"Just wanted to know if you were listening." But I'd learned a bit more. "So where do we go from here?"

"I need certain information from you—the name of the man who's to meet our friend at Gonggar, the type of aircraft I must look for, the time of its arrival."

There were four minutes to go, give or take a bit to allow for mental-clock error, and the nerves were tight now, the adrenaline coming into flow. I took a step toward him, five feet away, slightly less, but still not close enough.

"Oh, for Christ's sake," I said, "how on earth do you think you can put him on a plane at Gonggar, get him past the security, the police, the PSB agents, the military?"

"More easily than you. I'm not a wanted man."

"But they'll recognize *him*, don't you know that?"

Nerves in my voice, it was a shade too loud, a slight slackening in control, and dangerous, I'd have to watch for that. We were getting down to the center of things now and the rational fear of my getting killed had given way to the overwhelming thought that these people would take Xingyu Baibing to Gonggar and try to get him through and lose him to the police or the military, *finis.*

"In winter here," Trotter said reasonably, "everyone is wrapped up in hats and scarves, as you know."

"Listen, anyone trying to leave Gonggar is going to be told to take off his hat and his scarves and stand under a bloody floodlight, you're not even *thinking*, Trotter."

His eyes flickered again; he didn't like being told off. "You got him through Hong Kong," he said, "and Chengdu, and Gonggar. If—"

"At that time the whole of the People's Liberation Army wasn't hunting him down."

And he'd had a mask on. Couldn't tell him that.

Look, there's this to be said: he had a point, I was a risk. If he were really trying to get Xingyu into Beijing I could stop him in his tracks if the police picked me up and I couldn't get to the capsule and they beat everything out of my skull— they'd start hunting for this man too and find Xingyu, *capito*.

"You can't get him airborne at Gonggar," I said, "unless I remain alive."

I had the mask.

"That is untrue, in my opinion." Quietly said, but with an edge: he was starting to dislike me. That would be useful to work on, get him riled, off-balance.

"Look, Trotter,what's your motivation? Who's running you?"

"No one is *running* me. I'm engaged in this enterprise because of my profound love for China and her people— and because of what happened to them in Tiananmen Square." Black eyes smoldering. "*There* is my motivation— in Tiananmen."

"Off on your own little crusade. Tell you this, Trotter, you can *not* get him out of Tibet if you kill me off, because there's a certain element involved that will *guarantee* his getting through Gonggar and onto the plane, and you haven't got it, and I have."

He watched me carefully, seemed interested. "An *element*. Would you be more specific?"

"As good as a passport, as good as a *laissez-passer*, the only *certain* means of getting him through."

In a moment, " 'Element' . . . 'means' . . . I'm sorry, but I don't believe you. Unless you're prepared to tell me precisely what it is."

"Not bloody likely."

He looked offended. There was something frighteningly genuine about this man. He was telling me quite simply that it was regrettably necessary to kill me off and that I was expected to feel consoled to know that at least Xingyu Baibing would reach Beijing, and he seemed surprised that I wasn't totally ecstatic about the idea. I was missing something.

Then I got it.

Tiananmen.

He'd spelled it out for me, after all, but it hadn't connected. His rage at Tiananmen was all-consuming, and the only thing he had in his mind was to turn it into action, put the messiah back in the capital and kick out the geriatric junta there and let the people free, lay the bloodied ghosts of Tiananmen. And compared to *that*, the life of one solitary spook, already hunted by the police, already on his way to the execution yard, was not to be counted.

"Then I'm afraid we must proceed," he said.

"Do what you like. Kill me, you lose him, you lose everything." Needed time to think.

Trade? Time to think about *that*. Trade my life for the mask, let him take me to Xingyu and fit the mask and let them go on their way, and then get under the ground and tunnel my way out of Tibet like a bloody mole.

We may start to think like that when things get tricky, when it looks as if there's not a single chance left of staying alive, it's natural enough, the grave's got a certain smell to it, can turn your stomach.

"The other information I shall need," Trotter said, "concerns Beijing. I want the name of the PLA general who has committed his forces in your support, and the arrangements for having our friend escorted to the Great—"

"Oh for Christ's sake give him a name, can't you, *Xingyu*, Dr. Xingyu *Baibing*, this 'our friend' thing is so bloody coy, and incidentally I'm surprised to hear you still need so much information, I thought you'd got the whole thing buttoned up."

I turned away from him and walked for a bit, just a few

paces, wanting to think, wanting urgently to think without his face in front of me, the face of my executioner, and when I came back I stopped a bit closer to him, four feet now, call it striking distance if I had to go for it.

"Sojourner died," Trotter said, "before we could get everything."

"What? Oh." Hadn't got the name of the general, so forth, yes. I hadn't been paying attention because in those few paces I'd done some thinking and it had shaken me quite a bit, because listen, I might *have* to trade the mask, not for my life but for the mission.

We get vain, you know, the longer we're in this trade, the more we get used to bringing the bacon home time after time with nothing much more than a broken ankle or a shark bite or a bullet lodged somewhere in the organism, we start thinking we can go on like that, start thinking we're invincible, that only we can see it through to the objective, bring it home. I suppose it's the same in most professions, but in this one it's a lot more dangerous if one day we find we're wrong.

The objective for *Bamboo* was to get Xingyu Baibing back into the Chinese capital, and I was in possession of the mask and the critical information that Trotter wanted from me, but my chances of taking Xingyu even as far as Gonggar airport were appallingly thin—all right, yes, grab him if I could and run the gauntlet with him through the streets and try to keep him buried somewhere in a cellar or a cave until we had to keep the rendezvous with the bomber, hell or high water, so forth, but that could simply be an act of braggadocio, of professional vanity.

The alternative looked better. Give this man the information he needed, give him the mask, let him keep Xingyu here in this temple, a place where the military had already made their search, where he wouldn't be disturbed, and let Trotter take him to the airport, openly, as a man already familiar to the police and to an extent trusted—*they're used to me by now, you see, and I help them sometimes*—and let the mission run its course without impediment to its objective. *Because I was the impediment.*

Must be mad.

"All right," I said, "tell me what you're going to do."

Needed more time to think. Not mad, perhaps saner than I knew. But I couldn't go through with a thing like this without London's approval. Trotter would have to let me signal, before we did anything else.

You're suggesting that you hand over the mission?

London. Croder or Hyde or Bureau One.

Yes.

To a stranger, running a private cell?

Look, I know it sounds—

Have you conferred with your director in the field?

He can't make a decision this big. It's got to come from you.

Please confer with your DIF immediately and ask him to signal his report.

Look, there isn't time, and you don't know the facts.

Confer with your DIF.

Let me give you the facts—

Your instructions are to report immediately to your DIF.

They'd think I was mad. The instant I put the phone down they'd pick up theirs and get Pepperidge on the hotline through Cheltenham, tell him to pull me in and take me off the mission, send me home.

Head was throbbing again, I was pushing things, hadn't slept since the night before last, hadn't eaten, needed a break, wouldn't get one, but don't let go, for Christ's sake don't let go, there's got to be a decision made and not in London but here, where I was standing now with the lamps on the walls sending shadows beating in silence like great wings across the airy spaces, their bone-white beaks—*watch it*—the airy spaces of the burial ground—*God's sake watch it you're*—yes, straighten up a little, losing things, drugged my bloody tea and that hadn't helped, not just the lack of sleep—

"Would you like to sit down?"

"What? No."

Watching me carefully, the man with the big black beard.

Four feet away, less, an inch or two less by my reckoning, go for it now, not the carotid-nerve thing, a heel-palm, drive the nosebone into the brain and take the other man as he came for me, not as difficult, then stay by the door and wait till they came in here and go for them in whatever way I had to, go for the kill to make it certain, done it before, do it again, but there's no future in that scenario, no future in it now, because he'd have more chance than I would, Trotter, getting Xingyu through to Beijing.

"I think we should sit down," he was saying.

"What?" I made an effort to get him in focus.

"You look a little done-in," Trotter said. "Don't make things hard for yourself. Here," he pulled the stool over for me.

Didn't sit down. "How many people have you got?"

"People?"

"Men."

"Oh, enough. But—"

"What sort of training have they had?"

"I'm sorry, but we've got to get on now. Dr. Chen?"

The Chinese went over to the plinth and opened a black leather case, took out a few things and laid them near one end of the blankets where I'd been lying. Hypodermic syringe, roll of needles, box with a picture on it—alcohol swabs, I suppose—small plastic tray with three glass phials.

Trotter turned back to me. "What I would really like is for you to give me the information I need of your own free will, including the nature of what you call the 'element.' Are you willing to do that?"

Hate syringes, they're so bloody sinister, ritualistic, I'd been having a bad enough time with the insulin thing.

"I've got to telephone London," I said.

He looked a bit sideways. "I'm afraid you can't do that. I need—"

"Thing is, Trotter, you could have a point. You might get him through Gonggar better than I could. But not without the information and the 'element.' I think on the face of it I'm prepared to let you have them, give you a much greater chance. But it's a decision I can't make for myself; it means handing you the mission. But they might let me do it, if I spell things out for them, in London."

He watched me, surprised. "Why would you want to hand me your mission?"

"I've told you. I think you've got a better chance of flying him out."

In a moment, "It sounds a little altruistic."

"Dirty word, I know. But I want that man in Beijing, and I don't care how I do it. Completes the mission for me, and you don't know what that means. It's the Holy Grail syndrome, completing the mission, risk our lives for it all the time, so I'm not—"

"Oh, I see," he said. "You're ready to make a deal for your life."

"Not really. That's less important. I mean he's such a bloody good man, isn't he, and he could work miracles for all those people you love so much, if we could only get him to Beijing. I mean imagine the headlines—*China Free*—spectacular. I want to make it happen, you see."

It wasn't absolutely certain they'd say no in London, not absolutely, you come up against the most bizarre situations in this trade.

"That's very touching." Edge of sarcasm, but only an edge; I think he was a charitable man at heart, had a certain amount of compassion. "But your life is surely one half of the deal."

"Not essentially."

There's an overweening confidence, as I've told you, in our own ability to look after ourselves. There could be a chance, somewhere along the line, for me to cut and run.

"You're an unusual man," Trotter said.

"They broke the mold."

"I would of course be tempted to accept your offer, Mr. Locke; but there's no telephone here, and that would mean risking exposure in the street. And you'll give me the information I need in any case, and name the mysterious 'element.' They've made great advances in the field of psychiatric drugs, and unless you're willing to speak of your own volition, Dr. Chen will induce your full cooperation. When I have what I need, he will ease your passage to the hereafter. There is of course no question of pain, except my own." The reflection of the lamps behind me made a spark in each of his dark intelligent eyes; there was nothing I could see in them, no hostility, no enmity, perhaps if anything a hint, yes, of pain, reluctance. "What do you say? Will you speak freely?"

We'd come down to the wire rather fast and the sweat glands were reacting and I could feel the old familiar heat of adrenaline in the blood.

"I can't," I said, "without London's okay. I really mean that. Neither of us is joking, is he? There's so much in the balance. All I need is a telephone."

He turned away for a moment, had his back to me, and the muscles pulled tight and I was set to go, already in the zone where all the mind has got to do is say yes and stand back and let it happen, the targets selected and different now because he'd got his back to me, a *chudan mae keage* to the coccyx to paralyze the legs and a heel-palm to the occipital area to produce concussion and deaden the optic nerve, but it still wasn't the answer: the organism had simply noted the chance when the opponent had turned his back, that was all, it had had enough training, God knows, to do things without being told.

Go for him.

No.

It's you or him and he's exposed, he's—

I think we can get London in if I work on him.

Kill him for God's sake before he kills you—

Shuddup.

It's his life or—

Bloody well *shuddup.*

Turning back, Trotter was turning back.

"You'll really have to listen to me," I said. "I can't offer you more than the mission, and it'd work, you'd get him through to Beijing."

He didn't answer for a moment. His face had changed in some way, his eyes, his expression, because of whatever he'd been thinking about, I suppose, while he'd stood there with his back to me. There was a softness about him, and it worried me.

In a moment—"My dear fellow, you still don't understand. I appreciate your thinking, but there's nothing you can offer me. It's for the taking." And then—"Are you a Catholic, by any chance?"

Said no.

With hesitation—"I thought you might, perhaps, be willing to give me . . . absolution."

It was a moment before I got it. Absolution for taking my life.

"What the fuck are you talking about, I'm not a priest." Shocked him, did me good. "And if I were a priest I'd damn you to hell."

Do you know what a rattlesnake does when it injects its venom? It's partly of course to paralyze the prey, to kill it, but it's partly *to digest its body*. I mean it's to start the process of assimilation, to soften and prepare the tissues. I suppose other snakes do it too, cobras, for that matter, but I happen to know rattlers, lived with them for a bit. But isn't that awful, don't you think, for something to start *digesting* you before you're even dead? It gives me the bloody creeps.

"I understand your feelings, of course," his voice very quiet.

"You bloody well don't."

There'd been fright in his eyes, I'd noticed, when I'd talked about damning him to hell. He took his faith seriously, perhaps I could work on *that*. I didn't like him now, forget the compassion bit, this bastard had started *digesting* me.

He didn't say anything more, looked at the Chinese and

gave a little nod, and Chen started getting things ready, breaking a needle out of the packet and pressing it onto the syringe, and I didn't like that, I was beginning to wonder why Trotter hadn't made an honest approach, come to me earlier and put it on the table and tell me his ambition was the same as my own, instead of dodging me like a bloody *espion* and setting me up for an interrogation thing under the needle and then the final insult, what had he called it, *easing your passage to the hereafter*, bloody hypocrite, meant kill me, kill me like a dog and hadn't got the guts to say so, but there was this thought above all—I was prepared to believe he wanted to get Xingyu Baibing into Beijing but for the first time *I was beginning to question why*.

It wasn't *necessarily* for the benefit of his beloved Chinese. He could be selling Dr. Xingyu Baibing down the river in some way, and I didn't like that, Xingyu was *mine*, he was under my protection, he was the whole of the mission, *Bamboo*, and I didn't trust this man anymore, this man Trotter, and he went down but he'd seen it coming and swung away, very fast for such a big man, took only half the weight of the strike and was still conscious, shouting the place down, and I didn't have time to follow up with the killer because they were in here now, three of them, coming at the double with their guns out and I took the first one head on and heard the bone go, heard the bone go driving upward into the brain and he screamed very briefly and then it was cut off as he died, the second one coming but I wasn't quite ready because the whole weight of my body had gone into the strike and the momentum was still trying to carry me forward and I needed to recover, wasn't correctly set up—

"Zhūa zhù ta! Bíe kaī qīang!"

Trotter, shouting again as the second man came at me and I did what I could, broke his arm but it didn't stop his momentum, his gun went clattering across the floor but he wouldn't have used it anyway, none of them could, Trotter wanted a live brain lying there under the needle and they knew that, he would have told them, instructed them, one of his hands trying to get a grip on my triceps and I smashed a hammerfist down but the target was too insensitive and he hung on and another man began locking my legs at the ankle and all I could do was try for an eye gouge and got it half right, got another scream but it didn't mean anything useful, they were hanging on me like dogs on a fox, Trotter's face somewhere above me, blood shining on it because I'd raked the skin open with the strike, his eyes frightened, because if he lost me now he'd lose the whole thing, tried one more strike, a strong *hiji-uchi* with enough force behind it to break whatever it hit, but it didn't connect because I was on the floor now and Trotter was up there, huge, dripping with blood, while they wrapped something around my ankles and he lifted me by the shoulders and they took my feet and between them they laid me on the blankets, on the plinth where I'd been before, got in a quick tiger-claw and drew blood again but technically it was ineffective, simply an attempt to save face.

They held me down, the three of them, Trotter and the two surviving Chinese, while Dr. Chen broke open the top of one of the little phials and wiped it with an alcohol swab, from habit I suppose, there wouldn't be time for me to get any kind of infection, would there, the head throbbing a lot now because one of them had opened the wound under the bandage when we'd been milling about, I watched the Chinese, Dr. Chen, as he pushed some air into the phial and tilted it and began suction with the plunger, *they've made great advances in the field of psychiatric drugs*, I could believe that, Trotter was an intelligent man, would know what he was doing, the weight of his huge hands on my shoulders keeping me down, I've never had to deal with anyone so strong, blood on his black beard, his eyes watching the syringe, the plunger still drawing the stuff in, quite a lot of it, we were nearing the 5cc mark on the barrel, I hate these bloody things.

One of the hit men was sniveling a bit because of the eye gouge I'd used on him, didn't look pretty, mucus dripping from his nose, couldn't wipe it away, had to keep both his hands on my legs, I tried a last essay, jerking my knees to connect with his face but it was no go, they'd been waiting for me to do something, didn't trust me anymore, bloody shame, my eyes closing against the flickering light of the lamp over there, *watch it*, yes, *God's sake stay with it*, yes indeed, one must remain conscious, mustn't one, opened my eyes again and slowed the breathing, deepened it, sought prana, drew it into the lungs, felt better, a little better now, he was stopping at 5cc, pulled the needle out of the phial and tilted the syringe, pressed the air out and got another swab, asking one of them to pull my sleeve higher, wiped my arm and dropped the swab and brought the syringe into position and I said, "Trotter, you'd better listen to this."

Chen looked across at him but Trotter shook his head, keep going, I suppose it meant.

"When I got him through Hong Kong and Chengdu and Gonggar," I said, "it was because he was wearing a mask. The 'element.' I couldn't have got him through without it. You won't get him through to Beijing without it either."

"Zhàn zhù."

Dr. Chen was holding the syringe like a dart, ready to stab, but he didn't move now, watched Trotter.

I said, "Listen, if this stuff is as good as you say it is, I'll tell you where the mask is, but it won't do you any good because you won't know how to put it on his face. It requires skill and experience, takes nearly an hour, and you haven't been trained, and I have. I'm the only one who can put that mask on, Trotter, so you'd better tell the good doctor, hadn't you, to put that bloody thing away."

Chapter 24

Fugue

I suppose Trotter would have given it some thought but there wasn't time because the doors of the temple blew open and the whole place shuddered and I saw the light of the explosion on his face before the air blast reached the lamps and blew them out and I twisted and rolled and dropped and got onto my feet and began running through the dark toward the patch of moonlight where the doors had been.

"In there," I told Chong and he lobbed the next one into the Buddha room and the force came in a wave and I went down under the blast and hit something with my shoulder and spun away and got up again, a few seconds of darkness after the flash and then the moonlight came back, filtering through the smoke where the roof had blown out.

Shot, whining close and bouncing against stone, someone had survived in there but the light was too tricky to let him do any more than shoot wild and I checked the vestibule on my left and didn't find anything more than rubble, crossed through the line of fire at a run and called for Chong to look after things and he lobbed another one through the doorway and the building bellowed again and I squeezed my eyes shut against the flash and waited for them to accommodate and then took the room on the other side and found him there, Xingyu, another man with him and I went for a certain kill and called out to Chong—*"Where is the truck?"*

Xingyu was conscious and on his feet and I found his flight bag and checked it for the insulin by the light of the flames that had broken out in the Buddha room and then got him through the rubble, another shot and I called out to Chong again but he didn't answer, we needed another bomb in there, Xingyu felt heavy against me and I had to half-carry him, smoke in the lungs and the light deceptive, shadows everywhere as the fire took hold and began blazing.

"Chong!"

Crackling of timber and a beam came down with a crash and sparks flew, a billow of smoke rolling through the doorway and clouding gray in the moonlight, the eyes stinging as we reached the open and I saw the truck, *"Chong!"* but no answer.

I got Xingyu into the Dongfeng and checked for the radio and the map and started the engine and waited. *"Chong, we're going!"*

The whole place was roaring and I thought I saw Trotter, his huge body silhouetted against the flames as I hit the gear in and rolled the thing out of harm's way, still no sign of Chong, but there was a sweep of bright light coming in from the highway and I got into motion again with the headlights off and took a dirt track where the smoke was rolling, used it for cover and kept going as more lights silvered the landscape and I saw a personnel carrier, red star on the cab, it must have been in the area and I suppose you can't blow a temple up in the dark without attracting attention, *Chong,* where was *Chong,* we had to keep going before the military picked us up in their headlights, I think the first time I'd called out to him without getting an answer was just after the shot, the second one, so it could be that.

Something bumping against me in the cab, Xingyu, and I pushed him upright, *"When did you last get insulin?"*

"Who are you?"

He sounded lethargic, slurred, sat there lolling, so I reached over and got his seat belt around him and hit the door lock down, *who are you,* stressed out of his mind.

The dirt track was coming to an end and I turned the lights on and kicked the dip switch and took the road to the right, away from the blazing temple, throttling up and shifting into top, the main town to the left, to the north, the river on the other side, Gonggar behind us in the west but forget Gonggar, find shelter, it was all we could do now, I'd been with Chong when he'd drawn the map, sitting in the truck while I was watching for Su-May.

"Okay, this is where the foothills begin, so this is where they are, along this line here."

The caves.

"Which one should we make for?"

"Listen, we take our pick, a whole lot of them are going to be big enough to hide the truck, so we can set up our base facing the south, keep a watch on the road, this one here, the only way in and it ain't that hot anyway, mostly rocks, but if they take the search parties that far it's the road they'll use."

We checked our radios and synchronized watches and he started peeling a fresh stick of gum and I said, "All right, this is what we'll do if I can get them to pick me up. You'll take over the truck and keep me in sight until you see where they're taking me. If it's in the town or where anyone else can get hurt, report on your radio to my DIF and he'll bring in support. If it's anywhere remote, where you can use your bombs, do it at your own discretion."

He thought for a moment. "Okay. Zero?"

"Eighteen hundred hours. I'll work around that. But you're only a backup, Chong. If I can do anything on my own, I'd rather do it. A bomb is a blanket weapon and if Xingyu's there I don't want him endangered."

He dropped the Wrigley's wrapper onto the floor. "Like to kind of modify that," his tone a little hurt, "I mean you can pick locks with those babies, you do it right."

"No offense."

We talked about where to bring the truck, covering a dozen assumed sites, urban and remote and in between. We talked about signaling if any were possible, access, egress, how to keep Xingyu protected, how to get him clear. And finally we talked about eventualities and their appropriate action. "If one of us can't get away," I said, "he's left behind, and the other one takes Xingyu."

"Gotcha."

He'd got out of the cab of the truck and buried himself among the equipment we were carrying back there, and began waiting it out.

"Where are we going?"

Xingyu. I looked across at him in the backwash from the headlights. He was crouched into his coat, his face drawn, his eyes dull, but he sounded interested in who I was, where we were going.

"Dr. Xingyu, it's a few minutes past six in the evening. When did you have your last shot of insulin?"

"I cannot remember. Are we going to Beijing?"

"Yes. To meet your wife." No particular reaction, perhaps a look of cynicism. "How much warning," I asked him, "do you get when you're running low on insulin?"

He turned his head to look at me. "A little while."

"What do you mean by a little while? Ten minutes or an hour or what?"

"About half an hour."

"Then I want you to tell me as soon as you feel you're ready for another shot." He didn't say anything. "Do you understand?"

"Yes."

"Are you hungry?"

"No."

"Thirsty?"

"No."

"All right. Let me know if you need anything."

Chong had dumped a bag of provisions in the back of the truck when he'd kept the rendezvous, and I'd asked him to include a first-aid kit. The mask was still in its cheap cardboard box wedged behind the seat, and I would have liked to use it, but we'd need fresh water, clean hands, and time, up to an hour. The risk of taking this man along a highway in a truck tonight without the mask on was appalling, but the risk of being stopped by the police or the military was worse, if I tried fitting the mask and failed to get it right: they'd detect it and rip it off his face, *finito*. The risk of pulling up anywhere to look for shelter was the worst of all, and the only chance we had was to get to the foothills and the caves and stay there until Pepperidge could work something out.

The blaze was well behind us when I looked back, a bright ember against the horizon that left a trail of orange fire reflected along the river. Headlights were sweeping the area as the emergency teams moved in, and two vehicles, quite distinct, were behind us on the road out of the town. I noted them, because they could be military.

I picked up the radio and switched it on.

"Calling DIF, DIF, DIF."

"Hear you."

"Subject is in my care."

In a moment: *"Very good."*

Since we'd broken radio contact soon after noon today Pepperidge had been sitting in his hotel room trying to make himself believe that I'd somehow manage to stay alive, because he'd known I meant to get in their way and that's something the directors in the field always hate and always try to keep you from doing: the risk is of course totally calculated but wickedly high. He hadn't expected jam on it: I'd located and secured Xingyu Baibing.

"I'm proceeding according to plan." It was all he needed: I'd told Chong to take him a copy of the map and it showed the caves. "We should be there in an hour."

"No precise location at this point."

"No. I'll send that." I watched the two sets of headlights in the mirror. The distant vehicle had pulled up on the one immediately behind me. "There's a temple on fire southeast of the town and the emergency crews—and I assume the police and military—are already on the scene. There are several dead. One of them might be Chong."

In a moment: *"Noted."*

"He did very well. The subject appears physically normal except for stress and extreme fatigue."

"You have insulin?"

"Yes. But please note: I estimate that we shall be exposed for another half hour on a public highway, and the Koichi artifact is not in place, repeat *not* in place."

Hesitation, then, *"Half an hour."*

"Estimated."

I gave him time to think. I'd located and secured the subject but the chances of getting him under cover were shockingly thin, with his face undisguised and a major search operation by the military still in progress. There was also an added risk: if any of them had got out of that temple alive they would have tried to follow this truck. One of those people had still managed to pull off a couple of shots after the first bomb had gone in, or it could even have been two of them, each with a gun. Trotter had been running a first-class cell with highly trained personnel and if he'd been killed in the Buddha room, any surviving hit man would know what he'd got to do. If Trotter couldn't fly Xingyu into Beijing himself, he'd want one of them to do it.

"Obviously you have no alternative."

Pepperidge. No alternative but to try getting Xingyu to a cave in the hills through a military dragnet.

"No. It's the least risk."

"So be it. Anything more?"

"Nothing more."

"What's your condition?"

"Fully active."

That wasn't inaccurate. If I didn't get some sleep before too long I was going to drop in my tracks and the drug they'd put in my tea had left the motor nerves a degree sluggish and my reflexes were less fast than I was used to and the head wound was still throbbing, but if anything critically active started I'd be all right because the adrenaline would make up the difference: once the survival mechanism is triggered and you're functioning in the zone, the body chemistry shifts into a different equation and the strength-of-ten-men syndrome kicks in.

"You could probably use some support."

"It's not feasible. The only chance we've got is to keep a strictly low profile."

Things had changed, in the mirror: the vehicle immediately behind had peeled off, and I saw the red star on the side. The other one was closing on us; I would have said it was a Beijing jeep by the short distance between the headlights. There was now a bit of traffic starting to come the other way, and I kicked the dip switch.

"If you felt you needed support, would you ask for it?"

"Yes."

He'd got my thinking straight on that point before: the man slumped beside me in the cab was potentially the most powerful figure in the Asian hemisphere and if I thought that even one support agent could help me protect him then I would say so.

"If the situation changes," Pepperidge said, *"I can send in a whole cadre."*

He was worried, thought I was digging my heels in; no director in the field's all that happy when the executive's walking a tightrope with the subject of the mission in his arms.

"Noted."

We were going to have to find a hole, Xingyu and I, find a hole in the night and stay there, sleep there, hibernate until the dawn, and any kind of support would attract attention, flush us out.

"I'll signal Control. Remain in contact."

"Will do."

I switched to receive-only and put the radio on the seat. It'd cheer them up a bit at the board in London, *Executive has located and secured the subject,* so forth.

A truck came past from ahead of us and in the glare of its lights I saw the red star again and a huddle of soldiers swaying in the back. I checked on Xingyu before the light had gone; he was sitting more upright now, staring through the windshield, and he squeezed his eyes shut and jerked backward against the seat as the shot smashed through the rear window and into the windshield and it snowed out and I hit a hole in it and got the truck straight again.

"Keep down."

Shot hit a tire and it blew and the truck lurched and I got it back and bits of snowed glass flew inward as Xingyu started hitting at it, shouted at him again, *keep down*, headlights coming the other way and the glare blinding, wiping everything out, and I felt the truck lurch again and then the tire came off and we were on the rim, took my foot off the throttle, lights again, there was a whole line of stuff coming past, *keep down* I told him, right in the line of fire for Christ's sake.

The twin lights of the jeep behind us were jazzing around in the mirror and I tilted it and tried to see where the road was, there was no border, it just ran into a waste of flat land with boulders standing black on one side, silvered on the other by the lights, a whole string of them, this was an army convoy, red stars glowing on the sides, *shot* and the mirror went, the force of the bullet throwing it forward until it caught the windrush and blew back into the cab, *Christ's sake keep down* I told Xingyu.

The Dongfeng lurched again and a truck coming past us the other way had to swerve but it wasn't enough and we clipped his fender and the driver leaned on the horn, the Doppler effect bringing it down to a moan in the night as I dragged at the wheel and went for the flat land and kicked the headlights full on and watched out for the boulders and then things began happening behind us, lights sweeping in an arc across the terrain and then another shot but it was wild, and I suppose one of the army trucks had made a U-turn to come back and overhaul the jeep and ask them what they were popping off a gun for, either that or it was the truck I'd hit, coming back to talk about the damage, you don't, you do *not* hit an official vehicle of the People's Liberation Army without being asked some questions, it was no go, it was no bloody go in this thing and I chose a boulder and got to the other side of it and used the brakes and slewed the Dongfeng at an angle and hit Xingyu's seat-belt buckle, *"Out, we're getting out."*

I hooked the radio into my coat and got his flight bag and the provisions from the back and found him wandering in the moonlight, a cold wind cutting across the scree, *"Come on,"* threw an arm around his shoulders, *"Come on, quicker than that,"* huddled against the wind, the two of us, leaning on it, tripping on stones, the lights on the road very active and men shouting but no more shots, I suppose it was all he'd been able to do, keep on firing even though he knew they'd ask questions, keep on firing in the hope of a killing shot, and he'd come close, hit that bloody mirror a foot from Xingyu's spine.

"I must go to Beijing."

His voice thin against the wind.

"What?" Out of his mind. "Of course, yes, Beijing."

Sweat running on me because we'd left the Dongfeng less than a hundred yards from the road and if they started sweeping their lights across the scree they'd see it and we hadn't got far enough yet, not far enough along the road to Beijing, dear God, what was he talking about, *what had they done to him in that temple,* lurching along together like a couple of drunks and not fast enough, not *nearly* fast enough, I could see the dark rim of the foothills against the stars but it looked like five miles, could be more, and I didn't know if he could make it on his feet or if I'd have to carry him, get him far enough before the need for sleep knocked me over, the rim of the hills dipping as I watched it, rising and dipping, the air coming into the lungs like knives and the stones loose underfoot.

Shots down there, some shots, back along the road, no particular theory coming to mind, they were trying to take him I suppose or both of them if there'd been two, and they wanted to keep on our track, shouting again, a lot of shouting as the line of trucks shunted to a halt, the officers wanting to know what was going on, another shot and that was the last I heard, Xingyu heavy against me, "We've got to walk quicker than this," I told him.

"Yes. I must go to Beijing."

Merciful God. "Listen, Dr. Xingyu, they are soldiers back there, and we've got to get away from them." I didn't know how much he understood about things. "We've got to keep going."

"Yes. Keep going."

Snow on the wind, flurries of it like last night.

"Listen to me," I said. "If anyone follows us on foot, I want you to go that way, toward Sirius—you see Sirius?"

"Yes."

"That's your direction, if we have to separate. Go that way, to the east, and find shelter and lie low. I'll go in the other direction, you understand? I'll lead them away. Now do you *understand*?"

"Yes."

But I couldn't tell if he did, or if he were just saying it, this *bloody* wind freezing against the skin, the eyes streaming. "I'll give you your bag, and the insulin's there, all right? All you do is lie low and wait, and I'll send for help. *Understand*?"

"Yes."

All he could say, like an automaton, lurching over the stones. "I'll radio your position, as close as I can get, if I have to send for help." *If the situation changes*—Pepperidge —*I can send in a whole cadre.* "All you do is *lie low*, and use the insulin when you need to. Are you *listening* to me?"

"Yes."

He tripped and started to go down and I pulled him upright, poor little bastard, doing his best, facing straight ahead of him against the wind with tears freezing on his cheeks, one foot in front of the other, soldiering on, I must *not* let them get this man, he was the messiah, potentially a name to go down in history if I could get him to walk faster, for Christ's sake, faster than this, we could still hear them shouting down there and all it wanted was for one of them to turn his truck and pick up our Dongfeng in his lights and we'd have to separate because they'd take a look at it and find the engine warm and then they'd start looking for the driver, *finis*.

Snow on the wind, flakes sticking to our faces and freezing the skin, he tripped again and I caught him, held him closer, an arm around his shoulders, the rim of the foothills rising and dipping and the stars swinging, I would like to sleep, swinging across the night sky and swinging back, the stones loose underfoot, treacherous, the night treacherous with stones and soldiery, Lord, I will lay me down to sleep in another mile, another mile of this, lay me down to sleep.

"I must get to Beijing," he said, Xingyu, and tripped and dropped like a dead weight and I wasn't quick enough and he stayed there on his knees, a dark shapeless bundle against the stones, the messiah, head hanging like a dog's, the wind howling among the boulders and his voice crying in it, "I must get to Beijing," his gloved hands hitting the ground in frustration, and I dragged him onto his feet and he started walking, my arm around him again, walking into the wind and the whirling snow, and I said to him, "Yes, you must go to Beijing."

Chapter 25

Pendulum

*I*t was very quiet.

There was a hole in the sky and I watched it.

Feet ached, my feet ached, those bloody boots. Feet were cold, too, frozen, looked down at them, felt them, no boots on, that was the trouble, I'd pulled them off when we got here.

"I must go to Beijing."

"What?" Then everything came back and I said, "Yes," and looked at the luminous digits of my watch, slept for three hours, I'd slept for three hours and six minutes because I'd checked the time when we'd got here and reported to my DIF.

Not a hole in the sky, this was the cave and the hole was the entrance down there, full of moonlight.

Missing something.

"Dr. Xingyu, are you all right?"

"Yes."

"Need insulin?"

"No."

I was missing something and it worried me; I didn't know what it was, but I knew it was something important. Xingyu was sitting upright against the wall of the cave, looking straight in front of him, and I felt gooseflesh along my arms; this man had changed; he was different now, giving me answers like an automaton, yes and no, sitting bolt upright like that and staring in front of him, saying he'd got to go

291

to Beijing, hadn't said it before, at the monastery, so what was in his mind, I didn't like this, there were things I wanted to know.

Oh Jesus yes, got up and staggered as far as the mouth of the cave and switched to send—"DIF, DIF D—"

"*Hear you.*"

"Have you been trying to raise me?"

"*No.*"

So relax, but I wasn't terribly pleased with myself; there was a bloody mountain on top of this cave and he couldn't have raised me if he'd wanted to. The last time I'd signaled him we'd been still outside in the open.

"Three hours' sleep."

"*Excellent.*"

Sounded happy about that. Part of the job of your DIF is to look after your welfare, hour by hour, and Pepperidge had known when I'd last got any sleep because I'd reported on it.

"Subject is with me, no injuries."

I confirmed the bearing I'd given Pepperidge when we'd got here three hours ago and then began giving him the general picture, not terribly reassuring.

The snow was still coming down in flurries, making a hazy screen across the terrain below the hills, and through it I saw lights moving. This cave was the third opening along from a granite bluff an estimated four miles south by southeast of the road where it turned north in a wide curve with an estimated radius of one mile; it was the fifth opening from a low escarpment in the other direction that jutted at thirty degrees from the lie of the hills. There were no other landmarks except for the boulders, some of them huge, ten or fifteen feet high, but they were strewn across the scree at random like thrown dice.

They'd set up a roadblock, the military, halfway through the curve in the road. They'd been alerted by the shooting from the jeep behind me and the obvious decision would have been to trap all traffic in the area: there'd be another roadblock set up toward the west, though I couldn't see its lights from here because of the snow. But I could see the lights of the convoy; it was still stationary, most of the vehicles facing west, the way we'd come in from the temple. It was difficult to say how many vehicles there were down there: perhaps twenty, twenty-five; the ones that had passed me from the east had been personnel carriers. Estimate, then, three hundred armed troops, *at least* three hundred. Some of the vehicles had been swung at various angles to the road, providing a fan of light southward toward the hills and containing 180 degrees.

From this distance and with the snow flurries blowing I couldn't see the Dongfeng truck we'd abandoned near the road, or if I could see it I wouldn't be able to distinguish it from the boulders. But it would be there, standing in the fan of light, and they would have checked it out, three hours ago, and found the engine warm, and they would now be looking for the driver and any passengers. Those were the moving lights I could see as the soldiers spread out in a systematic search. They were already a mile from the road, making their way across the scree like a tide rising toward the hills, toward the cave.

I reported this to Pepperidge.

The line of soldiers was at ninety degrees to my angle of vision, and we'd have to allow a margin of error: perhaps fifteen, even twenty percent. This being given, I estimated that they would reach the caves in the hillside before morning, at the latest.

This too I reported.

Nothing but static for a moment or two, then: "And at the earliest?"

"I can't predict that. If they increase their speed they could be here sooner than that."

I didn't like telling him, I did *not* like telling him this, crouching here in the cave mouth in the freezing wind with that man inside there looking so strange, talking so strangely, giving me ideas, one of them so appalling that I couldn't express it to my director in the field until I'd tested it out, because it would change everything, it would blow *Bamboo* into Christendom.

"But if it occurs to them," I told Pepperidge, "that the people in the truck might have headed for the caves, they'll logically send troops in three or four files straight in this direction and spread out and start a search at this level."

Static. I waited. *"They could reach you, then, in two or three hours."*

"Yes."

Waited again.

"What are your plans?"

"All I can do is play it by ear. I can get out of here and take him deeper into the hills, or stay here and explore the cave and hope to find a bolt hole and cover our tracks. If we start moving higher we'll be making a race of it with three hundred men and I don't think we could win it. On my own, yes, but I don't know how long he can hold out. I haven't questioned him yet. If we stay here, there's the chance that you might be able to do something, you or London."

He'd said earlier tonight: *I can give you a whole cadre if you need one.*

We'd need a regiment.

In a moment: *"I signaled London the moment you reported you were at the caves. I said it was impossible for you to get him to Gonggar, that you had no transport, that the Koichi artifact was not in place. That was correct?"*

"Yes."

"But now the situation is fully urgent."

Argot. In any signal, any briefing, any instructions, *fully urgent* has ultra priority and takes precedence over everything else: it means sound the alarms, freeze all other action, bring Bureau One into the signals room and clear all communications lines to and from London through the intelligence mast in Cheltenham and the DIF controlling the field in the host country, using scramblers or speech code or audio-grids or whatever means that will pull the whole network together and keep the shadow executive in constant touch with London Control and the signals board and the agents-in-place and the sleepers and support groups and courier lines right across the spectrum of the mission, and if I told Pepperidge yes, the situation was fully urgent, that whole process would kick in and start running.

Said yes.

A beat, then: *"How much time have we got, would you say, before you could be discovered, if they began sending probes into the foothills and the caves directly? What is my deadline?"*

I looked down through the drifting screen of snow at the string of lights in the valley. The soldiers would be three miles away by now, as a rough estimate, and the terrain was rough, loose, and inclined at something like ten or fifteen degrees. There was moonlight, but under the snow flurries it didn't amount to much more than a glimmering sheen across the scree, with no real shadows. Across this kind of terrain a man couldn't go too fast without risking a broken ankle, and at this altitude the lungs would be starved of oxygen to a critical degree: we'd reached here, Xingyu and I, exhausted.

I said into the radio: "Two hours."

Waited.

"Two hours. That is my deadline."

"Yes."

A wind gust came, cutting across my face and leaving snow whirling into the cave mouth.

"Very well." That tone of cheerfulness again, got on my nerves, made things worse because he only ever used it when things were tricky in the extreme. *"A great deal can be done in two hours. A great deal. Unless there's anything you want to add, I'll get on with things right away."*

There was nothing important. I'd been going to report the suspicions I'd had earlier tonight when we'd been lurching across the scree to the caves: a couple of times I thought I'd heard faint sounds behind us, closer than the road down there, and once I'd told Xingyu we were going to take a rest, and I'd sat there listening to the rushing of the wind across the stones, but that was all I'd heard. I hadn't thought about it since then.

"Nothing to add," I said.

"Then stay open to receive."

I went into the cave.

"I must go to Beijing."

Sitting there staring at nothing, a shadow humped against the rock face.

"Dr. Xingyu, I'd like you to move a bit nearer the mouth of the cave. I've got to be there to monitor the radio."

"Radio?"

I spelled it out for him, saying that the signals we'd be receiving would help us to get him to Beijing, and he tried to stand up and I gave him a hand and we managed it. Snow was coming into the cave mouth and we sat crouched with our backs to it.

"It's a bit colder here, I'm afraid."

"I don't mind."

Small talk, I'd descended to small talk, putting off the question that had to be asked, that had to be answered, before we could do anything more, before even London could order the fully-urgent process into action—because if it was the wrong answer I would have to signal Pepperidge at once.

"You don't need any insulin yet, Dr. Xingyu?"

"No."

"Nothing to eat?"

"No."

The question.

"Night like this," I said, "a nice tot of rum would go down rather well."

"Rum?"

He turned to look at me, face blank.

Ask the question.

"Never mind," I said.

The wind buffeted the rocks, moaning.

Now.

He sat huddled into his coat, staring in front of him.

"Dr. Xingyu, why must you go to Beijing?"

He turned to look at me again, the moonlight throwing a sheen on his pale face. "To tell the students they were wrong, in Tiananmen. Democracy is not the way."

Mother of God.

"Hear you."

The snow whirled against my face.

"He's been brainwashed," I said.

Chapter 26

Shadow

"*Zhègè yīngguórén sì duìde.*"

I tapped the pendulum.

"In English, please, Baibing. You don't mind if I call you Baibing?" It would set him more at ease, invite his trust in me.

"No."

The snow had eased over the last half hour, as it had done last night, when Chong had seen to the sergeant out there; the moon was brighter now, shining on the pendulum. I'd taken the silver paper from the packet of syringes in Xingyu's flight bag, and wrapped it around a stone and hung it on a bit of string from one of the stalactites in the roof of the cave, and set it swinging.

It had taken a long time to persuade Xingyu to keep his eyes on the pendulum: *There are things you don't remember, important things. You'll have to remember them, or we can't take you to Beijing.*

Swung the pendulum.

But I haven't forgotten anything.

Yes, you have. I want you to remember everything, or you can't go home and see your wife again.

To and fro . . . to and fro, a tiny silver moon a little distance from his eyes. I watched his eyes.

There is nothing I want to tell you.

Taken a long time, fifteen or twenty minutes, wearing him down, he'd never get to Beijing, never see his wife, over

299

and over again, tapping the pendulum. But now he was deep in theta waves and under my control.

"*Zhège yīngguórén sì duìde.*"

"In English, Baibing."

They'd talked to him in Mandarin, of course, in the temple, Trotter or the man who'd been with Xingyu when I'd found him, or both; but it wouldn't make any difference: I was asking him for images, ideas, not speech patterns.

"The Englishman is right," he said.

"Is he? Right about what?"

He didn't answer, went on staring at the tiny silver moon. I was up against a block, something he felt was very important, important not to divulge.

"Right about democracy?" I asked him, and that broke his resistance.

"Yes. There is no future in democracy for the People's Republic, no room for it. You can see what democracy has done to Europe and America. We cannot contemplate that happening in China."

I touched the stone to keep it swinging. "What has it done, Baibing, to Europe and America?"

In a moment—"It's all there, in the manifesto."

"What manifesto?"

"Of course it is. But I forget where you put it. The manifesto."

Silence. He was having to find his way mentally through a bewildering field of concepts: his own fierce convictions before Trotter had gone to work on him, then the doubts Trotter had put into his mind, then the new convictions he'd been given under hypnosis. And now I was starting to ask worrying questions.

"We can't go to Beijing," I told him, "without the manifesto."

Swinging the pendulum.

"He said he would give me a copy of it, on the flight to Beijing."

"What's it about? The manifesto?"

"It is the blueprint for the New China."

"Under democracy?"

Hesitation, noted. "No."

"Under Communism?"

"Yes."

"Under your present leaders?"

"No."

Oh really.

"Under what leaders?"

"Under Xu Yun."

Making some progress now. Xu Yun was on the second level of the hierarchy, a young minister, said to be brilliant and on his way up; but he'd been given a rap on the knuckles for going personally into Tiananmen Square in June 1989 to talk to the students and peddle a soft line to bring the tension down.

"What will Xu Yun do for China?"

"He will at first seem to favor democracy, then gradually swing the ideas of the people toward the new Communism. He is very clever, and the students approved of his actions in Tiananmen, when he went to listen to them."

"Good. And what is the *new* Communism?"

"A society in which all people are truly equal, with no rich and poor as we see in Europe and America, with no millionaires and homeless sharing the same streets, with no pollution as the end product of industrial greed, no crime waves induced by social inequality, no drug culture spawned by the egocentric devotion to the self instead of the state. it is in the manifesto."

Gooseflesh again, as I listened to Trotter speaking with Xingyu Baibing's voice. And a sense of revelation, because I was beginning to learn more about the Englishman and the dream that had driven him.

"That's very interesting, Baibing. Would you like to tell me more?"

He hesitated again: the question seemed to worry him. "I have not read the manifesto."

"But our friend Mr. Trotter talked to you, didn't he, for quite a long time. Tell me a little more."

In a moment—"The human race has so far proved itself the least intelligent of all living species; man is the only animal incapable of living within its natural environment and accepting nature as its earth mother instead of a system to be conquered and controlled. By the use of fossil fuels, the construction of nuclear power stations, the destruction of the rain forests and of life in the oceans, we are destroying the planet itself, its surface and its protective envelope."

His tone was easier now, less hesitant: he was on his own ground here, speaking of ideas he'd held long before he'd come under Trotter's influence.

"And the new Communism will be able to do something about that?"

"Not immediately. It will take ten or twenty years. But it must be done, for the planet and human life to survive. Instead of nuclear power, with its unconscionable problem of Chernobyl-like disasters and lethal waste disposal, we need to harness the infinitely greater power of the sun's heat and the force of the winds and the oceans. Instead of fossil fuel, with its equally unconscionable problems of the increasingly lethal accumulation of poison gas in the atmosphere, we need electric transportation, much of it solar-powered. Instead of impoverishing the soil and saturating food products with toxic chemicals and irradiation, we need to allow the land to enrich itself again by disciplined crop rotation and the development of organic fertilizers. All this can be achieved. It is in the manifesto."

I stood up to check on things outside. The snow had stopped, and moonlight flooded the scree. As the wind shifted I could hear sounds from below, the banging of tailboards and the murmur of engines. The line of light had crept higher, away from the road and toward the hills; the soldiers were still too far away for me to pick out individuals, but their line was nearer now.

Tempted to pick up the radio: *Your deadline was two hours*

and there's ninety minutes left. Have you done anything? Are those bastards awake in London? The tide was rising, and all I could do was to go back in there and listen to Trotter's vision of a brave new world.

Xingyu was still sitting bolt upright, absorbed by the rush of concepts and images going through his mind. "I must get to Beijing," he said.

Not really. Not now.

"So China can achieve all that," I said, "in a matter of a decade, two decades?"

"If fossil fuel suddenly dried up overnight, the United States of America would have an efficient electric automobile industry within two *years*, otherwise trillions of dollars would be lost. Industry is very inventive, the lure of gold being its mainspring. In the People's Republic we can be equally inventive, otherwise life itself will be lost."

I leaned against the rockface, feeling its chill through my coat, feeling its reality. I needed life, too, and even more than that I needed to vouchsafe the life of this man here, because the mission is the Holy Grail and held to be above the survival of the executive, and the mission tonight was to protect Dr. Xingyu Baibing, the messiah, the little robot sitting here regurgitating a romantic's manifesto. I found myself sitting very still, my back to the freezing rockface and my eyes on the moonlit sky and my mind suddenly close to the Englishman's, to Trotter's, as if a mental zoom had closed the distance between us.

He had lied very little, that man, and then only by omission. His objective had been precisely the same as mine: to get Xingyu Baibing to Beijing and in front of the cameras. He had wanted the geriatric tyrants there to be thrown out of power, as we did. He had protected my operation all along the line, just as he'd said, *because he didn't have the dissident commander's tanks readied to defend the people, as we did, in Tiananmen Square, didn't have the contacts, the coordination, the military escort that would lead Xingyu to the cameras after Premier Li Peng had been seized and put under military arrest.*

So Trotter had used the Bureau.

Had used me.

Our aims are the same, my dear fellow, I do hope you understand.

The same, up to a point. Not just as far as getting Xingyu out of Tibet, not just as far as getting him into Beijing and through the streets and into the Great Hall of the People, but to the very point when the lights would come on and the cameras start rolling and he would appear on the television screens right across the nation.

And speak not for democracy but for the new Communism under Xu Yun as its leader.

Sat very still, shutting my eyes, absorbing the light of revelation.

I do hope you understand, my dear fellow.

Yes, I think so.

He'd wanted, as we had, to put this man on the television screens—but with a robot's brain.

"When they came for you at the monastery, Baibing, was Mr. Trotter there?"

"Yes."

"And what did he say to you?"

"That I would not be hurt."

"I see."

The object had not of course been to hurt Xingyu Baibing but to keep him sequestered in the temple and subjected to intensive brainwashing, probably under the influence of a hypnogenic drug from Dr. Chen's little black bag.

"Did they give you an injection? I don't mean insulin."

"I don't remember."

It wasn't important; it would simply have been useful to know what kind of brain change I was dealing with: psychochemical or hypnotic.

"Did Mr. Trotter tell you that he'd be letting you go free?"

Hesitation again, quite pronounced this time. "He said I would be returned to your protection."

"Yes, I see."

He was, then, to have been released in such a way that I would 'discover' him and take him somewhere to safety and finally to Beijing, the same man but not with the same mission.

And then I'd mucked everything up for Mr. Trotter by deciding to get in his way and find Xingyu for myself.

I do hope you understand, my dear fellow.

Actually yes.

"Were you given posthypnotic instructions, Baibing?"

I don't know what he would have said because the radio crackled and Pepperidge came on and I acknowledged and began listening.

Chapter 27

Eta

"**W**hat is your situation?"

"They're closer," I told him.

I watched the ragged line of light in the valley below.

"By how much?"

"Half a mile, a mile, it's difficult to tell."

I could pick out individual lights now, individual soldiers.

"Are they looking for you, or Xingyu Baibing? Or both?"

I thought about that. "The military were alerted by two things, the fire in the temple and someone shooting at us from a Beijing jeep behind us. I think Trotter could have been in the jeep, alone or with one of his hit men. Or it could have been just a hit man, or two of them. I think Trotter was probably injured by the bombs, could be dead by now."

The line of light seemed to be breaking up in one or two places. Either one or two of the soldiers were moving up faster than the rest because of easier ground, or the officer in command had ordered probes to move directly into the hills to search the caves.

I didn't report this. I wasn't certain yet.

"What might have happened," I said into the radio, "is that the military caught whoever was firing at me from the jeep, and put him straight under interrogation."

"And he told them you were somewhere in the area?"

"Yes, with Xingyu. They wouldn't have mounted a search on this scale for me alone. The police and the PSB agents are looking for me, but not the army."

I waited.

My position was not good; it was probably lethal; but I preferred it to what Pepperidge was going through. He'd been pleased to take this one on, had been courteous enough to say he'd be honored to direct me in the field, and we'd done well together, got the Chinese Communist government's most dangerous political opponent through the trap in Hong Kong and the trap in Chengdu and got him into hiding. Then Trotter and his private cell had moved in and the objective for *Bamboo* had changed totally. It wasn't that we could no longer hope to fly Xingyu into the Chinese capital: we no longer wanted to. It was the last thing we must do. All that was left of the mission was a static rearguard action outnumbered by something like a hundred and fifty to one, and my final instructions from London would simply be to save this man's life if I could.

I did not envy my director in the field. He was talking to me from his lonely room in that shabby hotel, the link between London Control and his beleaguered executive trapped in a mountain cave in Tibet, with no further objective except to survive.

His voice, of course, was perfectly steady, and that helped.

"They haven't brought helicopters in?"

"God forbid."

"Quite so. But if they do, please report at once."

"Understood."

"Have you explored the cave?"

"Yes. There's no hiding place."

"Will you decide to leave there, do you think, since the search is closing on you?"

"Yes, unless there's something you can do."

Better to be overtaken in the open and on the run than raked out of a hole like a couple of bloody badgers.

In a moment: *"I signaled you to tell you that London has been very active indeed since I reported our predicament. Through the embassy in Beijing and our courier line they have contacted General Yang.''*

"Yang?"

"He is the commander who would have supported Xingyu Baibing's television appearance with a tank corps in Tiananmen Square. He was told of Dr. Xingyu's critical situation and agreed to send one of his colonels immediately to Gonggar airport to see if anything can be done." There was a crackle of static suddenly and then his voice came in again. *"Was . . . course . . . originally hoped that he might be able to help us get the subject to Beijing, until you reported that he had been compromised."* Read brainwashed. *"If the colonel can do anything now—his name is Zhou—it will be to attempt to rescue both of you from the cave. London reports that he has already left Beijing in a MiG 23 fighter-bomber and should arrive Gonggar in a little less than two hours. I have no information on what he will do then, but I assume he'll use his rank and try to halt the search that is now in progress. But that is conjecture."*

I didn't answer immediately. It would be pleasant to catch some gleam of hope in what London had set in motion, but it would also be indefensible. If there were going to be *any* chance of getting this man out alive it could only be taken by a strictly cool appraisal of the facts, and I didn't believe that a tactical fighter-bomber now airborne over central China could have any real connection with the line of soldiers less than two miles from where I was crouched at the cave mouth.

Pressed to transmit. "I wish the colonel a pleasant journey."

Regretted it immediately but of course too late.

"We must not despair, my friend. We must not despair."

"Noted."

Static again, and I looked down into the valley, but there was no helicopter in sight. I think another military vehicle had moved in, a big one, and it could be that.

"How is the subject bearing up?"

"He's all right physically, but not totally all there, doesn't really know what's going on. I think he was still under drugs when I got him out of the temple."

"Structions . . . Lond . . . as possible . . ."

"There's some static. I didn't get—oh, *Christ.*"

Bright flood of light fanning suddenly across the scree down there from the vehicle that had just moved in.

"Information?"

"They've brought in a mobile searchlight."

"Will that affect your position?"

"Not directly, it's down by the road. There's a lot of terrain to cover and they obviously don't think anyone could have got as far as the caves. But it means they're dead set on finding us, throwing everything in but the kitchen sink. Did you say something about instructions?"

The huge light beam swung slowly across and across the landscape, the soldiers moving in it like insects, hundreds of them, *hundreds*, silver-green because of the light on their uniforms and throwing long black shadows. They'd make better headway now, could see where they were going.

"Yes. Your instructions from Control are to protect the subject as far as humanly possible. That is your final objective."

Poor little bugger, sitting there dreaming about his bloody windmills, *a fine man, he'd been a fine man* before that black-bearded bloody maniac had gone to work on him.

Said I understood.

"I'm in constant signals with Control, of course," the tone cheerful, rallying.

"Good-o." But they couldn't do anything now, they could do *nothing*. "Look, I'm going to take him higher into the hills, all right?" The snow had given over and the sky was clearing and I'd be able to get a fix on Polaris when we went into the open. "I'm going to head due north, so if that colonel wants to know where to find us we'll be somewhere along that line." He'd already got a bearing on the cave.

In a moment, *"Can you wait another thirty minutes before you leave cover?"*

I looked down into the valley. The soldiers were making better headway but there were no probes breaking their line yet.

"Why?"

"I don't like the idea of your leaving cover. At least not yet."

"Look, that colonel can't get here in time. No one can do anything. We're on our own now."

Insects down there, ants on the move. But they'd be much bigger when they got here and they'd be carrying assault rifles.

"You haven't been party to signals. General Yang has committed himself totally to saving this well-loved and eminent man. Colonel Zhou was chosen for his reputation for high intelligence and courage." A beat. *"It would do us no good to underestimate him, do you understand?"*

I thought about it. "All right, we'll stay put for thirty minutes, if those are your instructions."

I wouldn't have listened to those bastards Loman or Fane or Welford but I would listen to this man. He wouldn't give up on us.

"They are not my instructions. It's more important than that. I value your life, perhaps more than you do."

"Point taken. Thirty minutes."

"Please stay open."

I turned back into the cave. I didn't care much for trekking north from here myself, but if we left the cave it was the only direction we could take, and it was uphill and rough going and there might not be another refuge for miles and we couldn't go that far, we couldn't go for miles, he was a diabetic and he'd been drugged and manhandled and put into shock and all he wanted to do was sit here and think about his windmills and his solar-powered people's cars, thousands of them, millions, enough for all those millions of lucky ants.

I sat down facing him. "How do you feel?"

"Very well." Spoke in a monotone: he was still under.

"So tell me some more about the new Communism. Why should it fall to China to bring about these great changes?"

"It is the ideal cradle for change. The Chinese created a civilization before all others; we are a cultured people. We

311

possess vast territories, vast manpower, vast natural resources."

"I see. But this man Xu Yun, your potential leader—he's
going to start things off with a lie, so you've said, telling the
people he's going to give them democracy and then leading
them down the same old garden path. I'd call him a bloody
hypocrite."

Turning his head to look at me, saying with great force—
"But there is no other man to lead us!"

"No one but a bloody hypocrite?"

Something was happening. I didn't know what it was.

"He is for the *people!*"

"So was Chairman Mao, for God's sake, he had you walking about with your noses stuck into a little red book, don't
you *remember* that?"

He was changing, Xingyu. Eyes different, looked different. He was surfacing, and I snapped the string of the pendulum and let it fall.

"Mao was wrong. He was for the people in the beginning—"

"They're *always* for the people, Baibing, it was the *People's*
Liberation army that murdered the *people* in Tiananmen
Square, their *own* army, surely you remember *that.*" I went
on talking, because something was happening to Xingyu
Baibing and this wasn't a political argument anymore, it was
something much bigger than that. "Communist leaders are
always the same, you know that, they're either shoving your
nose in a book or a gun down your throat. They—"

"But I was told other things."

Breakthrough.

I didn't say anything.

He sat staring at me, but now there was intelligence in
his eyes; he'd lost that look of a zombie. I didn't know what
had happened to him but it could have been that the effects
of the drugs had worn off or that I'd challenged him for the
first time instead of listening to his precious manifesto, cor-
rection, let me correct something, I *did* know what had hap-

pened, *they'd only got so far*, Trotter and his Dr. Chen, *only so far with him*, and this man's integrity of mind had resisted them and gone on resisting because all his life he'd had the convictions of a revolutionary, a rebel born for the barricades, and the stuff had gone in all right, the utopian bit, *but it hadn't stuck*, there hadn't been time before Chong had got there and blown the whole thing up, this man wasn't *brain-washed*, he'd just had a half-baked manifesto shoved into his subconscious and he'd brought it all out again, got rid of it, and the change that had come into his eyes was because he'd surfaced from the effects of the drug and was coming back into beta waves.

"I was told other things," he said again.

"Yes. But you can forget them now."

"He is a very persuasive man."

"Yes. And a bloody Communist."

I understood something else: Trotter had *known* he hadn't got far enough with Xingyu; there hadn't been time to saturate his brain with the tenets of the manifesto to the point where he could safely go in front of the cameras in the Great Hall of the People and spread the new Communism right across the nation, and *that* was why the jeep had followed us away from the temple and the shots had come and the windshield was smashed and the mirror had gone flying, because if Dr. Xingyu Baibing couldn't go on the screens with his mind fully indoctrinated then he couldn't be allowed to live.

Glow on the roof of the cave from the distant searchlight.

"His practical ideas," Xingyu said, "have a certain merit. His technical ideas."

I looked at him. We'd need to do a little work.

"Yes. But the West is also waking up to things, and if there's still time to save life on earth, it won't be run as a slave planet. This man Xu Yun—what are your thoughts about him?"

He looked surprised. "He is a Communist too, as I have told you."

"That doesn't answer my question."

"My thoughts, then, are that—" He hesitated, and I thought, *Christ, we haven't got any time left for this*—"while he is genuinely for the people—"

"Listen, Baibing, Chairman Mao was for the people and he brought them to their knees and Deng Xiaoping was for the people and he ordered a bloodbath in Tiananmen and now you're saying that Xu Yun is for the people and you think he's going to turn out to be a fucking *saint*?" I shifted closer to him, got down on my hands and knees to face him. "You are the only hope left for China, Baibing, the most powerful voice in the land, but the Communist credo has rubbed off a little on you, even on you, and you've *got* to understand that any man getting up on his feet in a Communist state and talking about the good of the people—the people—the *people*—has got to be told to shut up and sit down and if he won't shut up and sit down then he's got to be taken away and *shot* before he becomes too dangerous." Lowered my voice. "Baibing, you're a man of enormous intelligence and you have *got* to get rid of the idea that Communism in your country will ever see its people with anything more to their name but a half-empty rice bowl. That man Xu Yun will have nothing to offer you but servitude, suffering, and blood in the streets. Are you *listening* to me?"

In a moment: "Yes."

Silence again, and in the silence I could hear the sound of the engines below, and voices now, carried on the wind, as the light across the roof of the cave grew stronger.

"So what are your thoughts on Xu Yun?"

"He is potentially dangerous. He—"

"Can you trust him, then?"

"No, I cannot—"

"He's a Communist, Baibing. What are your thoughts on *that?*"

"He is to be mistrusted. He will only bring suffering."

Sweat on his temples, I didn't know why, bright on his temples.

"You help to put that man in power, Baibing, and what will he do?"

"He will perpetuate Communism in China—"

"And you'll have blood back in the streets, *blood back in the streets*."

"Yes, it must not happen, it—"

"If we can get you in front of the cameras, Baibing, what will you tell the people?"

"That they must establish a democracy, a true democracy—"

"As the only way, *the only way*?"

"Yes, of course, as the only way—"

"Democracy as the only way—"

"But yes, of course, it is what I have been saying to them in Beijing for so long—"

"Then you can say it *again* if we can get you there, and not just on the campus, Baibing, *but right across China*."

"Right across China, yes. It seems to me," he said, and he lifted a hand to stop me interrupting again, "it seems to me that I have come very close, dreadfully close, to being turned into a traitor to my own people. Dreadfully close," the sweat trickling on his face and now I knew why.

"But that's over now."

Felt tired suddenly, should have been the other way, shouting glory hallelujah, so forth, but didn't, just felt very tired.

"Yes, over now," he said, and lifted a hand again, this time in a kind of appeal, or that was my impression. "Do you think I am fully recovered, Mr. Locke?"

I made an effort, got to my feet, picked up the radio. "Probably. But if we can get you onto a plane there'll be enough time to put you through it again, make sure we know what you're going to say when you get to Beijing. Don't think about it, just take it easy, I'd say you're back in your own mind now."

Pressed to transmit.

"DIF, DIF, DI—"

"Hear you, I hear you. I was just going—"

"Listen, this is for London. He's come out of it now. They didn't have enough time to do a proper job. I think he could go in front of the cameras. I know it's probably academic, but London ought to know, you agree?"

Static. I watched the soldiers below, and the flood of light across the rocks. We'd have to get out of here now, whatever Pepperidge said, whatever London said, have to save our skins if we could.

"London must indeed know. This changes everything." Static again and I didn't know if I'd missed anything. *"...Case... going... signal you. London has been in direct contact with Colonel Zhou in flight, and so have I. His ETA Gonggar is twenty-one-oh-five hours, in thirty-two minutes from now."*

Xingyu had got onto his feet for the first time since we'd reached the cave, stood stretching his legs, and I motioned him to keep back in the shadows. I said to Pepperidge: "Thirty-two minutes is nothing like good enough. Gonggar's sixty kilometers away and he'd have to get right through the town and God knows how many roadblocks."

I could see their guns now, the searchlight sweeping across them, the whole scene silvered, the stark shadows of the boulders angling over the scree as a beam of light swung across them, and Pepperidge came in again.

"Colonel Zhou has raised the military garrison at Gonggar from his plane and ordered an MI9 helicopter to stand by for him with a pilot and navigator by the time he lands. The maximum speed of the MI9 is two-fifty kph, so allowing for changing planes and lift-off he estimates he can arrive your area by twenty-two hundred hours, in fifty-five minutes from now."

Xingyu was standing there watching me. I didn't know if he could hear Pepperidge's voice clearly enough, but he could hear mine.

"It's still not good enough."

Heard myself saying it, having to say it.

"Then you must work something out."

Yes indeed, those were the only instructions my director

316

in the field could give me—they were as close as that.

"I can hear their voices now, and you're talking about fifty-five minutes."

"You must work something out. I expect you to work something out, and so does London Control."

He'd caught my tone, the color of my speech, and heard I was tired, close to exhaustion, been a thick night, two nights, the mission had been running four days now and the pressure hadn't let up, listen, if I'd been fresh I'd have got Xingyu out of here and higher into the hills, on my back if I'd had to, but I wasn't fresh and Pepperidge knew that and all he could do was to try putting some energy into me, enough faith and energy to work the magic.

No magic left.

"I'm going to take him north with me," I told him, "all I can do, it's all I can work out. We won't get very far, so if that colonel can find the cave he'll have to look for us north of there, maybe a few hundred yards due north, tell him that."

In a moment: *"If that is your decision."*

"We can't stay here. They're too close now." Too close *and oh Jesus look down there.* "They've also moved a helicopter in, and it's putting a light beam across the ground. We're getting out, you understand, all we can do now."

Xingyu Baibing watched me from the cave, his eyes large and alert, concentrating on what I was saying. I believed he would give me no trouble, lend what strength he'd got left, push himself up that bloody hill if I helped him.

Pepperidge came in again. *"I will tell Colonel Zhou where to look for you. Now these are your instructions: he will fly both of you to Gonggar and put the subject into the fighter-bomber and take him to Beijing. You will be placed in the hands of two dissident PLA captains, ostensibly under arrest. They will take you by military plane to Chengdu, and will personally see you aboard a civilian flight to Hong Kong. Do I need to repeat any of those instructions?"*

Said no.

Running things *much* too close for the colonel to do any-

317

thing, that *bloody* chopper down there, tracing a line of light from east to west, turning and moving closer toward the caves, west to east, the sound of its rotor slapping at the night, but perhaps it was the fatigue, perhaps I didn't have the nervous energy to believe there was a chance now, one in a thousand.

Put faith in him then, faith in Pepperidge, believe in the thousandth chance.

"Please stay open to receive," his voice came through the static.

"Will do." Then on an impulse, perhaps just to hear myself say it, give it substance "Maybe he can make it in time."

"Say again?"

"This colonel. Maybe he can get here in time."

"But of course he will."

I put the radio down and went back inside the cave to talk to Xingyu, the acid glow from the searchlight spreading brighter now across the roof and then suddenly the huge black shadow rearing above us and I spun around as he came for us, Trotter.

Chapter 28

Cigarette

T he voices of the soldiers had been reaching as far as the cave on the soft night wind, but I couldn't hear them anymore because the search helicopter was flooding the ground with light much closer now to the foothills and the beat of its rotor covered all other sounds.

The whole terrain out there must be awash with light now that the helicopter had arrived. It would help Colonel Zhou, when he came, if he came, if there were going to be anything left here for him to come for; he would see the lights from a long way off.

I am very tired, my friend.

The roof of the cave changed as the light changed, darkening and brightening as the helicopter made its run from east to west, from west to east, and the shadow of the stalactites stood like bristles across the rockface, slanting and straightening and slanting again as the helicopter flew past. Some of the stalactites had broken away, over the centuries, and were lying on the ground.

Reek of kerosene on the air, a sickening smell. When you are tired, very tired, heavy odors are unwelcome, aren't they, get on your stomach, make one irritable.

I feel irritable, my good friend.

Beat of the rotor blades, drumming in the mouth of the cave, throbbing against the ears.

Xingyu was over there, on the ground, Dr. Xingyu Baibing, lying on the ground.

Trotter was with me. *He moved again* and I tightened the lock on his throat but *oh my God* he was strong and rolled half over and I had to bring my knee up in another strike for the spine but it didn't have enough force because this man had drained most of the strength out of me since he'd come in here and gone for Xingyu first because he was the priority target and I'd managed a hook-kick to throw him before he could make his kill and it had started from that point and there was blood on the floor of the cave, his and mine, and all I could do now was keep the hold I'd got on his throat and see how long he could go without the oxygen he needed: his breath was a low sawing close beside me.

Moved again and I almost lost it, the sweat running on him and making the lock slippery and that was dangerous, could be lethal. I was appalled at the degree of strength still left in the man: he must have caught a shot down there before he'd started crawling after us across the rocks—there'd already been blood on his face when he'd reared above us in the cave mouth. But it hadn't weakened him.

Beat of the rotor, the light brightening, lowering, the stink of exhaust gas.

I thought Xingyu was coming to, trying to raise his head. I would have to tell him not to come any closer, he must keep out of this man's reach because the last of the strength I still possessed was diminishing over the seconds, draining away.

Kept moving my other hand, my free hand, over the floor of the cave; they made a faint metallic ringing, the broken stalactites, as I groped among them and at last found one that felt good enough, long enough.

Pepperidge was signaling me: I'd left the radio switched to receive as he'd instructed. But I couldn't hear what he was saying because of the noise, the helicopter.

He moved again, Trotter, feeling the point of the stalactite against his skin. He moved with appalling strength, and I received it, received his strength, and was in awe of it, and made it my own, drawing it into my arm and forcing the lock tighter, letting my mind float to bring the tension down, concentrating on his enormous strength as I let it flow into me and through my arm until the lock was tight enough to keep him still and I drove the stalactite in, *I was wondering if you'd give me absolution, my dear fellow*, drove it deeper through the running of the blood, *there is nothing personal, you understand, in this*, drove it to the hilt of my clenched hand until the sawing of his breath became liquid and it frightened him and he found the last degree of strength that we can only find when survival itself demands it, and broke my armlock and threw me off him and I rolled away across the metallic-sounding shards, rolled away as he came after me, huge, a huge man, his blood shining in the light from the helicopter as it flowed from him and he came forward again, hanging on his hands and knees like a monstrous quadruped, his black eyes wide and watching me, came forward again and then stopped, hanging on all fours again with no further will to move, or that was my impression, his eyes watching me in a blank stare, *I am for the dark, am I not, my dear fellow, I am for the dark now, I believe*, watching me until his black eyes dulled and he dropped like a dead bull.

Felt very tired now. I felt very tired.

They were like little bells, the shards, the stalactites, a delicate tintinnabulation in my ears as boots moved over them, blood congealing on my bare hand, *"Can you hear me,"* my face against the rough floor of the cave, *"Can you hear me,"* Xingyu looking down at me saying, "It is the radio."

Tried to get up and he helped me, his eyes staring, perhaps he'd thought I was dead too, been sleeping, that was all, *I had been sleeping*, oh sweet Jesus for how long, *for how long?*

"Can you hear me?"

Swaying on my feet, the light sweeping across the cave mouth, a wave of exhaust gas blowing in, and when the sound of the rotor died away I could hear their voices, the soldiers calling to one another, and I picked up the radio.

"Hear you, I hear you."

"Colonel Zhou's ETA should—"

"Look, it's too late, we can't leave the cave. They're too close now, they'd see us."

Beat of the rotor, the chopper coming back.

Static, then—"*Colonel Zhou's ETA should bring him directly over your location at this moment. I will repeat . . .*"

Beat of the rotor, its downdraft picking up a vortex of grit from the rocks and whirling it into the mouth of the cave and I shouted for Xingyu to keep back but there was no light flooding down, this was a different machine, a bigger machine, the landing skids putting down on the loose shale and tilting and straightening again as a door swung open and a man dropped onto the ground and came jogging toward the cave and I went to meet him.

"I am Colonel Zhou. We must hurry, please."

I turned and beckoned to Xingyu, but he went on standing there, seemed uncertain, or the damage that Trotter had done to him had left him groggy, so I went and got an arm around his shoulders and shielded his face from the flying grit and brought him to the helicopter.

I watched from the windows of the military shed at Gonggar, two PLA captains with me, one on each side, as the fighter-bomber lifted from the runway and left a storm of sound booming among the buildings.

He had looked grubby and dog-tired, Xingyu, his face drawn and his eyes nervy as they'd helped him into his flying gear, but he would catch some sleep on the flight and they'd clean him up in Beijing and he'd look all right on the screen, that was what mattered.

"Take."

"What?"

One of the captains was holding out a packet of cigarettes, the end torn open. "Take."

I pulled one out and he struck a match for me and we stood together with its light on our faces.

"You help China people."

"Well, hope so," took a quick puff as a gesture.